Woman
of the
Aeroplanes

Also by Kojo Laing
Search Sweet Country

WOMAN
of the
AEROPLANES

Kojo Laing

William Morrow and Company, Inc.
New York

Recognizing the importance of preserving what has been written, it is the policy of William Morrow and Company, Inc., and its imprints and affiliates to have the books it publishes printed on acid-free paper, and we exert our best efforts to that end.

Library of Congress Cataloging-in-Publication Data

Laing, Kojo.
    Woman of the aeroplanes / Kojo Laing.
        p.   cm.
    ISBN 0-688-07941-5
    I. Title.
    PR 9379.9.L35W66   1990
    823—dc20   89-49593
                                                                                CIP

Printed in the United States of America

First U. S. Edition

1   2   3   4   5   6   7   8   9   10

To my children

CLASS ONE

Kwame Atta was the bad twin, and his chin was strong enough to box with, even with the sun on his tongue. He kept his science in his chin. Now, he was so agitated that when he inadvertently picked up a piece of rubbish on the clean streets of Tukwan, he threw himself in the bin instead, with the rubbish motionless in his left footprint. His words misted the tall glass of akpeteshie in his hand: 'Save that building there! I have lots of love buried under the old stairs! I was leaning over the window-sill as a child when it was being built . . . and now that I am old enough to buy it, you are pulling it down . . . I beg you in the name of the black stools of the ancestors to spare the baked blocks, to spare the hastily mixed cement. Otherwise I will take out sharp my home-made Asante gun, and prove that I am a real gunsmith in heart as well as in hand! Have you no pity for this strange town that has been banished here by Kumasi? Have you ever heard of a whole town being banished, land, goats, elephants, ducks, lakes, latrines and lawyers? Well, you are a stranger here, working on the orders of the authorities, but beware! We shall overwhelm you with kindness! I am using leaves to induce a divine gentleness whose power is limitless . . . I warn you not to pull that building down; besides it will destroy that pawpaw tree here, that tree that has been pressing its fruit against the walls for the last two years. We have a big beautiful woman boss here in this town of trot. Trot? History never walks here, it runs in any direction. We have been building something different here for years and years, and you just want to come and discover a whole town by accident, then pull down a house that doesn't conform to building regulations in Kumasi! What have we had to do with Kumasi since it banished us for subversive activity, for refusing to listen to *all* the songs of the ancestors? A quarter of the spirits of the ancestors will do, we shall fill up the other three-quarters. We shall unregulate you immediately under the coconut trees if you don't jump out of here with your cruel traxcavator! God bless you with as many alleluyas as you can squeeze into this moaning biting

— 1 —

machine. Pokuaa will get you! She will produce so much wealth in Tukwan here that not even all the gold of Asante will challenge it! Go to Obuasi, go to Mampamhwe, go to Konongo, go to Obenemasi, we in Tukwan will outstrip you; we go dooo!' Kwame Atta surged forward with the crowd of Tukwan people, and voices shouting, 'We go dooo, we shall score you, we shall put pepper in your eye, we shall score you!' They demanded an answer from the poised traxcavator.

True, Kaki the driver of the machine who had been eating bofrots fried crisp near the tasty palace, was torn between tearing down the building, and tearing off his work clothes to go and hug and join these people who were ready to be so kind or so cantankerous. Kofi Senya the spiritual shrinemaster bossed something in the ear of Zolozolo the boy-man of the shrine. Zolozolo with the cool hands raced up a coconut tree, and tore off the fibre from one coconut with his bare hands. 'I agree with immediate effect to let the building stand,' shouted Kaki the driver, with a smile so strong that it could switch off the engine of the beast-machine. There was much cheering of the same intensity, except for the calm Kofi Senya. He stood there as usual, smoking his thick wooden pipe, with a vulture perched on it. Kaki stared at Senya, and put out his hand to receive gratitude or forgiveness, extending a begging look straight into the eyes of the vulture. Senya's pipe smoke swirled round Kaki's hands, and he was told in that calm Kofi voice that now that he was here, it would be difficult to return to Kumasi, and reveal so soon that the banished town was thriving after all . . . which would be a double subversive banishment. 'The man smiles too much, allow me to reduce his lips,' Kwame Atta growled, eating the pawpaw that leaned against the building that was saved at last.

Kwaku de Babo was the good twin, coming with the nearsame face as the other one, Kwame. The twins were a bigitive force in the town, even if it was suspected that they only had half a buttock each in common . . . Atta having an advanced chin, which was developed by some stylishly deep holding when he was inventing; and Babo powerful knees that refused to knock even when he was entering Pokuaa's house, knees that were strong enough to hold the large Minutes Book of the town. Babo was the chief secretary to the town, and he wrote everything with his pen and his chalk – parts of the book were slate – even when there were no meetings koraa. When they were children, Kwame would often borrow Kwaku's hairstyle whenever he found it tidy; and when they quarrelled, they would sit and touch the four soles of their feet and push hard to see who would give way. Kwaku. Or they would see who could cover a whole plantain leaf with urine first. Kwame. Kwame used to laugh at coconut trees because he would say that they were just growing up to have their coconuts cut, kwasia. But what would really annoy Kwaku was that sometimes Kwame ran off with his name out of sheer wickedness, taking biscuits and goat's milk that were meant for him. Thus Kwaku, suddenly without identity, would give out more goodness in compensation: nameless, he scrubbed people's floors, nameless, he would bath reluctant dogs. But as soon as Kwaku got his name back, sometimes through fresh compensatory khebab from Dogo, he would resew it on his soul and dare his twin to steal it bio. Even then, Atta loved the glamour of his own name. The mother of the twins, Sister Mansa, sugared Kwaku sweet with her wisdom paa, but Atta would never listen to her. She would tell Kwaku that care was close to goodness, and that you could meet the world on a cedi, and die on a pesewa angry . . . nothing to show for your life. Thus Kwaku grew up desperate against the biskitisation of life, crumbs in the morals, crumbs under the table of life. In life, he would think, you ate the bread whole, you pushed your chalk hard!

Now, Atta's boasting and tricks remained: he could slip in and out of the raindrops without getting wet; he could chase his twin out of the story of his own life, and then misuse his absence small. As Atta took his fine stand against the demolition of the building, Kwaku just smiled to himself: the main reason that Atta was being so-so loud was that he had in the first place sold this building without authority, and he didn't want the anger of the buyer on his head, once it was demolished, you Dogo the buyer. And how could he stoop so low as to sell a family house with some dizzy stories about some instant inheritance . . . Where were the town's sworn qualities of freedom, honesty, and good politics? Inventiveness, yes, but Atta was patapaa first class. So he agreed to share in compensation the patent with Dogo, on his new cassava-grating machine, which sent cassava flakes over Pokuaa's plantain hotel, and dried them high in the sun before their descent. Babo found it amazing that rumours that Atta had seen the breasts of Pokuaa by accident still persisted. Both twins loved Pokuaa. And it troubled Kwaku that they said she was looking for some foolishness in her life – since it was already so successful – and that the best person to provide such a quality was Atta. Babo would warn them with a controlled anger to leave Pokuaa's skin out of their mad rumours . . . and that they should be more concerned with helping Atta to meet the shrine's warning: Atta had to invent more, before a single new house could be built beyond the present ninety-nine. And thus the historical trot prospered, with the onus of the forward thrust being much with the foolish Atta. Onus, anus, what was the difference, Atta would ask, since the emission of the thrust was backwards.

One day the twins met by surprise at a corner among the sweet-apple avenues, and stared at each other for a full two minutes. Oddly enough Kwaku did not take away his eyes first: he was remembering that when they were small, Kwame used to steal food from his mouth; and he usually forgave him by stealing it back. This now gave him strength to stare. And strength to remember that he was responsible for getting his twin baptised in church, years back: they were being baptised late after they could walk;

the stubborn Atta, even at this small age he was stubborn, he did the toilet without warning on the smiling priest. The smile changed to thunder, and there was consternation around the font; the priest had refused to continue until the wide-eyed Kwame had, small as he was, wiped the mess while his mother looked on struck, and begged the priest with an old bit of sugarcane to continue; the pulpit, pews and lectern begged him; and so, finally, after ostentatiously changing his sleeve the priest finished the ceremony quick, quick while one grandmother was trying to decide whether to faint or to pray. Now they stood, staring. Kwaku's cornerstep was dangerous: he was strongest at corners – where several perceptions usually met in his head and strengthened it – and he loved the surprise and space there. Someone somewhere would one day clap at the wonder of his cornerstep. 'Why do you have to stare so long? Have you forgotten that I'm the older twin? So you are always rescuing me. One day I will get you back for all that goodness! Kyere, give me way, I don't admire your stare koraa,' Atta shouted with disdain. It was just as well that Kwaku knew the pain of being accused of too much goodness, for he walked off with a slight stoop, swinging his arm with regret, wondering when his twin would die, and then forgiving himself for such a wild thought. His mother would tell him that there was a good reason for his good height: he was so tall that when he met the truth it couldn't go over him, so it stayed in his heart, the heart being the shortest space available.

Bra Kwaku wanted to walk towards all the four bosses of Tukwan at once – Pokuaa, Kofi Senya, Nana Bontox, and the lake – but he ended up on the path to Pokuaa's house. She had planted scores and scores of pepper around this house, so that it could be a hot walk up the garden path. He remembered that when she was poor and struggling, Pokuaa once charged him workmanship for making him and his twin rice and stew double. Kwame Atta had rushed fully into the brown rice, his face covered in grains, and he had rejoiced in the stew because he knew that he had a better chance of having his love for her returned than Kwaku did. Atta too, his legs were alanta; and anytime Kwaku felt like resenting Atta, he added a contrite heart to the feeling, and it burst. One day, Kwaku thought, he would respect the rain in his brother's mouth, even if it was spit mixed with words and tobacco. He could see Pokuaa in the distance bending her side the same curve as the arches in her house . . . they in fact built the arches to her bend exactly. Pokuaa was a contractress who usually supervised with her head at one side, then at another. Her beauty started at her heels and ended up breathless on her eyebrows. She was the mistress of two small aeroplanes which both stood at the level of her lips: one at her upper lip, and the other at her lower lip. She perfumed her aeroplanes every morning with frangipani lavender. The planes were owned in trust for the town by

Pokuaa: she bought them, and had arranged for the town to buy them back by exporting palm-nuts and cassava to a sister town in the UK. She was a kind buy-and-sell woman, she was an arrangement alombo. She was prepared to take anything up into the sky to let the town prosper. Recently she had to travel to London to see the edge of somebody's tongue: to look into Roy Mackie's mouth to clinch the deal of aeroplanes and farms. She went covered in entry permits. But when she came back she was so angry that she ordered one of her steamrollers to go over Atta's hands: he had ransacked her house in her absence, and used many of her documents to buy fried yam. He only saved himself by rushing to the various bola heaps and retrieving the soiled papers, and by inventing a new paper-cleaning fluid that made them almost new again. Pokuaa was angry only twice a year. Atta had stood there before her anger, rain filling his pockets as he begged; but he was prepared to rush up and bite the steamroller driver, if she were really serious about the slow drive onto his hands. . . .

People were sceptical about Pokuaa's intentions until she miraculously brought the aeroplanes. Now they were waiting patiently for one great thing: to make a journey to the sister town, Levensvale, a journey that they hoped would lead to prosperity. The shrine said the travelling was necessary, but that those to travel had to be carefully chosen. So every now and again a fever to travel would grip Tukwan, a fever burning food, stirring the lake, and scattering the elephants back into the forest. Pokuaa received Kwaku with open arms but closed them before he could have a hug. There she was jumping out of his dreams again! 'Come and sit down, then stand up straight away and help me to plant more pepper. We could export it later,' Pokuaa said with her smile. They peppered in silence planting. Pokuaa, go into his dreams, go into his dreams, but leave your skin out if you wish! Occasionally Pokuaa would get married. What? She believed in traditional weddings that wedded her to any spirit she liked. She had even married Kwaku de Babo once, admiring his simplicity. And she would have married one of the blue elephants – two were blue in mutation, six were very grey – if de Babo hadn't rushed to her at midnight to remind her that the only way to get the whole town to move along with her was not to be too free and too capricious. She listened to her spiritual husband and did not marry the elephant; and she thus continued to lead the town through the different calabashes of history, even if it meant having frozen palm-wine in the northern territories of the UK. Tukwan would go anywhere to survive, said the busy shrine. Kwaku de Babo advanced into noise: 'Is it true you want to love my twin brother?' Pokuaa gave a sideways look as if she was supervising the building of the tarmac for the aeroplanes. She was silent but shook her head. Perhaps she half-loved the idea of falling in love at the age of twenty- eight, but she was too tough to reveal the other half. 'The shrine once told me, without Kofi Senya's authority, that I needed a little foolishness in my life before I could move into the larger life; but when I asked the shrinemaster himself, he just laughed and told me to be careful with the boy-man of the shrine for sometimes he spoke out of hunger,' she said slowly. 'I know you will never marry my skin,' Babo added both emphatically and hopefully. 'No?' answered Pokuaa with a gentle doubt. 'Then don't consider my brother either,' Kwaku shouted with a misplaced heat. There was that silence now. It was as if his name had been stolen again. He held a seedling tightly and broke it. 'Give me my name back,' he said without thinking.

Mr Cornerstep truly wanted to manage his heart better than this, so he tightened his chest muscles, breathed deeply in the scent of guava flowers . . . which bisected, with massive regret, the smell of wild creepers from the forest beyond. 'We shall travel?' was all Kwaku de Babo asked. 'We shall travel,' Pokuaa replied, reaching out for his neck and patting it, but these were not fingerprints of love, these were kind utilitarian fingers papaapa.

Since Kwaku de Babo knew that the journey was almost definite, everything became tarmac. The town slid into bitumen, into rehearsed goodbyes, into lobbying for seats and positions, into preparing farms for export; but above all into that nonchalance of day-to-day living that betrayed the pressure of new expectations, new houses, new money, enhanced spirits, a oneness with all humanity, and ntromo and koobi . . . which Pokuaa had introduced into her Plantain Hotel to prepare stomachs indeed with something new locally for the journey. So when people spoke you never knew whether they spoke with an ordinary mouth, or with a mouth working above the tarmac under construction. The mouth could be goodbye.

This town of Tukwan, of doubtful existence to the rest of the country, to which it was invisible, had the most beautiful yawns in the world: its ancestors had moved and stolen people from region to region so fast so breathlessly that no one had had much chance to sleep while this was going on. And now, this stored sleep burst out in long artistic yawns, which had especially captivated Kaki the traxcavator driver. As our forebears worked, goats must have run into the wrong forests, bush rats must have tunnelled into fresher graves, and pride of tribe must have become useless except for festivals. And the eternal mist round Tukwan would speak: this town was near enough Kumasi to be far enough away never to be seen by residents of that city, except rarely; and if it had not been situated over one hundred miles from Accra but was nearer Koforidua than Ho, you would not have seen how far it was from Bolgatanga. The mist made the myth easier, ampa; for as the town grew, it didn't: the houses grew into forties fifties sixties seventies eighties and nineties, but created a dam for history when they got stuck at ninety-nine. It was a shame that the pressure to break this history rested with the bad twin, who was obviously one of the biskitisers of life. How could you forgive a man who marched into Pastor Korner Mensah's church in a frugal kente, made himself prostrate on the altar to everybody's surprise, and begged and begged for forgiveness, only to steal the collection plate when the congregation diverted its eyes to pray for him? Ewurade one million! But the gods got him back, even after he had declared himself a muslim probably as a doctrinal trick to save himself: for the next few days he dreamt that every time he urinated, coins came out and rolled back to the church, until all the money went back. 'More jimiso kakraba!' Atta would shout in his sleep, hoping that he would make more money by forcing himself to urinate more. Out of disgust, the two policemen of the town did not arrest him; besides, everybody thought, rightly or wrongly, that Atta was under the wing of Pokuaa. But.

Moro was not Yes but No like Opanyin Akorsah, he was suspicious of everything; and he thought the twins were wrong: wrong to be born, wrong to have anything to do with the development of Tukwan. To Moro even Kwaku the good twin was libilibious, and ought to have thorns on the paths he walked. As for Kwame Atta, Moro wanted to devote a whole association to him: the association for the sticking of broken bits of snailshell into the tiny tooshies of Kwame Atta the irreformable rogue. Moro the cola farmer was serious about two things if you leave out his friendly hard-to-touch wife: his Mercedes Benz and his ambition to co-rule Tukwan; the other co was Lawyer Tay or Nana Bontox, whom he considered soft enough to be led by the head. His Mercedes Benz was decorated to the extent of having blue underwear, plastic, to keep the world away. While Moro was frowning he looked up and saw the whole sky crowded with descending cassava flakes. When he became angry and shouted, some went into his mouth. 'Ewurade TooGood save us! What is this nonsense about a fool inventing something that leads to the whole town fool-full of cassava shadow! They will say they are practising for snow next! My wife Fatima, come and save me from this foolishness . . . now you people here think that this drunken twin with tricks over his tongue and thievery under it will take you somewhere? May I chew the cola in Allah's mouth! All he wants to do is to go and chop women in the cold. Me I will not contribute a pesewa towards his fokofoko bed-bills! Fatima my wife, come and believe what I am saying immediately, you hear!' Moro's sweat went into his wife's sweat. Fatima was a sweet smart wife who was equal to her husband, and fought his excesses peacefully: whenever he talked too much she would b-u-n-d-l-e him gently under the Benz, and hold his mouth until he fell asleep. He could then talk as much as he wanted, provided he did this in his sleep. And he was unique at Tukwan in that he was capable of making extremely short yawns in his bed.

It was Nana Bontox who suggested that yawns should be measured in case such statistics were required abroad. And when people laughed at this he insisted that the laughter too would have to be measured. He had his best thoughts when surrounded by his wives. They shoogled his flesh proper especially when they were quarrelling. There was Nana sharing his skin among them, a little more for his favourite wife; and slipping with majesty around the thighs knees and wrists with a full glass of akpeteshie. He preached on peace while the women hurled abuses at each other. But Nana was bold: when he ascended the stool, he immediately descended, complaining that the wisdom required was beyond him. 'But this is exactly what we want of our chief: unwiser than everyone else, including some children, so that he may have something different from the head to offer,' Kofi Senya had said with his emphatic whispering. Nana did not disappoint his people: he continued to make a fool of himself as often as possible, so that the people rested assured that he was faithfully showing the opposite of qualities he should offer; so that whenever there was a defeat for the town, he would – in his relentless trend of opposites – turn it into a victory fast. 'Nana, which one of us will go with you to the cold lands?' the wives asked in the middle of their fighting. 'None!' shouted the chief, 'none. Don't you want me to taste any other woman in any other country? Don't be greedy. Besides you are all having too much of me! There will be nothing left of me very soon. I am transferring my body to another country sharp!' Nana's

sharp

favourite wife took her favourite smile away. He watched her buttocks move as she walked to the old refrain: to whom to whom to whom to whom does this bottom belong, to whom to whom? Nana's favourite wife was called Corporal. 'Corporal, come and lie down in front of me . . . goood. Now give me my smile . . . good. You are the best, I lie?' Nana shouted. He soothed Corporal with a pat on her forehead, then put fifty cedis in coins on her breasts. She rose haughtily, gathered the coins, and strode out without a word, knowing that she usually got what she wanted. 'Today there will be no second-favourite wife, I declare!' Nana said. Then he fell asleep.

You could say that Lawyer Tay was a semi-boss. Gulder beer had created a belly that was usually on the verge of take-off: they would joke that this was his contribution to the coming journey, this belly. He thought everybody should be a lawyer so that each would be as intelligent as he was. In fact, he believed that most people gained in intelligence when they came into contact with him. He was a guard of the brain. But sometimes his perception wasn't as sharp as his logic, so that he let his hate for Opanyin Akorsah get the better of him; and also he tried to find little ways of annoying Pokuaa who was more powerful than he was. He did this because she once defeated him over a land case. He sometimes believed also that Pokuaa was in league with his wife to destroy him, to boot him out of the court of life. Nkwasiasem. One of the many things he was honest about was money: he was honest about using any means to get it. When Kwaku de Babo reached the good lawyer's house he found a batik gown drying on a palm tree – the lawyer was original enough to reject black gowns.

Everybody had to have one element of originality before he or she could continue to stay in the town. The lawyer had a son, twelve years old, who was impossible. Sala often carried the quarrels from his father's mouth to his mother's mouth and back again. He did this with an arrogant frown. 'Is your father in, Sala?' Kwaku asked him. Silence. 'Is your father . . .' 'He is searching in palm-soup for snails, but he has told me to tell anybody who comes that he is not in,' Sala replied, without looking up. He was busy with the tail of a wall jeko, so he had nothing more to tell. 'How small would I have to cut each bit of the tail for the different bits to die, Owura Babo? Is the smallest living bit just one inch?' Sala asked, then without waiting for any answer, rushed through and shouted to his father, 'Father Lawyer, it is only Kwaku de Babo, and I have told him already that you are not in. What shall I say to him now now now?' There was an outraged pause from within, there was an emphatic silence. When the shower was turned on from the bathroom, there was a song under it: LT was singing to save the situation. Then he came out wet, in middle towel, and apologised with water dribbling down from either side of his mouth. He offered: 'If my son were not some super good ally against my loving wife, I would beat him everyday . . .' 'Father Lawyer I would take out a writ against you in toto,' Sala shouted in from the tail of the jeko. LT ignored his son and went on, 'I believe Nana has sent you with a message. He phoned me in this elephant country – do I mean a trunk call – and told me that he had sent you with a message. He even told me the message. What's the logic in that? But he insisted that I should hear the message again from you. I am very happy we have a silly chief, sebi, but it does allow intelligence to grow all over the place, does it not, my good and better twin! Look at me, I'm laughing wet! Ah, and I always believe in scrubbing my tongue; it allows more law in that way . . .'

LT usually took turns at being both solemn and gay; when he was solemn he became gay, and when he was gay he became . . . He had now shut his face against his laugh. 'I believe the impending journey is causing a little hysteria in the town. I want to come out with a decree banning all expectations of the immediate future. . . ,' the lawyer said in his half-naked thoughtful pose. 'That is if money doesn't belong to the future,' Kwaku added innocently. LT glared at him with one eye dry. De Babo continued, 'Nana says that he has agreed with Pokuaa and Kofi Senya that there should be a full town meeting to discuss many things wonderful and that if he is only half-sober you should not complain about the other half.' Lawyer Tay smiled until he was almost dry, but there was little mirth in his mouth: he was only gloating over the fact that Nana Bontox was having to consult him more and more. His towel dropped involuntarily, but he was not in the least embarrassed by the sight of his own middling member his pittance popylonkwe. 'Sala, be sharp,' he shouted, 'come and pick up my towel for me. We must not keep our twin guest looking at me direct without any shame!' Two minutes of utter silence later Sala strolled in to cover his father, without a word. 'I think this boy may have some brains later, and that's another reason why I don't beat him . . .' The lawyer went back to search for snails in his soup, and cursed his wife for the fact that he found only six there. Kwaku went on.

At first Kwaku de Babo could not see Kofi Senya's head for the vulture on his pipe. Senya had been tutoring Zolozolo on how to increase his spirituality. Zolozolo never failed to curse the vulture at the mouth of the shrinemaster, for the beast of feathers usually had bits of food that he would otherwise have had. Admire the master, admonish the vulture. 'Will the meeting be tomorrow? Some want it tomorrow, some next year, others after eternity is over. Yet they all want to travel. It is because you want us all to assess ourselves that some don't want a quick African meeting at which they may be disgraced . . .' Kofi Senya could blow words out of his pipe, as others blew smoke rings. This was when he did not want to talk. The words would rise up blue in elegant short sentences, and then disappear when the vulture flapped its wings. His smoke told de Babo this: 'This is the time to have a meeting. The journey will come. But we can only go with purified hearts. Tell the rest fast.' If Kwame Atta were to be around he would have kweed an answer back, perhaps; but Kwaku read the words carefully before they were flapped away. Kwaku went on, smarter . . .

This time towards the fourth boss: the lake with its sacred ducks that some nevertheless sometimes hunted, much to his outrage. De Babo was the tender of rough ducks. They were a quack to watch. The reeds, forced to hold onto some elephant grass in the way of the wind down to the lake, murmured and complained in green and slimside silver. As the smartest Kwaku entered the rolling banks, many ducks rose in welcome, some bouncing off his shoulder, others rubbing their beaks on his leg. The hills could slip mist and show their tops when the ducks rose. A lone lamp-post with a pale fluorescent light brightened the lake night and day. Kwaku the duck shepherd usually did something strange at the lake a few times a week: at night under the love of the light he would catch and scrub ten ducks with sapo and guardian soap; and then use some of Pokuaa's aeroplane perfume on them. The lake would take the new smell into its ripples which never ended. That afternoon the cassava flakes had reached the lake, and ducks, moss and reeds were changing colour in very fine layers of white – either Asante snow, or snow was originally Asante cassava. Even here the good twin could feel the presence of the bad twin. And Kwaku pictured Pokuaa asleep, with her little cat beside her. The only woman in the world who sometimes forgot that she owned a hotel: she built the hotel but she did not manage it, and when she managed it she forgot she built it. There stood Babo with his hotel legs – legs of hospitality – serving himself with the hope that one day, his goodness would disappear and that she would order some passionate love from the sky for the two of them to share with dignity. Alleluya to the good twin, around whom the ducks swam in ever-increasing circles, until they had all reached the centre of the lake and were no longer concerned with human beings. He pressed the greenest moss of the fourth boss of Tukwan; some ducks would have to make the journey, a bottle of lake water would have to go as shrinewater to bless all these people here who wanted so many new things.

It was after he pressed the moss with love that he found a huge cake by the lake. It was an electric cake – earthed for the teeth – conceived by Kwame Atta, and baked by Pokuaa for Zolozolo to chop under the cassava sky: the idea was to offer salaka for the spiritual town with its flesh showing. Kwaku bowed down with his heart low, for here was another example of a link between his brother and his spiritual wife. The wires of the heart should not lead to cake by the grass. And Zolozolo was approaching, pulling up fresh stalks of grass to chew, preparing his mouth for an attack on the cake whose decorative wires he removed first. De Babo adjusted his joromi, counted the ripples, and rushed off to the town as the ducks flew the cross formations of his heart. The town rushed back at Kwaku. That simple sly dusk had created a noisy cock near the small churchhouse of Pastor Korner Mensah. De Babo settled within the cry of the cock, shivering, pushing memories of hurt deeper into the beak and the feathers. When all failed you could arrest the language and appropriate, painfully, the worlds behind. It was after the cock swallowed the memories that Kwaku bumped into the hurrying pastor. Korner Mensah noticed Mr Kwaku Cornerstep shaking, and said, 'Has the Holy Ghost finally got to your stubborn heart, my good non-practising parishioner? I don't understand you koraa. You are good, or at least better than your brother; you feel for people; you cry for the world. Yet you won't attend church or shrine. But I will tell you a secret before the meeting: we have churchified the shrine and we have enshrined the church; so should that not make things a little easier for you thinkers and doubters, kakra? Kofi Senya has agreed to this temporary union to help make the coming journey easier for the soul. You realise I was in the middle of lecturing at my own very new theological school in Accra when I was stolen for this town. . . . I was whizzed through Aburi Nkawkaw and Juaso before I could even complete the sign of the cross, and then left panting at the outskirts of this wonderful village. I completed the other half of the sign of the cross quick/quickly. As I crawled in trance and revelation I blessed the bush, I touched heads with a persistent frog that was jumping the same path as me . . . so here I am, fond of my Guinness and my God, ready to eat anywhere, and prone to malaria once a quarter. I allow ducks, elephants – the blue ones on Sundays only – and freshly skinned grasscutters into the church any time at all necessary. And one day I will win you for church and shrine. Hey I am happy to tell you that I have been able to convert Lawyer Tay's wife Dadoona to the church; but the only difficulty was this: she was so big that she couldn't get through the door. So the choice was either to push her through a stained glass window, already broken and not yet mended – with African saints I am happy to say – or to widen the door. Manu the carpenter was called to do the latter, but he couldn't come because he was on penance for trying to mishandle Sister Akyaa the wife of Azziz. Ah, bear with me young man, I can see you are shaking less . . . Well, Dadoona Tay – her name is a celebration for the shrine – had to stand at the narrow church door for three days until our sole carpenter widened the door. She did everything at the door, cook and all that, except excuse me to say fornicate. I am not a good priest, far too worldly and far too interested in magic. . . .' With that the pastor jumped off with his polished theology: one belief for each sandal on extremely clean feet. He would not touch a frog soon.

Kwaku de Babo watched the small laugh of the pastor disappearing, a laugh whose sound was gone, but whose shape was still wide on the lips. The shivering had disappeared but came back immediately when he saw Kwame Atta bursting out of the forest on a horse and galloping up beside him. 'Brother Kwaku, my better twin! Why are you always trying to avoid best

me? We are of the same blood, even though mine is darker! and even though your knee is more advanced than my chin. I am riding on Pokuaa's horse, but my plan is to transfer to an elephant in mid-gallop without dismounting. You see here the more you invent the more you are forgiven. Come up and ride, so that when I jump from horse to elephant and back to horse, you will be able to help me by controlling one or the other . . .' Kwaku refused with a frown, and said, 'You are overdoing your spending bills. I'm paying too much on your behalf . . .' Atta tried to spit at Kwaku as he galloped past with a laugh, shouting, 'The only reason you were born into this world is to suffer me, haha! And if you ask that stupid Zolo the Zolo – everybody's Zozo – he will tell you that I demanded and got some of his spiritual electric cake . . .' Kwaku stood firm and made his shivers go.

Kwaku wanted a hill and he had it, lying on top of one watching the people gathering slowly for the meeting. In the darklanded forests you could arrange a job for the eye: beyond the thinning distances you could start the savannas spreading, you could give the valleys a cut of eye from treetops to fast crabgrass. Go higher again: on one oval hill with very soft lovegrass stood a big blue cross, sometimes neon, put there by Pastor Mensah. He was going to put up a white one soon, so that the two crosses would make it difficult for anyone to double-cross God, he had said. There was one hill behind another always; for in geology too you had your watchmen. And one of the finest sights from a hilltop was when all the animals, birds and insects of the forest decided to have a race, to end up while in the instant freedom of the savanna beyond; and then to turn round back to the forest with wild cries, squealing, humming, barking and moaning; with the wild pig leading surprisingly, and pushing the mosquito off its impudent snout to cross the forest first . . . and the blue elephants were last, with beetles on their tails. Kwaku de B spent the whole night on the hill without realising it. They could not have the late meeting without him. This pleased Moro who had always insisted that as tradition demanded important matters should be discussed at dawn. Kwaku, rose, fell asleep, rose, and fell asleep again, only to rise yet again and rush to the chattering town which was getting ready to fill the slow misty dawn with its jots and joys.

And some feet moved so slowly, turning over the doubt in their soles, wondering whether it was wise at all to make one's life an experiment. The feet would send a message to the head: walking hard enough could mean ending up in simpler towns where custom was custom, and where a town growing into a city was a simple fact. Even with the safety of reincarnation, there was often a terror for the new. The feet cut their own walking, and wanted to about-turn and leave the ability to form history altogether to other people. But in Tukwan there was always a ground-swell of wholeness and excitement that the prodigal feet would return to, reversing the message to the brain instantly: the head should continue to let the feet march towards the hills, to rush towards those ideas that would retain Tukwan as the happy renegade of history. Climb up and up to the meeting on the sacred hill, you feet! . . .

CLASS TWO

Several shiny chamber-pots first class with much Izal were brought to the tops of two hills – one of them the miracle hill – which were almost bigger than the valleys they held: this was for the meeting, so that no one would have to roll down the slopes to pass water. The lake was adjusted, merely by pulling the ripples, so that it could come nearer the meeting and interrupt the wisdom if it got too much. The grass around the big blue cross was dancing even before the wind came slowly. The voice of Azziz followed de Babo's ear and found it: 'It's a private matter whether I want my wife's buttocks to touch an elephant or not, whether blue or grey. My wife Akyaa she sweet me complete with some gentle body, but I will not allow Manu the carpenter to look at the elephants touching her; and don't the beasts have hearts and a very good eye for beauty. Forest beauty even if we are meeting in the savanna. She the ladylady has been long independent but short too knowknow: she sometimes even questions my good mornings. Nevertheless true, she's good for my poor heart . . .' Azziz was swaggering up the hill, for the last letter of the alphabet was friendly to his name. With his shoulders as thick as his thighs, he sometimes considered love a tight corset: he would burst and jump out of it, landing in an unreal infatuation for Pokuaa which his wife sometimes tolerated. 'Today be today,' he added to Kwaku. At this moment Kwaku was guarding his language against all intrusions so he said nothing, and he said it with a nod. He was the secretary but his shadow was something else: the carrier of especially long and sorrowful yawns this morning, for the vacancy at the corner of his mouth was not yet for words . . . and there was somebody else speaking to him, Appa the quarrelsome young blacksmith stolen into the village from Yeji by Pokuaa's travelling earth recently banished. One of his favourite occupations was watching old old crows moving from mouth to mouth fortifying the talk there; so he was confused by Kwaku's silence, but wanted to quarrel about it: 'So you too, kyere, what is your mouth closed for? Is it because it is your pen that is supposed to work and scribe this morning?

Wake up and be as bold as your twin! I know you are older than me but so is my father, and I'm wiser than he is. Me I blacksmith everything . . . and the metal of my A-levels was very hard to crack. Move your big feet small so that I too can walk in your footsteps quick!' Appa was confident that he would go on the journey, because he had already taught himself to fly an aeroplane without having entered one. This was sheer metal intuition, he said, nodding uncontrollably.

Amoa the twenty-year-old Aponkyi Man was once buried by mistake just because he was sleeping long over a bench with his body divided on and off, long division sleep. But he was saved by Kofi Senya who dragged him out of the grave, while his vulture stood a cemetery stand, waiting to reperch on the pipe. Now Amoa was even more confident than before he was buried. He insisted on the privileges of reincarnation, claiming that no one could really tell whether he actually died or not, since he was the only one in the box. Senya's smile could swallow him. Now, however, Amoa was carrying a dictionary among the swamps before the hills, wondering how many words Kwaku de Babo would ask him to look up in case the language was stronger than he thought. Several zinnia held each other around his ankles in the breeze. There was Amoa remembering: in spite of his bright smile he was a man of coffins: when the old tailor died – he cut his broken heart out by mistake with his scissors, for his fine new ugly girl had left him for an even older man – Amoa had gone to the afro-bluffing burial box and had knocked at its door, demanding that the old man finish his trousers before they buried him; and when they were pulling him away, he spat on the coffin, shouting that after all the old man was his friend and that why shouldn't he part with a spit of parting. One controversial custom that Kofi Senya had introduced was this: a few days after each death, a tractor had to move round the town collecting as much laughter as possible to crowd into the big box; bales of laughter, metres of laughter, jugs of it, sheets of it . . . and after that those who were courageous enough to do so could cry far into the night. If you could hoot at hunger, like the Gas, then you could hoot at death too. Cry, you tough people with copper hearts, for reincarnation was always round the corner.

Climbing up the hill proper with a bell ringing at each side of his waist was Dogo the man with not a little money whom Kwame Atta sold part of his patent for the grating machine to. Dogo made his money from selling khebab, but sometimes his khebab was roasted rotten, said Appa. Being a man of much meat, he was usually stubborn when his meat was tough. So his character was assessed in bites, sometimes tender sometimes tough. He caught up with Kwaku, saying, 'Kwaku de Twin, am I not a fool selling meat when the gods have given me a mouth that prefers fish! I quarrel with my wife every day about fishbones: her mouth is made of meat, so she doesn't bother about whether my fishbones are soft or not. I am supaparticular paaa about my fish . . . and I will soon buy a bicycle because it is better to ride after fish than to walk after meat, I lie? . . . What are you saying my friend? You are saying that you can't hear me for my bells? Allah! All these years you have still not got used to my selling bells. Well, it's unto youououou, be careful they don't cccccconsider your goodness awam! And meet me there!' When Dogo was sad he became bones. But today this soul meat was extremely wide open for smiling and selling, wide for flesh.

Opanyin Akorsah was walking up the hill with one leg. The other leg was tripping behind. Since Akorsah was often close to evil, Kofi Senya sometimes nullified one leg and made it walk behind the other. It was not only such a walk that made him vulnerable, that tempered the evil with a touch of mortality: he was also not sure of his wife's faithfulness. Nor was his wife. Ei, this be serious asem matter, he thought. Obaa Yaa had married her husband's cocoa and cassava farms, but since she found that she could not love a pod and a root, nor his sarcastic skin, she started to dream about where to put her love. When Akorsah realised this he tried to double his sarcasm, so that he would test her into getting her senses back. This was not koko at all, for she was a woman prepared to go her own way straight or crooked. Pity sometimes to the man who walked with his leg following later. 'This meeting too is a big waste of time, cocoa time, cassava time. Your Pokuaa woman wants to make highhigh profit so that we clap for her forever. Me, I'm wise about everything except my wife. I married her for the wrong reasons but I love her for the right ones . . . on to the meeting we go!'

And the path was busy making way for hundreds of feet; and in the end each footprint was a different direction, so that to remain straight the path had to be miraculous. And the bosses half-arrived in a trial run of the lower-lip aeroplane. They had to walk the other half, since the tarmac was not yet finished. Nana Bontox was sweeping the grass with his cloth as he walked. Pokuaa the simple, the cunning, was there. Kofi Senya was whispering to the lake to keep its ripples quiet. But Kwame Atta was there high in the middle of the water on stilts, putting sensation there. As a chair divided the ground into four points, so the stilts divided the lake into two levels of ripple: one group of ripples snapping at the stilts to break them, and the other group rushing away in concentric rolling. The ducks were perched disdainfully on the bank. Kwaku de Babo looked down with pain at his twin. At his tricks again. When Atta waved up with a snort, his hand was in ripples. 'Can't you all see that I'm trying to make an experiment that will allow the ducks to flap the water along faster, and then make it possible for the aeroplanes to land on a ripple-free lake if the tarmac is not ready in time . . . you free-ripple nnipa, you silly people don't respect me, and yet you are all waiting for me to fill the invention room with ideas that will allow you to travel and to build again. I will also exact my price! I will steal your money, I will chase your alombos, I will be cheeky in your shrines and your churches . . .' They rushed at him with saws with Manu the carpenter leading. 'Leave my stilts alone!' Atta screamed as he fell with a huge splash into the water, cursing them and threatening that he would stop thinking very soon so that they all rotted in their stagnation. But he did not disturb the elephants at all; they continued to drink the lake and to spit it back out onto their backs at their leisure; and sometimes a lucky duck would catch a stray fish expelled from a trunk . . . prod the blue elephants and they would groan through the grey water; prod the grey and they would groan through the blue.

As the aeroplanes roared by the banks, refusing to go into the lake for Atta's experiment, Akyaa walked among the ankle-happy zinnias knocking against the pinks and the whites with her best friend Maimuna. Maimuna gladly lived alone and considered that men were worse than their own shadows, even though she was not interested enough to have anything against them. But she planned that one day she would grab one man, have a quick baby with him, then throw him back into his own shadow again. Akyaa and Maimuna had made a mistake this dawn: they had mixed up their earrings and were wearing one each of the other's. They might as well have changed ears, for they often heard the same music coming from the world. And sometimes when they chattered you could not hear which mouth the words came from; so that Akyaa used Maimuna's mouth, and Maimuna used Akyaa's mouth. 'But does your Azziz still have some love for Pokuaa?' Maimuna asked, knowing that Akyaa was only half-interested in this. 'Why, do you want him to love you instead?' Akyaa answered laughing. They shared the same laugh, and when they let their hands go, the laughter stopped. Maimuna was chewing cola bought from Moro's farms. 'Have you decided which man will be your baby's father yet, my sister?' Akyaa asked trying to keep the sparkle in her eye secret; but where would you put a very broad smile if your friend didn't take it . . . 'Think about the meeting you Akyaa of Azziz's wife, and stop bringing men into my head this morning!' Maimuna was irritated. 'Into your head? I thought they would be better in your small ginger bed!' They walked a little distance apart, Akyaa's mirth separating them; but they came together again when they reached the middle of the meeting, their cheeks almost touching, one earring against another and a laugh in between.

The bosses without the lake were sitting in the middle of the meeting in time and place, except Nana Bontox who was sitting in the usual traditional semi-circle with his elders. One marvel that Nana and his elders had created under the direction of his senior linguist Nana Kofi Kasa was this: today they all wore one uncut continuous cloth, so that what Nana wore round his ample shoulder went round uncut to Nana Krontihehe, then to Nana Nifahehe, then to Nana Benkumhene. Today the cloth of eternity did not have scissors working on it; and what was hu and marvellous was that Kwame Atta had invented some geometric shapes at the point of separation to each shoulder, so that each of the elders could move for half a mile without dragging the other in the same direction. And when they all decided to walk in different directions at once, the ten yards of cloth for the border of the shoulder made fine and sometimes symbolic patterns; at other times the long unbroken cloth blocked the sun for children and for shorter people. But now Nana was sitting and building the words: 'Now that we have finished with libation, pass me the biggest chamber-pot . . .' There were murmurs of disapproval as the sound of royal urine met chamber-pot and was amplified through the microphone. Somebody was just asking what kind of chief this was, when Nana rose and crouched, rose and crouched, and then demanded his snuff bag. 'Please switch off this loud loud microphone so that when I sneeze you won't hear my nose . . . and some of you think I am a child in the head. Well, let me tell you that I believe in receiving all your dignity free. I have none myself koraa. But because I talk true I hope to build up my own dignity store. I will draw on it in real battle, and you will see me as a different person . . . I believe in bodily functions, be natural my subjects and objects . . .' Nana was deeper than you thought: when most eyes had left him in impatient disgust, he then had the time to call his second-favourite wife and slap her doona with a hand hidden by his fan . . . and all this time he had been urinating under his cloth – out of necessity he had perfected the five-minute pee – into a special pot that emptied its cargo automatically and secretly and came back for more. Kofi Senya's vulture flew round his pipe three times and resettled on it hot.

Then Pokuaa took out a white handkerchief which the sun caught and heated with love. She waved it, and scores and scores of other handkerchiefs waved back. Nothing was said for ten minutes as the hands waved and waved. Kwaku the secretary to the town sat down and wrote all the silence, did not forget the commas in the waving of the dawn. Everything was true. And Pastor Mensah rushed up a higher hill with his lean panting so that he could bless everybody including those not blessable; and he prayed that God would rush up even higher, with the ancestors at His heels, and be profligate with joy for this town that was different in the soul; this town that showed that the future should be the humanity of travel inner, travel outer. Pokuaa had a voice that went deeper at the end of each sentence. She was vulnerable in the face, tough in the head, and open in the heart. So that when she spoke, her words had a prepared place to lie among the people: 'One hundred people, two hundred people, three hundred people, we are to live hard before some of us travel. The soul must burst out full before we take it to another land for a short time. Shouldn't we scrub our sheep more, give the invention room more head and heart, plan more and more business, and then enjoy the joy of change!' . . . yes my dear newnew sister you are talking the kind of meat that is good for the sense . . . Pokuaa, you should be our chief, and not just our queenmother, bring us every change, be our woman, odoyewu . . . we all trust the wave in your handkerchief . . .

But Moro was sour. He disregarded the joy, and strode up to Pokuaa, demanding, 'Give us the details of your deal to better us. We demand to know how many cassavas and palm-nuts will pay for one aeroplane.' Moro had a way of swivelling his shoulders opposite his neck. His integrated Northern face had a cough in it, followed by a handkerchief wiping it. And when he was angry, the anger killed his face, except for the bright eyes which were of different colours, one deeper brown than the other, with the whites yellow and slightly green. His face was a stereo cemetry by the cross. 'Ask the serious questions later, Alhaji Moro! Your face is too hard for such a soft-hearted meeting!' It was Nana Bontox talking, with that touch that spoke for almost everybody. But Akorsah had put of course his face to the service of Moro's anger, doubling it thus; and the two of them stood among the crab grass defiant, one a cola man, and the other a man of palm-nuts. But the middle of the meeting was too cool for them for now; so they postponed their heat.

As the ducks flew in and out of armpits and other spaces, Pokuaa came in cool: 'What problems are we going to solve before we travel? Nana is here, Kofi Senya is here . . . and the lawyer is here. Are we going . . .' '. . . to reveal the secrets of what everybody was doing before being pulled into the strange time of this village? Are we going to see how thieves, murderers, and destroyers came to be admitted to this place? Are we going to praise this town-village for being free and new when we all know there are big gaps in our hearts and minds . . .' Kwame Atta had at last removed his stilts, and had rushed up the hill to give his mouth some talking revenge for the big splash. 'Stop your foolish seriousness!' screamed Nana, as the okyeame-hene echoed the scream. The bad twin suddenly bolted, but not out of fear or defeat: in his anger he had forgotten that he had put a jot lit into his belt to hold it: his trousers were on fire, and the righteous laughter could not put it out. Kwaku the good twin rushed after his brother involuntarily, leaving his pen suspended above its paper. He got a scornful thanks after he had helped to put the flames out, but he ignored this and went back up to write, above the dotted swamps: the ducks were either colons explaining other ducks, or they were question-marks doubting how high each could fly before becoming a dot above the skyline. Down below them in patches of colour up and down the hillside there was just enough eating among the townspeople to allow some huddling and talking. Atta had caused a shock by what he had said about thieves murderers and destroyers: the past could be destroyed by living meaningfully in the present; and the new joy was never easy, for it did not close the humanity they lived and wanted. 'What was I before my spirit was stolen into this town? Am I an ancestor living out my ancestry in this mortal Ashanti time?' Appa asked these questions of De Babo because he thought that if they were answered well enough, they could be fashioned in metal with his A-level at the tip of it. But Kwaku told him to eat his breakfast fufu and soup so that the chewing would give him enough sense to keep silent before the big questions of life. 'But that is not fair at all. Some of you have asked so many questions that some of these questions have turned into their own answers, I lie anaaa?' 'Here in this place where most of us want only the few to do the magic and the thinking for us?' was all Kwaku asked, shaking his head at the brightest clump of grass near one small swamp below. 'Why do you want to be so good?' asked Appa persistently. Kwaku de Babo stared at him in disbelief, patted him on the head, and then tripped over a heated argument between Amoa and Dogo about who was living in which time where, now and previously. 'You Dogo the logo, how can you talk about time, when all you do is to sell and make money? Your time is measured in pesewas, meat, bells and smocks. I know I am young pass you koraa but I have the wisdom of death to carry around with me . . .' 'O stop that talk <u>now</u>! You think I don't sabe the trick you made when you were going to let them bury you dead! You are alagmai crawling into your hole of lies. You only want to be famous before the journey so that they take you on the aeroplane sharp . . .' Amoa snorted and farted fully, then moved off, leaving Dogo's open mouth wide enough to put in the last bit of meat left for sale; he chewed so long and he was so scunnered by what Amoa did that he created some big suspension of the mouth.

Opanyin Akorsah came and cut Dogo's time of the hanging mousa: 'Are you not a seller of meat? Go down and get some more, catch your goat quick. I can't buy something that's finished, can I? Add some fresh white yam if possible . . .' 'Leave the yam out of it, Opanyin Akorsah! Since when did you see me sell my fine yams. They are for two stomachs only: me Dogo and my wife!' 'These days asking for a small favour is a crime. You know how difficult my wife can be. I must have some yam.' Opanin Akorsah was almost pleading. Dogo was the only one he pleaded with sometimes. 'How much will you pay me for the trouble?' Dogo asked with a look of triumph. He was proud about his unspoken control over Akorsah, but never pushed it too far. 'Leave money out of the food I want to eat!' Akorsah growled. When later Dogo came crawling up the hill brightening the morning with new yam, Akorsah paid what he had to pay, simple; and when he chewed beyond the microphone he had a sad look on his face, to make up for the aggression of his eating.

Fresh yam, whether white or golden, was a fine journey for the jaw. But the mother of Kwaku and Kwame was not chewing. She was coming down from a geologically fresher hill, in inner anger: for years she had rejected the claim that the twins came from different fathers, wondering how it was possible for her to regroup her thighs away from her lazy and doting husband. He loved her so much that she had to ask a score of whys every day to explain such bigitive love . . . may he rest in peace even if he was now just having a morning nap one hour after rising from a bed that would have him no more. So there was Sister Mansa, worrying down a younger hill with her finished stoop: she had no more space to stoop over, her current stoop had used it all walking to the correct hill where they all were. Then she heard, to her surprise, her husband's voice behind her: 'Mansa, there I've caught you walking down the wrong hill. I know you only did it to avoid them for a bit, with their talk about the twins coming from different fathers . . . and that's an insult to myself, lazy though that I am! I have also brought you more love in my bag, nonono don't frown, how lucky you are at your age to be receiving so much love. After all you will soon be sixty . . . and as Kwaku is like you, so Kwame is like me. We are the bad ones me and Kwame, true . . . let me help you up the hill by pushing your shakyshaky buttocks. . . !' 'Sososo much love, and in front of people too,' Mansa said with a frown at Papa Ntow and looking up to see whether anyone was watching. Only her triple so, thought Ntow. Still, she let him push her thus all the way to the crowd; and she preferred the teasing to the insinuations she usually got.

Pokuaa had gone back to the microphone, after Kwame's interruption, and had asked the same question stubbornly, though adding that thieves and destroyers could be solved too: what lives, what problems did they want solved before the journey? Atta sat sullenly on the ground beside her, trying hard to give the impression that he was close to her. Some of her words bounced off his head, since the microphone was working so hard. There was this sudden silence which Dogo's bells refuted. The rusty bells could ring their worries away, for small joys were possible when you were trying to make a fresh start with your life with your hills and with your ancestors. Ring a soul, Dogo, ring a soul for all of us to hear. Even Kwame Atta, who had suddenly risen from somewhere near Pokuaa's elbows . . . in order to appear detached and masterful in their eyes: he thought that it required courage to move away from rather than towards Pokuaa's skin. And he was running, this Atta with ideas lodged impudently in his belly; he was running down the hill with a dog, but all the dog was doing was running up and down his back barking while he ran unaware that he was carrying a passenger. When the dog was descending Atta's forehead, it howled into the latter's grunt of annoyance. Carrying dogs next, he thought. People watched Pokuaa curiously as she reclaimed the microphone and shouted into it with some heat, 'Get that mad dog off him, he has some inventing to do! If we don't give him some love, he will sail up the rivulets straight out of our lives, and we shall never have our house number one hundred, and we shall not travel . . .' She stopped talking when she realised their gazing; but she gave their staring back, bringing her toughness into her eyes, and deciding to ignore whether they thought her outburst was a sign of attraction for a rather ludicrous man or not. When the dog finally jumped off Atta's back it had left its smell and a few hairs on his head. He jumped into the lake, took out some soap he had hidden under the bed of water, and scrubbed until his confidence came back. He loved to hide soap in lakes and watch the soap survive. Beyond, the crows stood on the aeroplanes standing on the tarmac. Kwame walked there.

The time of the meeting was in the running of the stream beyond the disused townhall . . . why meet in the dampness of an old hall when the psychedelic cross and the hills were fresher? The frogs below tossed themselves by the lake, and the elephant grass was bending with tiny birds resting on and on. Lawyer Tay rose with his kente gown – they didn't understand why he had to wear the gown everywhere – and went to the rural microphone. His heart was shut under his cap, his voice uncharacteristically quiet: 'Me as a lawyer, I don't like free emotion, I leave it to my wife to cry for the things the world does to us . . . though I know she will tell you that she cries at me and not usually for me. Shouldn't she help me more than that . . . you know the system: there is too much strain when I have to prosecute as well as defend every case that comes up in the one court. I make cases against myself and defend cases against myself. I came here to do something new, and to get money and . . .' '. . . power, power!' Appa inserted quickly. The lawyer looked at him with his large bright eyes and then continued, 'But if this Kwame Atta wants us to do some public confessions, then he's striking at the roots of my being here at all . . . what sort of a man is he anyway? He commands no respect yet he commands influence! How can I tell you what type of life I was leading before I came or was brought to this town? And I am getting suspicious of Kwame Atta because sometimes he boasts he can invent a truth machine! And if he does that he will reduce the cubic capacity of my calibre! I will slip on the status banana . . .' 'Ah!' shouted Appa, 'it looks as if the lawyer has already swallowed the guava of truth!' Six men were running at full speed 440 taking the laughter from one person to the other; but there was tension: they felt that the lawyer was about to reveal something that may force them to reveal some of their own secrets. Aponkyi Amoa was irreverent with other people's tension; he gloated in the little spaces that others suffered in: 'Is Lawyer Tay going to tell us about the time he cheated both the defence and the prosecution, pocketing thousands of cedis fresh? Or about the time he tried to pay the boy-menace Zolozolo to kill Opanin Akorsah? Let his fatty bombole wife tell us about the time she caught her beloved husband trying to force a lady clerk of the court behind the magistrate's chair to do some legal logologo . . .' 'Hey leave my fat out of it!' shouted Sosuaa Dadoona, the lawyer's wife, advancing threateningly towards Amoa, and sensing that she had to protect her husband even if this was in her own interest. 'The elders are free here, but you must still respect them.' Nana Bontox rose quickly; he wanted to conduct the uproar, but he was almost pulled down by the tug of the single communal cloth: one elder had moved beyond the statutory distance of Atta's textile invention . . . and it was only Nana's superior weight that stopped him from being pulled to the ground. 'Order, order!' Nana shouted into the microphone. 'You don't arrive at togetherness by playing at hopscotch with our history!' 'Don't mind that foolish boy!' boomed Dadoona in triumph as Amoa ran off down the hill, 'he's running away to find another coffin to pretend he's dead in!' 'I beg you to buy more khebab, entertain your mouth with the hottest kyinkyinga!' shouted Dogo behind his bells, sneaking a useless appeal into the microphone. But Kwame Atta's mood of accusation and confession had caught the lawyer first, and was catching others . . . Kwaku de Babo, chief secretary and good twin, Mr Cornerstep, and duck shepherd, did not know what to write but wrote when he had to. He was listening to the uneven flow of the hearts opening.

'Me too I am guilty,' said Nana Bontox sitting. His sedentary but drunk guilt led to some silence, so he continued: 'I am the one that killed Kwame Agyei spiritually, poor Kwaam is gone through my wickedness.' There was a stunned silence. Then Moro shouted, 'Let us destool and try him, I will then ask the kingmakers to nominate somebody like me for the vacant stool . . .' Nana's stool executioners who had never executed anything, and were usually drunk, surrounded him protectively . . . for tomorrow was when they got their bi-weekly ration of akpeteshie. 'You Moro keep quiet!' answered Lawyer Tay in anger and resentment: he sometimes saw Moro as a rival for his grasp for power. 'You Moro, you think just because your Mercedes Benz has got underwear, has got some engineering pioto, you think you can hide your sins! You think I don't know that you secretly stole some of the late Akoto's land? You got the surveyor to work at midnight under the tiny light of fireflies, and then rushed to Kumasi to forge a plan. Cheat! Akoto told me on his death bed when I was making his will . . . but he told me that he would attack you spiritually, and that I shouldn't sue you yet . . . besides Nana is only drunk.' Tay had a heated smirk on his face. When Akorsah rose to speak, shaking slightly, no one paid much attention to him until they heard what he was saying: 'It is me the one who really killed Kwame Agyei spiritually! I killed him first! He was becoming too rich and powerful with his charcoal and transport business. Besides he had discovered the secrets of the shrine.' 'The only secret the shrine has is that it can control time,' Kofi Senya declared from his vulture corner, with a seriousness that thickened his smoke. His eyes were smouldering, so that some were afraid, for he had never been angry before. 'And we now want to find a way of commoting time outside the shrine instead of only inside.' Zolozolo added with a furtive and hungry look. Who killed Kwame Agyei whether spiritually or physically, was what all the eyes asked. 'So now we have two people killing one man without the knowledge of either killer! Ewurade, this is a banished town indeed!' Amoa exclaimed after a quiet reentry.' Keep quiet and let the elders speak' someone shouted. The pause led to Zolozolo: 'How could you both have killed him at all when he was rather taken away from this world to go and reorganise the ancestors, to give the past its proper path? I swear you want some bad fame for a killing you no dooo kapereba . . . you want power over the past! But the shrine has it already!' When Zolozolo was saying this he had that same stupid look on his face that he was famous for; and his right hand was perpetually extended begging for gifts, for anything from bananas to boots. And the subtle stops in his speech were meant to be pauses to remind people to give, give; so that one phrase was worth one banana if necessary. But now Kofi Senya his master took him by the wrist, led him all the way back down to the shrine, and gently locked him in, adding, 'Eat and pray and practise until I come to open you soon.' 'Kofi Senya my master, did I talk unwise, was my palaver too plenty?' There was fleeting anxiety on Zolozolo's face, but the shrinemaster had already gone.

One sign of the worried man was an involuntary sigh, which came out of the face of Zolo the Zolo, crept up the hills, and swiftly hissed through the frowns of Nana Bontox: Nana was clever enough to know how stupid he was: he was prepared to make his confessions if it led to the damaging confessions of others. And there he was, expectant, his flywhisk upside-down and chasing the flies the wrong way. 'More confessions, more confessions!' a voice rose from the flowering dandelions. Lawyer Tay sat by a group of thin thistles. His large frame contradicted what he thought was his small build: he must have been forgiven any sins he had committed before coming here . . . that was part of the agreement worked out with Pokuaa, Senya, and the ancestors, with the gods somewhere in the background. But any sins committed here were a definition of perfection: compromise, a compromise usually under the uneven gaze of Pastor Mensah . . . and under the pipe of Kofi Senya. LT, the man with the legal mouth, could not bear to be under any authority at all: he had a deep emotional feeling of ultimate independence; and after a long discussion with Korner Mensah one day he arrived at the conclusion that the pastor should reinvent God with a different form so that he, Tay, could worship him. The lawyer had no problem with the ancestors, nor with the lesser gods of the shrine, for he felt they were close enough to be sarcastic with when necessary . . . especially when fate had dealt a blow that he thought they could easily have absorbed. Besides, Kofi Senya was so remote, so mysterious that LT usually tried to avoid him in case he would bring all the magnificent law in his lawyer's head under a preternatural spell. And there was a wild rumour that Pokuaa was really the younger sister of Senya, and that the town would one day become a dynasty. It was also sometimes said that Pastor Mensah had hidden much money right in the middle of the altar . . . that the altar was a huge safe . . . But this rumour made it easier for the lawyer to relate to the pastor: they both seemed smaller than the theological discussions they held; especially after Korner Mensah gave blessings with a trace of Guinness on his hand. But at this moment this pastor did not want to mix religion with the kyinkyinga, the chamber-pots, the swamps, nor the ducks. There could, however, be some theological considerations for the elephants of the mutant kind, for the hearts part-open part-shut, and for the direction of meaning in the town, this town that had decided decades ago to be conscious about everything except its own being . . .

Lawyer Tay was sometimes deeper than the swamps he sat by. He had wanted to take the sky into his jaw, so that the angle at which it met the horizon could not be crossed by aeroplanes: if they wanted to fly over his heart and judge the confessions there, then he had already put the barriers high. He would accept nothing, he would deny nothing; and all that he would do was to sleep at night on the possibilities of the following day. 'Sleep faster, lawyer, sleep faster!' shouted Appa the metal man, 'for the deeper you sleep the faster you will escape their insinuations! We don't want your law to get less . . .' LT's sleep so sudden was interpreted as something deep and suspicious. 'Pass the questions onto someone else!' shouted Kwame Atta rebursting onto the scene. 'It's all your fault. You are taking far too long to make a major invention that the gods would approve, Kwame Atta! It is because you are a scoundrel!' Akyaa shouted, raising her courage for the elders, shoogling her irritation beyond her husband's shoulder. 'Ah, there you all go attacking me again! But give me the chance and I will transform the ninety-nine houses into one thousand!' 'But we don't like your high price!' retorted Opanin Akorsah. 'Now everything for the high
journey is ready even though I don't agree with this everything . . .' 'So you don't agree with getting pounds for your harvests, and then contributing to the buying of the aeroplanes . . .' Amoa asked, keeping a safe distance from Dadoona. 'I say let the abongo boys take over the aeroplanes!' came Akorsah's reply. 'A fool is always a fool!' Amoa shouted to Opanin Akorsah, this Amoa running down the hill for the second time in flight. 'All I want is I don't want anybody to fool us . . .' announced Akorsah through the microphone. Then he tripped over a minor cross which fell down at the same time as he did. In the uproar, Dogo used two khebab sticks to chook the cross, to steady it; and when they hooted at him – not necessarily for expressing his views – he rushed down into the half-attentive embraces of his wife who was in the middle of counting the pods and bunches and roots of his farms for her benefit. Poor Akorsah! Everything grew in his farms except his hopes; and everything was good in his life except his evil.

'My confession is that I want this town built on love so that I can get some of this love transferred to me,' Pokuaa said loudly and without warning. 'Is it love of Kwame Atta?' asked LT bold and awake. She resented the general silence, but she filled it all the same: 'Love of the living, love of the dead.' There was some clapping, but someone else asked, 'Do you love the rotted bones of the dead, or do you love their skin just before it putrifies . . .' 'Leave the aeroplane lady alone!' boomed Appa's voice. 'You too keep your mogantic mouth shut,' an elder retorted. 'Do you younger ones want to control everything or what?' 'If you trouble her too much she will take her love and wealth elsewhere,' Kaki the driver said, his mouth louder than his traxcavator. 'O, no she won't!' replied the contradictory Moro, 'she won't because there are too many people hanging onto her love, if it's really true love that is . . .' Moro never failed to sleep under his Benz, augmenting the absorbers with snores; but he was now wide awake, seeing what subtle wounds he could make in Pokuaa's many-sided skin. 'But it was not only love that brought the aeroplanes,' Moro went on, 'it was fighting, manoeuvring, and tricks on tricks forever!' 'But Moro, Papa Moro,' Pokuaa said with genial heat, 'you know that some of us fight hard in strange countries, and then bring the gentleness to our own country . . . How did you manage to let your cola and your Mercedes Benz grow together like that? Don't hate me because I have no hate to give back to you . . .' There were many cheers and much meat eaten at the same time. Moro stood there defiant, far fatter than the spaces between the lines of his elaborate batakari. Fatima stood by him supporting his flesh but criticising his spirit.

Fatima was as tall as sixty-six of Moro's different-coloured cola piled up sensibly. Her wisdom was usually written by de Babo the secretary, but this did not make any difference to her since she never wanted to be overconscious of the world about her. She was one of those that fitted well in the town without desiring anything new or anything high. She sweetened Moro's life with her long sugar-cane legs, and made love best under the stiffness of the Benz. But the two soft sharp girls arguing about whose left buttock was softer were not written by de Babo: for he was afraid of bursting the Minutes Book if he put all time place and thing in it. The world wore the sun high at noon. Kwaku also refused to record one outrageous fact manufactured by Manu the carpenter out of pique that he was caught trying to comadi Akyaa: that Azziz's popylonkwe was so small that he had to have two erections in a row fast before poor Akyaa could even see it; and out of righteous anger – not that there was anything wrong with a tiny popylo, he thought – the only thing that Azziz could do and did was to bare himself to Manu in the full view of others . . . after all what kind of morals would Kofi Senya sanction, in free discussion, for a town that had very few seams? The confessions continued to burn at different parts of the meeting, so that at one point Nana Bontox had to beat an electronic gong-gong to announce that the point had been reached where people had to tell some temporary lies about themselves in order that the town did not disintegrate; so many had committed sins of such magnitude that each found his neighbour sordid . . . and out of fear that even the truly revered ones would reveal something profane, Kofi Senya was forbidden by consensus to reveal his past, much against the wish of people like Lawyer Tay. And then Pastor Mensah saved the day by declaring that there was a deep difference between sin and crime; and that crimes could be considered after the journey, while sins could be forgiven now provided that a spiritual debt to the future was agreed, a few cedis. And when the agreed lies came Kwame A was in his element:

everything bad he had ever done was reversed in his gleeful moral headstands; and he wanted to be appointed a shrine priest, or a church saint immediately if that failed.

After touching the face of somebody's wife as a prelude to carefully calibrated concubinage – this being refused by the irate husband who wanted someone else to take his wife from him – Kwame Atta calmed
$$\overline{A}$$
himself down by drinking two handfuls of wild honey, and going into the invention room only to rush out in a rage because he feared that nothing was inventable. But before he returned to the meeting he had what he called a major idea: the democratisation of family genetics. He had decided, without the authority of the ancestors, that there was a finite number of human types available in Tukwan; and that once this number was reached, any human characteristic – whether physical or mental – was a repeat of what was already available over an agreed time span of two thousand years: so that if you talked about inheriting a leg, then you could easily inherit it out of the family pool. This would increase togetherness, and rope all bones into a potential oneness. He swore that this would also reduce guilt, tribe – which barely existed in the town anyway – and then would, paradoxically, increase the space of individuality available to each person. When they laughed at him, he laughed back and re-presented the idea right at the same meeting. 'This idea will make it easier to choose the right people for the journey without any trouble,' he declared, with a look of ludicrous seriousness. 'But it doesn't sound very scientific to me,' the morose Moro said doubtfully. As soon as most people saw that Moro doubted the idea, then they agreed with it, knowing that to be successful at cola did not mean to be successful at genetics. Atta was getting more and more confident during the meeting. He reminded the meeting: 'Remember that the abstract, the idea and the speculation have been reblessed by the ancestors as ways of living, but that they must not control us . . .'

The beautiful yawns got longer, especially from Nana Bontox who secretly wished that the wisdom of proverbs and ritual in tradition would occupy the head alone. But he did not dare say this since it was generally agreed that new things were as wise as the old at Tukwan, and that the opposition between the two was welcome and controllable. And this town was so new and so strange that it had even given Kwaku de Babo the task of modernising all proverbs from all tribes. And also, all ritual outside the shrine was declared instant, creative and individual, as long as they were all reassessed once a year, and given a very broad direction by Kofi Senya, who obviously kept some of his wisdom in the mouth of his vulture. Kwame Atta the inventor was drinking from two glasses at once, and sometimes his tongue got stuck in between them. He looked at Pokuaa triumphantly, wondering whether she would contradict the silence that meant consent with his new idea. 'But what is genetics?' Maimuna asked with scorn. 'Ah,'

Kwame began with a smirk, 'genetics is the origin of your other leg that you thought belonged to your uncle when it really comes from somebody unrelated at all!' 'He only wants a cheap way of earning the right to travel!' a voice came from among the hihe, 'and after all if the shrine says we must travel, why should we seek any other reasons? Me I think we are overdoing all this knowknow thing!' It was Azziz, holding onto Akyaa's hand while he talked and squeezing it too hard out of forgetfulness. Her little squeal made him more obstinate: 'What is wrong with having ninety-nine houses anyway . . .' 'It's too crowded!' shouted Appa in disgust, 'and remember, we have vowed to move ahead. Let's not question the ground we are standing on now! It's too late for bigitive questions!' Pokuaa and Kofi Senya nodded in agreement at the same time. 'There's a big space ahead of us for questions,' Senya said simply, 'but if we start now, Kumasi will attack us.' Blue words, blue pipe smoke.

So the new genetics got off to a fine start when one hundred ritual hens, each with a candle on its back, surrounded the dusk of the meeting, fluttering out of fright for the flames on their backs . . . with the ducks proud standing slightly below on the banks of the raised lake, wondering why the good duckmaster had left them out of the spectacle. And the insects were gathering, spending their sounds so hard, choosing their space and shouting in it, choosing their skin and biting it. The pastor had already installed the second cross so white, while they were busy talking; and there was Christ doubled on the hills. Dogo was mixing good profits and good bells all the way downhill. The silver chamber-pots were being cleaned slowly by the executioners . . . who kept on asking when they would exercise their real functions. The long unbroken communal cloth for the elders was cut by Kofi Senya. 'My inventions are working!' A/Atta shouted with triumph; and the elders could at last walk the extra metres without relying on the power of an unusual invention, nor on the power of being pulled back rudely by their own cloths. Your Appas Maimunas and Amoas were already gone, and could thus not hear Pokuaa saying, 'As soon as we finish the tarmac, we will move forward on the journey. But we haven't solved our lives and problems yet. Anyone who wants pepper or guavas to help with the thinking should come to my house in the morning.' The moon had made the crosses and the grasses exciting as they descended at different speeds. Kwaku de Babo was left alone up there in the dark. For now, the top of his head looked exactly like the top of the hill, take away a descending swamp or two. Every firefly was the moon, fireflies on the minutes book, fireflies forming his steps in sudden stairs of light down the little-used side of the hill . . . and the good twin went on and devoured kenkey and kyenam.

CLASS THREE

Freed from the tyranny of narrowly inherited legs, Kwame Atta had developed a new walk: every fourth or fifth step you would think his legs came together and crossed in mid-air, and then returned in perfect rhythm back to the waiting, skipping earth. And his hands were lovers: they held each other hard, and then pulled the town together, scooping flesh, festivals and tarmacs into his head to see what would come out new, even over his super chin. His great ambition when he was sober was to reveal the town to the rest of the country, after the inventions and after the journey. Although he had a way of dancing into responsibility and kicking it, he deeply resented the reduction of his worth whenever he was not appreciated: when this happened he would accordingly reduce his name by dividing it with its first letter, and then he would destroy the remaining letters in an anger of alphabetical suicide: $\frac{Atta}{A} = 0$. Usually his muted individualism would erase its own adjective, so that his desires and excesses were open for all to view and to mock. $\frac{Atta}{A}$ had not invented a truth machine, otherwise he would have invented immediately its opposite and used it to suppress everything about himself, except his inventions and his love for Pokuaa. After all he could still discern a few alleluyas left in his soul: he wanted the town to survive and grow. Though he did not show it often, he loved the calm honesty of his twin brother Kwaku, but felt that this goodness should be stored in a jar of Marmite: to be kept and shown sparely only to people of unusual tastes. He would say to the scorners: know me! For if they wanted him to lead them from the back, then some of the values too would come from the back.

Kwame Atta collected information about himself freely: he was wise enough to believe that since he was rejected so often, he had to be firm about himself: left sandal slightly heavier than the right sandal because of the greater sweating there and the faster gathering of dust; an extraordinary screaming before the noonday sun every six months, since the heat burned so hard at such a physically cool man; a belief in the power of an advanced chest: a chest that could take all the horse and elephant riding, and then all the jots plus the akpeteshie, was a blessed chest, an unbootable chest . . . though he sometimes wheezed beyond the trees. Kwame Atta's love language was spoken in coughs, for he accused Pokuaa of being the cause of that vast store of misplaced and unrequited love in his withering heart; and this made him cough on and on. And his khaki shorts, being long at the thigh and short at the knee, did nothing about the emotion above . . . they rather tweaked the tooshie and then squeezed them ten times smaller than an elephant's. On to the invention room where Zolozolo often unthinkingly interrupted Atta's inventive thinking, making those ideas that did not deserve it appear ridiculous. In the thinking room, where sweetapples and coconuts lay to give fruit to his thoughts, he remembered this: he only saw Pokuaa's breasts by accident as she lay under her pepper bushes planning her tarmac. Atta had roared with desire as she covered herself in her own time. Then he had asked her, 'Why do you make yourself so simple, yet not simple enough for me to hold?' He had asked this while trotting on the same spot and lighting a jot at the same time. She had looked at him with pity, at the foolishness that wanted to come into her life, and then had disappeared inside her shoulder-stooping compound arches and had fallen asleep, having forgotten all about him. It was a productive sleep, for as soon as she dreamt that Kwame Atta was stealing a bottle of brandy from her house, she woke up just in time to see him actually doing so. She had no intention of chasing him, but he himself went off with a huge bound . . . and tripped over his fourth or fifth step mid-air legs, sprawling with a curse among the broken bits of glass, and still trying to drink the rivulets of brandy spilled in the glass. 'I am just too good for you!' Atta shouted with an authority that was full of smoke descended and brandy muddied, 'I am far better than my twin so consider well well well where you want to put your love! Consider that any children fathered by me will be both head-head children and kind too . . . I can arrange that their bones come from beyond the new genetics . . .' But a wink and a yawn from Pokuaa were enough to send him away.

Atta always saw more after being playfully rejected, for he appreciated that the play was meant to temper the rejection. This though did not stop him from that feeling of revenge that need not be directed at Pokuaa, but either at himself rather, or something different altogether. He had watched the land being stolen and moved centuries ago; and then, in the days when he was a good ancestor, he had been present when the gods and other ancestors – on behalf of God their skymaster – had decided that the same inhabitants of Tukwan would be born over and over again until all the changes required had been met. This decision had been made under a huge dawadawa tree laced to the sky with fruit and birds. So that everybody except Kaki the driver was a series of incarnations, yet some were a little earlier than others. So that the Pokuaa you saw now was in herself a plenitude of generations; the sheep and goats wore the same renewed skin of centuries. And it was only Kofi Senya, Babo – and sometimes Pokuaa – that saw his desperate need to burst out of this recycled immortality! There lay his foolishness as Senya would say: if Atta had been given an immortality that he was usually only dimly aware of, where then was the need to break this immortality? Who would dare say that change came only from the wound and death of mortality . . . and Kofi Senya – sometimes in the company of Atta, sometimes not – would smile at himself and wonder when some of the people would see this: to break the barrier of ninety-nine houses was a mortal act; to travel for profit and renewal was also a mortal act: so that the gods were giving Tukwan a final choice: the more change it made, the more mortal it became, the lighter its being grew. It was the fear that Kofi Senya had some wonderful secret or knowledge that kept most people away from him and yet drew others to him. And he did have this secret: his peace and quiet came from the original SMASH that he got from the knowledge that the gods were so close to breaking the pedalling of immortality; that Tukwan would cease to exist in a time that moved in any dimension. Yet when you saw change coming, you hugged it, or you hugged the parts that would leave less blood on you. And the vulture was suspended above the perpetual smoke of the pipe, above the bare feet that Senya used to walk and to run, above the burr on his scratched and hairy legs.

Kwame Atta walked on assessing the avenues with their ice-plant hedges. Very few of the streets were tarred, but they were neat and could be touched. The pawpaw trees had shortened by the dwarf banana shoots, so that both trees held their fruit at the same height . . . but below the skin-ringed neck of Tukwan's chief inventor; the tiny pink-flowered stomach herbs, the milk-juice rabbit leaves, the blackberry thorns, the velvet leaved cough bush all grew in lines of deliberately controlled weed; circular rows of wild crab grass tightened the streets and met the yellow-flowering milk bushes, daring the planners of the streets to continue to use weeds creatively. When he reached that hillock, God's geological bump, he met his twin Mr Cornerstep eating a coconut by a breeze that seemed to come from his hands.

For a while they did not say a word to each other, which was quite surprising for Atta the bad and garrulous twin. They both watched the smoke from all the kitchen chimneys of the town. Everybody cooked on wood, everybody loved the smell, or. And the forest gave the wood plenty for they replanted what they used, except Pokuaa who replanted twice all the time. When Kwaku de Babo closed his hands the breeze was shut, and Kwame Atta was sweating . . . but for a different reason. He got up from the coconut that gave its fruit to be stolen, raised both hands in triumph and then shouted, 'I will steal the aeroplanes! This is what happens when they do not give you love!' De Babo looked up from the coconut; his expression was a quiet husk: what was his mad brother saying now? So he wanted to steal two aeroplanes . . . Atta read his thoughts: 'O, I will stick one aeroplane on my head, and then drive the other one away; I am sick of the insults!' When Atta raced off Kwaku didn't take him seriously; and the elephant grass beyond the borders shook with the race. 'Up up up into the sky!' came Atta's voice with the new breeze. Kwaku rose with his tall look, rubbing the grass from his elbows. A hawk and a crow chasing each other playfully in the sky were immediately above the aeroplanes. And they scattered as the great roar of the upper-lip engines went up. But Atta could not move: the lower-lip aeroplane was stuck in his head; and when he finally adjusted his head, it fell off skidding in circles towards Kwaku's arms. Kwaku had arrived in a rush when he heard the engines. 'Stop what you are doing! The tarmac was changed yesterday, it's not long enough!' But Atta answered from the sky, 'If it's long enough to take off, then it's long enough to land, and that's life!' But can't you see them shortening it again now? They haven't seen you, so they are continuing with their work. You are a fool forgive me! The tarmac is shorter now than before you went up!' screamed Kwaku. 'But can you see now that I have freed the other plane from my head? I want to travel alone . . . after all, I invent alone!' Atta shouted back with a grunt in his voice. And when he spat from a hundred metres up it almost ended up in the eye of his brother. Kwaku looked down hard so that he could look up double in the glare. After the spit there was the urine released from on high, and this got his back. Kwaku practised his goodness against the descending wastes, and did not give a curse at all. He wondered rather how his brother would come down safely.

Atta descended fifty metres and shouted, 'Up here, I am dealing with suspended truth! No one can call me a fool here, for after all the air is more and most foolish to be holding me up! And when I blow off in my fine releases of kwee, I just add to the air that makes me float!' 'You have slanted your life in the name of shame!' de Babo shouted up without thinking, and then ran towards the house of Pokuaa, his coconut, suddenly intelligent, rolling after him.

When he reached her, she was already looking up the sky in consternation. As soon as she heard the engines she rushed to Kofi Senya. Senya just smiled as he took off his ring and threw it into the sky, so that it expanded and then surrounded the aeroplane, it trapped it. Ring round plane in the deepening sky. Atta could only fly in diameters of one hundred metres, cursing at each radius of flight from a centre of enormously confused love. Then he fouled the sky above the groans of Pokuaa by releasing two turds in unison and then racing down after them in a mad dive. 'You will crash and spoil our hopes!' screamed the distressed Pokuaa. 'I don't understand a magic that can put a ring round an aeroplane yet fail to bring it down,' de Babo hissed to himself, hoping Kofi Senya would hear. He did, and replied with a growing grin: 'Intermediate magic always finds its own way later!' They both stared at him, puzzled. Hiss replied hiss. Pokuaa shouted to Kwaku, 'Please go, go with Appa and assess the lives of those being considered to go on the journey, so that by the time you have finished, we may have brought this Kwame Atta down and finished the tarmac ready to go . . .' And she never let that one tear in her eye fall, for after all if you cried, the rain always fell first. Kwaku heard a shout from the aerial Atta as he left. 'Try to invent a ladder of air, Pokuaa my love, so that I can land without using this stupid and shortening tarmac; as the tarmac shortens, so does my smile. Kwasia to the whole town! This is one of my small revenges! It is the love revenge!'

Ready, get set, gooo! went Kwaku's heart as he went to Appa's house with his coconut following, and gathered him from the bed that still held him fast; and the first person they went to unfortunately was Moro the man who wanted more and more of the universe. Fatima was washing her new baby boy born under the Benz, and rain washed him too. She had just finished chewing into her husband's ear for ten minutes because he loved the chewing to calm him down: he was whimpering a bit since he had just escaped being run over by his own car: he had forgotten to tell Fatima that he would sleep under the Benz without her that evening. So she was about to move the car when his loud snores reached her. She went over only one toe – which had a curious shape anyway – and thus a combination of snore, scream and crunch saved him. Moro was talking back under the Mercedes Benz, 'It's a bad omen, an omen for all men, that I was almost killed when you came! Why have you come to assess me? I am unassessable! Is this a dictatorship by a woman that wants all lives gone into before we travel? Why don't we just throw a dice to see who has the luck to go? After all, everybody in this town is worthy, or they wouldn't be here at all!' 'It was a decision taken by everyone,' Kwaku reminded Moro, with Appa impatiently quiet in the background. 'Well, I can't go . . .' began Moro. 'Don't you want a spiritual experience?' Appa asked with scorn. 'Nonsense!' shouted the no longer whimpering Moro. 'How much money will we get, and how many women will some of you chop in the snow! Me all I want to do is to listen to my wife's jaws chewing!' 'All right,' said the quiet Babo, 'but we must still assess you . . .' 'Go away with your assessment! I will not tell you that all I do is to struggle with my cola farms, I will not tell you that I worked so hard and prices are so low that I could only buy my Benz in bits. I began first with the plastic underwear, then I went onto the absorbers, then the engine, then the brakes, the transmission . . .' 'But all you want is power here!' said Appa, cutting Moro short.

There was a pause which Moro's expression of scorn and triumph filled: 'Now tell me of any hardworking man who is prepared to watch others exercise power without him! My work, apart from its own reward, deserves the reward of power!' 'But we share this power here,' protested Babo, 'and the mistake some of us make is to want reward beyond our life's vocation . . .' 'Don't bring your goodness here to me koraa!' boomed Moro. 'But my dear husband, goodness should be taken everywhere!' interrupted Fatima holding her soft screamy baby with his bot like her bot. Moro never failed to admire the softness of his hard-to-touch wife. He felt he had the strength to rule Tukwan, but that his wife kept him in touch with the vagaries of humanity. And sometimes felt that power would drag him into death. Besides there was nothing to beat a fine frolic under the Benz with Fatima, especially on Sunday nights, when Moro, with that thick and strong back, would appear almost childlike in his playfulness; and that batakari which he wore specially for Sundays, would shake with love. Now Fatima bathed and rebathed the baby out of forgetfulness until she was told by Moro's cola mouth to stop the soap skin and water show. The intelligent coconut, losing some speed, rolled from foot to foot as they talked, with Appa jumping up in mock fright whenever it approached him. Moro totally ignored it, only too ready to link it with what he felt were Kwame Atta's ludicrous inventions. 'Now my dear wife, are you speaking up for these visitors? . . .' began Moro curving his lip with a question-mark. 'Papa Moro,' said the everready brilliantly simple Fatima, 'this Kwaku here gave me soap for my baby, and this soap is so good that it has never finished. You know that his brother invented it, and it has saved us cash-cash. Everybody uses the everlasting soap . . .' 'Yes but it finishes whenever you tell a lie,' said the blacksmithing Appa. 'O yes!' agreed the glowing Fatima, 'and that is why I never let my husband use it! O . . .' There was an embarrassed silence which Moro broke with a queer but loving look at his wife: 'Anyway I am not going to any cold land where everyday the primitive people there will force me Moro the great cola farmer with Allah on my lips, to prove whether I'm human or not! What sort of deep and filthy nonsense is this! I will not go to such a primitive place!' Fatima held the hands of both baby and Moro, and said with a deep, ironic and civil smile, 'Don't worry my husband, when any of the cold landed people come here, we shall make them so human and so much cleverer . . .' 'That they will lose half their mad technology!' said Appa, inscrutable for once. 'Nono!' shouted de Babo adjusting his feet against the ever-advancing coconut, 'if you are really human, you don't have to lose anything you have invented before you remember its human source, before . . .' he took a bite at the automatic coconut, '. . . before you realise that keeping your humanity is the supreme intelligence!' Appa stared at Moro staring at Babo. 'Are we here to solve the cold and heat of man, or are we here to decide whether me Moro will travel or not? Behave your mouths I tell you! When you go you will solve nothing! and when you come back you will bring more problems . . .' Moro's sarcasm moved from irony to contempt as his wife looked at him with pity. 'If Papa Moro says he will not travel, then he will not travel,' she said looking at her baby with devotion and bewilderment. She closed the talk as de Babo threw a quick thank-you to the valleys and rushed off with Appa to the next house. After all, what time was there to spare when the aeroplane stolen by Atta was still high above in its suspended truth . . .

Two automatic and intelligent coconuts followed them to the house of Azziz and Akyaa. So in kube too you have twins, Allah. Azziz noticed that his wife had been sitting on used palm-nuts ready for cracking, each of which made an impression on her wonderfully soft yet muscular doona. 'My dear and soft Akyaa, please pull the posting of your cloth out of your excuse-me-to-say tu, because we have visitors . . .' Akyaa accepted her softness with ease, saying, 'Please Azziz, my pig-rearing husband, do it for me, for I'm too-too busy cracking the nuts . . .' Akyaa had the knack of growing in status without growing in intelligence or wealth . . . her constant look of half-surprise half-annoyance did this; and both wife and husband had fine forms, his biceps being more or less equal to the jut of her breasts, and his back to the curve of her navel. 'Ah, here comes Kwaku the duckmaster who by regular bathing has cleared all lice from the sacred ducks! O, and the metal man follows him! Sit down and enjoy the coolest water from that freezer of ours that keeps freezing alive our chickens which sneak into it for our stored corn whenever our careless children leave it open and then shut it later too late. The ways of God are often seen in the mysteries of frozen feathers! And don't mind my wife koraa, she thinks I love Pokuaa when I just admire her . . . of course I won't tell you exactly *where* I want to admire her!' Akyaa had a vision of beauty: the gods recreating sense into the elementary head of Azziz the good husband with bad habits. 'Ah, I know your mission already,' continued Azziz the farmer of pineapples, 'I know you want to know who should know about travelling! But never worry, wherever my wife goes I go . . . the secret being that we share the same shadow . . .' 'Except when we are lying down my dear husband!' interrupted Akyaa.

'What sort of life would you offer for the journey?' asked the impatient Appa who was often uncomfortable in the presence of love that he did not generate. 'O life!' purred the fastidious Akyaa who at twenty-eight looked eighteen, 'my husband tells me we haven't started living it yet! I honestly think that love can get in the way . . .' Azziz looked around in shock at this. 'O my dear and ever-faithful husband sometimes, I mean that if I didn't love you so much I would have made more money sharp. But I jump to say that the more money I don't make the more love I have for you . . . and we want to tell you our fine visitors that we offer love as a good standard for the journey.' Akyaa presented her smile as fruit of the freshest order. 'But we can't assess only a smile and a love for such an important journey,' Appa declared, as Kwaku smiled into his declaration. 'Ah!' exclaimed Azziz the of ah man, 'Why don't we offer pig-rearing as a source of strength for the journey . . .' 'In other words, our dear visitors, my husband wants to be a pig in the United Kingdom!' Akyaa offered between her nut-cracking. Azziz's laugh was the squeak of the fresh bacon still walking about on African soil red; and he added, 'But the pastor blesses our pigs near the times of slaughtering, so I don't see why we can't make something holy out of the trotters for all the feeding physical and spiritual I do with pigs and pineapples. And I understand they have pine as well as apples in UK, not forgetting the fact that I stopped being a muslim so that I could rear and eat pork. Do we qualify for the travelling or do we not, Kwaku the Cornerstep, chief windy man of the breezes?' Husband and wife both stood there, full of intense but deflected expectation. To travel was not an obsession for Akyaa; but for Azziz to make money in pounds for pineapples was another thing altogether. 'We shall make our recommendation to the Elders' Council sharp and sooner,' said Appa moving off and grabbing de Babo's hand with him. By the time Akyaa screamed at the moving coconuts, it was too late: they had left, rolling after their masters Babo and Appa, and had expertly avoided the dives and lurches of the two small children of the house of pigs and pineapples.

Gooooo! on to the sleeping house, one room, of Amoa the newest reincarnated adult of Tukwan went the astute and assessing team . . . whom the outraged Amoa joined by force: 'How dare you come here to assess me for the journey when you should already know that I must be part of the assessing team! I will be going on the deep and long skyflight with immediate effect, since I am Appa's best friend, and since I have secrets of the dead to reveal in the hilly ices and snows abroad!'

So they moved on into that palace of gentle akpeteshie whose storage place was in the belly of Nana Bontox; and it was to find out whether Nana was taking his favourite wife abroad, or. Nana was asleep but he stirred when his heaviest wife lay on him for effect. The effect wakened him quickly. 'I thought Pokuaa would have come herself,' drawled Nana trying to cope with that long yawn pulling him back into sleep, 'but never mind, she must have some reason . . .' 'She is trying to bring down the upper-lip aeroplane,' said Appa with only a perfunctory greeting which Kwaku corrected with a double emphasis on his. 'I will eat the young raw one day, especially those that greet half,' Nana said with force, a second Tukwan yawn flowering behind his frown. Appa readjusted his greeting without the slightest trace of remorse.

The coconuts remained outside the palace, knocking against each other in the rhythms of kete; and beyond the walls some late-March rain was threatening the hurrying shoulders bent against the wind. Much to everyone's surprise in the town, the same year somewhere in the 1950s had shown itself for the last three weeks, during which the sun had been saved from the sweat of running in and out of different decades in the same week . . . and it sometimes became so bad that two different houses experienced two different parts of the same breathless calendar; and when Tuesday finally caught up with Wednesday, it was a different year altogether. Time was slowing down before the journey, was jumping about less . . . so that Nana's skin could rest small: 'Please bring my wives now, but go and get a dice first so that I can see which one will go with me, but already I know it will be Corporal . . .' There was uproar in the uxorial rooms, for the wives knew that none of them was going to travel. Corporal stood in triumph, holding the seniority in her immaculately cut jaw. 'I will go, me I will go!' she cried defiantly to the other wives. When the rain finally came down onto the pen of Babo, Nana too had to come down with promises to the other wives, all of whom were financially independent of him, but who remained with him for the status and for the stability of tradition. When Akosua Corporal finally walked down the compound under the stares of the other wives, shoogling the elegant locomotion of her magnificent tooshies, she said to herself quite loudly, 'Ewurade, continue to let your blessings to me be one thousand more! If you give me pepper I will give you soup, if you show me sweat I will give you a bigbig towel . . .' Akoss, only your walk cut to fit the rain, cut to fit your joy! But Akoss couldn't make the plane: she fell asleep, none of the other wives wakened her.

After Kwaku had put up with a ridiculous argument from Appa about whose back should receive more rain, and thus keep the other drier, they arrived at the residence of Lawyer Tay, with Appa falling into the mud in front and earning from Kwaku a wipe gratis.

The muddy Appa greeted the impeccable Tay with Kwaku's goodness lost somewhere in between. 'Gentlemen of the mud and the pen, akwaaba! I know your mission already, since Nana phoned me through the rain. It may have been a trunk call with the grey elephant standing beside him. I have just eaten a very fat bush rat, obviously the ekusie of the month, and this has given me much thought about my next case, which as you know is always a double case fought for either side. Now, my latest problem is that my wife is corresponding too much with Pokuaa, and at the same time she has become so religious that it shows through her soups . . . when you start cooking for God instead of for Lawyer then things get serious. So I have decided that since God may have no one to cook for Him if Dadoona travels with me, she should stay and do so. She resents this since she considers that the Almighty may get more protein in London with her cooking there, but I was firm with her. I reminded her that she has a son Sala who loves salad – no, he has no relation to his own eating – and whose impudence needs careful watch by either parent . . .' 'But Papa Lawyer, I am coming,' declared Sala. LT raised his eyebrows and kept them raised as Dadoona ambled in supporting her son with whom she did not get on too well: caught between religion and the law, Sala chose the law to break the catch. 'All right, father and son will go, myself and half myself,' Lawyer Tay said, edging towards his visitors with a new conspiratorial air: 'But I would advise you not to go to the house of the magistrate, for as you know he is a most difficult man, especially to travel with, and since he has no training in law, he has trained himself in highly offensive arrogance, some magistratus arroganzus!' There were always inexplicable passes in the lawyer's laughter, spaces of silence among the noise. When they were going out the visitors had to go through the window, for the good Madame Dadoona had got stuck in her own sitting-room door while in the middle of a sudden prayer, thus duplicating her chuch door sticking. She would boot her husband's laughter if she could!

Then on to the bean-deep atmosphere of the fusty-coated magistrate who ate many balls of mashed beans fried in deep fat, especially before his judgements. He was so stern that he had refused to reveal his name when he arrived in the town; and it was only the intervention of the successive reincarnations of Kofi Senya that allowed him to stay. Even the ever-accommodating Pokuaa hesitated, and was only persuaded when the magistrate reluctantly hinted that he could have been born on a Tuesday. Mr Kwabena, K for short, had decorated his small house in deep brown, the same colour as his chin; and without wife but with an impudent and hardworking maidservant or child, he kept his house immaculate, filling it with beans and cashew-nuts every Tuesday, his krada. He had already ordered his coffin, lined with deep-brown cloth; and he did this without permission: in this town you had to apply to the elders to do two things: to emigrate and to die without reincarnation. He made no secret of his desire to die once and for all, scorning with extreme arrogance the reincarnated world he lived in, and handing out heavy sentences of manual work whenever possible. He thought it ridiculous to exchange greetings, and he would give a withering look to anyone who wished him good morning . . . with an even more withering look for the carriers of good evening. For the elders, a pained wave of the hand was sufficient. Why was he in Tukwan then, they asked. 'We want as many spirits as different as possible, since we all want such a wide wide freedom so much,' Kofi Senya would reply. Before de Babo and Appa could speak, Mr K glared at them and said, 'I have a nature nurtured by beans, my name is unassessable. Your journey is a luxury, for all the answers you want are here. I judge people because I have from years back been the severest judge of myself . . .' 'But we want to teach others something too of this town,' broke in Appa with the soul of ore. 'You only teach after you learn,' Mr K said with traces of a distant smile which he immediately wiped off. There was an intense silence in the brown sitting-room; an old cat, with bigger brown over it than under it, slinked by glared at by the magistrate, who said with a change of mood, 'I have a brother in the UK, an anthropologist of all things, and when you people reach there he will arrange a conference for all of you to do your teaching and learning in the foreign lands!' There was a mischievous glow in Mr K's eyes. 'Are you tribally inclined, sir,' asked Appa without warning. The short, fine-motowayed Mr K got up brusquely and started to push his two visitors out. Appa pushed back, but Babo had already coaxed him out, asking Mr K in a throw-back of the voice, 'What is your brother's name?' There was a cheeky whistle in Appa's mouth which Mr K ignored, and he answered Babo: 'Find out his name when you get there, but don't think that because you will know my brother's name you will also get to know mine . . .' The cat walked between his master's legs, in and out, in and out. Kwaku had just started to wave with a coconut round his hands when Mr K stormed back into his room, carrying his cat by its front legs.

The moon was close to a pig's face when our two brave assessors rushed out of the livid Opanin Akorsah's house with a thrown sharp knife following; they were saved by the relentless prancing of the coconuts: the knife got stuck in one. And this was all because Appa had flaunted his A-levels before Akorsah by saying that he should have more sense and open his eyes to the eyes of his wife who obviously looked at everybody except her husband, and who spent the days counting his potential wealth. Whether Obaa Yaa had really been unfaithful or not was not legally important in Tukwan, though it was traditionally so . . . but it was the burning of the hearts behind the law that agitated some. Akorsah had first given Appa a surprising Makola suspension, creasing the latter's already shabby batakari; but Appa found it quite easy to blast Akorsah's arms away with his metal arms. Then that was when the knife started. Try to assess the shortest of souls in the quickest of times, and you rather get the sharpest edge of a rage.

The next morning – which saw the regurgitation of Independence by an erratic time, with buntings appearing in the streets involuntarily and quickly taken down by the unsentimental people in the town, especially Moro – arrived with both the sun laughing and the rain crying at the same time. Kwaku's undertongue had taken on slightly more lime, a semi-sharpness that came from all the wailing, all the disappointments, all the abuses, and all the attacks that were offered in his rounds with Appa and now Amoa. Amoa had come late because he could not find his belt, and when he tried to change his waist instead Zolozolo burst onto the scene and laughed the idea away: 'So just because you were buried you think you can bamboozle your own body . . .' Zolozolo the shrineboy had said with the white chalk on his face shining. Kwaku de Babo could not understand the reactions: this was supposed to be a free town with few things hidden, but very much a part of the country; and any profits from the journey would be enjoyed by everybody. So why the rush to ascend the polluted skies abroad? He himself would have stayed if he were allowed to. Dogo too had expressed his anger through his kyinkyinga, hot meat sharp sticks, and had threatened to stab Amoa in unseemly places if he did not withdraw his claim that sometimes his meat was so tough that you had to recycle the chewing. And Dogo had a problem: as soon as he stressed the need to make profits out of his khebab sold in London or wherever, then he would wail in case he was not chosen; but as soon as he wailed then his popylonkwe rose in wild unison . . . so that his consternated guests did not know whether to stare at the wailing mouth or at the funny erect longspoon trying to stir it. It was finally agreed that Dogo was to export his mad meat, but was to stay behind, not only to keep an eye on Moro but to help an elder's council, soon to be reconstituted, to run Tukwan in the time of the journey.

Pokuaa and Kofi Senya listened to the travails of the assessing team at her house . . . the team had to stand firm against Manu the carpenter – who was half drunk – because he was outraged that he was punished just for trying to touch somebody's wife . . . after all poor Akyaa was supposed to have buttocks that, naturally, shook too much, and Azziz in an unusual and wild jealousy, had spent hours with his wife trying to teach her a new and less provocative walk; but she had laughed back into her own natural perambulation. Manu was threatening that he would refuse to build the wooden trailers for the aeroplanes; at which point Appa had offered to build the more expensive metal ones. But with the estimates ready now and the hearts flying, Manu was warned to behave, to send his lust to the free women that did not have the shadow of a man crowded in their bodies. Though lies were of course temporarily allowed in the town to keep it together, Kwaku de Babo did not cease to be amazed at the attempts of most to appear in new light. How long would the lies shine, especially when everyone knew about them? Dogo had never used a rotten goat in his life, not even for kyinkyinga secretly exported to Kumasi; and his selling bells were of course taken from an ancient shrine-cathedral, but not bought from the market at Amakom cheap. Dogo insisted that he always sinned in fresh meat, sinned in fresh yam: all his sins were clean! and they could be chewed if necessary.

Pastor Mensah was causing a sensation by wearing extremely short cassocks as a way of saving cloth money towards the journey. He was being material. When the team visited him, he caused something bigger: he burst open the altar and thousands of coins ran out flooding the streets. He insisted that this was his contribution towards that opening of the soul that was necessary before the journey. The children rejoiced in the rain, throwing coins, scooping them into their faces, and then trying to buy the whole town wet. 'But we could have built a new church from all this!'

shouted the bewildered flock to the deeply meditating short-cassock pastor. 'The journey will bring us a new and bigger church,' Korner Mensah replied. The team toured the church, pushing aside coins, goats, and incense, and found that the pastor could be an asset in the strange lands. So the Korner arranged for some newly composed prayers in advance, to be used, surprisingly, by Mr K the magistrate who was given the ultimatum of acting as the priest in addition to his duties, or revealing his name immediately. Since he was not yet ready to leave this town, he agreed with a frightening and lugubrious expression, to do the priestly work; but he swore to himself that everything he did in the church would be done in silence; the worshippers would never enjoy so much silence! And he suddenly introduced deep green into his house, to atone for the sacrilege of the invasion of his privacy.

And the young team went to the lake in which the entire forest was reflected hard. It took an adjustment of the sun to clear the lake of reflections again. But it was a sign that the forest too must be visited, must be assessed against the savanna. Kofi Senya's vulture would sometimes eat the smoke from his pipe and flap burning into the forest rather than the lake to release it as all the animals stood still, expecting it to bring great news from its master's pipe . . . The lake was now more than a jewel, making most of the sun and changing shape frequently with the rain; the grasses were majestic, holding the breeze and riding it with long dances. Never mind the colours of the ducks pushing their darker patches out for greater assessment. But there was a wild flight when it was revealed to the lake that only two ducks would travel, plus one elephant grass and one crab grass uprooted. The ducks would hold the soul during the journey, and the lake would remain here to breed greater sunsum, greater joy. The angry ducks minus two could tear the sky; but when Kwaku secretly left the team and washed them safely, the quacks were silent, the wings did not flap their ripples. The decision was accepted in quiet as the coconuts rolled finally into the lake.

De Babo was there by the lake quietly brushing the ducks when Amoa came to tell him that the tarmac had now been made long enough for Kwame Atta, so exhausted, to land and certainly to be punished. There was an anger to Pokuaa's face: this Atta had stolen then rescued her documents; this Atta was now trying to steal her aeroplane. She walked in haste over the thousands of coins in the streets to the landed plane. She stared at the profusely sweating Atta, and her gaze was so intense that it needed an intermediary, someone to soften the piercing of Atta's vulnerable madness. 'If you were not the one to drive one plane, you would have stayed behind to do penance!' Atta did not speak. He shivered, and was lost in the light of thousands of coins rolling up to the tarmac. But in a sad attempt to redeem himself he dived into the pesewas, roared into the cedi coins, and then, still lying down tossed single coins, saying, 'coat-of-arms you kill me, cocoa you forgive me, coat-of-arms you kill me, cocoa you love me small . . .' When Pokuaa tried to take his temperature deep in the oxter, he just tried to get closer and closer, and then finally shouted, 'All the heat is in my balls, woman, all the heat is shua hot!' They all left him except his brother, and Pokuaa left him quite sure that his heat was certainly not of the body, but of the mind. She went slowly to pick her peppers small for the last; if only she could pull the plants into the aeroplanes. Pokuaa, only your kpakpo shitohs, only your white, orange, yellow, double-green, violet and very red peppers.

It was only after the two brothers sat down on the ground that they knew which bot belonged to whom. The world had ceased to be firm for them for different reasons: Kwaku was overwhelmed by the different reactions of people, and Kwame was desperately trying to shed his own body to let a better person occupy it. You could see their noses were the same but Kwame said that the snort was different. 'Let us be snortified,' Kwame said still roaring to be himself less and less but achieving the opposite. Kwaku got up to go, but sat down out of pity and shame for his brother. 'That is the problem about twins,' Babo said more to himself than anything, 'sometimes they share the same heart and end up . . .' '. . . being beaten by the same beat,' Atta concluded. He rose under the lower-lip aeroplane, gave the wing an upper pat, and said, getting some of his nonchalance back, 'I will pilot this, and Appa will drive the other one. This town can't do without me . . .' Babo ignored him, and besides his pen was frozen, there was no longer any heart left in the ink.

Then the message from Pokuaa to the sitting brothers was this: check all tasks, the final list has been approved, prepare the aeroplanes of the lip. The twins went through all tasks as best as they could 440. The webs of the travelling ducks have been duly polished, Yes? And the requisite number of feathers have been pruned, pulled out for the weight, or painted, No? A few men will continue to be busy sweeping dead reeds off the lake, for that was the best way for the water to breathe and still is. And brooms on the water became excessively clean. Fine, if we want to be twin to twin, then we must check thoroughly the double system of caves so that there are no speleological problems left to see. Me Babo I will reduce the hills before the journey by passing a string through their centres, and I will raise them again on our return. If Atta looked at Babo it was to detect some new pride that may not last beyond the journey. Everybody should freshen the tomatoes and the coconuts, not forgetting the peppers on our return. It was possible that a mistake was made in appointing the odd Mr K to perform naming ceremonies for infants, and also to baptise. We the twins do not want some crude and rabjibeeb ceremonies, for sometimes you protected more what you did not fully believe in, as if some doubt led to greater certainty. All sphincters travelling must be fortified against attacks on race, humanity and intelligence, and yet there must be that type of fortification that allowed a measure of kindness to flow in strange lands . . . flow for business and flow to prevent bitterness. Ejaje! Moro is not to make a coup in the absence of the elders and other rulers, for his great selfishness does not have any width to temper it. When the forest was assessed it was decided that the cries of the various animals, the wild pigs titrew, would be taped and played abroad at any time thought appropriate, especially when the group was in any way being attacked psychologically. So the forest had love. Anybody that was vulnerable and loving simultaneously, like Pokuaa, would most probably be reassessed when all the money hoped for became available, in case there was any danger of the town being suffocated with kindness . . . according to Atta. The eating of beef, akrantie, and extremely rich wood-maggots was forbidden for the duration of the journey. Kaki the driver was not to drive his Kumasi traxcavator towards any inordinate sinners; and the altar was to be resealed against the hoarding of coins, even though the pastor objected through a quick prayer to this. The jumps of frogs would be enumerated daily, and related to any hearts that appeared to be withering, so that no crying was to wither or jump.

Sala was to leave his photograph for his mother the ever-praying Sosuaa Dadoona to cane his absence with whenever he misbehaved either abroad or his shadow at home. Nana's wives were to quarrel as much as possible, but were not to resort to any slashes of the flesh with long nail or snail shell. Frost was to be experienced in advance through the inordinate buying of ice for the travellers for the next few days. It was to be re-emphasised that no snake was to make any appearance in any public place during the time of travelling, paths in remote farms being included. Kwame Atta, much to his worry and consternation, was to be abused openly and frequently in his absence as punishment for his immediate sins, including the stealing of the aeroplane. Why do you people, why do you treat a boogie-long man like me like this, Atta would hiss. Zolozolo was not to be tempted with any special tasks at the shrine unless a telegram was sent pronto to Kofi Senya first. No apparent or real enemies were to be destroyed. Since all the palm-nuts and cassava were to be exported, especially through the trailers of the aeroplanes, yam and groundnut farming was to be encouraged. One clean long-legged sheep was to be allowed inside the church, provided it would cross its legs upside down and allow them to be used as living crosses during any service, no bleating allowed. No automatic coconuts were to be tolerated. If anybody wanted to sell any property, no property was to be sold, except as approved by the interim council which shall be liberal. We twins know how to drive the earth because our vehicle is the town. Two doves jealous of the ducks have landed on Kwaku's shoulder with jealous chattering. Kwame would shoot and eat them there and then if allowed. Only five clocks were to be used at different times simultaneously. Fetch gin and food regularly for the gods and for the ancestors, some of whom – after they have chosen themselves perhaps by the toss of golden coins – would visit the strange lands when necessary. Don't wear the communal uncut cloth koraa; and the Tumtuhene was to pour libation to the stools and count them on and on. Lawyer Tay should not fight with Opanin Akorsah abroad. The town must construct a fine maze round itself in case Kumasi decided to attack in addition to banishment.

No more stray residents were to be accepted from there until the return. Every animal, human, thing, or presence was to be treated as equal in being, in principle, to everything else. Boom, boom, roared the engines twice, on trial with Appa there too now. Atta said that the town should continue to have geeology, cytoOlogy, biology, odology, and philosophy so that there would be no vacuum for the mind on the return, or, and what about being akpeteshique or sikadimous in the void that does not exist in Tukwan? 'Open the soul out, open the soul out!' shouted Pokuaa appearing and powdering the aeroplanes. She was copious with her lavender too; and she even touched Kwame Atta in forgiveness. The avenues were ushering the people to the tarmac, all birds flew in formation; and those that wanted to cry out their goodbyes ate sugar-cane instead, for life was sweet if you already had some soul and then there was the possibility of money coming to test this same soul. Bring out the brass band! was the general cry of waving hard!

May rain threatened in 1965, but with three other watches at different years on different wrists, time was African-free and controlled at the same instant . . . the free was in the belief that precision was for carpenters, and that outer time was ultimately below the imprecise yet more intelligent thrust of the inner. If there were to be as many leaves as raindrops, all the fast and thick rain could be received one on each leaf. As the suitcases thudded onto the aeroplanes, as the brass band blew memories that cut across the generations, Kwaku de Babo stared with an eye that seemed to freeze the town: at the moment of parting the eye could cry with the intensity of its last look. When would this town be unbanished? When would it become visible to the rest of the country? The fine white hairs on sugar-cane leaves could be seen close by Bra Kwaku; several lower lips were being held by lower teeth in anxiety: the gods should let the journey be safe, be profitable, and many many presents should be brought whether material or spiritual. In spite of the music, there was singing. Libation was an extension of spiritual skin, and they looked at the skin of Nana Bontox as he stood there witnessing the pouring by his Okyeamehene Nana Kasa, skin that took on the fatality of parting; Achimota date-trees crossed and tossed their small birds among them; all the advice about what to do and what not to do raged back and forth across the large forehead of Kofi Senya as he stood there shirtless, with his thin medium height, counting the sixteen travellers over and over again. And the non-travellers talked: . . . don't forget us-oooo and don't live there forever . . . in this short time you are going don't let them cheat you or break your spirit . . . if you want to bring back any wives or husbands send us a telegram first . . . be careful that you don't get lost in the sky, otherwise the cassava will rot there . . . Pokuaa don't let them pollute your beauty, and if you come back with a new sense of time we shall destroy it! . . . come back with a touch of skin and trees under the gadgets . . . and treat the natives kindly even if they think they created every universal quality Ewurade! . . . and give them a punch or two, but don't forget to eat their food, you foodians . . . and remember that their present rulers will always hate you . . . mon nanti yie! God go with you, don't worry about the lake, the avenues, the forest, the crosses and the lowered hills! Remember the traxcavator, remember the ducks and the frogs, the coconuts and the pawpaws, the blue elephants and the grey too, remember that the truth does not only go over your height but it goes through you too, remember the houses stagnating even if they have fine and original shapes in baked mud and small cement, remember that the people you have left here will be waiting for you, and they all have real blood, real feelings, real thoughts, and are not to be thrown out of the head when you are studying biology or computer science or electronics or atomic physics; remember that we want *everything*, including the impossible!

And the two aeroplanes took off simultaneously, each with its wooden trailer suspended miraculously at the back, and crowded with palm-nuts and cassava; and as they were disappearing over the sad skyline, a terrible silence fell over Tukwan, the brass band beat only one drum. It was only after Dogo shouted, 'C'mon let's remember them in the true African style!' that the trumpets, the rest of the drums, and the dancing came back. Came back hard! But then there was a commotion on the horizon: one of the aeroplanes was coming back, without its trailer. 'Now what omen is this!' was the cry. There was utter confusion as the gong-gong was beaten for reassembly. As Appa landed his plane, Amoa rushed out and saw with a cheeky smile all the questions on the faces. 'Ah, my elders and brothers and sisters, fathers and mothers, uncles . . .' he began expansively. 'Hurry up and tell us what is wrong and where is the trailer? You see, I told you that this whole thing was useless!' shouted Moro. 'O no, there's nothing wrong . . . we just forgot our supply of koobi!' There was a roar of annoyance. 'So you let our hearts burn like this just because of some koobi . . . I am sure it was Nana's stomach that became so important in the sky!' shouted Maimuna with scorn. 'And I suppose the trailer is suspended in the sky waiting for you to return.' 'Yes, fine woman, yes you are right! Atta's inventions can keep the trailers floating in the waiting sky! Please grow your sweet goodbyes again, but use only half because this one plane is going again! A big byyyye to you, a big bye to youou!'

So there were the two aeroplanes afloat with their cargo trailers, aeroplanes surrounded by two clouds of similar shape that made the fuselages cough. The seats were made with dry hardened moss at the request of Pokuaa, so that if anyone were to shed a tear for the future, there would be slime to receive it. Everything else was normal for small jets, even the complaints that Sala was taking far too long in the ridiculously small toilet of the plane opposite to the one his father was in. The plane with the law in it, LT, and driven by Kwame Atta who was becoming majestic with his constant irony in the sky, had already done two somersaults and had thus been turned into an aerial court by Lawyer Tay's instant proceedings against him for fright and for upset. 'But I am only trying on the joy of travelling!' Atta complained, 'And don't forget that if you sentence me up here, I will take the plane down by force!' The vulture had left Kofi Senya's pipe and was perched on the wing. When tired, it went and perched on the other aeroplane. The two planes could communicate, and thus one conversation that was not finished in one could end up in the other. And sometimes the wing of the vulture equalled the wing of the aeroplane. 'What sort of nonsense soul is this that we have ended up with, travelling away from this new town that we have set up ourselves through our own engineered ancestry? What do we want with money or with ideas that we already have enough of . . .' This was Pastor Mensah being pensive through the discomfort he felt at being so high from his crosses. He did not consider that theology should be so tall. And up here he was even more afraid of one thing: the minute Tukwan struck a true balance of life, it would either be invaded or destroyed, he thought. He ate a slow and stiff orange.

Bra Kwaku de Babo now loosened his language, under the pressure of the cabin, and asked whether the pastor was going to complicate the journey with some shrine eschatology . . . to which the pastor replied that he was already uncomfortable enough to feel shrunk and scatalogical rather; besides, his nephew had forgotten to pack his Guinness between his cassocks; and that vulture that sometimes smoked jots without, pre-sumably, its master's knowledge, had in a most dastardly and unTukwan manner released its toilet on the fiftieth page of his new draft book on African theology. To deflect his distraught mood Korner Mensah asked the dozing Babo this, 'What will happen to the English language when we arrive among the natives?' Kwaku gazed at him in irritated wonder, but said nothing. The pastor persisted: 'You have appointed yourself in that quiet and cunning way of yours, as the custodian of the English language . . .' 'But everything else is in Twi,' de Babo said, 'and you are not going to get me to be defensive about a foreign language that I knew before I could walk . . .' 'O no!' interjected Mensah, 'I too love the language, but I have not set myself up as the ridiculous master of it, nor do I consider that its native speakers have become soft and self-indulgent with it . . .' 'Then consider your position again!' Babo shouted uncharacteristically to the pastor, 'for you are out of date!' The aeroplanes droned on, they all argued, dozed, ate, fought, and prayed. They all flew above the rain.

CLASS FOUR

The Valley of Levensvale was crowded with ten canons from the Scottish Episcopal Church, fine sherry-drinking priests in this town that couldn't find its geography to rest in. It was towards the end of a fine summer which had many brambles in it green, red, black, and then rotten. God's good men, some with faintly English accents, were at the house of David Mackie on a unique mission: Mackie, businessman plenipotentiary, and a man whose morals were sometimes a cut above his thick moustache, had arranged a good business deal with Pokuaa of Tukwan over aeroplanes, cassava and palm-nuts. He was a man who usually jumped into things with one foot, but found that he often had to go nack for the other foot indeed. Ewurade. His risk was this: some thought he could have brought better business from the Japanese, or even from South America, better business for a town that thought it was dying – giving up the ghost to Clydebank, yieee – until it found itself outside time altogether, stuck to oatcakes that were made in any decade. There was nothing new about clearances and travel round the globe, but when Levensvale found that it had a magical link with Tukwan in central Ghana, it had to increase the production and consumption of Scotch broth . . . in order to build the courage not only to live beyond its means, but to live beyond itself, ampa.

Now the canons were in the valley of the Mackies' garden as part of the welcoming team: Mackie had some influence with the church through his well-placed but basically sincere contributions to its many congregations. He could rush to a sale of work with an extraordinary number of pigs' trotters – he was accused of turning his own feet into trotters, that tripped – and sell them free for a worthy cause such as free dinners – none of your lunch here my friend – for the old folk. Levensvale was becoming evangelical proper about history: it got passionate about preaching its existence and experience beyond its borders, but when it received visitors, it remained ordinary, and thus only the especially perceptive could see its dance of time and culture. But very unfortunately the two aeroplanes of the lip had not arrived at the appointed time, and the priests could not wait; so there was this grand welcoming party without the guests being present, holy smoke. Margaret Mackie was frantic with the absence of the Gold Coasters as she called her prospective guests . . . she considered this more romantic than calling them Ghanaians. Being timeless, if Margaret hadn't been around fifty-two, and she was perhaps forty-eight, then she would have been fifty. She had an unconsciously seductive manner that pleased the priests, even though they all had noses of different lengths, half of them with pipe smoke descending the nasal bridge. So there was Mackie the female, going round the sitting-room at exactly the same speed as her husband was stirring his tea, placing many good-byes on cassocks and dog-collars, and wishing that the aeroplanes would arrive out of a sudden sky. David M was sharp paa: he gave his wife a rest by reducing the speed of his controlling teaspoon. This was one reason that the Mackies survived the usual tea quarrels that plagued the Levensvale valleys – vale to you – the tea being drunk after the strong stuff, hmmm.

When David and Margaret first met thirty years ago into the future, it was among a patch of outrageously pink rhubarb; and they had cultivated that patch ever since, bursting their hearts into four, and then spreading the pieces in such a way that the present always remained less substantial that time before or after it. Rhubarb leaves had an affinity to nkontommire. When all the guests left Margaret made sure that she had her jots to entertain her, so that she could safely look forward to the past: her middle name was Shebelda, a name that even she did not know whence it came; but she was quite well educated, depending on which part of her head you were looking at when. When she was sitting her qualifying, or eleven-plus as the Sassenachs called it, she found that she had eaten so much tablet and peanuts that the terrible examination turned into the eleven-minus, into the disqualifying experience. She never regained her intellectual confidence again. She grew with this hurt baako baako, until she became immensely knowledgeable about her own ignorance. That was when her shrewd husband rushed past her brains, throwing back the dust of his pride at her, pride that grew from his judicious reading coupled with the gift for some bold and frontally erect decisions. All this made it easier to be extremely intimate about not getting too close at all koraa . . . The deal concluded between Mackie and Pokuaa would make it possible for a margarine and starch industry to be established in this town; and Marge was a little starchy about her creeping suspicion among the ivy that David had a crush on Pokuaa, and that the latter had been able to work out a deal more beneficial to Tukwan than to Levensvale, or. Shebelda wanted to shun the whole shebang, but she seemed to be irresistibly drawn to the visitors at the same time: she secretly wanted to wear a tama, so that she could unite her waist to Africa; and perhaps she would be introduced to aboloo too.

Mackie the male knew that he was suspected of emotional finance: of getting rent on his heart from other places. But there was nothing more gratifying than to be accused of the wrong crime, so that one could have the hurt of being accused at all in the first place while enjoying the triumph of proving oneself innocent later. Yes he had three apartments in his heart for three women: one for Shebelda the Margaret, one for an old dead girlfriend whose name was too painful to mention, and a recent one for Pokuaa. The trouble was that they all saw through him, even his late sweetheart who reacted in exactly the same way Pokuaa did: laughter at the sacred doors of the Mackie heart! 'Do you really think I would come these thousands of miles just to commit my body or my heart to *you*!' Pokuaa would say with a merry irony that stiffened both nostrils. So Mackie packed his love away from her, but was ready to unpack anytime she forgot that she did not take him too seriously. Mackie's girl was buried in the next county, and he was overwhelmed with a joyful deep sorrow that he was able to hold her hard just before she died. But the advantage about Margaret was that he could safely laugh back at her, resent her fully, then possibly meet for a hug later. He loved her loving him, especially when he produced his wonderful post-presby braggadocio about his latest deals: she admired him for five minutes but was sarcastic for the next ten. David had refused to reach the age of sixty, and thus, with that manoeuvrability of time shared with Tukwan, was allotted fifty-five years with a lantern to brighten any year necessary. This David with so much business in his groin had shortlong hair, grey at the tips, massively rough eyebrows, and debonair tweeds that made him a risky experience for the conventional to be ordinary with; and he believed much in the emblem of the town: a claymore with which to whack history hard. 'O David!' shouted Margaret, 'one of your canons has dropped his crucifix in a sherry glass.' 'O he'll come back for it, old MacCleod, he wants to see whether there are any men of the cloth among the visitors . . .' 'He'll come back for what?' asked Margaret without thinking. 'He'll come back for the sherry he didn't finish! and see the Ghanaians later . . .' answered David Mackie, twisting his mouth around his pipe, and hoping that for once the budgie wouldn't settle on it. The stone wall of the house had white heather on one side, and then the usual pink heather on the other side. 'Joy to the different cultures!' shouted Mackie through the microphone of a late whisky. 'Joy to my hefty wife . . .' Mackie went out of the room, his laughter mixing with his smoke, but Shebelda held the seriousness back down in the room, washing dishes faster with it; and she knew that marriage was a kitchen: the right amounts of cynicism, originality, bedlove, and warmth kept the brew going.

The subject of her thoughts interrupted them: Mackie ran in from the gate, having administered a dusk midgie with a slap in mid-rush, and roared, 'I have just got a belated telegram from our visitors saying their aeroplanes have trailers, and so we have to bend the tarmac at the end since the trailers curve the jets an angle of forty-five degrees for the last fifty metres of stopping. And they will arrive tomorrow! Help ma Goad! Get Ed, hen, get Ed! We have to solve this instantly curved tarmac if we don't want our exports of the pocket to blow up!' Margaret contained the rush, for she remained slow, and then went up to him and wiped a bead of sweat on his forehead with her tongue. 'Woman. . . !' screamed the harried male. 'Man!' replied Margaret with a sneer softened. She never ceased to find him especially fine in his sharp and sudden agitations. Margaret with her tongue back in her mouth ran down the avenues of pine, thistle wild, and heather, to call Eddie Gilmour; she went with that forward-bent queer run of hers, her feet leaving the ground several times. David himself bounded the other way, just next door, to go and call Jack MacTaggart, the old bulldozer driver with the permanent sorrow in his eyes. Old Jack could look so gnarled that sometimes, apart from his cap, you couldn't tell the difference between him and an old winter tree; besides, his arms could be several branches, moving his pipe, frequently and jerkily to different parts of his dry lips. His sorrow of the front of the eyes came from what he termed the sly death of his beloved wife. Sly? Well, they had both taken a bigitive decision to buy two heavy pine coffins which were put away with the dust of the store cupboard. But one day Ma MacTaggart did something sly: she died: when it was a fine African summer out of which she and Jack had made much bramble jelly and elderberry wine; they would even go quite far for wild raspberries, and then come back to Ma's old speciality, potted hough; Jack would smoke in the late evenings still light, Ma would knit in the everlasting dusk that the summer had stretched. The evening of life had a morning vigour. But the night before she died Ma had dusted one of the coffins, without explanation; Jack had laughed and slapped at her arthritis, telling her not to be morbid. Ma had replied, 'But morbid is the word, Jack, morbid is the word.' The next day after a quick dinner of pie and beans, Jack had gone down to bet on the dogs; and he had had a terrible suspicion which he did not articulate, for Ma had insisted on giving his cheek a hard peck. So he had come back and found poor Ma cramped into the upright coffin. And she had died standing up, leaning. Jack now dusted his own coffin, every morning hard.

'Quick Jack!' screamed David Mackie, 'you've got to extend the tarmac! You've got to curve it!' Jack's patience was in a puff, so he said nothing. 'Quick, I'll give you a hundred hot pies plus double time!' Mackie rescreamed, trying to lift the old man into the sleeping bulldozer. 'Put me down lad. Do you want to kill me into my wife? You've got to control that urge of yours to tar the whole world!' Mackie stared at MacTaggart without recognition for a second, then rushed back to his own house to receive Eddie Gilmour his rather informal partner. And there was Ed the Ted, as Mackie was wont to call him, ensconced on the settee with a glass of the waters of life. 'Drink your whisky later, Ted, later! We must rush to the tarmac to resurvey it for old Jack to curve it!' shouted Mackie, his face beetroot paaa. 'Ah, there's a tarmac loose aboot the hoose,' Ed mumbled, his lips still curved round the glass. 'But are you going bonkers or what! We want a curve on the tarmac not a drunken curve on your drunken lips!' said Mackie, serious now, but trying to arrange to laugh later . . . if only this Gilmour that looked like a gourd with whisky in it would rise. 'Money!' Mackie shouted into Gilmour's ear. The latter shot up. 'Now you're talking,' he said. 'For god's sake, mon, your language won't get the fuel for the bulldozer, get cracking; and then on to the tarmac.' There was Shebelda sitting hard on the easy chair, her face almost portentous with desire: her man was being agitated again! Disbelief now at other people's lack of urgency was Mackie's thing: and he used it to look at his wife. And then shot off without the Ted to the tarmac, his pipe smoke flying behind him . . . and then had to rush back: there was the talonted budgie holding on for dear life onto his pipe. Mackie threw budgie into house rough, and budgie flew upside down into Shebelda's hands.

Ed was a tall thin man with his hair in sarcastic waves. He worked in a solicitor's office but he never laid down the law in his house, since his wife and daughter were too strong for him; hence the sea in his hair. He was with Mackie part-time, even though he liked him, for this informal association made it possible for Ed to have a few moments of triumph in his house: when money came extra, he lorded it over his family for fifteen minutes. He would picture the Africans coming, in coins of expectation; he would picture them with their drums and inventions, in little aerial skites over Glen Coe, ready to drum a dirge for the MacDonalds now, while eating palm soup spoonless. In his minutes of masterfulness he would stand confidently in sausages, sliced and links; he would shake himself free of mince and tatties with a nod at the kitchen mirror; and then as the litres of whisky lasted less he would declare that his money was his precipice: financial jumps down down slopes of sheer penury. Supply more food, bring on more chewing! Mackie would vamoose the intermittent poverty one time! Ed thus reached the tarmac muttering to himself as Jack and David worked plenty.

Any pine trees spruced up in arithmetic and image could enter a dream one plus one and whistle in it. For those like Mackie who slept with one eye open, a garden of ferns could reflect in the open eye, and then disappear with an unrecorded snore in the other eye shut. A nap on the tarmac had led to the three working men falling asleep, and perhaps dreaming of being collected later by a wife or two. But since the very same wives had also fallen asleep waiting, and were dreaming too of the responsibility of trudging to the tarmac and bringing the men down, there was a useless correspondence of dreams. And in this town of smoky sleep the genetics changed at night: scores of limbs became scores of other limbs, elbows touched and changed their bones, and under almost every tongue was a new territory, a new language just for the night. The morning would be as usual looking at a dream with the eyes wide open. And this tarmac too that held the sleeping men had reached the level of a rabbits' shoulder; and its curve was the waist beads and the waist bend of a fantastic woman who was prepared to walk around every corner in sight naked – Miss Cornerstep to Babo's Mr Cornerstep – provided she was looked at with wisdom and turned into that type of memory that was beyond both her gender and her daring. 'Eddie, how dare you dream about the same woman I was dreaming about!' mumbled Mackie, waking up cold to the early morning dongs of a three-o'clock church tower. 'What sort of work is this,' said the bewildered MacTaggart, 'this cold will give my death to pneumonia.' There was a spirit in a wild rabbit's eyes, thought the old man, wondering whether the soul of his wife had now rested in a rabbit. Eddie Gilmour was the plus sign that answered their surprise at sleeping out without any intention at all: he added to their outrage that no member of the family came for them, by making a screech of annoyance. And the screech brought Shebelda with her beautifully clumsy run. Mackie combined a feeling of huff and glare: 'So woman why did you not venture out to come and waken us as we slaved and slept . . .' 'But I was coming up when the bogey man whipped me back. I'm telling you the truth! It's that meths drinker who wants to send us back to the time of ordinary raspberries!' 'Where's his neck till I squeeze it!' Mackie said. 'Right here behind you!' screamed a hoarse old voice. They all swivelled in surprise. 'Ah, so you Alec Bogey, you meths midget, you had the cheek to try to whip my wife last night . . .' 'Hold your horses Mackie, I am sober in two coughs! I saved her from something far worse: she was so tired that she was going to walk into the path of your stupid bulldozer. Now you ungrateful people of this mad town, you will never listen to me. The minute you start treating me kindly, like a human being, you will have your proper weather, your proper streets, your proper hearts back! I am here to damn you awake! to . . .' 'To pinch the turnips on our farms, to frighten our children, to put sand in our engines . . .' Mackie continued, getting angry. 'Hey Alec, you know it's only David here who has been saving you from the wrath of other people. He thinks you will change. Change! If you don't behave while the visitors are here, I will tell him to have you arrested! And what is this lie about the bulldozer going to knock me down? I was nowhere near it . . .' 'Then look at your footsteps,' Alec the bogey man pointed down in triumph. 'You people keep forgetting about your funny time, sometimes you lose it without knowing . . .' They did not bother to look in their anger, but Jack did: and saw a footmark or two, which he did not bother to assess; but he wondered whether the rabbit's eye he had seen with his wife in them were not human eyes after all, perhaps Margaret's if she fell away from the whip. This whip was snatched from Alec by Ed the Ted, and they all left the dirty-coated drunken old man of the meths vintage all alone on the fresh and curvaceous tarmac.

Alic Murray the bogey man had taken his Highers and would have entered the university if he had not become a metal man like Appa, but of a very different kind: he had a revelation that he had to make obscene little sculpturesque pieces of man and woman, with discarded wire; and he kept sending these pieces to distinguished priests and academics all over Scotland. After years of debauchery in cellars and sleazy pubs, he fell through a small hole in time, right into Levensvale, having put on twenty extra years plus a huge resentment against humanity for his own faults. It was only an insight or two, and the kindness of David Mackie that kept him alive and drinking in the town; and he was sometimes fed from the kitchens of the Lord Provost, correct. So Alec fell asleep on the tarmac, dragging and dreaming his urge for status and power and recognition all over the early-misted vale.

A few miles beyond the tarmac the elbows of the dawn held the lippy aeroplanes, with traces of darkness trapped under the wings. The tarmac was wise for those that were desperate to land on it: Appa's plane had run out of fuel, and had landed expertly on top of Atta's, with the two trailers mating in the sky. The shitoh, kyenam, and kenkey, still wonderfully fresh after a day and half's flying, was being eaten in a one-storey fashion, one plane above, one plane below, with the teeth chewing or chattering with the cold. One plane was heaped with the eating of another. Having baptised the celestial dawn with much of his own often unanswered laughter, Kwame Atta was now trying to sleep through his piloting; but was wakened several times by those with no respect for the automatic pilot. The few especially strong termites taken along to be thrown into the primitive piotos of any possible racists, had made a hole in the upper fuselage of the lower-lip aeroplane, so that anyone could crawl from one plane to the other free. Manu the carpenter was trying to construct a ladder two-hundred metres up, so that those who did not believe that the aeroplane-carrying plane could land safely, could jump out, after the descent of the ladder. Nana Bontox was indignant and full of palaver about objections to his decision to descend the ladder and jump; dignity in the sky for a chief was very important, some thought, especially Nana Kasa: if chief jumped, Okyeame jumped with beads and amulets flying fast in the Scottish mist. 'Buttocks are double but not aeroplanes!' Nana shouted in a rage. 'I am chief of the sky as well as the earth, and I will not agree or be party to a one-storey landing! And I swear you have to double the earth first!' Appa's piloting was now a matter of balancing his plane on top of Kwame Atta's, and he was feeling irritable: 'If I had been allowed to pilot and make a metal ladder at the same time, things would have been easier, and Nana would have enjoyed the sound of his rings and pendants against the metal. Ho, look at Amoa with clouds around his chin! Because of the wood rather than the iron, I believe that Nana is wrong, but since we have already agreed on aerial democracy, then we should allow him to come down the wooden ladder when it's made, rather than experience the joy of a double landing.'

'We're in a different country now ooo, we're in a different country! We're here to tighten our logic! to feel the brain feeding on itself and going squinty! power to the originality that forced us to come here to extend it! please hold on while I urinate and see whether it can fall on the northern leaves of what they call the sycamore tree . . . let the chief jump, just in case he does not survive, Ewurade!' 'Stop your bodanfo chattering and pilot properly, otherwise we shall all use the ladder to go down!' shouted Opanin Akorsah impatiently. Atta the pilot spread his laughter higher, ignoring the intense scrutiny of his laughing back, scrutiny that worried whether he would get them all safely down or not, after his miscalculation on fuel. In her cloth of sankofa patterns, Akyaa relished her non sequiturs: 'But what do the people in this non mango country eat anyway, my dear husband? Ah, Azziz my husband, stop sleeping on my wrist!' 'Ah yes,' said the interfering Amoa, 'I think, Sister Akyaa, that they eat a form of natural needles: pines and thistles, and after they have digested the thistles, they immediately make it their national flower . . .' Kofi Senya called his vulture inside and brushed it after rubbing sheabutter on its breast. His skin, as the remote sun rose, had taken on a burnished brown, with his delicately long nose multiplying the shape of his pipe. They thought he was going to speak to the two aeroplanes at once, and so they were quiet. But he just gave them the longest yawn yet emitted, reminding them of the original journey that gave the beautiful yawns in the first place. The travelling Tukwan earth was resting, with its people travelling now. Then Atta shouted with as much glee as glum, 'But there's someone sleeping on the tarmac!' Stretch a smile and it could burst into laughter: they thought he was joking until they saw the prostrate snoring form of Bogey Alec Murray, with his jot dead and hanging out of his dribbling mouth. 'Manoeuvre round him of course,' declared Appa with authority. 'And do they all look like the man down there?' Akyaa asked with faint disgust. 'God's children are everywhere,' answered Pastor Mensah flatly. He had kept his mouth long enough in the Bible, and he felt a few words should be uttered in this uncomfortable sky. 'But he looks drunk to me,' Akyaa persisted, ignoring Azziz of the sleeping wrist, 'and looks: mist and wrist!' A few heads turned in her direction, wondering whether the height was adversely linked to her sanity, but Akyaa no be craze: there were two sudden bracelets of mist on her wrists when she pushed her hands out of the plane in exasperation. The face of Azziz had slipped off her sharp and was snoring in another nasal territory. Pokuaa sharp

passed round peppermints above and below the aeroplane. With her hair plaited in brilliant folds of excitement, she adjusted her heart accordingly: raised beats, and joy for the future! Kwaku de Babo, strangely quiet throughout the journey, had ducks in his inner, and ducks in his outer: having bathed the two sacred ducks in a tight and crowded corner of the upper-lip plane, he went to sleep and dreamt about exactly what he had been doing; and then woke up in a sweat because he next dreamt that his pen was busy writing without him, finding that this was precisely what his chalky pen was doing . . . 'Safety belts please you gari-chopping momoni-chewing people, I beg!' shouted Amoa and Akyaa sharing the words among them. There was a sudden rhythmic pounding, with Nana Bontox screaming that he told them that this was the end of the aeroplanes. They ascended and descended the planes in consternation. 'Am I seeing right?' asked Lawyer Tay in loud disbelief. 'Is that Amoa and my son Sala pounding fufu in the upper aeroplane? Ewurade Nyankopon! Halt your pounding! I put an injunction on you straight away! Foolish Amoa and impudent twelve-year-old Sala, how dare you force me to be legal in the sky . . .' They rushed at the pounders as the aeroplanes lurched. The wings tripped.

Nana Bontox had begun to forcibly descend the half-finished ladder. But Manu was smart for once: he made the last missing rungs so quickly that they fitted perfectly into each descending royal footstep. Others refused to follow Nana, arguing that since they were now in a different country they had to modify tradition. No bontox threatening sign made any difference, except that some said they had to stay to look after the few gold rings brought by Nana. Nana asked his dear subjects, 'So are you saying that you are prepared to save the rings, but to abandon the finger that wears them! You will see how long you will remain to enjoy my confidence.' 'O Nana,' purred kool kat Okyeame adjusting the alphabet in his mouth, 'you know that we love you tootoo much, and we will love you even more if you survive the jump . . .' There was a roar as Nana jumped with a curse, from fifty metres, closely followed by Amoa . . . and landed with a thud on the sleeping Murray . . . who would have been crushed completely if Amoa had not got caught high on a nearby spruce. There was a huge groan from the methylated lips. There was a brilliant new sun as Nana rose to inspect the unconscious form of Alec the bogey. He still wore his royal cloth perfectly, as Nana Kasa too descended the same spruce with surprisingly sprightly limbs, after jumping. 'Of course it is my eating of bokoboko that gives me strength. One day these young men will force me to swear the ntam kese against them to survive! Nana, is that man you fell on dead? I can smell his boozy mouth from up on this tree. O, pity him!' There was a second series of groans from Alec the Sleaze. 'Kofi Senya will come down and treat him quick. Meanwhile, give him water from that little stream, in case he dies and has to be resurrected if we decide that he is a worthy human being,' said Nana with a look of concern, which suddenly changed to alarm when he saw Murray urinating involuntarily through his trousers. Nana Okyeame said with some sad haste as he waved up frantically to the aeroplanes, 'In this world you can pee through cloth before you die koraa.'

Up in the aeroplanes which Kwame Atta made dance grotesquely in this moment of crisis, Manu the carpenter was refusing to make any more rungs. He was annoyed: 'What sort of a journey is this? No one told me that in an aeroplane when you blow off, excuse-me-to-say, your wind goes up. My hands are exhausted with nails! Let Appa continue with his metal ladder . . .' 'But Appa is busy balancing the second plane,' Opanin Akorsah said, making the obvious equal to the irritable. He and LT exchanged their usual looks of hate for nothing. 'Me, I no jolly this air koraa!' Azziz said rerising from his wife's wrist into the commotion. 'Please relax your bots, I am about to land now!' shouted the merry Atta, enjoying the general discomfort immensely. 'Here comes the belly flop! And me I fear no peace kapereba . . .' And when some nervous laughter came Atta trebled it. 'Up the customarists and down the pilots please onto the tarmac, for the former beat the latter down,' said the equally merry Amoa from below, Amoa who had decided that next time he pounded fufu in an aeroplane, he would use the mortar to pound the pestle . . . 'Get set, ready your alombos, goooo!' screamed Kwame, laughing and smoking at the same time. Four wings shook and turned the sun among themselves; the wheels in the lower plane came out and met the disappearing mist; the rhythm of the fuselage was exactly like the waving of the two Nanas below; chestnuts, pines, spruce and sycamores were generous with their different leaves in the breeze below. The planes lowered with Appa doing a miracle of balancing by piloting the stillest plane in the sky. 'Come down safely you aeroplanes,' said the vulture, eating slyly the tobacco in its master's pipe; the ducks slapped their wings in annoyance, and their last and only flea fell out of the open jet windows. And the earth was coming up, tightening its tarmac shoulders as Atta landed near the large and sleeping feet of Alec Murray. One bump called another, with Akyaa's frightened shout in between. There was an incline of silence between the early birds and the moan of an overpressed jet. And ducks and vulture raced along with the landed planes, as the surprised Mackies and Gilmour rushed to do their welcoming. 'O my God, I have fewer oatcakes than I thought,' exclaimed the marvellously running Shebelda.

Nana Bontox stood there with the friendly arrogance of his new descending experience of ladders, hand outstretched to receive the running Mackie who hugged him instead, with the former's hand protruding through the armpit of the latter. Kofi Senya had already come out of the still-moving aeroplanes and was tending Murray with an instant mixture of Tukwan and Levensvale herbs. There was relief and welcome in everyone's eyes, except the continuing laughter in Atta's, and Amoa's too. The hosts stared incredulous at the carrying of one aeroplane by another; and then at the slow rising of Alec under the hands of Kofi Senya. Akwaaba was brought out by the hosts, Okyeamehene took out the schnapps and placed it beyond the heather, to pour libation after the exchange of greetings. 'David, don't they look so beautiful in their browns greens yellow and reds!' exclaimed Margaret in her Shebelda voice. 'Woman, woman, I am wearing black,' said the bellyful Tay, releasing his large smile in jumping lines of approval and pride. 'Let me hug everybody, especially our three and a half hosts!' roared Atta the menacing pilot with the semi-alanta legs. 'OOooo, Mr David Mackie, your wife has some shea-smooth buttered skin!' The visitors looked askance at him. 'There must be time to pray after the libation,' said Pastor Mensah with a cassock so starched that you could stiffen the theology in it; there were cracks when he moved. 'And where are the priests?' Korner Mensah asked suddenly. 'Gone, all gone to their altars!' replied the smiling Mackie, 'for when we were expecting you, you didn't come, and when you came we were not expecting you . . .' 'Up the good people of this wild land!' Amoa said, bursting his words with laughter, 'and I hope you have your profits ready now now now, ha!' 'You too Amoa what, you do something too mech, what. Keep your silly youth under control!' boomed Azziz. 'My youth or my mouth?' Amoa asked defiantly to nobody's answer, to nobody's notice.

Libation was being poured, but it had not been noticed that while the gin was going down to the hallowed earth, down, down, old Alec the bogey had crawled between many legs, and had put his open mouth right in line with the descending drink, and had swallowed hard twice before he was finally seen by Appa who dragged him away with a curse, with Nana shouting in turmoil that to steal the drink of the earth, the gods and the ancestors was sacrilege. Okyeame continued, one foot on his sandal, as if he hadn't heard or seen anything at all. So when Murray finally stood up, he was drunk again, this time on vintage orange-based akpeteshie. Sala for some reason was holding Pokuaa's hand, asking her constantly, 'Is this Abrokyiri, is this the UK . . . or is it only the northern part of it? Let me ask you something else: is this town equal to ours, or are we both the different points in history books all together, bommm? My father tells me about history whenever he quarrels with my mother . . .' Pokuaa had given ten answers, and with each one Sala had held her hand tighter, until she tightened hers to bring him back to abnormal. 'Where is our half-a-host? Ah, I'm sure he's searching a stream to see whether there's any alcohol in it. Are we going to stand under the pine and yearn for seats? Don't bother to send for a car for our luggage and language, the bulldozer will do. I demand a sherry with all respect!' said Kwame Atta the speaker of persiflage, 'and let me correct one thing straight away before you offer me a pomegranate or a glass of home-made blackcurrent juice: we in Tukwan, and in the rest of the country too, are not a sensual people at all: we are merely perceptive with our bodies, rhythm is the beginning of the universe, and once you lose it, then you start world wars, haha! Mrs Mackie, where is your superscribed lipsticky smile? . . .' 'My good lad,' replied Margaret cheerily, 'I do not wear red on my lips, they just appear extra pink every time the sun rises.' 'Bring the gourd for laughter!' added Atta, suddenly jumping up and down, and rushing to a pine to pee his acceptance of the welcome.

Kofi Senya smiled at his empty pipe, and tweaked the guilty vulture at once. There stood the aeroplanes, like tremendous adowa dancers still, and Appa had gently driven the upperlip plane down from the lower, with the tiniest fuel left, and they all clapped, including Murray who was sitting down clapping with his feet, after releasing a huge kwee; with Appa adding, 'Is it true that in England the incidence of farts is faithfully recorded from volunteers that eat many beans?' David Mackie had prepared himself for questions of the back and below, and he put up his hands helplessly, saying, 'Some of the things the English do, we're trying to get the Scottish National Party to ban when it comes to power . . .' Hosts and guests roared their different roars, except Opanin Akorsah who watched the whole proceedings with distaste in his eyes: apart from his fully envious nature, he actually wanted to taste something with his mouth. 'Give me gari quick,' was all he said to no one in particular. During the lull, there was a sudden cry from one of the trailers: 'Open me, open me!' The flummoxed ones flocked there, except Kofi Senya and David Mackie who passed a mutual respect between them for the few seconds that they were alone. And there hidden in the trailer with a good supply of her favourite nkonkonte was Aba Yaa the sometimes superbumptious seller of crabs in Tukwan, crabs which she caught herself. Aba jumped out holding her exquisite chin, greeted everybody, and said in one breath, 'Forgive me elders and Pokuaa because I had to do it, I had to hide in the trailer without authority, because I knew that it was my duty to come with you to the UK to catch crabs, so that we could compare the different crawling. I would like to show you my walkings! Don't I look nice with my waist small and my back shaking and all that . . . I suffered in the trailer, and I almost screamed out for help complete, I cried into my duku. Forgive me and welcome me fast!' Nana Bontox cleared the look of indignation on his face with a cough, and Nana Kasa coughed to interpret it. Pokuaa called Aba and hugged her, telling her not to embarrass everyone with her crabs in the sky again. Aba curtsied, and whenever anyone was curt to her for her trick, she curtsied again. Kwaku de Babo wrote down Aba's presence and sat down smiling.

It was the ducks which guided the trailers down when the planes were landing; they did this by pulling at them with their beaks, left and then right; and their sacred beaks had completely ignored Alec Murray when he had said to them only that if an oaf liked an oat, then this would be a porridge landing. These selected years never remained in their proper slots, and you could have a duck dancing with one foot in one year, and the other foot in another year. The state umbrellas were up, challenging the fast-disappearing rainbow. For a moment all the tobacco looked multi-coloured; and good morning could come from 1960, while good afternoon came from 1965. Atta too, Atta too, he insisted on counting each hug that Pokuaa had. 'God has created in us a rainbow of the flesh,' was what he said to try and drive away the sudden jealousy he felt for Pokuaa. Azziz often held his wife's waist involuntarily, especially when he was looking at Pokuaa. 'Do you like the glen and the burns?' Shebelda asked as they walked towards the house. 'Ah, explain to them woman, what a burn is, or they'll think that you are careless with your cooking!' In order to win the world, the Tukwan visitors were singing 'Yen ara yen asaase . . .' down the glen. Travelling on the travelling earth proved the world belonged to all, Babo thought. Glen and burn: in this place he had to attack a new language, paa.

Hosts and guests walked more or less in unison through the bracken, the gorse, and the burning streams, sun, or the streaming burns, rain. There was a stillness, even through Atta's chattering, a stillness that de Babo felt a little uncomfortable with; then there was a smell of peppermints twice: hey without warning two stout people, man and woman, sprang out of the gorse and faced the motley group. The two were absolutely silent, but they held up two superscriptions reading: Immigration Officers On Duty. There was an irate puzzle in Mackie's tammy: he knew he had cleared all this up with the Lord Provost long ago. 'Agooooo,' said Lawyer Tay impatiently, waiting for the two strangers to pass or to speak. 'Speaka da lingo?' drawled Murray without his Alec. 'This is an outrage!' roared Mackie, his cheek unconsciously touching his wife's for support. Supporter Margaret nodded vigorously into the current outrage, restraining herself hard this time from enjoying her husband's attraction in anger. 'My deepest apologies,' Mackie said, facing the visitors.' 'Shall we bulldoze them over?' asked Amoa, pointing to Jack MacTaggart. 'May I ask what you want with us here in the braes that make my home?' thundered Mackie. Immigration John spoke at last, though Immigration Jessie kept silent, probably with the pressure of the disdainful triumph on her face. 'We believe not all of the party has visas, we believe; nor do we consider that the proper quarantine procedures were taken for the accompanying birds and animals, goat if you care to have the proper description. Also it may be considered a threat to the public to have the aeroplanes landing the way they did. My female counterpart . . .' 'Did he say counterfart . . .' began Appa. '. . . almost had a heart attack . . .'

'She's grossly overweight dodo,' broke in Atta. 'Do restrain your frisky elements . . .' 'Frisky elements, eh, good lord, no wonder one cheek is fatter than the other,' shouted Ed the Ted to everybody's surprise, since he had a somewhat quieter style that he was showing now. 'Do you want these fine people to take their business elsewhere?' asked Mackie in anger. 'We are doing our work, nothing more nothing less,' Imm John said to the nods of Her Jessie. No one moved; each leaf reflected the silence of its stem. At last Mackie said, with a growl, 'I would wish to contact the Lord Provost . . .' 'Politics won't get you anywhere in this case, for we have taken the opportunity to warn the Provost of the political consequences of unorthodox measures in immigration matters such as this. I mean look, imagine entering British air space with the help of ducks without authority. And it would well be a public nuisance to have a hastily constructed ladder protruding out of an aeroplane with two noisy people coming down it . . .' preached John Immi the superogatory, with Jessie as usual pushing the words along with her nods. 'Where is your office?' asked LT prodding his legal belly smaller. 'In the grass if necessary,' the male officer answered, 'but I am afraid we must be asking the questions, and not you.'

'How many midges are in the grass?' asked Shebelda, with massive irritation in the handkerchief that Akyaa had just given to her. There was no answer, there was just an equally massive double gathering of stiffness on the upper lip. So Jessie spoke, and her voice was so high and in such contrast with her corpulence that they thought it was the squeak of a rodent in pain: 'The cheek is getting a bit too much, and we may have to extend our authority to matters of proper decorum . . .' 'Midges, whatever they are, could be a subject for a decorous utterance depending on which side of the law your brain is on,' said Lawyer Tay with gravitas and wile, watching the dawn disappear with one eye. He continued, 'And you may have to redefine the nature of some of the living beings with us here sharp: our ducks can talk, our vulture may be the repository of a certain type of sacred soul, our goat can jump and balance on a pesewa creating patterns with its feet that any artist may envy . . . we come from an ancient civilisation that worked beautifully in gold . . .' 'You may come from heaven if you like, but we are here in the line of duty . . .' John the-Grationman said matter-of-factly. When the ducks talked, Jessie recorded it. 'One of them is English, the man, but the woman is local,' Pokuaa stated, putting on her duku against the wind, and then sauntering off. 'Please stay here, young woman.' 'I know it will be woman for foreigners, and lady for the natives,' Korner Mensah said, crackling in his cassock, and sitting in the ferns with a prayer suspended casually on one knee. Nobody wanted to be real before the official forms. Pokuaa walked on regardless. 'In the name of the law, halt!' screamed the professional but profusely sweating ImmiJohn, taking out a small polished trumpet and blowing it.

Out came two constables, one with his baton being chewed by the Tukwan termites while he hid in the bracken; out they came in full charge . . . but in the wrong direction, for they had misjudged the sound of the trumpet. Policeman One said, 'Och I don't know which direction I'm charging, but I warned the fool to get a bigger trumpet!' 'Aye, y'are right,' panted Policeman Two, suddenly crashing into a baby pine. 'Pick me up for the recharge, I'm dizzy. Or better, continue with the charge, and collect me later! Never mind if our force has been reduced by fifty percent . . . besides you are fatter than me!' Policeman One agreed but continued in the wrong direction fast . . . and the two of them lost their words to each other. And Kofi Senya took over Policeman One's legs and ran them right out of the county. 'Where are your policemen now?' mocked the slowly sobering Murray. The two immigrationing officers conferred, they shared their fat close. Then Jessie squeaked, 'We have drawn a line across the valleys and the burns over which no one here is to cross except with authority.' 'But don't you see that Pokuaa and Nana Bontox are already over it, Nana that you are calling noisy . . . you will have to pay for this,' growled Azziz. And the ducks flew and landed on the heads of the two officers, who had decided in advance, considering the nature of the operation, to react with the utmost calm to provocation. They stood there stiff and writing as the ducks beaked their hair, and flew off with a plop in John's hair that looked like brylcreem brutal. And Jessie's small smile was summerweight. The entire group had now crossed the imaginary line, the blatant border. Johnny and Jessie rushed round them, asking questions with a hiss each, writing down outrageously squiggly information. 'I hope these devils are not going to be racist,' shouted Amoa, looking for an answer from Kofi Senya. Senya just adjusted the vulture on his pipe, and put a smile where it was. 'Do not defame me, I have never raced a human being before!' hissed Jessie. 'Ah,' replied Atta, 'never trust a woman who makes a verb out of race! They do not like us, they do not like us!' 'Yes, and we wish, we twins, to extend the territory of our humanity to include even those who deny us . . .' added Babo with the saddest frown in the world. 'Fine, fine, but let's attack them first!' screamed the calm Appa, his A-levels on fire. Forward, forward! was the cry.

When Atta went into the plane and blew its terribly loud horn used in the sky to scare off ghosts, there was an answering blow . . . from the Austin Princess of the Lord Provost now ascending the vale. The tossing of horns continued, with Mackie's head sticking out of the window of the car. In the car, apart from Mackie, was the deputy senior assistant to the senior principal deputy of the Lord Provost, who was so efficient that when he took a quick shower in the summer afternoons, somebody acted for him. Mackie jumped out of the car even before it stopped, waving many papers in triumph at the faces of the glen-dominated immigration prestidigitators with their forms covered in burr. 'We have everything, now!' Mackie shouted. 'We have visas for human beings, for half-vulture half-souls, for sacred ducks, for goats, for Aba Yaa, and laśt and most difficult for the termites!' 'Precisely,' crowed LT glaring at Akorsah for little reason, 'precisely. I put it to you that if it's termites you want us to have visas for, we have got them. If it's spirits we should procure visas for, we have got them! Long live Mackie the man ready to receive business!' Jessie had mellowed slightly in the face of the strong evidence, but Immigration One, with morals of the john, scrutinised the new papers ever so carefully double. John the -Gration was hot paaa, but could say nothing against the evidence of the triumphant forms: every living thing on the two aeroplanes was to be classed as a human being for the next three months, after which, if there was any evidence that anyone or anything had become a spirit, or that any animal wished to become a human being and could prove that this was a possibility, all applications of an ontological or supernatural nature should be presented anew. If the soul was to be kept in a form, the form too could be kept in the soul; the ducks tasted the pine needles with half a shudder each. Some officers will chop kerosine one time, wo be wi kerosine papaaapa! Only Alec the bogey was left wet with the officers there, Alec the old soaker soaking in his soakage. Officer and officette marched down the valleys with one shrug between them. They passed Mackie's house fast, where Aba was crying because she feared she was going to be asked to prove that she was a human being whose soul was fit to be admitted into the Benighted or Blighted Kingdom.

CLASS FIVE

Fresh eggs, fresh cobwebs were the lot of David Mackie's disused hotel, which he forgot he owned even when he was managing it. He used to have a waiter whose undertongue showed when he smiled onesidedly, thus showing later many of the underhand deals. So the hotel broke; and now the visitors were in it, its walls spruced the pines. The sun of the second morning in Levensvale was borrowed from Tukwan – learning to rent the weather – but the afternoon was local, was native, with its elements of rain at the seams, rain on grey streets, rain on black slates and brown stone. New bright-green moss claimed patches of the outside walls. Any heart could have such patches of dark brooding over fears of losing Pokuaa altogether in this new place, without even capturing her in the first place. Kwame, the best way to transfer the pain when you banged your head in absent-minded rumination was what you said: bang the gods, for how far-fetched they had made fate. Yesterday Alec Murray had caused a scandal by standing in the middle of the town square trying to auction his genitals for the price of a bottle of malt whisky. And the fresh parts – private and scrubbed for the public – were put on a fine porcelain plate with an obscure heraldry; and were almost bought with a dud cheque by a fellow meths drinker: Amoa passing by coincidence struck the popylonkwe off the shining plate and into the trousers; then pulled Murray along the streets until he left him near the hotel, his drunken head against a wet wall, which could now boast of rare vulture dung. Aba had dried her tears when she saw kindness from her hosts, but this morning she was overwhelmed with homesickness. She packed all her things, without yet seeing any crabs let alone catching any, and went and lay on the tarmac motionless; she kept counting the blue in the sky whenever any came through, and she called it joyful home blue. There lay Aba packed in heart and suitcase, with the birds passing and repassing her in different types of rush and flutter. But there was no aeroplane coming or going, and she had not been able to persuade the vulture to desert its pipe and take her on its back, back to Tukwan. Aba Yaa, only your staring ooooo! But the tarmac was not a good bed in the intermittent rain, and her cloth was all wet, and she could only open one eye up to the rain when it drizzled. And it was at the end of one eye that she saw a young man with long hair and a scraggly beard looking at her. She gave a start, and if she had been in a different mood she would have tried to run away, hoping the gorse would not prick her.

'So you are sleeping in the rain?' the young man said, more burr in his mouth than in the vale. Aba gave a snort and returned to her mood. 'I have just come down from the hills, I am David Mackie's son, I look for meaning in the glens, I hitchhike, then I travel in trains, and I am broken-hearted just now: my girl-friend left me just because she was able to make university and I didn't, even though I'm cleverer than she is . . .' Angus Mackie, train traveller and wandering factotum, gauged Aba's frown. She said, 'That's what happens when you go round quick-quick with a heart heavier than it should be!' Her frown was now mixed with words, out of which burst a synthesis of laughter: 'But why are you so untidy when your parents are so neat? What is the nature of this beard of yours that can't decide whether it's coming or it's going! Why did your mother and father not tell us that they have a son? . . .' 'They are often ashamed of me, especially the old geyser!' 'The old what?' 'The old man.' There was a pause, during which Angus turned round and quickly combed his hair for effect. 'Can I lie beside you? I like your courage in lying all packed in the rain. Are you leaving us so soon?' Angus was asking with a voice faster than he meant. 'You can lie beside me if you like but I'm getting up first,' she replied, slow, and with a grimace. As soon as Aba rose the rain went off. 'So magic maker of the rain, you won't let me lie beside you! Remember I have a broken heart . . .' Angus was laughing from that part of his mouth that brought pain with the laughter. 'Please help me to take my suitcase and chopboxes back, I have been waiting for any stray aeroplanes that would swoop and stop and take me back to my country. I even tried to whistle them closer but they didn't mind me in the sky koraa, aasemni!' Aba complained, walking off with one box. Angus followed.

Levensvale could neither escape the genetics nor the geology: true, some of the rock of Levensvale had been scooped out and made into a supplement for many hills at Tukwan, and of course vice versa; but two small stones so foreign, had returned to each town, rolling about hard, rolling up and down people when and when not necessary. Thus the people of the shared hills took their changes of history and rock in the form of bone, flesh, and mind that was still mixing. People of originality did everything twice: one for themselves, and one for the world, up the hearts down the crying, in the soul and out of its back. The Tukwan law of genetics was accepted in Levensvale, even by the Lord Provost who was so busy that he had only been able to see Nana Bontox and Nana Kasa, with Pokuaa in the background, and Kofi Senya even further back . . . so far that his lordship saw him with only one eye. Now, since a snore in Levensvale could originate in Tukwan, and since an elbow in Tukwan could have its counterpart in Levensvale, everybody was free to be and to do what he or she like. There was a blast of freedom from freely-mixed bodies and worlds, ampa.

At last Aba and Angus reached the newly renamed Plantain Hotel, existing exclusively for the Tukwan guests and any well-wishers. Since Angus was exhausted, it obviously didn't suit him carrying the cases. But they walked into a commotion: Appa's nods had come back again. His nods were so strong that they could send him flying onto the floor. So they tried to put it between the ducks; but when they suggested hospital, he speeded up his nods and warned them that nodding uncontrollably was one of the seats of his soul, and that he didn't need a doctor at all, kapere. There were Vauxhall nods, and there were Toyota nods, though it was the African Datsuns that finally stopped the nods . . . but it was too late, for others still had a residue of nods made in sympathy, so that if some wanted to speak, they would tame the nodding first. 'Just as well this didn't happen when you were driving the aeroplane,' ventured Akyaa, 'otherwise we would have been leap-frogging in the sky.' After the nods, Angus met the guests, and he felt a bit thin doing so, since the welcomes were so thick and so warm. Pastor Mensah even added a prayer onto his head. And every morning Margaret would bustle in with her breakfast of bacon and eggs and potato-scones with sliced sausages; after which some guests secretly ate kenkey, shitoh and kyenam. 'But I love the food here!' Nana Kasa would tell Nana Bontox whenever he demanded home food as a supplement. 'Yes, so do I sometimes, but that shouldn't stop you from going to arrange something from home for me now,' Nana would reply, irritated with the ritual of his wing-chief's independence . . . which he was determined was inappropriate in the new land. Thus the visitors were settling down, were allowing the worlds around to seep through, while throwing their own worlds in a corresponding spread when required. There was yet no talk of the business deal. There was no talk yet of curing Jack MacTaggart of the pain in his wife's death: he walked around the hotel every morning, holding a fried egg in one hand with a tear in one eye, and wishing everyone a painful good morning. Bulldozer of the raining eye, driver of the historical machine that made it possible for one town to land in another. But the afternoon with visions of an early evening could shorten; the little knots of time pulled ropes of people ahead, so that what Babo thought he was doing with his own elbow was really Gilmour's elbow; for the blast of freedom came without warning, and could come in bits: one hole from one nose measured exactly like another, some nostril metamorphosis. And there was Amoa with his afternoon-turned-evening nap, with a dream towards the north of night-mare – the south remained awake – which created a picture of everybody's head broken because history had come to stop in one town but not in another. Shebelda adjusted a jaw that she suddenly shared with Aba, even though she had just wanted Pokuaa's jaw. Could Jack fit his quiet wailing into someone else's heart, perhaps someone like Amoa with vast holes of youthful and reincarnated joy. Appa, the tip of your tongue was different! for there was less metal, and it came from the ferns. The snoring Akorsah couldn't talk in his dream since a pipe from somewhere had ended up in his mouth. You could get a wrist somewhere in the eighteenth century freeee from either continent koraa. And one duck lost its head in an outrageous exchange with the vulture, but it screamed against eternity hard enough to have its head back. But just before the genetics disappeared Kofi Senya had been busy adjusting souls by talking to and quickly touching everyone: 'Grow with your world!' he whispered at each sleeping person, so that by the time the morning came, several people were fresher than the newest shitoh, the choicest plum.

For some reason, the hotel had sunk three inches since the arrival of the guests – the weight of truth, Korner Mensah the pastor had said – and the marshy hill below which it was built had increased its height by the same length; which gave the pastor the chance, knowing it was the equivalent of the hill of miracles on which they held meetings at Tukwan, to plant a big black and white cross. But the miracle hill was obstinate: it threw the cross miles away through a sudden upsurge of stones, and then created its own crossrock, much like the stones that made the wall for the turnip field beyond. One of the miracles about the hill was that on your first ascent, you could climb two sides of the hill at once, but the tough heather on the opposite side would soften while the near side hardened, becoming almost wiry. After this first climb, things would return to normal. So the pastor preached to the hill indignantly about the shortness of its magic; and then tried to slyly bamboozle this impudent geology: he tried different disguises – even going to the length of wearing a kilt – so that the hill would not know him, and thus allow him to climb two sides at once again. But the pastor failed miserably, and fell down at the foot of the hill on top. Finally, however, through loving persistence, the hill allowed Korner Mensah to put round it a huge necklace of polished pine cones which Manu the carpenter had laboriously varnished first. And in the mornings sparrows would come and perch on every second cone, created a pattern that started to haunt the Levensvale people to such an extent that some started to go to church again, and others began to create instant shrines with short lives, made of any bric-a-brac, and with leaves and flowers too.

And it was Sala that managed to fire the town further: he had found a discarded corset probably twenty years old, and had worn it boldly, after slipping past his law-tutoring father . . . How much law could you teach a quietly flamboyant and opinionated boy who felt greater than his father?

Sala's intention was to go through the town and interview the children to see whose grandmother the corset belonged to quick and to see what skin they could share. But it look longer than he thought, for he had to slip out several days in a row. The first day had armfuls of sun and a brilliant spread of brambles in flower and fruit simultaneously. He had crawled out between the drying slacks of Pokuaa, and could have sworn that her absent toe touched him in a trick. When he reached Donald Shearer's house, by sheer coincidence, he met Donald playing at conkers with a champion chestnut wizened and tough; Donald had red hair and a rush of freckles resting on his nose. He laughed at Sala's corset but wore it later to be laughed at too. Playing under stone bridges and rushing into turnip fields to eat and to make lanterns too early for Hallowe'en, Sala said gravely to the corseted Donald: 'Never forget when you grow up that you played with a boy called Sala, with a different skin, and with as much life and play in this skin as you have in yours, never forget!' And then the two friends exchanged one guava one plum, and swore to meet later. You had to meet the rain of the following day with buckets; and the famous corset was all wet . . . it was still in Sala's possession for Donald's grandmother had rejected it with a frown and a laugh at the same time. Sala in the rain which the drains chopped fast ended up at the house of Iain McKay, a tall blondish laughing boy who insisted on three metres of laughter for every sentence he uttered. Sala went with Iain to pick wild raspberries in an old disused yard far away on the horse-shoe road that slowly surrounded the town. And fresh cow's milk at a nearby farm was too fresh for Sala. Sala pontificated on the corset, saying that if it couldn't bring all the children of the world together then it was a useless corset trying to gather spineless children rather. He said to Iain with his face serious and sad: 'Never forget that when you grow up, it is your duty to remember this day of playing as often as you can, and that however different my food or my worship is, we are the same!'

Again the corset was rejected, and thrown playfully on his head, with the last metres of laughter following. On the third day which had one side of the Main Street sunny and the other side raining, Sala went and accosted Kwaku de Babo and took him along towards the terraced and semi-detached back gardens where children swung and ran, but did not get the chance to experience gari. Kwaku had brought along the ducks, the goat and the termites but couldn't persuade the vulture to leave the napping Kofi Senya's pipe. The termites engaged each other in small and biting talk, and made Billy and Ann and Daisy and Dizzy and Alex and Geordie laugh by executing minute undertobolo jumps into each other's mouths; while the ducks made unbending quacks of yards and yards; and they roared when the goat lay on its back with an ancient bleat, and tried to use its balls as a microphone to chatter in. De Babo shouted in his written voice, 'Love us all here as we love you all, for we are here to help you helping us! Never forget!'

He threw up gari high, and everybody danced under it for seconds until it lay on the shoulders in a baptism of trust. When Sala returned to the teaching of his father, Kofi Senya gave him the egg of a vulture, but refused to say whether it was laid by his vulture or not. He was to keep the egg whole until they returned to Tukwan. The rest of the group went about their own rest, and tasks too; unloading the cassava after watching a John Cassavetes film; preparing for the tug-of-war of business talk; preparing to meet the Lord Provost probably in the townsquare; getting ready to send telegrams to Tukwan and receiving some; preparing to use one aeroplane as an inter-county trotro; discussing the possibility of one or two Levensvale people going on a quick visit to Tukwan, while the rest of the visitors minus Kwame Atta who may lead this short visit, stayed; and the conference too would come, where it was expected to drink palm-wine as a small import, and where kyinkyinga would be devoured crossculturally.

Was it not Kwame Atta up an oak tree, pushing his head to the top of the leaves, and congratulating Sala sitting at his father's feet, for making a wise splash in town; something he wanted to do later himself: if he could not get all the recognition he wanted in Tukwan, he had to supplement it in Levensvale. He decided to try a bit of seriousness, and he went to Donald's grandmother the smiling scowler; he looked at her throat and found some of the swallowed history that he thought his twin brother should rather be searching for . . . there was nothing like a smattering of historical fact to boost the business talk. Atta told grandma to hold her throat for a few minutes while he went to bring his brother who, he added, was a far more serious person than he was. There were finger marks on the old lady's throat when she removed her hand after they came: Donald could count six fading pressure marks. She told them that Levensvale was open to oral history, and that she hated the written kind since all the alphabet was a glorified spider party: the town could be written by the likes of Babo – her voice shook whenever she pronounced Babo, for she said the name reminded her of a recurring nightmare involving distilled streamwater that always turned into all the urine deliberately gathered at a 1930s football match. She was one of the rangers over her Celtic origins. Levensvale was once prosperous, quite high in kalabule. It could shut out invaders at will, except when they came through the Oban caves and prevented the domination of Loch Fyne herring and the reinvention of malt whisky. Thankfully, invaders had bedabbled feet that could slip out of history, though nothing except valour prevented them from slipping back in. Grandma's mouth was getting smaller and smaller as she talked. Kwaku felt an overwhelming sympathy for her, since it was obvious that every event of history had a deep terror for her: she fastened her heart round everything, and then watched it burst. Kwame Atta joined his talking with grandma's, so that while she talked about Levensvale in metamorphosis, he surrounded her talk fast with his point that she could quickly declare herself an ancestor of Tukwan to see whether she could comfort herself by examining Africa's history of slavery. She laughed – she always laughed when the pain got too much – and then revealed her great addiction to sliced raw turnip. She announced that she knew exactly when Levensvale became almost invisible to the rest of the country: it was when David Mackie's ancestor announced with a totally debauched look on his face – as if he was salacious about abstract things – that his town had rejected all the usual categories of life and thought, and that from that day onwards, no train that left Levensvale was to come back. And it was astonishing to Kwame and Kwaku that the old woman knew that Pokuaa had cried over two rusty nails-pointed omens – and that the minute the tears fell over each one, Levensvale and Tukwan became almost one in soul. One contractor's nail in Tukwan, one contractor's nail in Levensvale . . . though it was in London that Mackie first met Pokuaa.

So both towns wanted a prosperity of the pocket to go with the reincarnating prosperity of the soul, as if to remain immortal took too long, and that money would shorten things a bit. David Mackie stood before the mirror this morning, trying to select the most financial smile to face Pokuaa with over the rhubarb patches, true. He had inundated himself with tweeds of a dazzling nature. And when he strolled over to call Atta and Babo from grandma's – her mouth had finally disappeared the minute she stopped talking – his sartorial dazzle made them think he was a walking painting, O you painted Mackie. Pokuaa and the twins faced Mackie and Gilmour, with LT walking in and out of the points. There was at first a cross-legged silence which Pokuaa broke by uncrossing her legs: 'It seems that you want cedis and we from Tukwan want pounds, the idea being that you will agree to spring the cedi as a marvellous surprise on the rest of the country after we are all rich . . .' Pokuaa had sprung eyes waiting to spring back in case Mackie made any objections. There was a shout from Shebelda from the bedrooms, 'David dear, please be careful that you make a good deal and you are not cheated.' Pokuaa raised her eyebrows and looked at her twins, one eye each. Mackie stuck out his chest, and gave a long stretch. Stretches were long in Levensvale, yawns were longer in Tukwan. 'I feel that we shouldn't jump to conclusions about springing currency on anyone, until we have assessed the quality of the produce you brought . . .' 'First class!' shouted Kwame Atta instantly. 'Yes first class public relations,' added Eddie Gilmour wryly. 'Now, my friend, I do not wear a batakari for nothing,' said the smiling Atta, 'I am an inventor, and the only thing I haven't invented in this world is money!'

David Mackie decided to select another smile: serious. 'Do you have any complaints about the aeroplanes?' 'Of course not,' said Pokuaa with an incandescent smile, 'but only that they were a bit small, and we had to build trailers to supplement our cargo space . . .' 'And a lot of love made the invention of the trailers possible,' said Atta with his elbows propping up arms propping a heavy chin in an otherwise light face with thin features sliced almost into nothing. 'But there is the small matter of the expenditure I have written here on the trailers . . .' said Babo, with his bland honest smile. 'Now let's get a few things straight here, are you people from eternity or are you not?' asked the exasperated Mackie. 'But my dear David, you know we share our immortality together,' said Pokuaa, putting sugar in her reasonableness . . . and stirring it, 'and your tea is so-so nice.' 'I do not agree that expenses on the trailers should come into account,' Mackie said flatly. 'Now now, now, we must be fair,' Pokuaa said half as flatly with a sly smile in the other half, 'we also know you made some extra expenses on the curving of the tarmac, I lie?' There was a suspicious pause. 'What is the relationship between the cedi and the pound?' asked Gilmour. Atta was fidgeting: 'Now you honourable gentlemen already know the answers to some of your own questions, so what game are you playing at . . . your ignorance is your profit ampa!' 'I spent hours weighing the produce with Margaret, and the tonnage of both cassava and palm-nuts was exact; in fact one cassava and one nut were extra,' Mackie said, adjusting his third smile. Then without warning, Opanin Akorsah stormed in, shouting, 'But why are you having this meeting without me? I know you have a committee, but I have now decided that I should have been on it. Besides I want to sell my own cassava direct . . .' Pokuaa was irritated, and said, 'that was not the agreement before we left, and besides it's not only your cassava that you came for; it's Moro's too, and he hasn't given you permission to sell it solo has he?' Her irritation disappeared into her duku, her smile came out of her kabasort instead. Akorsah looked at his enemy, the brooding and uncharacteristically silent Lawyer Tay, and then stormed back out to think about what to do. LT said at last, 'You see the agreement must be restudied one by one, baako baako; and then we will arrive at a just exchange rate, after which we will decide what percentage to take each for when Appa goes trotro with the aeroplane.' 'And we are not going to get some reparation kitikiti for the few but shameful years that that one ancestor of yours engaged in slavery?' Atta said with a grin. 'All right!' Mackie said with the same grin doubled. 'Shall we then allow one percent of net profits for any such historical sins?'

There was some laughter, but the one percent was written all the same by Babo. 'But take one quarter percent off the reparations for guilt,' Pokuaa offered, looking mysterious. 'Guilt?' asked the perplexed Gilmour. 'Ah, Ed, you're slow, gay slow today! What the lady means is that those of us here who sometimes suffer a feeling of guilt for what some of our ancestors did to the slaves so-called of Africa, are to enjoy a guilt allowance of one quarter percent of profits in this deal under discussion, isn't the lady smart!' said Mackie in one breath. But my dead friend, what do you mean so-called asked the puzzled LT. 'Ah Lawyer, you're slow small today! What the good gentleman means is that you cannot define a person merely as a slave; for if you do that you destroy what remains of his humanity, isn't our host gentleman smart!' enthused the clapping Kwame Atta, touching his heel with his toe through the blue chalewate. 'David dear, try and be serious with our kind visitors because you may lose an advantage through the laughter,' Margaret called through the curlers of her hair. 'I am smiling, woman, I am smiling, not laughing! Can you be a little more discreet with your comments please!' Mackie hissed through the half-open bedroom door, his ears pressed against his head in irritation. There was a gentle shuffling of feet all round. Atta broke the silence: 'Has Appa still got the crows going round his language?' LT rose in triumph, shouting, 'Did I not tell you that this banku pilot would come and disgrace us here! We are talking seriously about our livelihood and he brings in the beaks of crows nibbling at the language! Alleluya, sack him from the committee!'

Just then Kofi Senya stole in, the biggest thief of time – tiefmann of eternity – but he did it so quietly that no one heard him one pesewa. The vulture had been left indignant in the hallway. 'Now that we are getting ready to eat the money, you lawyer two-bits, you are bringing my dignity in again. I warn you that I do not drive an aeroplane for nothing! I have sustained you all these months with my head-head palavers and inventions, so you do not have the right to insult my person one bit . . . nor two bits Mr Lawyer if I may add!' LT made his livid forehead bold as a rock, Atta followed, hardening his in turn. The two geologies stared inches away from each other; but Shebelda had already rushed in with home-made pancakes, and judicious touches of port in very small wine glasses. 'What a fine dose!' exclaimed Atta. He had forgotten all about his near-fight with LT, and had already downed his port, with the pancake following suit. LT still stood stiff in his anger for a few seconds before he took his considerable belly to the armchair, waiting to be served, and muttering about the need for some decorum. 'But another complaint we have is that you brought so much of your own food that all that David asked me to store frozen has become superfluous . . .' complained Margaret Shebelda. Kofi Senya caught her words and released them again through his pipe. His smoking made them see him at last. 'I always feel more comfortable with Mr Senya around,' said Mackie absent-mindedly. Atta said, 'My dear boogie hostess, as for your food we have been chopping, and we shall continue to chop! In these cold lands we have to eat more, half yours, half ours. I know you are Scottish, but you are not mean at all as the jokes say . . . except that your husband was telling us that the food bill is part of the total expenses . . .' '. . . provided that there is an equal amount of eating when or if a small return visit is made to Tukwan; but anyway as I said, we can include the food bill in the factory costs when we have finished our negotiations,' Mackie said slightly exasperated: he had good mathematical anger, being able to instantly subtract heat from his temper. 'But we have a complaint too that the factory bill is too high,' stated Babo, opening his mouth at last and putting the end of his pen in it. 'Well, well,' mused Eddie Gilmour, 'what exactly are the terms of trade we are using? Are we calculating in the same economic year?' 'How can we calculate in the same economic year when we are children of eternity?' asked LT with a face portentous with innocence. 'Now shall we have some sanity here please, especially after the pancakes,' Mackie began, and paused, continuing, 'shall we then agree on the year in which we are talking? I thought we were sharing 1963 . . .' 'O certainly not! because 1963 was a bad year for me legally, for I lost so many cases against myself . . .' 'And if you want to choose 1959, you'll find that that would be unfortunate because that was the year I hurt my popylonkwe . . .' 'Your what?' asked Mackie. 'My popylonkwe, my ttthing! I hurt it when I was trying to sheabutter it in readiness for any eventuality . . . ooooomy . . .' 'Shut up Kwame Atta, close your atapkame mouth! and why are you stammering?' shouted Opanin Akorsah with indignation. He was certain that these young fools would make the journey worthless. 'Bbbbut I thought you knew sharp that whenever I mmmmention my popylonkwe, I stammer, I multiply the language . . .'

LT stormed out with his head in his hands and his belly shaking. 'Dream is better than reality here!' he shouted out as he entered the toilet. 'Then dream urine!' hurled Kwame Atta, determined to break his own image further, so that it would scatter over all of them, including Pokuaa who these days did not often come to his aid. 'And I will refuse to drive the aeroplane again!' he added. They ignored that, but LT shouted, 'twiaaaa!' from the toilet doorway. Gilmour without the Ted didn't know which cheek to use to smile surreptitiously. 'Can we please return to the years?' Mackie pleaded, his voice deepening into business. 'Me no one can sack me from the committee! If you sack me I too will sack you on top, and then you can take all the committeeless decisions you want, indeed I say!': Atta was still on the attack. 'I suggest the year 1965 because that was a sensible year; that was the year when corn was plentiful, when sugar-cane was sweeter; and when Kwame Atta made a gliding aeroplane with bamboo,' Pokuaa said very calmly, getting up and straightening her cloth with finality. Kofi Senya hummed to himself to back her sanity. The vulture flew in stylishly without permission, right back onto the pipe . . . which wasn't even in the shrinemaster's mouth. The year 1965 was accepted by acclaim. 'But the records show that both currencies fluctuated wildly in that year,' Gilmour said, scrutinising some printed matter. 'That's all right,' replied Babo just returned with his cornerstep from a quick stand at the hotel corner to breathe in some soul, 'we can use the same degree of fluctuation to work the rates out, and I have already done it.' 'And what was the result I pray?'

asked Mackie feeling helpless enough to let some sarcasm out. 'The cedi appreciated on many occasions, and eventually left the pound exhausted with three depreciations in a row; but when we take the average . . .' '. . . when we take the average hemmed in between the mean owl and the median grasscutter, we find that every part of the aeroplane is less valuable than every part of the palm-nuts and the cassava,' interrupted Atta, bulldozing the words of his brother aside. But Babo persisted, 'The average being this: there should be fifty cedis to every pound.'

There was some educated silence, as both sides worked frantically with their own figures in order to gauge the advantage. 'But I thought only one twin was silly, kwasia!' screamed Opanin Akorsah. 'How can this Babo be such a fool as to try to be so honest with these richer people! The safest thing richest to do is to try to dupe them small. Then they should also try and dupe us small, home trade style! And what is more honest than this: cheating somebody and knowing that somebody is cheating you too! Equal draw! 'Don't mind this man one tigernut, his brain is atadwe. Ewurade one million! If we can't have some subtlety in an advanced state of rein-carnation, then how can we be children of immortality? Me, I eat law as much as possible! And the beauty is to relate the law to cashew-nuts for the purposes of breaking both and eating them. We have got new categories, and we want more, more!' the lawyer said fast. 'What do you think is the ethics of a humble businessman like me?' asked Mackie suddenly of Pokuaa, for he just now found her voice and lips irresistible, and ethics was the best way through which to deflect the desire. 'The ethics is to have mercy on the exchange rate, and to minimise the expenses,' she answered quickly on a piece of paper: she didn't want to speak; what was she doing writing just when he was so desperate to hear her voice, which had a pinhead of vulnerability at the end of it? 'Good morning!' Mackie said to Pokuaa in desperation, still bent on hearing her voice. 'Good morning,' she wrote: 'I have a sore throat, but it will be better in five minutes.' Mackie's neon tweeds dimmed a bit. Let the woman keep her silence for five minutes, he said to himself.

'Are your thoughts straying a wee bit away from the business, David?' Margaret asked with her new solicitousness, which was prone to want to spar more than the old. Mackie's natural nature was to be a bit gruff, but a series of new situations and new pressures had created a sort of mad restraint that was now straining at the seams. Presently he seemed to be a man of seams. But his thick eyebrows and dashing moustache still gave his look a worldliness that was sometimes risqué. The sun slipped through the open window, and it was strange to see some of the visitors put their hands out to catch it . . . for it had been so scarce, the real sun, scarcer than Tukwan itself. 'The sun makes me ashamed of myself,' Atta declared all of a sudden, 'because . . .' 'Now the man is going to tell the truth about that long-chewed chewing-gum character of his!' LT interrupted. '. . . because it is so clear and I am not and nor is the lawyer, I may add,' Atta continued, 'but let me stand in for my brother who, true, is sitting in now now, and tell you about the details of our accounts . . .' 'If only Kwaku will agree, for after all he is the secretary,' Pokuaa said finding her voice again. Babo glowed inside, but since he had long decided to bury his love for Pokuaa, he just nodded to Atta to proceed. 'Certainly we have some expenses which are spiritual, like the workmanship of waiting for several days at the shrine for the proper divination over the journey . . . we are not saying you have to pay for everything but we must tell you . . . and of course we had to make money available for town meetings for khebab and sometimes yam, from Dogo, otherwise we wouldn't have the energy to make the big-big decision to travel. In addition we had goat's beef . . .' 'I demand you explain goat's beef, since when did goats . . .' shouted LT scornfully. 'I go to the invention room at the shrine to study, so when I say goat's beef I am talking shrine language: it's a goat killed on a cow and roasted together so that you can't tell the difference . . . goat's beef to feed the stools with. We have brought you fresh sugar-cane free. What is the cost of a chew between friends of the same time! But as for the technological expenses and advancements we have some bambala estimates: nothing less than half a million cedis for that alone. Then of course we can get down to minute irritants like aeroplane grease; and we did some screwing . . .' 'I beg your pardon?' said the bushy eye-brows with Mackie behind them. '. . . into nuts that did not understand the nature of my desire . . . to check how firm the alloys of the wings were, and then to reach a number of climaxes with screwdrivers . . .' 'What on earth is your man blethering about?' asked Ed the Ted, throwing his hands in the air. 'What is he getting sexual about accounts for?' 'Me nua, hold it hold it . . . no, no, I didn't literally mean hold *it*, you stupid Amoa that shouldn't be in this room koraa. I am talking about the workmanship for making holes and then putting something into them, aeroplane maintenance. Altogether when you add the cost of the produce . . .' 'Hold it! no Amoa, not that, are you mad, get out of here with your tricks . . . don't say another word, Kwame Atta. We shall not reveal the final figure for legal reasons until our hosts have also gone through the details of their transactions,' Lawyer Tay said firmly.

There was a pause during which everybody turned to look at Kofi Senya for guidance, but he had vanished. Mackie rose impatiently, ready to spill the accounts, with his automatic eyebrows raising themselves every few seconds: 'We had to deepen Loch Divina with dredges to make more water available for the construction of the planes.' He paused to see the effect of this; and then he let his eyebrows down just as the others were raising theirs. A shout from Shebelda came from the rooms, 'David, don't overdo it, remember your links with the Canons of the church, and tell the truth as often as possible!' Mackie ignored his wife by holding his chin harder: 'The dredging was a complex operation needing the services of a much-bytten and nibbled computer. And because of our time scale, so fast, we had too many Burns Nights on the calendar, and therefore lost much productivity among the bracken where we were all falling in love with the growing aeroplanes . . . incidentally we are aware that you have some patents to sell, for example your trailers; well, we also have a few things we invented locally concerning computers and then walking-sticks that actually walk beside you so that you don't have to lean on them as eminent rabdopilists!' 'Can we please have something stronger than tea and port of the Tema variety, so that we can adjust to the power of the information you are revealing?' came the deliberately lowered voice of Atta. 'Certainly . . .' replied the agreeing Mackie, rubbing his hands. '. . . Not!' completed Margaret from yonder, 'the whisky is already finished. I found Alec Murray completely pissed if I may say so, crawling about the cellar . . .' '. . . trying to use his popy-lonkwe as a walking-stick!' ended Amoa true. 'All right, all right, if no whisky, then no whisky. Let me continue . . .' said the ridiculously imperious Atta. 'Kindly let me finish!' protested Mackie, still rubbing his hands with radish and relish, savouring his aeronautic accounts, 'Now let me remind you that we have already agreed on two important things: ten percent of profits goes to the African National Congress of South Africa, and then one percent to a mutual research fund whose purpose is to assess the quality of our inventions; and that's because we have already agreed on one fundamental principle: to invent something in wood, bamboo even, or moss – like your plane seats – is equal to anything else invented in harder metals. We think this is a breakthrough, since we will all then be dealing with the pure idea . . .'

'It's wonderful for the two towns to be together, isn't it!' enthused Pokuaa. 'And it is because of this last idea that we have brought you thousands of dead termites with the live ones, so that you can consider how we can store snake serum in them . . .' Hold the excitement, hold the excitement, was what Mackie thought, but he said instead: 'Our total outlay was £200,000!' There was a deep silence, during which Babo did a quick calculation: 'This agrees nicely with our total expenditure of ₵4.0 million!' The deep silence continued, until Kofi Senya walked into it. He said with a smile, if you have solved all the accounts, then let's get to work on unloading our things, helping with the building of the factories, planning the visit to Tukwan, flying the aerial trotro and everything else so good. Come!'

CLASS SIX

The peewit that missed its moors almost landed on the crying shoulders of Pokuaa, who was hidden deep in the heather. Sometimes for days at a time even when things were going well, Pokuaa would suffer bouts of absolute vulnerability: she would cry for the world, she would cry against the world; the thyme that brushed the old walls had watched her move back and forth, each time her fresh footprints getting caught in the old footprints. By the gnarled hawthorns with their descending berries, she raged, biting her forefinger small and snapping it against her thumb. Where were the boundaries of her life, this woman that they all thought so strong? The old Paul Anka song, Diana, was torn at its recurring climax as it wafted up from Angus's wireless far below. To her right, one hundred metres away was the necklace hill, with Pastor Mensah on it, half-hidden and praying, prayers directed at the crisis of Pokuaa, directed at Levensvale and Tukwan. The sun slipped behind the clouds and made them glow, above that handkerchief that could not hold all of her tears. A few metres to her left stood a furtive Alec Murray, well without his bogey, shivering with Pokuaa's shivering, holding his head as she held hers. In spite of his drunken and rather lurid sophistication, Murray could not understand how a fine, sharp leader of a woman could break down so hard and so without explanation. Some worms crawled under hard ground with very soft earth under it. Alec was surprised that Pokuaa had not driven him away with any sudden anger that should be guarding her crying: he was reminded of his own vulnerability before the failed opportunity of his education, and then before his wild living.

If you stood higher up, as Kwaku de Babo did regretfully, you would see a composite picture: Pastor Mensah praying in agitation round his huge necklace of hill pine, Pokuaa desolate in the middle and Alec Murray duplicating this desolation with his odd and jerky movements. Kofi Senya would sometimes appear by her with a grave manner, and rub leaves on her arms. No one else knew of her crisis, though Kwame Atta was missing her

— 77 —

and wondering, without success, where she was. The same with David Mackie, who for two days had been wearing more restrained tweeds. Senya shouted over to Korner Mensah not knowing whether he heard or not: 'When you cry for time, it's hard to stop; but the joy will soon come!' Alec Murray had taken out a jot, with his ash under a mountain ash; and that one birdtable by that one stream that he always found ridiculous, he now found surprising in the valley. Old and mouldy crumbs filled this table half-rejected by birds of all feathers. Babo did not dare reveal himself to Pokuaa, for he was terrified to see her sorrow, especially a sorrow that was general and not down to one hurt. Why should she make her heart so large, when she hadn't even solved what she was going to do with it? Babo could not write, not even when one wansana pobee, one bluebottle, landed on his pen to help. His ankles were itching. Murray waved once or twice in restrained recognition of Pokuaa, but she seemed to ignore him in his unworthiness, as he thought with a deep stab of regret. He wanted to make this woman from the far, hot lands the focus of his future recovery; to be known not as the man who bared himself to the world, but as the wide, wide man who bore the world. Pastor Mensah crawled in and out of the pine necklace, repeating Pokuaa many times for each pine cone that he passed; as if to exorcise the short body of her anurous renunciation of the world, some hot-shitoh damnation so pure that it was tailless, and shellless, or. You couldn't burst her out of it yet, you couldn't burst her further into it either. Memaaameeeeii! Come and do some maths and subtract Pokuaa from her suffering! In this mood, Pokuaa could turn ferociously upon herself: she damned herself for having no children yet, for she knew she had so much love to give to her child, so much freedom; she condemned herself for her material success, wondering where that hard part of herself came from; and at the worst moments, she even thought that she should apply to the ancestors to live in ordinary time again, to be removed from the weight of the new and the adventurous. Ebei!

It was when the Lord Provost himself heard of this cosmic crying that he decided to send secretly his little six-year-old girl who often had a verve that went through the wounded heart. So little Pamela was down in the valley of the afternoons – when it seemed most beautiful – and was slowly climbing up to where Pokuaa was. She periodically skipped among the nettles in her blue slacks, and she smiled with an intensity and a directness that brightened the chrysanthemums far away, a smile tossed like Shebelda's pancakes and never caught again. And that smile reached Pokuaa, disembodied, long before Pamela herself. 'I play the violin,' Pamela said immediately, 'and I have brought you a nice present: two handkerchiefs joined double, white and blue, one part for one eye, the other part for the other eye. My mother tells my daddy that he has no time for us, and that when he dies, they will bury him with his politics. I like my daddy laughing, because it means he will give me sherbet ten minutes later. My father is my sherbet; and in twenty minutes it will be fruit gums. Why are you crying? Hurry up and take the double hanky, and I will hold your hand – no hanky panky, promise – and we will play at skipping.' Pokuaa had disappeared altogether under the bracken, but with her eyes getting stronger. She with no warning at all lifted the laughing Pamela down the hill. They were laughing together and holding each other's hair; and there was Alec Murray in hot pursuit, manipulating his bones between the mocking gorse. Pastor Korner Mensah continued to pray, but this time with both hands touching the hill, and not with one lost for Pokuaa. De Babo was delighted, but with a deep underlay of forlornness: he was hoping to draw Pokuaa out of her dark night of the soul, with that hand that always held that pen of chalk that was constantly writing. But if the little girl had done it, there was no point in hiding his joy with the little regret below it. Mr Cornerstep Babo was deliberately creating corners by going round even the smallest trees, so that it took him the whole afternoon to transfer himself onto the necklace hill.

Pastor Mensah was poking his prayers into the shrubs and grass, and had shoulders stooping towards the eastern cross of rock. He looked up on one knee, and then jumped from the other too, saying, 'Kwaku Babo, Kwaku Babo, so have you now come to me at last to worship? Have you waited until we have reached this strange land to do it?' Kwaku Kornerstep joined corners with the pastor, but shook his head, saying that he had come to see how heavy the necklace was. The daylight of the summer Levensvale evening was the equivalent of the Tukwan yawn: so long. Babo just watched Korner Mensah praying, a prayer to each cone in religious pine; and the midges were coming. On which side of the hill was the thicker heather spread? Who was going to adjust the vulture's wings so that it could fly up and down the chimneys, now that the fires were out? The lonely women making bramble jelly had lived full lives, but were now not too sure where to put their old age, not even after some post-wise elderberry wine; thus they adored the visitors because in Tukwan growing old was no real problem, and Levensvale wanted to learn, learn. 'The cross has lost yet another stone to children! I don't understand why they have to come up here koraa to steal a sacred stone to throw!' Pastor Mensah shouted down to the retreating Babo. 'And can't you come up so that we can pray together?' Babo waved in reply, but continued to descend with gathering speed, one bit of ground meeting him and throwing him onto another bit with alarming momentum. The earth shared him fast. And he couldn't stop, poor Babo, raising his knees in a stinging hurtle over the nettles, rushing into a hedge of big beech and scattering a nest there with the birdling about to be fed wearing a huge frown bigger than its beak; and squashed under his propelled feet were prized and extremely late daffodils with the owner abusing him to the rhythm of the running: 'You, just as well you are not the moss-seated aeroplane inventor or I would cane your stampeding thighs . . . he was here the other day drinking my . . .' Babo couldn't hear the rest for the rush. There he was, having covered two decades already with his insane running, touching the fifties with the left thigh, bump, and grazing the sixties with the right thigh, thump. And they screamed under his thighs, especially those suffering murder, war, disaster and racism, those coffee skins being forced to arrange their skin over blackboards so that the pink mathematicians would decide whether one plus one equals humanity or not. Up the ferns, down the gorse, for the scratches were growing on poor Babo's thighs, through this run of the mixture of past and present. And there was a mouth very high in the sky, its body buried long ago, a mouth shouting, 'Come here laddie, if they are hounding you, jump out of your skin and huddle blue or green, anything to escape from the white or the black, for I am a good purple colourless Scotsman myself! O I know that you have had a whole binful of good Presbyterians who were racists at the same time, for just when you would think they would be allies against the Sassenachs, then they would betray you: they would see the beautiful black in you as if you didn't exist, and then they would create some dubious connotations around your skin with their instantly primitive minds. Laddie, these men of the surface of the skin are the last primitives of this earth! Stop running, stop running, so that you can hear more . . .'

And another voice fastened onto his leg, 'Yes sonny, it was shocking to see Mothers' Union members hate a man for his skin, it was shocking to see professors of good Scottish universities claim that some skins were not equal to others and you could see that bestial and misplaced pride stiff on their faces. But of course their daughters would like you, for the sensible ones among them would certainly want something greater than skin. Run, my good black man, run, your speed will push away the insults, your inventions will make the sophisticated primitives turn their backs, again as if you didn't exist! Look at all the rrrubish of history, the buried lies, and the resurrected murder! Can I run beside you, you're going too fast, stop and run, stop and run!' Babo had bumped into six aunts, two grandmothers, one grandfather, thirteen sisters, forty brothers and one terrier which loved to bark at uncontrollable speed. Perhaps a pine would eventually stop him, perhaps his twin Atta would save him with a brotherly and drunken lunge; under the herring could lurk a betrayed king, whose majesty would have to be fumigated for all the dirty rotten things that were stuck to it. Babo broke the speed limit! His heel was stuck to a church for a while, until a saint in a stained-glass window stuck out a hand and freed him. 'Joy to the worshipping agnostic!' the saint said with a Glasgow accent, and it is possible that heaven may have very very few racists . . . Then the saint talked no more, for the glass was broken by the vandal's stone.

What on earth was Babo doing wearing roller skates through the history of this strange land? And as he rolled through the artificially salted Loch Divina with its cheeky herring that flipped off your plate even though they were pickled, he miraculously, through his speed, arranged for a heap of mussels about which songs were sung, to pile on his head; and by this he was given a greater right to rush into any souls available for scrutiny freeee: and there was Jessie the gloomy wee hen who would have loved to buy kelewele in Kumasi, but instead was trapped in the Gorbals up a dingy close that had the leak from the drainpipes rushing in with a directing breeze; and Jessie had been presented with two broken hearts on two broken plates – couldn't even give two wholesome plates for the job of destroying her soul – and now her former lover was living across the same street with a truly skinny undertobolo female gannet; and when the culprits cooked, the smell made her insanely jealous; and when she was drinking to warm her shivering heart, she had to take: gin and jealous. Come on Archie, you are equally lonely, go and rescue Jessie from the disgrace of a passion transferred across Nicholson Street. C'mon Archie, stop your argie bargie about the heart! Speed was the thing! Do you not see the young African Babo running through our streets with that caring of the soul that may make him think he owned them? Don't disappoint Babo, Archie; O we know that you can play the piano gay good, and that once you joined the Orange men in their ridiculous unAfrican dances through the staff-throwing drum-girl streets; well, let us tell you one secret: Jessie is a Fenian! But what's the Pope between friends? We will rely on your good judgment paaa, to bind the heart of Jessie. Hurry, or she may die of grief! Babo could make plantain grow in the middle of the Gorbals, or even at the Eye Infirmary when he could see better. So Archie was inspired, and rushed towards Jessie with his arms open and his heart wider . . . but after making the final surrender, he was told by Jessie that he should wait until she smoked a jot the other side of eternity. So Archie just died with an anti-Jessie bugle playing automatically on his coffin . . . Never give up Jessie, Babo thought; and he didn't even know her koraa. You are a stranger Babo, buying fish and chips meant your soul was on a sole potato! Brief the Levensvale streets on the time, and the heart of time that you were using, for all they knew was that you were running out of control, and that you had added one foolish cousin to the long list of people you had made a historical bump into. Shame, for even though they were an original town, they could not fathom how to stop a man from running eternally. Try love, try love, came the cry, for there was nothing slower than the heart. Bring Pokuaa and that would stop Babo running! You mean that Pokuaa that had just freed her very self from the dangers of time recurring, with the help of that Pamela that tamed time by behaving as if it didn't exist at all? Don't bring yourself!

Mr Cornerstep the Chief Secretary would write his own solution for his legs, would delocomote his own thighs, I swear! When Babo's speed finally led to an attack of asthma, Kofi Senya intervened hastily by wrapping the speeding legs in tempering vulture wings that almost made Babo vomit for all the carrion in the great bird's belly. The earth, the earth, no longer shared Kwaku de Babo, the earth gave him the slowest walk in the hills; and the sweat had changed his clothes entirely, and he wondered with the sly terror of responsibility whether Jessie the Jot was dead; or whether Jessie was Pokuaa, and Archie was Babo. 'Kwaku my brother, what has been happening to you and to Pokuaa? Is it because we are in a new land that you want to make some strange journeys inside your hearts or what! I believe in the habits of the properly drunk and inventive scientist! No one has ever called me a scientist before! If you don't respect me, you lie bad! If you had made me aware of your speed earlier I would have slowed you down now now now, ok! and old Senya would not have had to administer his vulture onto you!' shouted the panting Kwame Atta, holding a jot in one hand and a whisky in the other. Kwaku looked at him with a delayed stupor . . . and then went to look for Kofi Senya to thank him for stopping the clocks moving for a short and timely time. And the wind could be caught and pocketed again it was so slow this wind above the factories.

It was at the next breakfast, which had steps of thick traditional porridge leading to everybody, that de Babo realised that libation had already been poured at dawn for the starting of the two factory buildings; and that Nana Bontox had been highly annoyed to see only the Mackies, Murray and of course Okyeame Nana Kasa at the opening of the bottle of the praying gin. Kofi Senya had already got up, but was busy on the horizon suspending the dawn for a few minutes, so that the gin could pass smoothly under it. Cocks at the Mackies' semi-free range poultry couldn't crow this morning because that mad Murray had gone and glued their beaks together in anger: David had refused to give him any more drams of whisky, since it had been established, after Murray's sympathy with Pokuaa, that he could live a life without curving himself round a glass with waterfire in it. But the pressure had been too much for Alec the former bogey and Mackie caught him slowly crawling back into a glass with the intention of drinking himself within the glass whole if there was no whisky left. Mackie's abuse led Alec straight to the birds, which would have died of glue if Akyaa hadn't noticed the extraordinary poultry silence first. So Murray had been left stamping about refusing to feel shame at this cruel scandal of feathers; standing there sober but stamping to be drunk . . . and then he stepped without intention right on Babo's pen, crunching it. There he stood, his contorted face both contrite and triumphant. 'Ach what a pity. My face is my banner! Look at the flag of sorry on it! I hope young man that you are not going to say that all time will stop with your shattered pen . . . and if you give me the chance to shut those cocks up again, I may do it. After all they crow far too early! Filling up my world with those ridiculous feathery screams just will not, hic, do . . . and look at what is happening, hiccups on top of everything, hic!'

Babo looked at him with bland pity, and then slowly his eyes focused on the up-sauntering Atta; he looked at Murray and Atta with alarm, for they were looking at each other with mad recognition. 'Are you the human piffle who has been stealing my whisky in the dead of night when the ghosties are aboot?' asked M for Murray. A for Atta jumped with a sharp and sideways spring at M, saying, 'Me I will let you know sharp-sharp that you are only a perambulating cockroach crawling before me, and about to be crushed. I will commot you one time! How dare you accuse me of the truth! Of course I have been doing libilibi with your drinkable, but who are you to question the ethics of a distinguished akpokplonto? I will reserve my spleen for you dindiiiindin! I am a scientist I will have you know quick. I doubt that I believe in the thomas of your tomfoolery, nor do I believe in the loo of your lewdness. I will highjump you just now!' M for Murray had a look of intense recognition on his face. But he broke the look and said, 'Jesus Christ brother of my balls! I have finally met a drunken bastard like myself! Don't eff me loose there standing like Tam O' Shanter with an andy capp on. Respect my kilt immediately! Now if I had met you earlier in my disgraceful life I would never have become what I am now! I would have been both frightened and disgusted right off my own life. What you are doing now you scientist-you is to tell me that I have no right to complain of my whisky being stolen when I'm dozing half-time before I start on the booze again. What cheek!' A replied with an impossible hiss, 'Hey contrey, let me beat gongong with my mouth and announce your foolishness to this three-man durbar at once pronto, you kotiboto with an unshaven popylonkwe! Kwaku I beg you, bring the breeze quick, for my language is burning . . . or better, try and commot some small spirits for my pressurised mouth.' 'I knew it!' exclaimed the triumphant M, 'I knew it! You can't stand the pace, you need to be delivered from the singe of my mouth. Hurray to Murray!' A looked at M with scorn, and said, 'You tiefman accuser, it's the drink I'm after not your words bodamfo. At home you would be a discarded circle of smoked fish, but I like you. I can change you long before Pokuaa can: I invent wisdom for the wise, and foolishness for the fool. So shut up now now now, and we shall become friends with one aim: to be spiritual for ever . . .' M was going to speak but thought better of it, wondering whether this man of ether before him was going to take him backwards or forwards; and perhaps he would produce the drink quick too.

'Won't you two gentlemen stop your giftgabbing gibbers and continue with your work on the buildings?' asked Mackie, approaching with an exasperated laugh. 'Of course boss,' said the deeply bowing Murray, his rotten hat falling off as he bowed. 'I believe we shall be paid extra for helping to build the factories . . .' 'Absolutely right!' declared the expansive Mackie, for he had just finished calculating that there would be a quiet profit on the building itself, which of course would be shared 50–50 after various expenses were deducted: such as the expense of putting up with the likes of Atta and Murray. He tolerated Atta only as a man of invention and profitable foolishness . . . and he had also noticed that Pokuaa was sometimes protective towards this inventor. Mackie would not forget in a hurry the morning Atta woke up, stormed into his bedroom, just after he had given Shebelda a long and absent-minded hug, and asked him, 'Mackie, are you a European or a Europium? I will slam your metal eyes if you can't give me the rare answer I want . . .' Atta had then stormed off equally quickly without waiting for any answer; nevertheless he had a curse thrown after him by Mackie. Kwaku de Babo had long fallen asleep among the bantering. His all-sides pen was still chalk. Mackie looked at him solemnly and said, 'It's just as well you are to write and not to supervise, otherwise I would wake you up.' Mackie was restless for as the work went on he saw that most of the workers, guests and natives alike, wanted to be in supervisory grades. Eventually each just granted himself or herself promotion. So that you were left with everybody supervising only Mackie and Pokuaa, the originators of the scheme in the first place. Pokuaa looked at Mackie, Mackie looked at Pokuaa. Shebelda cooked, and her cooking this time included abenkwan, gari foto, dried snails, crabs from Aba Yaa, and fufu. The woman she try-O. Even Angus – who otherwise worked quite hard between some unproductive inventions – was supervising. But the trouble was that he was only supervising Aba very closely. She often pushed his supervision away, it was so close. Angus would think with great rue that he had still not managed to get a simple hug from her: she liked his eyes but she did not like his nose; she liked his elbows but she did not like his knees. She had in fact worked out a system of mathematical love and appraisal that cancelled out poor Angus altogether . . . Angus that admired her agile and warmly tototicular tooshies. Never believe in supervision when there was love for the mortar would cake on the hands while the heart remained drastically dry . . . for Angus, you Angus of the nascent beard.

Work went on. The two pioneer workers ditched their myriad supervisors and became bosses again. Sometimes the sky was a very blue penny you could flick away when its sun was hard on the working back. Ham sandwiches appeared on the skyline from Margaret, and they were eaten immediately. Expenses grew but remained painfully anticipated by Mackie . . . who flew into a rage when Murray the semi-bogey declared that all this time he found no difference between account and acunt, for a poor man could afford neither; besides M for Murray did not understand why the popylonkwe should always be the butt for risky jokes – especially by the visitors – and not its counterpart at all. It's not fair, black, it's not fair.

Work went on, but didn't: blocks were being laid carefully by the newest automatic machine jointly invented by Mackie and his son Angus, a machine that could with impudent ease lay one block in mid-air, horizontally or vertically suspended, move sideways to work somewhere else, and return to continue with the laying. But the trouble started when it tried to lay Amoa, who indignantly shouted that he was not a blockhead. The work didn't: there was an announcement that the Lord Provost would soon be ready at the town square for an introductory meeting with the visitors and the townspeople. 'So at last your coat-of-arms bogger mayor now wants to meet the proletariat,' drawled Appa with his mind more on the forthcoming trotro service of the sky than on dignitarians. 'Please have a proper sense of respect for our dear leader who is extremely informal, especially after he has tripped in that loveable way of his; he is so clumsy sometimes that after he's tripped over both feet, he'll find a third to trip over,' motioned Gilmour with his mouth. So they all walked over his words and went towards the townsquare . . . where the baroque townhall faced the rococo office and banquet rooms opposite; with a nudge from the backend of a college carrying all the way across to the phallic columns of a museum where as a surprise, large photographs of all the visitors decorated the walls. And everybody was smiling except Opanin Akorsah who was already standing by his photo, complaining that it did not make him handsome at all, and that his cocoa-watching wife would reject its image. 'Next time take a picture of my nose alone; my nose is a good thing because it can smell bush meat in the farms far away, even before the traps trap it, I swear,' Akorsah said, allowing one smile to move from his face into the mouth of the photograph and then back to the face again.

The state umbrellas were there, dancing in forward and upward thrusts to the drums . . . in answer to the bagpipes in the opposite corner. They reacted to each other's bars, music and beer: male and female drums embraced the wail of the bagpipe; and Kwame Atta talked through his stout to Bobby Maclean: 'Which one of all the women present do you think I love, my good friend?' Bobby looked at Kwame quizzically, took a noisy slurp, and added deadpan, 'Well it's not that fat yin yonder, for that good lassie is my wifie! What? O I assure you that it is English I'm speaking, but it's an enriched version, ye see.' 'I am a scientist in love,' Atta declared, his head higher over his neck than usual. 'Well, laddie, I thank ye for telling me, otherwise I would have had trouble guessing. I would be dancing in a tizzy instead of guessing. Believe me the furthest I got was that I surmised that you were an interesting human being with an endless gullet. OK! gullet for drinking, I mean . . . Do you sometimes wake up feeling foolish, mon? I always have that misfortune: I wake up feeling more foolish than when ah went to sleep, because of my dreams. Ma dreams are so wise that they give me myself an inferiority complex, I wake up a lesser man than myself, d'ye see what ah mean, mon? Aye . . .' 'O course I see what you mean, contrey, but I am telling you that try and judge my character by pointing out to me the woman you think I love,' Atta insisted, looking far away at Pokuaa who seemed to be beautifully animated this afternoon. 'You're a blether!' Maclean said with a laugh, and moved off to another empty glass for someone else to fill. But Atta pursued him, so he blurted out with a twinkle in one eye, 'Now laddie, surely everybody knows that your heart is just crazy for that beautiful lady over there with the wonderful neck. What d'ye cry her, Pokuaa or what? Is she not the woman who is strong enough to reject all the men loving her? There's a rumour that Mackie has fallen too . . .' But Atta had moved away in disgust, stroking the bar in rhythm to the music.

Pastor Korner Mensah had begun the rather informal function with an extremely long prayer that the bold interrupted with disdain, insisting he should stop putting everything to sleep and go back to his interesting necklace of the hill, beyond the crosses. The pastor felt crossed, for the Lord Provost had arrived in the middle of the prayers; so that he was caught between stopping the prayer and amplifying it. 'I insist you finish the prayer, I pray,' boomed Tommy Rae walking that stooped angular walk of his, and smiling for political reasons koraa. You bambala mayor, with the kind heart and the kind little daughter, and the busy head . . . a head that did not want to go into politics in the first place. They voted him into it by force: a man with a reasonable degree of honesty might as well go into this dirty business of ruling. 'Welcome everybody, and sorry I'm late! Synchronising my time to one hundred other times is no joke. But then the advantage sometimes is that you can eat and eat two big breakfasts one right after the other, and you won't feel guilty about stuffing yourself! O sorry, sorry, continue your prayer. The Canons would never forgive me for this interruption of the holy supplication, eh!' As the pastor continued, you would think that some bowed heads were nodding heads. Kwame Atta was outrageous: even during the praying, he continued to ask three more people to identify his possible love. The stylish lampposts came on unusually early. 'Just as well we did the libation earlier,' said Nana Kasa with a frown. 'Yes, and the dancing too. Always better to dance early,' added Nana Bontox, who had persuaded a reluctant Sala to sit beside him today as the embodiment of the soul of the stool. Today therefore there was a frowning soul by Nana. Appa was already revving the upper-lip aeroplane far away on the tarmac, but was dragged back by Lawyer Tay to listen to the civilities. 'Do we have the mandate of all of you here to retain this beautiful association with these great people from a great continent?' asked the effusive Tommy Rae, with hands raised. There was a huge Yes. 'Are we all going to make profit?' the effusion continued, under an equally big and second Yes. But there was a small voice from Jock the fish and chip man: 'But are we allowed to dislike any particular one of these good visitors?'

There was a silence that Azziz sneezed into. 'Well, well . . .' began the Lord Provost with a reluctant and democratic glow in his eye. 'I'm saying this because there's one man here who's been eating pounds and pounds of my fish and chips without paying. He always tells me that as soon as the woman he loves gives him some money straight from the heart, he will pay. I don't like him, because he's a cheat!' Kwame Atta looked innocently astonished. Kofi Senya had strolled up to Jock and whispered to him, 'All the money he owes you is in your till. Please go and check. It will never happen again.' There was a cheer as Jock did a little jig – a raw fish fell out of his overalls – and raced to verify the truth offered. 'It looks as if justice is foreign!' an admiring Levensvale voice said to Kofi Senya. 'Don't kid yourself!' another voice warned, 'They just want to butter us up to make more money to take back to the sun!'

There were appreciative wolf whistles from Levensvale when Pokuaa walked onto the dais and shouted with as much feeling as politics, 'We love you all, profit or no profit!' 'What about the genetics, my people?' asked Tommy Provost the Lord. 'Well, my honourable Tommy, I entreat you that the only thing I want to keep intact is my giant willy!' There was a roar as Alec Murray rushed away from his own words. 'Let us have some seriousness here,' thundered the Lord Provost. 'But my dear Lord Provo, too much seriousness drives out the democracy of the occasion. The hard look in the eye is not our style, is it,' said the curate of the Episcopal Church with his blatantly Anglican smile. 'Please allow us to reach the important decisions!' LT added irritably, adjusting his kente gown with frills worn especially for the occasion. The drum beat for silence after a burp.

Then the Lord Provost tripped; but nobody laughed because since they all by now knew of his famous tripping idiosyncracy, they had all laughed in advance. Tommy Rae and the Lord Provost had achieved a fine dispersal of each other: being one person too under the light of the large generator of reincarnation he had acquired advantages. He could separate the Tommy from the Lord, feed either with goat's milk when necessary, let one hide from the other, and then sleep noisily between the two selves. But the Provost and the Rae were more difficult: there was no philosophical affinity between the two: the Provost loved the manoeuvring of politics, especially when it was necessary to liase with the rest of the country, which did not have the advantages of time and reincarnation, nor even the temporary suspension of guilt by inadequate lives; the Rae, however, was deeply antipathetic to the pretensions of office, loved his family – especially his daughter Pamela who was usually the centre of his life – though his love did not prevent him from staring passionately at attractive girls, when the Provost was asleep.

Thus his head was honest, no deals with contractors and no trading of favours, but his thighs were doubtful. He considered himself beyond convention – he preferred invention to it – but retained his office by appearing both more ordinary and more unconventional than anyone else in Levensvale; and he never spoke with notes, not even when his advisers warned him that he strayed too often from topics that sometimes didn't even exist. 'Speech, speech!' cried Appa bored, for he wanted things to finish quickly so that he could transport the aeroplane across local skies, and learn to land in the shortest spaces. Tommy began, twirling his sidelevers as he was wont to do when beginning to speak in public, 'If you are dealing with history and fish and chips, then usually you can't have either: both towns have reached outside themselves, those with long noses, those with short; and as soon as you reach outside yourself, you have the problem of keeping intact the soul you started with. This has been the trouble with all invaders, and we have both had our fair and foul share of them: they forgot the humanity under their noses when they grabbed the land and the gold, no? I am here to say that we have the privilege of living within and without time, even though many of us live as if we are in ordinary time . . . as far as I'm concerned I may have died and risen many times since we began our meeting in Levensquare; and I still can't believe that my ancestors were involved with colonies and other cruelties . . . I weep for their damned and broken souls . . . but since most of them have improved by reincarnating themselves into us here, then I have hope in the future. I am bored with racism. It's so primitive, it shuts out so much, it dehumanises the doer and the done so much that I find it disgusting for a man or woman to show its stench and then go home and behave like a loving father brother or lover, or like a god fearing person. The good loving racist father . . .'

'Kudos to Lord P!' shouted Amoa with a grin which he had just received from Eddie Gilmour. 'Yes,' came Jock's wee voice again, 'yes, but I hope he's not just saying all this for profit . . .' There was some muttering: Jock seemed to be prodding in the wrong bins. 'I am a sincere man,' Tommy declared to a shower of cheers. 'And all our Tommy wants is a huge and ritual renunciation of skin in law, in heart, in churches – not your usual "it's bad, but" – in pubs, in death, in sport, in fashion, in, in, . . .' shouted Ed Gilmour, dancing rather stiffly to the sound of Kete. 'And after all,' enthused the Lord Provost, 'the man that goes to the moon can surely go to humanity! And you gain from me, I gain from you, eh!' 'Ah, I can see that you people want to make humanity both ordinary and glamorous!' said LT adjusting his ever-moving belly . . . which little Pamela with the joy in her eyes pushed out of the way to get to the dais to hold her father's hand, and wave a big white handkerchief given to her by Pokuaa. And out came all the handkerchiefs, the Levensvale natives learning to wave while waving and the visitors so used to it already that they danced the wave. And there was old Jessie crying into her hairdressing, for she always got less love than she needed, and the love was more sentimental for her when it was started by strangers; true Neil had been trying for years to hide a tenderness that insisted on coming out through the hole in his sock, so that as soon as his wife saw it and was preparing herself for some embarrassing inner exploration, he had the sock darned; alleluya, you wouldn't believe that Dr Stuart who stood so stiff above the visitors whether they were well or sick, was now trying with a slight reduction in stiffness to do a wild Adowa: heal your own dancing, Dr! They were all trying hard, heel for heel and toe for toe, to enter into each other's soul, even the cheeky Amoa who managed a good Gay Gordons under the prompting of a fair lassie of brunette hue; and as for Kwame Atta, he had touched many thighs, and caused a whole concertina of screams; Babo calmed the flustered women with several deep waves of his pen, as if to wave was to write the answers for life: his smile was as sweet as an Obuasi orange, but he used it as little as possible, in order to prevent the large reflexes of irony flowing from the same mouth. Just watch Jessie, she enjoys a good cry with either eye!

'Stop, everybody, stop!' came the roar from Eddie Gilmour, 'believe it or not, but the Presby church tower has been stolen, s-t-o-l-e-n!' There was an incredulous hush. 'Me I know we'll be blamed for this I told you so,' frowned Opanin Akorsah, straightening the same Adinkra cloth that he always wore, but he forgot to straighten his forehead. His mouth was an irascible divination. The growing murmurs were so involved that they joined the webs of spiders in the square. But Pastor Mensah and Appa were missing. Akyaa rushed to the microphone and shouted into it with a sense of discovery, 'I think that God came for His own tower; when we were all busy dancing and talking. Back home, our gods can move; they can make fun with the ancestors before the one bigitive God comes . . .' Then they heard the aeroplane landing, even though they didn't hear it take off. Pastor Mensah walked in a stately manner, with his automatic cassock shortening and lengthening, onto the dais and declared with an amazing calm, 'My theological schools have all collapsed, back home. But I must be frank with you: I have borrowed your tower, with the help of Appa, for a small religious experiment, kakra, an experiment of logic: if your churches are emptying, and my pine necklaces in the hills are filling up, then why not take a significant part of the church to the necklace, and hope that the latter cures the former . . .' 'Good god!' wailed Mackie. 'Just wait till the Canons come! They will be in a . . .' '. . . towering rage?' Amoa completed the words for Mackie, while eating soft and subtle greengages from someone else's poke. 'Run after your language, you man, hic, and catch it in the heather where it's lurking,' shouted the lurching Murray who had lost Atta hic. Whenever he lost Atta, he lost the memory of himself, as well as the opportunity to have more drink. 'And let me tell you good people with your rotten status-seeking that I have seen the stolen tower amongst the hills looking better than it ever did, lying down among the ferns,' Murray continued, hic. There was a rush to reach the giant necklace that housed the stolen tower. 'Anyway isn't it a new idea for worship?' asked the perplexed Lord Provost joining the trooping to the holy hill with the rock and neon crosses, 'but what beats me is that has the good pastor got planning permission for the transfer of that part of the church's anatomy?' But Pamela wasn't listening: 'Hurry Daddy, hurry, I want to see the tower lying down in the grass and sleeping beside the lovely necklace. Daddy, hurry, hurry more fast!' They went and they saw.

CLASS SEVEN

If the tired tower, dragged off its base by the piloting Appa, was still lying on its side staring into the bracken with its steeple eye, then things were quite different: it had been hauled up, spiritually erect again and with African antecedents, into a bold thing, a fine addition to the rockcross shrine . . . and birds could make their dung on it vertically again. Somebody had dropped a single toffee in the valleys, suck. Kwaku de Babo passed it, and put another one beside it on the spur of the moment. Two sweet towns. Azziz had been fishing in the stream when a new pound note floated by dry. He wet it when he tried to catch it but couldn't. He became suspicious when another dry pound came by; and he stormed upstream, wondering what Akyaa would make of this, only to discover Angus and Aba arguing about whose money would reach the big sycamore tree downstream first and dry. If Angus won he would get a hug, very short; if Aba won, she would continue to push him away. Money in the burn too, what's all this. Gently but impatiently Appa was far off on the tarmac, having spent an hour sleeping for the nearing dawn by the MacTaggart bulldozer. Appa had, in a rare request, begged Kofi Senya successfully for two minutes of magic. With this, he did something that he had always wanted to do: there he stood raising the aeroplane with the long end of his urine. Then he used the other minute of the magic to divert the stream onto Aba and Angus chatting loosely on the white and tiny bank about the meaning of life. They held their breath and spluttered the language; though it was only when they were dry that they wondered where the miracle came from; and whether the gods should make their miracles so wet again.

There was a hoot and steam in the distance: the old train at Levensvale was a sports train that went nowhere. It would zoom and hoot, hoot and zoom . . . in and out of doors ajar in town – it could easily leave its tracks in a leap of sporty whizz – and rush into laundry rooms to iron piotos and other things free by the heat of its wheels. The train felt threatened by the trotro aeroplane; the lower-lip plane was all right because it was supposed to rest during the visit here, but the upper-lip one was going to take away passengers who didn't want to go anywhere in particular anyway: everywhere was within walking distance, just like Tukwan. But the sports train found nothing more purposeful than rushing about town picking up passengers that wanted to go nowhere, but still wanted to reach there on time. But the only consolation for the mad locomotive was that the aeroplane would have longer distances between its stops; and it would be arguable whether people would prefer to go nowhere by air or by train. And a very dangerous thing happened to Appa when he tried to leap onto the plane without using the small gangway: his open penknife nearly sliced his popylonkwe . . . the way the knife was positioned, it cut poor Appa's initials on it, so that when he rushed in a mad and unauthorised dash in the bulldozer to Shebelda to ask for elastoplast, he confused her by refusing to reveal where the cut was. He muttered to himself, 'I am the only man in the universe who has raised an aeroplane with his urine, but now I was about to destroy the very thing that commoted this big-big record.' Appa had found himself a new habit: he cut his A-level certificate into two bits, and then stuck the bits one on each wing of the plane. But for his blacksmithing, the only way it showed now was in his hard eyes, hard to go in the air to fly tro by tro,

When the myriad needling wind of the morning blew through the pines, it caught Moro's telegram from Tukwan right at the door of the Levensvale post office, raised it among a company of leaves, rushed it into the betting corners, pushed it beyond the longest necks, and then released it to land noiselessly and intimately in Pokuaa's hand. The telegram was intimate but Moro was not, this cola-man's telexactitude. Half of Levensvale had jumped up to try and read the windy message, but Margaret had to jump up twice, for she had forgotten her glasses the first time. The telegram said: 'Please try and get that silly Kwame Atta to invent a stupidity machine for the people here: they are feeling so clever that they are questioning every decision, even those we all make together. Come back and have your power, woman, for I don't want it.' There was a hush, and so too was the puppy nibbling the shoes. 'O poor Moro . . .' began Opanin Akorsah. 'O shut up and let us all enjoy Moro's pain for a change!' shouted Amoa, as usual overstepping his own lip. 'Let's get on with the business,' Pokuaa said severely, without even bothering to get Amoa to apologise for his words to Akorsah. 'A stupidity machine indeed! and note that he calls me a silly man,' exclaimed Kwame Atta repolishing his indignation for show. There was a postscript at the end of the telegram: 'If Atta Akpeteshie is not clever enough to invent a stupidity machine, then go to the stores and buy one quick!'
quick
Mackie now walked into the perplexity, trying to squeeze a smile through

— 92 —

for lighter effect. 'This is exactly what the man with the Mercedes Benz underwear would do!' shouted the scunnered Atta. 'He fought and manoeuvred for a greater position, and now that he has it, he's throwing it away. I condemn him the Moro to be covered in pesewas, and then shaken till the coins enter his empty brain. Ewurade!' When LT was a little disturbed, he shuffled on one foot only. He lamented silently that Moro did not know how to scheme: if he knew that the old man was going to be so fickle with the power he had been given temporarily, he LT would have stayed behind, and possibly led a coup against the present dynasty, as he called it. The ducks flew around the reception room of the Plantain Hotel. Mackie suddenly said, veering off course, 'But you didn't tell me that you also have a Plantain Hotel in Tukwan, it was only yesterday I found out in 1968.' 'O sorry,' said the smiling Senya the cunning controller, 'you see, ours is the original, yours is the duplicate.' Mackie laughed with his mouth shut, and traces of pipe smoke came out of his ears. 'Sala, have you still got that filthy corset!' screamed Lawyer Tay as he watched his son pass up and down with imperial gait, wearing the famous cross-cultural corset, and completely ignoring his father's anger. Sala the kinglet just said, 'Father, I want to improve my science here. I have had enough of Law.' 'Then come to my metal, come to my metal!' exclaimed Appa up in the plane, but flying as low as possible so that he could hear what was going on through the roof. . . so low that he almost landed on Babo's forehead when he looked out of the window to check the sun. And he nursed his hurt popylonkwe. Then Aba burst in suddenly, shouting, 'I have caught my biggest crab, look at the mighty claws just out of the freshest water!' They looked at her with pained surprise, all except Angus who had followed her in, trying to hide some of the adoration on his face, and fervently hoping that the crab would bring him and Aba closer together. Pokuaa was rubbing her heels together, and looking at Kofi Senya in an absent-minded way. 'Well I think that the twins should be accompanied by Mr Mackie to Tukwan on a short visit, to investigate what is happening, and to return some of the hospitality we have been getting here. Mr Mackie the tweed must taste some Asante hospitality,' Lawyer Tay declared, scratching his belly ostentatiously and exacting a shoogle from it. Pokuaa looked doubtful, but Kofi Senya gave a quiet nod through the incline of his pipe. 'But what will I do without my twins?' she blurted out. Then she laughed and laughed as they looked at her. It took her three minutes to laugh, beside the apple.

Kwame Atta agreed finally to construct the stupidity machine, but his suggestion that Lawyer Tay form the nucleus of it caused an uproar; and the good lawyer only adjusted the snarl on his tongue to something gentler when the same Atta admitted that he admired Tay's legal dexterity in cross-examining himself in Mr K's court, and only meant that it was that part of LT that lost cases to himself that needed cleverising. Lawyer Tay stood in doubt holding a pink marshmallow in one hand and a white one in the other. And all he said was, 'I will not allow myself to be trikballed!' Then he accommodated the marshmallows in his mouth. The twin-scientist was now free to invent while the legal chewing proceeded: he went to the wet bit of ground near the stream where the crabs were on strike – they wouldn't allow their claws above a depth of one foot – in protest at the frequency of Aba's catching. Trap too many crabs and you change the stream. Atta went there to entice a few worms up which he cut in half, leaving the other halves generously in the ground. He put the truncated worms in a descending basket, in which he had made six cane steps for the reception of ideas within the framework of things: he took the concrete, powdered it, developed one abstract from it, then transformed it back to the concrete. This was true in his country, where that gum had held the abstract to the concrete would not be broken. Then he made a philosophical rush into the breezier areas of Levensvale, produced the concrete, abstracted it with no vision of the concrete at all, then created more and more abstracts in a mad legerdemain. Kwame Atta was quite joyful because if you gave him John Knox in his basket, he would immediately create Okomfo Anokye out of him; if you gave him a little Presbyterianism, with or without salt, he would make some high roaring Suame Pentecost out of it . . . and then return it a little singed. The machine was growing, but it needed a memory: the first time a girl saw his popylonkwe she laughed because it was pointing to the left, and was so serious-looking . . . Into the basket he threw an old comb from the battle of Bannockburn, and then some tobacco from the Mankesim Constitution, Levensvale's 1314, to Tukwan's 1871; elements of the claymore and the spear were ground together and sprinkled around the changing basket, which had shrunk, and which was now partly encased in metal from Appa. Part-circle part-square, the machine would sometimes change shape subtly, depending on who was looking at it at the time. It never changed shape with Kofi Senya, and did so only slightly with Pokuaa, Mackie, and Kwaku de Babo.

Atta the inventor had programmed his basket with a series of ludicrous questions which appeared when either the black or the white button was pressed; and it tailored its questions to the questioner: Pastor Korner was the first victim, for when he pressed the simple question 'why' he had the following outpour: 'You pastor with the automatic cassock who do you think you are fraternising with God like that? So all this time that you ran your afro theological schools, you couldn't bring yourself to unify your scattered beliefs into a coherent theological system of abenkwan! Shame! Do you think that it's sufficient to rush about the two historical towns scattering crosses all over the place and causing a rock one to be made? Why did you keep all those coins in your altar? You are not even afraid that Guinness will get between you and your God! We know you are no drunkard, but be careful that one day you don't sneak some beer into the sanctuary. Now, if you have really joined shrine and church, why don't you sometimes wear the matted hair and white cloths of the shrinal priest? And you like food too much! As for your other sins, we shouldn't talk about them too long: a quick glance at a woman, a desire to be famous, a sly feeling that you are ultimately superior to everyone else when you are celebrating the mass, if there were other priests in Tukwan you would litigate with them tiik, you often feel that if a priest was too gentle and too good he would be swept off the face of the earth with some mocking laughter. So you cultivate some toughness that sticks out of the cassock like a sore thumb, or better like an erect popylonkwe. Shame again! When last did you really try to minister unto the suffering in such a way that your status and your comfort were put under pressure . . .' Korner Mensah turned off the basket with an uncomfortable look in his eye. He looked round quickly to see whether anyone had been listening to the basket's high-pitched voice. Only Atta was standing by, looking unusually unscrutable, but finding it difficult to hide the triumph in one eye. 'They will ban that machine here, you watch,' was all the pastor said, 'for though I'm not a saint, I am not cynical either. I gather my crosses for love of the world.' Kwame Atta burst out laughing, but never took his eyes off the box, for it changed shape most when he was looking at it. Outside the rain was so soft that you would think it came from a dove's back.

In walked David Mackie with that grave confident walk of his that persuaded men of the cloth that he was a businessman with some conscience in his briefcase. 'Come and try my machine,' shouted Atta with a great glee of welcome. 'Of course my good man, I am for anything new,' Mackie answered, pressing the button he was shown. The basket voice squeaked: 'You Mackie, you have been desiring that Pokuaa for months now, even though you know that you are a central layman in the plans of many canons. You are still hoping to extract a few concessions of expenditure which a man of your stature should be wary of considering in your accounts with the visitors. You have encouraged your wife to be shrewd but not particularly knowledgeable, as if she should continue to reflect her mind in your brighter brains. Why do you show that you care more about Scottish history than you actually do? Is it not true that you are only interested in it as it profits the present? I suspect that it is only the anticipation of money that has kept your temper in check for so long, so don't let them give you any compliments for it! You are really hoping to grow old stylishly, are you not? Perhaps grow a few turnips, buy a Bentley, and acquire an older form of the Levensvale accent, and maybe finally replace the Lord Provost . . .' It was Mackie that was laughing this time, not the akpeteshie scientist. Atta watched the rich laughter until it disappeared round the corner, but by then Mackie was holding his head in his hands. Would this machine not have to be stopped, he thought to himself, for after all democracy was about people, not machines with a pretension to some inner wrangling. Och! Away with you.

The basket picked Pokuaa next even though she wasn't there, for Atta made it feel her vibrations: So you fine woman, don't you have the courage to tell all the men that love you that you are more interested in developing your world than in settling down with any of them? Why do you sometimes want to protect the twins when deep down you know you are only giving one or both of them false hopes? Are you afraid that you will not get all you want from life in your bold ventures? And is it true that the bolder the venture, like this journey, the less need there is for the heart to settle? You should consider yourself lucky to have the strength to outmanoeuvre so many worldly men. Where do you know Kofi Senya from that he supports you so much . . .' Then the machine itself went off, with Atta's face grave and broken: his heart had been made useless before Pokuaa again, but he would plod on, ampa.

True, the machine was put out of action, by Kwame Atta himself: it had calculated a way of preventing every second dawn from coming, and thus Atta was missing some rations of whisky with Murray. The circle was disconnected from the square, and the basket was stored safely in the aeroplanes until it was time to send it to Moro to help him in Tukwan, if that was what was required there. But the machine, the basket presence, did not give up as easily as that: even Kwame Atta the gin-scintillated scientist did not know that once the basket was disconnected, it began to work long-distance: it created a crisis by bringing in all sorts of characters, things and presences which did not necessarily have the same time-scales as Tukwan and Levensvale. And the first thing to call was a thingmy: a domiciled elephant with one tusk, a beast that was once a pigmy, but which burst out of its dwarfhood by growing its toenails extra long, and then transferring the dead cells to the pulsating life of the skin; this meant that the elephant was on top of the political life of the next county: it rushed into tarring contracts through which the various district chief executives got new tweeds, new boots, new whiskies with elements of akpeteshie – the Queen of England had to attempt orange-distilled gin, kiss me quick, before she was admitted through the elephant for an unreal visit to Tukwan first then Levensvale next – and then cleverly concealed acquisitions for executive mansions, such as computerised back-scratchers, dildos of Highland strength, and new wives with controlled burrs that went beyond the English heath.

The jumbobod would chair board meetings with a smoky atmosphere mellowed by love-hearts, Caramac, Bounty bars, fruit gums, and the sherbet that Mackie loved in his weak moments. Have you ever seen a grasshopper poised on a butterscotch and then getting stuck on it as it tried to jump off? That was the type of questions the elephant asked before rushing back to Levensvale to address the basket: 'I am the elephant with a difference, for they cannot tell whether I am an African elephant or an Indian elephant, nor even a third breed which was born in anyany zoo, that place of the bestial soul-once-removed; my trunk costs nothing to call, and whenever the Prime Minister wants me, it is not the telephone he/she uses but radar: I am usually a dangerous entry into the airspace of my own country, I slip in the sprays of water created by my own trunk, a very expensive trunk lined with gold from Obuasi and diamonds from Akwatia. I have come to this machine to try hard to find out whether the honourable Prime Minister is really racist or not: I must find out because I have a new ivory business in Zimbabwe – selling my own tusk a thousand times over to different buyers – and I must not be seen fraternising with leaders of dubious raceage, otherwise my grandfather, who was unfortuntely a human being but a human being who believed in reincarnation into elephants, would not approve of the transference of my soul to another planet (the first black elephant to found a white planet) in the biggest step ever taken in any reincarnation! To whom to whom, does this bottom belong! Elephants too love sex but sex through skins so tough that you have to triple every act to get results . . .'

The basket shook back at the shaking elephant, and had hardly recovered when a historical figure in the form of all the following figures appeared from the county next to the next county: Robert the Bruce extremely strong, leprosy or no leprosy later, gathering the Scots together in direct leaps against the Pope – at that time the Pope was receiving allowances from the CIA, the KGB, the Mafia, the Broederbund, the Nazis, Amin, and other genocidalists, but still managed to retain a pure morality that was admired by all especially the Press and all its barons whether in Accra, Siberia or Philadelphia, but above all by the Protestants – and then there was Nana Kwaku Dua shouting all over the place that the bush was stronger than Governor Pine's cannon, and that the governor should choose either the long stick for war or the short stick for peace; and Kwaku Dua rushed to die soon, and the basket couldn't make much of his war, even though it was continued by Kofi Karikari who didn't make any appearance in Levensvale. The next group to pay homage to the machine was ants: soldier ants, corporal ants, queen ants, termites, ants with huge popylonkwes, fresh ants, dirty ants, political ants, literary ants, and then ants that were philosophical on Mondays and then regressed to theology on Fridays (God could have at one point been inferior to His own universe, but now it was only a series of broken divine hearts, broken by the ways of the world). Now, the ants did not speak: they just bit and bit and bit: at scrolls, constitutions in the basket, irrevocable agreements between friendly nations presently at war, Accords but no Hondas, selected Cherries but no Datsuns, Fiats but no Uno who. The ants were biting the leaders of Ghana so that they may cause the first car to be locally made in Asante for the same ants to swarm over. Death to the antediluvian subversionists of military-cum-civilian vintage! The basket was machining the local sky.

And then there were Kwame Nkrumah and Kofi Busia engaged in a furious waltz over Tukwan – no Adowa no Kpanlogo no Kete were available at that instant in time – but forgetting that it was the people's heads they were dancing on: squashed heads, bleeding heads, swollen heads, bruised heads, kwashiorkor heads, and totally crushed brains. The basket was overheating in its binding metal, but the mad history coming out of its entrails refused to stop: Lieutenant-General Afrifa had become trivial and was talking to Andy Stewart about the Scottish soldier; Akuffo had sent his brilliant eyes into the face of Rob Roy, and the two stalwarts both agreed that Loch Lomond, minus its seductive islands like Inchmowan, should safely fit into Lake Bosomtwi, provided it was prepared to overflow its banks with the tears of all the wronged and the desecrated of this world! And there was General Ankrah, slipping alive in and out of the streets of Accra, looking out of the sad eyes of history, and recognising that all the grandeur that he got from a rather sceptical populace – charisma wasn't his strong point – was false and had been buried forever. Mackie, Mackie rushed up to the basket to try to switch off its flow of suspicious presences. He was doing this for humanitarian reasons, for everyone was confused about the time that was being created and the morality that was binding it: they would be bringing in Rawlings next, said the ants, but the Scottish National Party, more so Winnie Ewing, would not really allow that.

Danquah bowed before the exhausted basket, with his cruel wife condemning him in the background; your Macintoshes pontificated on UDI when everything was in smithereens at the political corner of some Scottish university: Kwaku de Babo rose among the paraphernalia of the basket and declared that all the pain of history was a personal pain, and that if the machine were to continue to force him to record everything, including the warts and the boils and the kookos and the bozi, the sasabro and the peripheral neuritis, then he would have to say NO to that same eternity that demanded so much positive neutrality of him. Babo was getting biased at everything except the single view . . . and that was because the single view simply did not exist except for the historically chosen fundamental issues, like the right to equal life, to equal love, and to equal skin. I lie?

The machine said: Subversion followed the analysis and the science, subversion followed the conference. Ideas would come from it. No one should constrict the spirit, alleluya. Mackie sent his certainties to the basket which sent them back with dollops of suet, mounds of gari, and long doubtful litres of Scotch broth. Memaaaamieeeei! Ibi hard-O! Mackie was sitting by the ripening blackcurrents, contemplating the possibility of travelling with Babo and Atta when Jock the fish and chip man sauntered into his front yard. 'Good evening, Davie,' said Jock after he saw that the afternoon was finished, 'I have come to you with another of my wee problems with the visitors . . . I know they are supposed to be renewing our spirit and all that, but in God's truth, they're bringing my chip shop nothing but shenanigans . . .' 'Ah, patience to you Jock, I want you to be as patient as the dead sole that you sell so well . . .' 'Well there'll be nothing left of my fish if they continue to stay here any longer. And I'm not the only one suffering. Some others are finding the rate of crazy inventions too much as well. I mean how can one of the lady visitors join two kilts together and then half a third one just to make a cloth to wear? . . .' 'But Jock,' broke in Mackie good-humouredly, 'Jock, you know the visitors are bringing us jobs, and new ways that we badly need to escape from some of the eternity we suffer from . . .' 'O, it's not that I don't like them. I admire them in fact, but I'm worried about my fish . . . you won't believe that they are trying to bring new ideas to fish and chips even! How can we tolerate that? When I think about fish and chips, that's all I want to think about: I don't want to be told that sometimes the fish must lie east to the chips and that if you add a touch of . . . shitoh, is that right? . . . then your fish and chips would be smashing . . . They'll start on the mince and tatties next, help ma goad!' Jock said with his streaky high voice. 'And wouldn't it improve it!' Mackie laughed, looking at Jock with a fond directness. 'And the little secret, Jock, is that listen to all the ideas, yes, but just take what you want and leave the rest. After all we have to take some. They take some of ours and we take some of theirs, that's the way to the new toughness of the world . . . and don't forget that we all have our little obligations to be new, new for this town to prosper, new to be mortal and free again. You get me Jock?' There was a doubtful silence with a fidget at the end of it. Jock spoke, conspiratorially, 'But I was hoping there would be one or two new things about sex . . .' Mackie put his fond into his laughter, and began, 'But . . .' 'No!, no buts,' screeched Jock, 'I have heard that their touch lasts longer, is it true? Please don't laugh, I am talking about a very important matter . . . old flame Jennifer has been won over by the new shrine, and she swears that I can only touch her four times a year . . . and that's still quite a long time even when I move my watch forward . . .' 'So that's your real problem!' said Mackie with a wise nod. 'Then fish is not really the problem, is it?' Jock shrugged himself mute, and sat down on a mouldy bench. 'Or am I growing old, Davie, am I growing old?' He asked the silent smiling Mackie who toned down his tweed trousers by moving into the shade, with sadness.

Into this quiet contemplation crept Kwame Atta on tiptoe. Jock's eyes rose to the deepening sky. 'I can't even have a few silent thoughts about growing old without the biggest free eater of fish and chips rushing in and interrupting it . . .' 'Hold on, hold on you middle-aged maker of chipped potatoes!' beamed Atta, spreading the mould on the bench by parking his bot too. 'First of all I must give you a hug! It's your fish and chips that have given me an extra jump in my walk. I used to bounce sometimes, but now there's a jump to my bounce! Second I want to remind you that don't worry about growing old because as you know the two towns share the same reincarnation and the same genetics. C'mon, test your energy, jump to my jump!' 'Well, I'm not surprised,' drawled Jock. 'It has been so free to you the fish, that I have only been saved by that polite gentleman with the vulture on his pipe . . . you notice, Davie, that it's an assault on my dreams to have to see a vulture on a pipe everyday . . . who pays for you; and sometimes your own twin pays for you too. But I'm afraid . . . I don't know what's coming next.' 'Now Mr Mackie, shall we solve the fish and chips later? We shall commot Mr Jock's worries in due course. Now what about the journey? It has been decided that Jock must accompany the three of us; this means you, Kwaku, myself, and then Jock the Fish And Chip. Some supertobolo surprise! I bet your uncle's cocoyam that Mr Jock is dying to experience our humble humidity!' Jock rose in consternation, saying, 'But how can you take a decision about me travelling when I don't know anything about it!' 'Don't worry,' soothed Atta, 'don't worry. Kwaku de Babo doesn't know he's travelling either!' 'But what the hell do I care whether he knows or not . . . I will protest to the Lord Provost . . .' 'Well, Mr Jockstrap, I have some fine-fine news for you. It was his Lordship himself who decided this. He was surely thinking that a few sole and chips could be exported to the sister town. What a good problem-asem!' cooed Kwame cool. Jock rerose and rushed to his shop and sold a rapid twenty pounds in anger.

Which anger did not stop the preparations for the journey. But there was a small crisis because Aba insisted that she too wanted to go back to Tukwan. She had already packed her suitcase and was now lying obstinately stiff by the tarmac. 'But how can we break the heart of our hosts' son by letting her leave like that? He has already suffered one heartache. If he keeps on suffering, he will not be able to do the small-small inventions he does, and he will become a delinquent of the heart,' LT said, walking in little semi-circles round Aba. 'Look at how she is behaving,' snorted Opanin Akorsah, 'imagine being a stowaway, and then after being forgiven, demanding a seat early back to Tukwan one time. She's just spoilt, enuanono. Some of you don't deserve to be immortal koraa . . .' But Pokuaa came late and sat by Aba, whispering. She said, 'Aba, Aba, how can you go back now when your work will help us to make more money for Tukwan? You are one of the most useful workers because whenever you are working, Angus works at double the speed, for himself and then for you, and then he makes a last effort always to try and persuade you just to look at him. You must stay.' There was a hint of the stern in the last words. Angus himself was standing almost within earshot, half-devastated. His mother and father had kept a discreet distance in this affair of the heart, though Shebelda was thinking that her son was making a bit of a fool of himself by declaring his love so openly before he was sure of having it returned. Throughout the lives of mother and son, whenever mother wanted to offer akoma support, son rejected it; and father walked quite comfortably between them, drawing from and giving to the two lives to the left and to the right of him, whenever he wanted. Finally Aba got up and shouted, 'All right I'll stay and catch crabs, but don't blame me if I try to persuade one of the ducks to take me on its back. Angus please help me back with my chop-boxes, and don't look so happy that I'm staying, it doesn't suit your short beard!' Angus loved the mangoes that were brought and he ate one with a long-suffering look which had joy at the edges. Old Jock was a guest of middle age, and fancied himself as a good walker with his knock knees. Much fish and chips was frozen and packed, and many sole and fresh potatoes were loaded onto the lower-lip aeroplane for export, but Appa took a rest from his trotro and shouted sardonically with his paining popy-lonkwe, 'Now who do you think is going to buy fish and chips in Tukwan? Who is going to allow an interval of the mouth for it between the waakye and the fufu and the ampesi and the everything? Don't be optimistic!' Then he flew back into the sky.

CLASS EIGHT

Pokuaa's lips were still aerodynamically useful, since the aeroplanes could still be measured by the open mouth; one lip could heighten a plane, another lip could lower it. In addition to the Mackies – mother and son – and to the Nana Bontoxes and Lawyer Tays, the Akyaas and other guests, the Murrays and the rest of the Levensvale faithful, sheep, mountain-goats, squirrels, wild rabbits, deer, dogs and cats also came to the tarmac to see off Kwame and Kwaku, David and Jock. Margaret was saying, 'You haven't yet drunk my coffee, David. You must do it if it's the last caring thing you do before you travel.' Mackie's answer was carried away by the bleat of a sheep, and nibbled by a squirrel, but he put a quiet hand on her shoulder to continue the language, mute. Pokuaa made a fuss of one twin, and then made a fuss of the other twin. Kwaku Babo took it rather uncomfortably, for as the secretaryship of his writing deepened with the never-ending recording of the heart, the hand, the head, and the soul, the more self-conscious and elusive became what was left of his love for Pokuaa. Whenever this happened, Pokuaa sent her eyes more to Atta than to him, for there was a touch of rebellion in them which said: Babo should not make her responsible for defining himself against her sometimes; besides she was always prepared to laugh at any love that was becoming more complex than she could ever dream of returning, even in her sleep. Six goats flanked Atta with serious bleats, and another six made lust beyond the heather in a mix with the Tukwan goat. The vulture had a new trick: it hopped from pipe to pipe, especially Senya's and Mackie's; and somebody had decorated its neck with a tiny string of beads. The two sacred ducks stood on one wing each of the aeroplane, while Atta pushed his way through the communing goats and sheep. All morning the weather had been coming in gusts aimed at hats, skirts, cloths and kilts. Atta continued to push but the goats would not let him out of their semi-circle: they immediately moved round to cover the empty half whenever he made an attempt to cross it to the cock-pit. A very dandy tweedy cock crowed on the tower shrine. 'Can we have some order here please, for the libation to be poured for the gods and ancestors to guide and guard the travellers!' boomed Nana Kasa. The sheep rebelled against the goat's wisdom, and allowed Atta to slip through the semi-circle at last, covered in the wool of the small struggle. It was imperative that the squirrel got off the tartan waistcoat belonging to Gilmour.

The Lord Provost had rushed on to the tarmac for the libation, and rushed back off to continue his mid-sentence in the office. 'Are you people sure that Jock is not going to misbehave all over the place with his quiet but cunning fish and chips?' asked Jack MacTaggart revving his bulldozer against the rabbits. 'Watch your tongue, MacTaggart! and stick to the ghost of your wife, otherwise I'll fill the vacant coffin in your store room with yourself . . .' 'Keep your mouth on the right track, Jock,' said Mackie shocked, even through all the noise, at the severity of Jock's riposte. Jack slipped into gear angrily in his bulldozer, and then drove in a sideways lurch towards the scattering Jock, who shouted back with a curse, 'Keep your flipping bulldozer out of it!' It was only after five minutes of frantic chasing around the bracken that Jock learned sense again, with a gruff apology to Jack. There was a sudden scream from under the plane: 'Which mad contreyman has vanished one of the aeroplane wheels?' Atta couldn't believe the anger in his own voice, 'There must be a search straight away. Is this part of the hospitality or what!' There was some groaning beyond the beech hedge. 'I bet you sharp that that groan we hear is guilty! Isn't it your own friend Murray groaning there because he has pawned the tyre? I saw something bulky under his jacket yesterday . . .' shouted Amoa, rushing to the hedge to spy the prostrate Murray, who answered back in the manner of his mentor Atta: 'How dare you accuse me of something that I am guilty of! Hic. As soon as I get my ration of whisky I will go and redeem the plane wheel. Help my hic!' Kwame Atta looked at Murray with angry disbelief, and then ran down with Amoa to the pawn shop where the fine wheel stood with an African glisten. Azziz had poured some of his pineapple juice on it, out of his anger that most of his pineapples had been left behind at Tukwan, though the agreement now was that the present travellers should bring a fresh tonnage when they were returning from Tukwan. Azziz had to smile in a new pineapple fashion, for his simple wife Akyaa had rushed to him, saying, 'Surely my husband Azziz, you don't have to send for the pineapples, because here they have the pine trees, and they have the apples too . . . never worry, we shall make our own applepines OK?' The tyre was retrieved with its pineapple juice, and put on after a ritual cleaning initiated by Kofi Senya. 'I vote that we transfer Murray to the nearest latrine!' shouted Appa down from his clouded trotro.

Pokuaa sprinkled the lavender on the aeroplane again, and Jock swore that he had never flown before, and that he didn't know how the quality of his fish would take it. Margaret demanded another embrace and then

— 103 —

laughed onto Mackie's neck when he was giving it. 'Alleluya to the tukwaning aeroplane!' shouted Appa from the upper-lip wings still in the sky, after dropping passengers at the hospital. Pokuaa gave the twins one long hug each, but Babo shortened his. She laughed longer. Kofi Senya slid down his own incantations. Lawyer Tay was insisting that there were certain legal lines in the sky that had to be followed: he warned Atta not to overreach himself by avoiding the lines and thus bumping into other aeroplanes or birds of a big nature. 'Believe me, ampa,' LT said with conviction, 'if I had my way, all courts would be in the sky: when somebody was guilty, he would just be given some regenerative koobi, and then thrown out of the plane, even on the rare occasions when there would be a shortage of parachutes . . .' Aba was looking wistfully at the aeroplane; and she had taken to walking her best crabs on a string leash, and painting some claws when necessary. 'Is the stupidity machine packed in the plane?' asked Babo. 'Of course,' answered the machine itself, receiving a cry from a goat and crying back. 'Don't forget to look at the sculpture with the most beautiful lips in the world near the church at Tukwan,' Pokuaa shouted as the engines roared. 'And I've never known how many of my smiles make my laughter,' Akyaa said with her fine new hat at the same angle as the tail of the plane. She was being inconsequential with yogurt and gari. The people and the animals had exhausted their blessings to the travellers . . . and there was a last blessing from Kofi Senya which the plane took in mid-air powerfully, letting it glow on the wings, so that a sudden pattern of sun and luck decorated it. But not for long: 'Ewurade! watch out!' screamed Atta, as Appa's plane hurtled towards him. Two sudden swerves, and the ducks fell off Babo's shoulders; a screech of singed tyres and a tiny touch of noses spun the aeroplanes round, and their tails touched instead of their fronts. Atta ran raging out of his still moving plane, climbed Appa's spluttering to a halt, and shook him hard, saying, 'You Appa, how did you manage to cause such a near crash! Are you mad or drunk? Or is this how you intend to operate the trotro sky in my absence? You almost killed us all!' 'I had just run out of fuel,' said the shaken Appa, wiping the sarcasm off his face for once. 'Well, next time, urinate into the tank and nothing will happen . . .' 'O I keep my urine for lifting the plane itself,' Appa said with an entirely straight face. 'Let's double our blessing then and everything will be all right,' Amoa said stroking a stag with a small necklace of pipes on its antlers, new style.

'I told you about the lines!' shouted LT with triumph, 'you never listen to me.' 'True, true. I never listen because I know you don't like me Mr Lawyer,' Atta replied severely. 'The eye can never use its own tears again, the heart gets tired but the spirit moves on . . .' Nana Bontox was quaffing his own wisdom with a glass of schnapps. '. . . And when you eat too many beans, your wind moves on too . . .' Amoa said, completing the wisdom, while piling a termite on top of a squirrel on top of a rabbit on top of a goat on top of a sheep on top of a magnificent stag with a second necklace on its tail; and below them all was Aba's crab crawling among the hearts and nibbling the fears authoritatively.

Depending on which end of the binoculars you were holding, it would mean you were leaving one culture in the evening of its freedom, and entering another in its dawn; you would be leaving one with a tradition of formal consciousness, so-so direct, to one where being was touched with a glancing step and then left alone in a mysterious relationship, or. One wanted less consciousness, one wanted more . . . but there was always the gari in between, and there was the mince. The carried dancing omanhene with malaria was a palanquinine; and the dying dancing warring highland chieftain shouted: clay no more. But the land of the cocoyam and the plantain had the most inclusive people ever seen; for the old body refused to be shed, and rock was rock, crying was crying; nothingness was something. The lower-lip aeroplane was going through raised collars of cold air into necks of cloud, with Kofi Senya's vulture impudently on its tail. The venturing vulture took the air coolly and nodded into it. 'We have to share our sleep, since you can also drive an aeroplane,' Atta said to Mackie, who had been wondering whether the vulture would carrion eating dead flesh. 'O I know what you mean, you piloting rascal . . . when you sleep I drive, and when you drive I guard your driving, no? . . . but to be serious I admire the vulture enormously, even without its pipe . . . though it sometimes chooses mine . . .' Mackie replied with a slow absent-mindedness. 'Can I rent a plot of ferns when we return to Levensvale?' Babo asked Mackie all of a sudden, still writing. Mackie looked at him for a long time, and said, 'Yes.' 'Then I'm glad,' Babo the quiet replied simply, the fernrenting sun-touched secretary. 'Och, the heart is very slow up here, isn't it?' asked Jock holding hard onto the moss seat. 'I am thinking that Mr Chip is afraid up here,' laughed Atta, touching Mackie's elbow in companionship. 'But he has his fish to comfort his sole.'
   Atta flew sharply under a flock of geese, which the vulture joined for a small cackle, and then returned. And to even cultural matters up, whenever Mackie peed, Atta just urinated, and the others would join in this confluence of urine when necessary. 'But has the sky got earth?' asked Jock in his fishy manner. 'I'm asking because I see a tree just outside the window . . .' 'O, you are only seeing things through the special glass I have installed beyond the right wing to reflect any interesting things below . . . especially any beautiful women bathing . . . you saw the greenhouse of a private botanical garden,' Atta said without looking back, expecting some derision that he didn't get. 'All this must be because of the folosofy some of you people practise,' Jock declared and then fell asleep. Atta turned round to look at the sleeping Jock, and said, 'With this character around, anything

huhudious can happen! Can somebody please close his mouth, the snores are challenging the aeroplane!' As they all slept with the exception of Atta and Mackie-half – he guarded the sleep with one eye – the discerning rain bathed the aeroplane . . . and continued to bathe it even when it flew above its clouds: all the rain had done was to start falling up, for mirrors on aeroplanes could do anything, and the magic of life was becoming democratised. Kwame Atta had got up to stretch his legs, looking through the window with no particular concern; but then his eyes popped to an amazing size, and he gasped: there in the skies stretching back for miles and miles was the neck of a duck whose feet were still standing in Levensvale: with the neck stuck to the wing, it had been stretched interminably. If Atta had not seen it when he did, it would have snapped. The aeroplane went into reverse for an equal number of miles – its massive horn blowing – until the elasticity of the neck was reduced, and the webbed feet could join the journey, its neck stretched longer by only three inches. Thus one sacred duck arrived in the aeroplane sky, for it was missing the lake terribly, its moss, its one lamppost, its creative ripples. 'Please feed the duck a sugared quack,' Atta said to the sleeping gallery, retrieving his astonishment from the window. Atta was savouring the silence; and silence was something he did not do much with when he wasn't inventing. He would do everything, including smoking and talking to himself, everything except introspection . . . which he would only engage in when it involved his resentment at people's treatment of him. One inventor plus one frustration equals resentment and the acceleration of the whisky-cum-akpeteshie experience, sot.

The lower-lip jet was running beautifully, and two of its moss seats had already been changed to heather by Angus Mackie. But there was a noise at the back, and two suspicious-looking crabs appeared in the passageway, followed by two old chestnuts, and three still-writhing worms. Behind them with his hands up apologetically was Donald, Sala's friend. Atta gave a roar of frustration: anytime he travelled, he got a stowaway on board. 'What on earth are you doing in the sky, young child!' Atta shouted. 'I'm harmless, it was my grandmother that said I should come and experience your land for the short time you were going . . .' 'What's happening?' asked Mackie in bewilderment, seeing Donald standing with his hands up in the plane, 'and what are you Donald doing here? Have you just arrived by immaculate conception or what?' The others woke up with the force of surprise. The vulture and the duck had come in and were staring benignly at Donald Shearer, twelve years old with a mop on top, his eyes like two exclamation marks pulled from a language still wary of them. Babo went and gave Donald a welcoming hug, and asked the others to forgive him immediately and blame his grandmother later. 'I'm sure Sala knew you were hiding here,' said Atta making some vindication in his mouth. 'Yes,' Donald answered simply, 'and he would have come too if he hadn't been invited to a party with his corset.' They looked at him helplessly, and he in turn held the helplessness in his tightened fists. 'Give the boy pineapples!' Atta shouted at last. 'He said give the boy pineapples right now!' echoed Jock merrily. They all looked at each other. Then Donald exclaimed, 'I know where the pineapples are, I've been eating them to survive!' 'Then go and chop some more,' Atta added, concentrating on his flying again. Donald went and sat beside the writing Babo. Some returned to their sleep, and things became quiet, except for Donald who could be recognised by his chew. The birds reperched on the wings. David Mackie was remembering his dead girl with a drone that matched the sorrow of the engines; a tiny impending tear was easily transformed into an ironic laugh. 'What is my co-pilot finding funny?' 'It's the sadness I'm finding funny. Was it really necessary to rush to Tukwan like this when we haven't earned all our money yet . . .' 'Don't go back pondering decisions already past,' Jock answered with surprising firmness, 'when I have decided that a particular fish is going to be fried and I have fried it, I don't waste time regretting its taste!' 'Yes, but fish are easier than hearts . . .' Atta said sadly, giving Mackie a sympathetic look. 'Nonsense!' insisted Jock. 'I have a human relationship with my fish, let me tell you! . . .' 'Of course,' answered Mackie, 'you share the same sole.' 'Davie, there must be more than a few ounces on top of that last pun . . .' Jock brushed the roof of his mouth with his tongue as he spoke. All their tongues stretched different inches, but Kwame Atta's was the longest, anokwere.

The darkness entered the aeroplane first before spreading to the rest of the sky, stars or no stars. The last thing Mackie said before he fell asleep was, 'I hope Pokuaa and Ed are supervising the last bits of work on the buildings.' Atta too fell asleep beside his bottle of akpeteshie. The lower-lip plane smelled the sky alone. There were no sets of eyes to see it along. This was dangerous for its passengers, but good for its independence: for this was an investigative aeroplane, and yesterday was its birthday. It could have chosen its birthday from several other days, knowing the secrets of time, but it chose yesterday and today because there was a glut of investigative feelings in its red nose: why not land somewhere near a deep forest or a desert, Central or North Africa, where carefully selected wild roses would brush the aeroplane beside the supplementing scents of the frangipani. So the plane started to lower itself, brushing aside ambitiously high mosquitoes as it went, tossing back the glare of the Sahara as the moon shined. The wonder of scents in the dark! thought the nose of the aeroplane. True the LLip plane did find a forest bordered by the vast desert and in between was a tiny natural tarmac, the size of which tested its landing ingenuity. The smooth and confident aeroplane landed with one leg cocked; and it had written on the computer in the cock-pit 'SELF-DRIVE, and for this bofrots are needed to guide the lower fuselage.' It was the deathly silence of the forest that partnered the desert that finally woke up Atta the sleeping pilot. He woke to the fragrance of more frangipani than his dream could take. 'Ewurade save us!' he screamed, wakening the others, 'Look at this impudent aeroplane, it has programmed itself to self-drive backed by bofrots, and has landed in the unknown . . .' 'The scented unknown, by the smell of it,' Mackie said, giving Atta an accusing look. 'O don't blame me for landing in my sleep! I thought you were supposed to be guarding this sleep . . .' Atta said in wild defence. There was an equally accusing silence. 'All right, blame me if you like . . . but I will soon get us out of this mess. Some of these aeroplanes are getting extremely cheeky these days, thinking they can outcommot their inventors . . . on second thoughts I think old David here should pilot us out, since he invented this plane with his son in the first place . . .' Atta was getting disjointed in the mouth. In the silence, the plane shook its metal tooshie.

'Hold it there all of you!' came a high threatening voice with one foot in the forest and one foot in the desert. The travellers turned round in surprise, and saw a wizened brown old man sweeping the desert of its sand and brushing the forest of its mosquitoes and beetles. The old man threw the broom down and proved the strength in his arms by making an arthritic bend and pushing the plane along for a few yards. 'Will you leave us alone to make our way back up to the sky?' Jock said with a vague fear, but ready to slap anything hard with a fresh fish in defence. 'Do not speak to an ex-prime minister like that!' ordered old man brown. Mackie always wanted to remain as ordinary as possible in extraordinary situations: 'It must be very interesting being an ex-prime minister . . . and of which country, may I ask?' The old man gave a growl. He was suspicious of questions, but answered, 'I was the prime minister of the forest until the desert was added. Now there are several of us, both black and white. We are now dead mercenaries scouting the forest and the desert for hostages of history to capture . . .' 'But we are completely outside history!' Mackie exclaimed with tragic triumph. 'Then you will have to come along with me to meet the rest to decide your fate,' the old man declared, 'and I hope they are in the mood of the forest, and not the mood of the desert, for the mood of the desert kills . . .' Kwaku de Babo continued to write as he would in any emergency, but Donald had not descended, and was hiding in his stowaway niche with the birds, crabs, chestnuts and worms. 'I am not budging an inch. Those of you that want to be captured can go,' said Jock. But before anyone could move several similar old men, brown, black and white, rushed onto the travellers and tied then with steel nets. There was a strange and overpowering urge not to resist: Mackie had a gun, but could not use it. 'Look at Babo still writing under the net. Incredible,' Mackie observed, his eyes lost under the unending squares of his net. 'What is your time?' Babo asked the old man and ignored the rest of the captors. The old man said nothing, but captor number two said, 'But you know it's almost four in the morning.' 'No it's not, it is midnight,' Babo replied, 'and what day of the week, what month, what year are we in?' 'Monday 1st July 1980,' another captor answered impatiently. They all had very high voices; two of them had their beards tied together, so that they had to share the same footsteps. 'But we certainly are not in 1980!' shouted Babo. 'So how can you capture us ahead of time? And we can't possibly be talking to you now, can we?' There was a long pause, during which Babo never stopped staring at them. The old man brushed his beard against a young teak while the sand rose and fell, rose and fell. 'Take them out of the nets,' he said. The others looked doubtfully at him, but he insisted. He seemed to have answers in his eyes. The nets were taken off. 'Are you out of the nets or are you still in them?' he asked. 'We are neither in nor out of them. We can't take part in something that hasn't happened yet. If you wait and capture us at the right time, there will be more of us, and we will have more money. But I haven't said anything because we standing here talking now do not exist koraa. And you know what happens to those that break the march of time by stealing events in advance, do you not, old man?' Atta was staring with disbelief at his brother.

The old man nodded to the snort of the next captor, and said, 'Yes the desert advances against the forest, and all our luck would be destroyed in advance. My beard would have to go onto someone else's chin.' Without any warning the tinlegge captors rushed into the forest and disappeared. 'Besides, you are already dead,' Babo shouted after them. The travellers jumped onto Babo with gratitude, wondering whether his pen was his microphone. Donald had come onto the tiny gangway, and was adjusting the sleep in his eye, saying, 'If you hadn't been taken out of the nets, the vulture and the duck would have come out to attack those funny men.' 'Some little flapping attack,' smiled Kwame Atta finding his voice at last, and patting Donald on the head. He added, 'My eyes are not truthworthy: when I think they're open, then they're shut. I just have to ban them from sleeping, that's all.' The aeroplane winked to the sky as its self-drive was destroyed by Atta: there could always be another nose to poke into things with, and flip flap went the wings for they could almost fly like a bird's. 'I have an idea,' said Jock, 'you talk me out of sleeping, he talks him out of sleeping, it talks them out of sleeping, and then I talk you all into staying awake, in case our own plane flipping hijacks us again.' As Kwame Atta was eating a grape he had the shock of his life: the vulture jumped up to him and took a whole grape out of his mouth with its beak as he yawned. Atta was absolutely speechless. He lunged for a stick to attack the vulture with, but he was advised not to do such things immediately after an adventure like this. Advise, adventure, advulture. When Kwame Atta stuck out his tongue in fury, it stretched past the nose of the plane, and led it further into the journey and he noticed that Bra Kwaku had rescued the team without the help of any corner in sight; Mr Cornerstep could step strong without his corner, even beside the desert. 'It's a pity there's no woman on the plane. My wife said she would send a tear ahead of me . . . I was almost hoping that Aba Yaa would stowaway again, and all we got was Donald . . .' Mackie said wistfully, as Donald raised his eyebrows, and dropped them again quite happily into the worms; and small as he was, he knew this: he could be forgiven and resented and forgiven as often as they liked, for they could not throw him out of the plane. Besides, he had a secret up his crabs: he once saw Murray peeing from a distance, and he could have sworn that it was a donkey's tail he was using; and of course this led him to have a hidden contempt or pity, depending on his mood, for all men in the act of passing water . . . especially any man that did not treat him kindly: how dare he trouble him when all that he had was a donkey's tail.

There was Atta perched on the upper reaches of his name, shivering: the aeroplane was falling down the sky for the second time, after a few days of peace. 'Hey but this time I'm not asleep!' screamed Atta losing control altogether. 'EEEeeech!' shouted Jock in a supplementary scream, 'I've forgotten what you say in your last words before you die . . .' 'You just say fish and your soul will be saved,' grunted Mackie in a mad grip of the plane floor. Jock looked at him with a touch of astonishment in his terror: 'Davie, you must be tough, for how can you joke when this mad machine is hurtling down to our death . . .' 'Cover the boy with vultures, ducks, worms, crabs and anything else to save him!' screeched Atta just as he looked at the control pit: and on it had appeared again, 'SELF-DRIVE, trying to save you by landing in the cassava field of an unknown country.' 'Are there no parachutes here in this contraption?' Jock begged the skies. 'Be calm, becalm,' said Babo still writing. 'Hold on, hold on! the aeroplane is landing itself by the nose in a semi-dive!' Atta managed to squeal out just before the thud of the forced landing. There was complete silence, no movement whatsoever, except for the frantic crawling of the crabs. Half an hour later Atta was the first to stir; then the spoon was the next: Donald was making tea on the vulture to revive everyone. And then the cassava leaves outside were the next, stirring in the mournful wind. Everyone thought that Jock was dead until they saw him crawl out from a sack of new potatoes, his face wearing a chipped anger: 'Davie Mackie, surely your wealth should produce better aeroplanes than this!' Mackie was so exhausted that he frowned with only a third of his face. He had wanted to say: it was probably the stupidity machine that had charmed the plane. And when he finally got up enough strength to investigate this machine, he couldn't find it: at its place in the plane was a note neatly typed out and pasted down on the floor. 'The stupidity machine has left in disgust to Tukwan, by its own volition, please hurry up!'

Just as the travellers were recovering fully and giving thanks for their escape, a stylish grasscutter, the akrantie with one golden eye, strutted past, saying, 'I warn you gentlemen not to spoil the king's cassava, because we are all on our way to the football match. I have attacked enough roots and sugarcane for the day, hence my golden eye. My other eye is silver. I come from several countries in golden Africa, and let me hint you that if you think it's one country you are in, then you have no idea what the universe is like! Now, as soon as the king has finished watching the football match, he will return here to inspect his cassava. You can come to the football match if you have enough whistles, because there's nothing the king likes more than several whistles blowing at once, especially if his favourite team for the day has been fouled. But before you can come to the football match you must cross a gorge of goats that guard the king against strangers like yourselves. Now these goats that love imported jelly are dangerous: they have small ladders tied to their backs, and when they bleat, the bleats climb the ladders which amplify them to dangerous decibels against the enemy. Here anyone who is not a friend of the king's is an enemy. Of course the enemy, after an enema of advice from the king's subjects, and after producing tons of subservience and gifts, can become a loyal subject . . .' 'Well, thank you very much,' said Mackie rather too curtly, 'we shall not attend the football match, nor become the king's friends . . . simply because we are in a hurry, and we may also find the arrangements here disgusting . . .' 'Be careful what you say, for the king has ears to hear everything that is said in his countries. He has women, very beautiful, and some of them have two sets of genitals each. I am only a grasscutter, but I am trying to arrange for my wife to have her genitals doubled, too. All right, all right, if you promise to dash me something I will sneak you into the football match by a secret way . . .' said the elegant akrantie. 'I want to see the football match,' demanded Donald getting bolder with his tea.

It was after the ferocious soldier ants – ball breakers – surrounded the plane that the travellers felt that it was the safest thing to do: to go to the football match. There was a huge crowd of black and brown people, with the black-and-brown king up there manipulating the huge scoreboard. The Left Back had dribbled himself into a philosophical cleftstick; moving forward would leave his flank open to the ravages of time; moving back would lead him towards an own-goal of patent absurdity. The king hated paradoxical situations, so he just shot the player to the great cheers of the spectators . . . who were all subjects as well as objects. When the Right Winger made a fantastic feint to the left, and sent the entire defence the wrong way, he found himself face to face with the king. When he dared to beat the king with a flick, he too was shot instantly. The king was everywhere, gathering approval on the turf, and finally scoring all the goals himself. But since he had shot half the spectators for not cheering enough, the volume of approbation had considerably reduced, sharp. The mouth-mouth show was finishing. 'The king is a fool, the king is a murderer!' shouted Atta to the stunned silence of the stadium. 'The king is a bogey, the king is a monster,' Mackie joined in with his tweeds flying in rage. 'We hate your football match!' shouted Jock, wondering how long his sudden courage would last. 'And as you can all see, the king is only a rat from a medium-sized hole! Get rid of him,' flashed Babo on the scoreboard. 'Run, run,' screamed the terrified grasscutter, 'run to your plane, or they will kill you too! And can I come with you . . .' They rushed down the secret passage with the golden-eyed akrantie; the poor animal's silver eye was missing, for the king had taken a shot at it in a great rage, pot. The guards swarmed after them, with Mackie shooting back in desperation. 'How long since I shot a gun!' he said sadly, 'and I never thought I would again.' And the beautiful women too were chasing them. 'And we didn't even see any special buttocks at all,' Atta complained into the running. 'If you had a daughter you wouldn't talk like that,' retorted Babo. 'But Kwaku, they're trying to kill us, so I have every right to attack their beauty and their murder.' But there was only one reason that no one was shooting at the travellers any more: the beautiful women and the massive soldiers were all running to climb on board the lower-lip plane, to escape from their king. To be free as the straw in Atta's hat! But the travellers were too fast, including Donald, and the repaired plane took off magnificently. 'Kill him and start anew!' Atta shouted down to the crowd. And the crowds raged towards the floundering king . . . 'When will we leave these terrors and arrive in the peace of Tukwan?' Babo asked with his pen suspended.

CLASS NINE

The best burps in certain circumstances were silent, and the lower wind too.
There was Atta with raised hands rubbing the marvellously slanting rain,
and releasing wind free which was not whistling wind. Mackie had sent the
vulture under the plane to fly hard there, to see whether it could prevent any
more adventures, aboa. The travellers were exchanging the music of the sky
from mouth to mouth, for they were in the best of spirits, Whitehorse.
Donald had already trained the crab to talk the lingo of the worm, and had
already created three balls for himself by wearing the chestnut; and he had a
bigitive nose for a boy: he who had a distinguished conk and was young
enough to play conkers so sincerely with Sala the tropical child, could
conquer anything. The we-go-do aeroplane played with the clouds, tossing
its wings among them like a lover's toss of hips; and it put more love in its
own deep air-pockets, and its jet emission was quietening with what the two
pilots thought was the metal intuition of approaching home: parking
aeroplanes near the sugar-cane farms was a factor of love. Atta was creating
fast tracks in the sky and in his head for thanking the universe for this
delayed deliverance to Tukwan. 'This plane paa, ibi too good, tricky but
good!' enthused Atta the farting pilot, letting the pidgin in his mouth fly
. . . straight to the redirected language in Mackie's mouth: 'Yes, down to
the hilly and humid lands where I can already see the giant trees touching!'
If the aeroplane could sing it would, but it droned instead, giving the same
truth a song would give. After a hard journey you rejoiced! Tukwan, lie
down for the snorting singing aeroplane to land with a smooth pull to the left
of you. 'Do we have the proper bearing?' asked Atta, pushing his way
through a glut of smiles to speak. 'Of course, we have always carried
outselves rather well, haven't we?' replied the jubilant Mackie. The shared
laughter survived the constant smiling. Jock's thighs touched and opened,
touched and opened. He rearranged his fish for the hundredth time, but left
the potatoes scattered nicely. There was the plane laughing; and never trust
a plane that laughed with its pilots, deebi. And Babo wrote out the different
gradients of joy so easily. Screech to the soul!

But O my god where was the tarmac! What sort of a pesewa fate was this that kept sending the large crunch to the reluctant jaw . . . and there was a sudden message from: the stupidity maaachine: 'Moro has dug up the tarmac for a large guava farm and there is therefore a new poorly made tarmac right by the forest. Adjust your bearing . . .' There was a look of terror on Atta's face as he had already released the wheels to land and was thus ttttten feet from the earth but ssssaw no tarmac; and he just had the time to raise his plane again and scream to the new tarmac under the guidance of the jimi machine. 'Mewuoooo!' screamed Atta as Donald duplicated the scream. They all covered their faces when they saw the condition of the new tarmac: mounds, pot-holes, ridges and lines galore. Agyeeeiii! And then the vulture spread its wings and touched the underside of the aeroplane, it guided the gentleness in its beak into the wheels; so that when they crash-landed, it was only semi. The lower-lip plane then raised its wings in a powerful and angry salute; and it snorted in a slow turn sideways when it realised that the last stretch of the tarmac was terrazzo. 'We will probably find that the elephants too have been terrazzoed!' exclaimed Atta in disgust. 'O, I wish the aeroplane wouldn't double its screeching like that,' complained Jock. 'Ah, Mr Fish, never enter a new land with a wail, for they would think you had a chip on your shoulder . . .' said Atta with a stern laugh on his face. 'Well, weren't you just wailing for your life just now!' Jock persisted, until he got a pained look from Mackie. 'O look at the coconuts, Mr Mackie!' shouted Donald. The duck sputtered in unison with the plane until the latter's throat halted the former's. 'Mr Babo, I want to buy some breeze here, because I don't know what to do with my new sweat,' said Donald adjusting his crabs and worms. 'O I've just remembered Pokuaa's nostrils! The god that cut them so beautifully was obviously a goldsmith to the Asantehene. And have you ever noticed the angles they are at? If you go quite close you would think the nostrils had continued to be cut right through to the upper bridge of the nose! How I wish this obaa beautiful was walking on the Tukwan earth right now . . .' Atta cried to the sound of the rivulet beyond. 'Give her a chance to walk Levensvale too!' Mackie laughed his fairness out. The hero vulture had already polished its bald motoway, and had arranged to stand near the smell of two frangipani staring across to each other with different colours. The old dawadawa tree held aloft its fruit. 'Ah, my good twin brother you haven't written your good morning to me today. Are you starting to get distant again just because we are back in the land of our ancestors or what. You too, what! Sometimes you do something too mech, ah. Ahhhh, the welcoming party, and look at the stupid confidence of that tarmac-changing Moro . . . still wearing the same underwear as his Benz,' said Atta with an off-hand joy, with a deflected intensity. The forest touched all its leaves, what a fine rustle.

So Moro gathered his batakari closely around him, and hugged each one of the travellers slowly, making sure that his almost bald head outshone that of the vulture, sheabutter. After a quick exchange of the traditional civilities, and the descent of schnapps to Asaase Yaa, Twediampong, Bosompem, Moro took on an offensive position meant for a defensive role: 'Now your narrow escape was not my fault. If the surveyed land tells us that the best farming land was under the tarmac, then what was I to do? This was one of the things they were always quarrelling with me about. I even had to shout the good magistrate down. Akwaaba, akwaaba again! We are glad to see you because that wise stupidity machine gives us plenty of advice, and then laughs and laughs when we ask any questions . . . I see there are three strangers. Mmrofo, akwaaba! The young boy can sleep under the Benz with my family if he likes.' Donald was already trying to climb a coconut tree with three boys of the town; and Jock had insisted on laying out his various fish after the instant presentation of a freezer from Pokuaa's house fish after fish after fish. 'What wonderfully odd architecture, and all swish . . .' 'Yes we love our atakpame walls!' interrupted Dogo the kyinkyinga man. Dogo had become slightly fatter, so that he looked exactly like that hot khebab he was holding right now. He said, 'My broders, I came to meat you, even though you can't cut and roast me for my words.' 'Where's my mother?' asked Atta. 'Is my father monopolising her as usual? Ewurade of the fufu pestle!' Mr K the magistrate kept his distance, kept the smell of beans in his handkerchief but he refused to talk yet about the church which he was supposed to keep watch over. There were so many questions being thrown at Atta and Babo, but very soon the three Levensvale visitors were left to wander as they liked. 'Food is well under way,' shouted Nana krontihene, 'but it looks as if the other stranger is already cooking too. Custom demands that he eats our palava sauce first, I lie?' But Jock was too busy in the kitchen of the twins' mother to bother about much else. Nana Bontox's wives insisted on a full report on Nana's activities before they helped with the cooking for the travellers. And whenever Moro got a chance, he would whisper into Mackie's ear, 'Is the money ready yet my friend? The way your eyebrows are so bushy, I have quick-quick confidence in you that you will make sure that we get all our money when they all return. Let's smoke a pipe together after you chop.'

Mackie, Jock and Donald made their base at the original Plantain Hotel, where the real plantain grew, and there were real pines too; but Donald did sometimes sleep under the Mercedes with his new friends. If you were not careful, you could snore into the exhaust-pipe. But Nana Baabi the krontihene thought nothing of entering the Plantain Hotel backwards, since he thought that his majesty could be ¾ too much: some warrior-like krontinising presence, which kept ¼ of its power back so that it could sometimes be kind, forwards. It was more human to offer a deflected frontal attack, tsooooboi, yei! Nana had made his smile available to himself, offering it second-hand to the visitors, yet very sincerely, so that his intention of being dashed something important before the visitors left, did not appear too open. Nana loved to beg double: when he was refused something once, he got it the next time. He admired Mackie's terraced eyebrows. 'I have come to learn how to speak with my mouth shut,' Nana said with his mouth agape, 'because I often see it in the flims.' 'Flims?' asked Jock with more than a trace of doubt. 'That is how we pronounce it here!' Nana Baabi declared, not prepared to tolerate any flimsy excuse. 'Well my good chief, I'm not quite prepared to teach you right now, since I'm too busy attending to the fish and chips . . .' 'But haven't you been told that the local dishes will outsell your fish and chips?' Nana asked. 'But how do your people know that I'm not going to sell my produce free?' Jock countered. Nana's feet were the same size as Jock's favourite herring, but they could dance much better, with or without sandals . . . but as a sub-chief he could only dance in the style of the former, provided he didn't step on the same-same herring. 'Donald!' Jock shouted in consternation, 'let go of the chief's ankles straight away! If you want to play a silly game lying on the ground to test your strength on someone else's ankles, don't choose this man! Besides you should have seen the beads there . . .' Donald had obviously become more sprightly since his arrival in Tukwan, for he loved coconuts and the hot and free weather. The krontihene looked at Donald the coconut with fatherly disdain, and then reclaimed his ankles with a royal jump, hup.

And landed in the rather cool glance of Maimuna the new hotel manager, no ress. Maimuna prided herself in getting the hotel organised, but was annoyed that that male stranger Jock had brought a ridiculous passion for hotel potatoes into the rooms. She wondered whether efficiency and little Jock were compatible. If she had her own way, which she didn't, she would arrange Jock and his cuisine on the bola. 'My goal in life is to bite as much money as possible,' announced Atta swaggering in while Nana Baabi walked out to the rhythm of his amulets. 'Now you Maimuna, why don't you like men at all? Were you not born of man and woman . . .' 'Keep your mouth shut, Kwame Atta,' ordered Maimuna the manager, no ress; 'if it's food you have come here for, then fill your mouth with it straight away . . . anything to stop your kwasia words coming out.' Atta stood and stared hard at her, wondering how she managed to make her eyes harder than her teeth so often. He tried to take her hand in mock friendship, she beat it with a fan; he tried to hold her in the play of some instant and rash romance, she slapped his solar plexus; Atta grabbed a nearby pawpaw, crushed it, and threw its seeds over her. Maimuna moved forward threateningly. 'Give me my food immediately before you beat me!' he ordered through his collapsing courage, and he was laughing into the gari foto that had been brought to him at the double. 'Now you are talking, my good woman! I ran out of my mother's house to eat here, because she was asking me moral questions, like why don't I think I have duties towards my mother, and do I think it's right to quaff so much spiritual solubility! or some verbal gari to that effect. And then coming here too my little jokes are taken by Maame Maimuna as attacks on her tiaaaa person, ah. This person with the temperament has obviously meant her temper . . .' Atta not only managed to finish eating while he was talking, but also wiped his mouth, which had lines of village cooking on it, and then slapped the cook on the hands before finally rushing out, shouting, 'The Plantain Hotel is a mere banana! and I don't care whether I love Pokuaa or not!' Maimuna nodded wisely into his foolishness, and restarted her contempt for Jock.

It was after everybody settled down that the problems became manifest in Tukwan. The lake was jealous of its two travelling ducks, and thus had refused to ripple for weeks. With one duck back, it was now crowded with uncompleted ripples, half fish, one-winged ducks, and semi-frogs. With the moss nearly dry and the pebbles partly cracked, it looked as if Moro's rule didn't suit the water at all: even the elephants didn't fill all of their trunks with water. What the stupidity machine was trying to do was to make Moro more democratic, and thus stop the rot at the lake; poor lake wouldn't be raised, poor lake wouldn't be lowered; and the flies were taking command there, until the machine turned its deep rust on them, killed them with its rotting metal . . . and then cleaned itself again. Since it was agreed before the journey that no automatic coconuts were to be tolerated, Babo discovered that what the coconuts were doing instead of following those they liked was this: moving and comparing their shapes from coconut tree to coconut tree; they palmed each other off and then took each other back. Kwaku de Babo wrote the movements of the coconuts, but they insisted on following him for several yards when they felt his presence . . . to the delight of Donald, who was used to a different type of magic. Apart from guava trees on the old tarmac, the yam and groundnuts that were to be encouraged were not there at all. Moro's authority was a handful of unplanted groundnuts. The machine had persuaded Dogo to grow some yam, fried, to go with his kyinkyinga, but the vines crawled so young and so few that they didn't solve anything for Moro, who had not been taking the advice of Fatima koraa. Kaki the driver had become so confident in the general disarray that he once tried to drive the traxcavator through the bamboo ramparts – steel hidden – of the town, and was ordered back by the ever-perceptive Maimuna; she saw him through a sliced okro. Moro would not listen to much advice from the council of elders either; so this meant that beef, akrantie, and wood-maggots were being eaten as often as before, with Dogo insisting that it was a silly decision anyway: how could he then sell his mighty khebaba? Zolozolo had stepped in to say that the shrine didn't mind beef being eaten, but that akrantie and maggots were to be left alone until further notice.

The crisis had thus spread into the kitchens and thickened the abenkan. 'Were the cries of the wild animals used abroad at all?' Moro would ask Babo every morning trying hard to find a way to criticise what Pokuaa and co would be doing in Levensvale. 'Use the cries, use the cries!' Moro would declare. 'Use the cries when they attack you . . . but haven't they attacked you at all yet? I don't believe you are enjoying that much asomdwe in the land of the frozen feet.' 'But we are both towns out of time, and skin is a joke,' Babo would answer as often as a centipede had legs. 'But at least we have resealed the altar!' Moro said later triumphantly. 'There are no coins in Christ any more! See that, even though I am the builder of this town's mosque . . .' Yes Moro had built the mosque in a series of bricks and boasts which Mohammed had tolerated up to the neck of the small round tower, but which was rejected outright at the still-unfinished tip, pity this sin at the tip. What saved Moro was his passion for his wife and for his Benz with each of whom he went to bed on alternate nights. His brow so cool.

It was the multi-coloured hen with the blue candle lit and tied to its back that walked up to Zolozolo the deputy shrinemaster and dropped its dung. It clucked with a confidence that came from its elegantly shaped wings; and tied to its right leg was a note written with a pen the same colour as the candle. It was a note from the Kumasi authorities, traditional and political, saying, 'We know you have been trying to run away from the map, and that you think you are immortal. This time when we find your land, we will not banish you; we will crush you. And we suspect you have kidnapped one of our subjects, plus his traxcavator. Release him immediately. Don't force us to swear any oaths against you.' Zolozolo went with his slow gait to the house of the krontihene, and showed the note, having fried and eaten the hen first, and used the blue candle to give light in a protective ritual, and to light a cigajot sharp. Nana Krontihene's first reaction was to panic and beat a furious gong-gong through the town, but he chewed tobacco instead, and sent for some elders, Moro, Dogo, Atta, Babo and yes Mackie. Dovi followed stupidly with his stupider son Agbozo, whose middle name was Jupiter. Jupiter was so much stupider. Some mangoes had been left around the compound casually for anyone who wanted to arrange for a bite. There was an interval of touching leaves, during which Nana Baabi rescued himself from the kind chattering around the chairs. 'See the note,' Nana said, building the potential for worry in his mouth. The note went round slowly, gathering the eyes as it went. Mackie cleared his throat, but Atta spoke first: 'Nana, put your worry in your pouch. They are bluffing us for wheee. This is the land of the recycled immortals, I lie? The land where to be immortal is not to cease to be human; where magic is made in bits but you don't become superhuman making it . . .' 'And where death is a junction that you die to cross, and then you resume eternity again . . .' added Babo. 'All right, all right, we thank the gentlemen for their twin wisdom, but in the absence of Kofi Senya and Pokuaa and Nana Bontox and Lawyer Tay, what do we do?' asked Nana Baabi irritably, a fly on his biggest ring. Zolozolo suddenly jumped onto an elephant, and jumped off again. 'He is getting ready for some divination,' Atta whispered sarcastically to Mackie who smiled sideways but looked grave forwards. 'Too late, too late I have divined first!' came the shrill voice of the stupidity machine. 'Now what you must do is to check the maze around the town. Dogo, Maimuna and Fatima planned it quite well, but didn't have the creative stupidity to make it impregnable. I am telling you to go and check the maze now . . .' Then the voice went off, the machine crawling and creaking in an attempt to stand near its master Kwame Atta. The machinemaster patted his work, and fed the gaping computerised mouth two lizards, some oil, and half a pound of mosquitoes. The stupidity machine swallowed and wailed with happiness. 'To the maze!' it repeated.

The mazy ramparts were a terrible combination of endlessly crossing paths, and interminably sliding inclines. Three paths would meet each other at the shoulder, and then scatter in opposite directions at the ankle; another path undulated sharply every three yards, and then carried its earth into a huge disguised hole; and yet another had no beginning and no end, starting in the middle and finding that that didn't exist either. Towards the west of the highest wall with its twin behind it, and its thick triplet behind that too, was a patch of turf with great big guavas growing out of its black soil; but with the last lunge to get the guavas you would fall down a gigantic east-west hole, into which the stupidity machine had inserted a wooden crusher that crushed tongues and threw the grisly bits into the footprints behind. Remnants of drumming – the dwarf sound – shot through the entire maze piii, but no tongues were caught. Mackie stared into the mysteries, adjusting his tweed shorts so that he could stare down longer. Then he nudged Atta, and whispered, 'I think I can hear someone groaning down there.' Atta switched on the S machine which screamed: 'I told you, I told you! There are two people down there, and one has broken a leg.' 'Wait, wait,' shouted Dogo with excitement, 'there are special ropes for going down, let me fetch them by the greasy hut near the hidden escalator that moves mud from trap to trap.'

Nana krontihene transferred his feet from ceremonial sandals to workaday ones, and ordered Babo to write everything he saw. Babo, who was doing so already, didn't even hear him; he heard rapid heartbeats instead. Babo and Atta decided to go down the ropes. 'Did you hear some contrapuntal snoring?' Atta asked his twin. 'It was two people groaning rather . . .' Babo replied with his ear to the ground. 'Watch where you step!' he shouted to Atta, 'you are putting earth in my ear!' The groans grew louder. Zolozolo had now finished his divination, and came to confirm the presence of two people from Kumasi in the maze. 'Mewuoooo, buiei! Save my foot over my leg. I am dying in hell but I don't deserve it!' came a strong voice from one of the holes immediately before the irresistible guavas. 'Switch on the escalators and they'll be pushed up to the detention slope . . .' Atta ordered, '. . . that slope where you can question anything and everybody at forty-five degree angles . . .' His mouth was looking for its long-lost jot. 'This is a serious moment,' came Mr K the magistrate's voice surprisingly from behind. And that's all he said, standing there with his long straight back, looking quite ayoungi. They had to transfer their staring from Mr K to the two men groaning up the moving escalator. One of them did seem to have a broken leg, and the other had a bad graze on his chin. 'Now,' began the bombolish man, with the chinny wound, 'we have rights as prisoners of war, no fears. You cannot kill us just like that. I am Donkor the wing chief of a wing chief. I do have confidence, no fears, and if hasmal go-go do, then we too we dey-O, proper! I can't understand why you have tortured us in your amazing maze like this. And all this scratching of my chin has robbed me of my beard. I tell you my enemy brothers that this beard-beard loss be serious-OOoo, and it will never be tolerated in the royal compounds . . .' 'Shut up, close your mouth! How can we take you prisoner, and then have to listen to some nyamanyama lecture or lecturity from you?' asked the angry Atta. 'And we shall not forget to treat your wounds after a few mandatory questions . . .' Mackie sauntered off to get something to treat the prisoners, without thinking . . . but he met Babo already coming back with first aid. Koomson was the one with the swollen leg, and he had not stopped groaning. 'But we will kak the confessions out of them paaa,' vowed Atta. 'But remember the town's code of gentleness,' reminded Mr K whose garrulity was becoming quite surprising: several sentences said or given in two months gratis, and with an extenuating smell of beans in both pockets. The detention slope let the prisoners speak in hunched-up angles, shouting for their stooping uncles and crying for their arthritic sisters.

Zolozolo finally took the prisoners to the shrine for healing, in a disinfected wheelbarrow kept for such an eventuality. The rain was starting to threaten, and Mackie felt he had cleared his throat for nothing. Was he expected to say something? He just went and polished the S machine, showing his massive eyebrows for effect, for a little gratuitous eye-high wisdom. And the rain came down this year, this afternoon; there were spears of it, bows of it, which the lake received with joy.

Zolozolo took only two hours to cure Donkor and Koomson. The rain had washed his healing clean. 'Now why didn't we have such mazes against the colonial presence?' Atta complained back in his mother's house with Babo and Mackie, and later his father, 'and I have the laziest dada in the world.' Papa Ntow raised one eyebrow against his son; he was too tired with rest to raise both. The house, built by his wife Sister Mansah with her petty trading, had a baked floor undulating with welcome and with easy architecture. The ceiling, with its unpainted plywood, was lower than necessary, because Papa Ntow insisted that the older one got the more one stooped, and thus the less space one needed from a ceiling. The words obviously bounced earlier to the undulatory floor, ball. When Ntow Papa was happy, he found it quite easy to dissect his laugh: the haha from an easy mouth, the hoho from the doubt of wasted lungs and a wasted life. 'I need to have my life properly cooked!' Ntow said with a happy yawn, 'and it is true, one time, that I was born to love . . .' 'OOooo,' complained Sister Mansah, 'can't you see that we have a stranger with us? All this talk of love . . .' 'I . . . is so true, and every stranger should know that it is true and good. This is not libilibi-labalaba love koraa!' Babo asked his father to take one last mouthful of Guinness to stop the flow of lazy words. 'Don't you sons know that you take more of your gifts from me than from your mother? . . .' Papa Nt asked puffing his chest with pride and cigarettes. The sons understood his truth with a great horde of laughter. 'Obviously your father is a gifted man,' declared Mackie with a severe pull at his pipe and eyebrows at the same time. 'O yes, O yes,' smiled Atta with a tug at his father's elbow, 'obviously my father likes receiving gifts, no doubt about that one pesewa.' Papa Ntow was silent. He gave his wife a wardrobe after marriage, and had a special love for her elbow which was exquisite, eldrobe. Babo got up and took his head to the bathroom, bathed it, shook it, dried it, combed it hard, held it in his hands, and then taught it to say, 'I'll be back soon after a small walk.' 'He's a deep one, this other son of mine. Even when he was a baby, I never understood him!' Papa Ntow shouted after his disappearing son. And continued: 'And now, Mr Mackie, you are a mature, dashing – how much will you dash me, haha – adventurous man, but there's one question you must help me to answer: is it possible to photograph a dream in your part of the world? No don't dum your pipe in wonder, I have been thinking this for the last five years; and for six months I debated whether I should voluntarily sign myself into an asylum. But unfortunately, there's no such institution here . . . which means we are all mad together and with nowhere to go! Seriously, seriously . . .' 'Always be careful of my father when he talks about being serious . . .' interrupted Atta, shifting from chair to chair with a mad and meaningless abandon.

Sister Mansah walked in demurely, and said with a very soft smile, 'My husband and my first twin usually have some freee show-show concert, so I beg you to go softly softly catch monkey.' 'Now, Mr Mackie, what do you think? Is it possible to photo a dream at all?' Before Mackie could say anything, in walked the stupidity machine. 'You see this mad machine is getting to be more and more like its inventor, my famous son of the aeroplanes! It is run-down, stiff in body, rusty, untidy, and no doubt runs on alcohol . . .' Atta roared in mock anger: he knew his father was trying to get his own back at his jibe of laziness. 'And you can attest to the fact that he's laughing at his own father right now! What sort of a lame bull is this son! He could easily have made more money by escaping from this crazy time here, and going to Accra or even Kumasi to live a normal life full of status for a clever engineer, but no! He makes a fool of himself by inventing all sorts of fantastic bolastic things that give him a history but no status, no money yet. Hmmm, sometimes I wish I had two daughters instead. Imagine if I gave birth to someone like Pokuaa? Yieee! I would be sweating with wealth and purpose! . . . but all I do now is to love and love a wife that complains about my loving: she calls it dotage, depending on which dictionary is at hand. Babo inherited his obsession with dictionaries from Sister Mansah's second brother. Isn't she beautiful! Here I go again . . . dot dote doting dotage, dote on tote, the old monkey of the heart!' 'I am the only machine in this world that can photograph a dream,' stated the S machine with its shrill and wise patter. It was all quiet, the breeze had surrounded the house and blown all its wooden windows shut. 'Pray, good machine invented by my son,' purred Ntow, 'show your majesty by letting us see the picture. I say you are a good dream yourself I swear!' The machine shook its lizards, grunted, and disappeared into the lowest point of a very deep rainbow. No one could speak.

Babo was walking among the tarmac guava, and pressing the elephant grass down to see further when he saw the S machine race out of the rainbow; it came so low on its way back to the house that it almost knocked him down. Collect yourself Babo, and go down towards the lake that you loved. It had shrunk rippleless before the advancing moss and mass of growing grass. Beyond the thousands of web-prints stood an elephant that you couldn't see: it was covered in resting ducks, so that when Babo jumped to scatter the ducks with love, he bumped his head against a suddenly revealed elephant now. The ducks flew in welcoming formations, carrying the surprise to every part of the sky, sky over the sugar-canes and the guavas, sky over the two prisoners, and sky over the stu machine. On the ground Babo ran the same patterns as the ducks in the sky. Mr cornerstep, you duckmaster you, there was much scrubbing to do, of beaks and feathers by you. And the first real ripple appeared for the first time in months. Babo was trying to bring the soul back to the lake, even for the long-dead fluorescent light from the lone lamppost. The chattering of the beaks was just getting too much when Zolozolo entered the noise with the two Kumasi prisoners. Donkor and Koomson were visibly shaken by the strange movement of time in Tukwan; and they had hoped to feel a little more at home when they saw Kaki with his old traxcavator; but Kaki had already devoured the new time, even though he sometimes reached the point of rebellion against his stay at Tukwan, especially in the absence of the usual elders of Tukwan. 'O menua Kaki, I'm sorry you are suffering the same fate . . .' 'What are you talking about, fate? I am here completely of my own free will. And the women like my heavy driving . . . it would be stupid of you to ask me to help rescue you. Rescue you from what?' Kaki asked defiantly. 'By the rock of my ancestral hills,' shouted Donkor, 'who has tricked you into forgetting all about Kumasi so soon? . . .' 'Shut up there my two dear prisoners,' ordered Zolozolo, 'we have come to the lake to check your truth in the reflection of the water. And if you refuse to say how you found the banned town, then I shall allow the ducks to pull your beard out one by one, while the other one suffers something else being pulled out!' 'What I love best is having the choice between telling the truth and telling a lie,' grinned Donkor with part of his mouth shut.

The stupidity machine passed low again, its rusty side the colour of rainbows and it was carrying a triumphant picture back to Papa Ntow, who had given up wanting an answer from David Mackie. 'Now,' shouted the machine high, 'I have the dream of a goat caught in this photo. It is a series of rainbow lines arranged according to the strength of each bleat. The dots are sexual actions and eating actions. The photo is an accurate image of an average goat's utterly useless dream.' 'But what did the goat have to say in the dream?' asked Papa Ntow. 'In the dream the goat asked the stupidity machine to get Papa Ntow to shut up immediately, whether he was satisfied with his answers or not,' said the high machine, waiting for its rations of lizard and mosquito, Allah. Atta saw his father touch his mother's tooshies gently, and moved his long-suffering look upwards. 'When there's so much love reaching the lower regions, I don't see why we must regulate Papa Ntow's madness at all, ah!'

Papa Ntow ignored all this, and went and sat, bom, by his cooking wife. 'Don't come and sit too near, Ntow, you don't want me to cook you by mistake do you?' Sister Mansah said with more seriousness than Ntow would have liked. He stroked the back of his own head, as he usually did when he felt a bit insecure. 'Why did you marry me at all?' he asked Mansah in selfpity. She looked at him with a quick sideways glance, and then smiled her way back to where her head was. At the tomatoes. After a short pause she decided to answer: 'So you Ntow after all these years of marriage you are asking me why I married you! Search your own heart for the answer, for you know it . . .' 'Do you mean that you love me more than you used to? O, I know you will not answer me seriously because of the twinkle in your eye; and it's always the left one when you want to trouble me small!' Ntow said, resting the Papa in his name, kakra. The garden-eggs and the okros spoke for their silence. 'Well, I certainly didn't fall for your laziness . . .' Mansah said dropping her Sister in exasperation, 'but if you really want to know, then I'll tell you: it's your forehead that brought us together. Do you remember when I first killed a mosquito on it? You said you adored my slap or something silly like that! But we are too old now to talk about love,' Mansah said Sister, attacking the onions. 'If you are going to heat the pot, heat my heart too!' said Papa Ntow with a desperate softness, remembering the forehead true, and Mansah's strong cool hands on and off the head in a flash. She continued with her cooking, refusing to put too much love in with the salt. 'You Ntow, one of these days you will let us forget that we are almost getting to sixty . . .' 'Yes, but our time is different . . .' answered Papa Ntow. 'Well, that's where you may be wrong my dear husband with the long thighs. My time is so-so traditional, I am the only one here that has lived all her years in single file, one year after another. Don't you know that, mr sabe! I am watching them all go after something new . . . what is good about the new things, and after all what is new about the new at all? I remember soon after I met you I hated marriage because I knew you were going to be somebody different. I didn't want anything different, but because of your forehead I gave you my love small small. And then you became lazy. I didn't understand it: the lazier you became the nicer your forehead too grew, and you gave me the excuse for the laziness: you said that you made the thinking of the twins big by thinking under their thinking. It was something nice to hear, a father multiplying the thoughts of his children by doing some underhead thinking himself. I couldn't dream what you were thinking about: gin? adoka? abe wine? the meaning of this strange town, whether it's more strange than normal or more normal than strange. But all this time they were worrying me about the fatherhood of my boys. Wait a minute while I go and get the goat meat . . .' Sister Mansah said, still concentrating more on what she was cooking than on what she was saying.

The dusk was coming and the windows couldn't stop it. Atta and Mackie were now sitting in the front yard, wondering when the stupidity machine would transfer its dream photos to the dreams of human beings. Mackie kept crossing his legs over his pipe smoke, and finally moved his chair towards the thickest puff, saying, 'Your houses are beautiful and local, as if they are an easy extension of the skin.' He looked at Atta hard, Atta with the extremely thin elbows, and then asked, 'Where exactly are the two towns going?' Atta looked at him with a merry frown, and said, 'Don't anticipate things, my brother, you know that the conference is coming and that supamammy thoughts like this will just have to come out during the organised talking. But I think the towns are the best things on this sorry globe! this riot of a football game they call life. You see, we have everything, from shrines and weeds and elephants and talking machines, to decorated pines, necklace hills, and your own private rocket that I secretly found . . . a rocket that rises and diffuses the anger in the heart. As soon as I discovered this rocket in your storeroom while I was looking for some old gloves, I knew the secret of your patience. And I love the way you talk about your canons . . .' When Mackie raised his eyebrows, you had to contend with the movement of some sort of forest there, but it was a silent forest: he said nothing, just smiled at last, and said, 'I agree with your views about the two towns, but . . .' And they went on chattering in the mixed-up smoke, and Atta was asking Mackie how many more times he was going to cross his legs, for it was not necessary: the smoke had lowered.

But Papa Ntow persisted: 'Sister I know I'm three months in advance with our time-table for love and fikifiki, but I beg you, can I have one more overdraft tonight? . . . please.' 'I know that all you want me to do is to break the dawn with an egg! To start the day tired paaa with your long moving up and moving down. Don't come and trouble my cooking! You will make the onions change koraa. Behave your age!' 'Exactly!' beamed Ntow, 'and hurry up with the cooking, hurry up! Never mind making it special for strangers . . .' 'Papa Ntow, I warn you not to hold my buttocks when I'm cooking! You are mad!'

Babo was rechecking the string passed through the hills to lower them. Rats had eaten it, so the hilly geology had lowered more than necessary. There was a small haemorrhage of small rocks through the holes made for the string. He sent the travelled goat with the sideways morals – it jumped laterally to increase the goodness in its life. The goat had arrived inexplicably from Levensvale, and the stupidity machine had refused to reveal whether it stole the goat and carried it here in its terminals or not. Stow goat away went seeing everything by the side; sides of hills, sides of animals that Moro did not treat equally with presences and human beings, sides of sorrow, and sides of time that Moro had encouraged in an attempt to bring in more mortality for the wrong reasons. Goat go, with more jump than run . . . right to Dovi's house, which had much laughter from Efida and her son Agbozo against Dovi the father, for he had done nothing with his life. Efida gave the goat the new string from under the laughing bed. On the way back the goat, glad in its leaps, and looking particularly testicular, met Dovi again. The emissary of string looked at Dovi with the string in its mouth. 'Can I carry the string for you small?' begged Dovi, looking for some unravelling of his life. The goat jumped over the morals: tried to butt Dovi with a strong side-leap. But even as the goat was in mid-air, Dovi insisted on some compassion for himself before it landed again. The goat gave a nodding grin, and off it went together with Dovi who had suddenly found great purpose in leaping like a goat on string. Babo received the string with a hug for the goat, and a hug for Dovi. And you wouldn't believe that there was half of Tukwan there, waiting to help pass the string through the hills, including the rats that ate the string in the first place. Hold the string with the new solignum on it, Tsooooboi, yei! There was joy in the sweat; as if the confidence that had reduced would rise again with the hills. 'Give us back the spirit, Babo, give it back to us, so that Pokuaa and Kofi Senya add more to it when they come back!' someone shouted. 'Even Nana Bontox will have a better spirit for us than Moro. Dogo tried hard with his soft kyinkyinga to help us with some joy, but he was disappointed with his meat that rotted in the aeroplane on the way to UK, so that he couldn't try any more,' another person said, dancing to the drums. Khebab sorrow. 'Hurry up and go and bring all the rest of our people back. We miss them, the lake misses them. Give us back our joy!' And Babo achieved his string.

CLASS TEN

There they were getting ready for the return journey to Levensvale, Babo, Mackie, Atta, Jock and Donald. 'Not soon enough, not soon enough!' all the people shouted except Moro. 'Go and bring back the rest, because we miss them, and because the two prisoners say that very soon Kumasi will find the path of eternity leading to Tukwan, and Tukwan will be attacked. They confessed this through their reflections in the lake . . . and they didn't want to suffer the torture of a million mosquitoes released at them in the hole of roses in the rampart maze. Go and bring them after they have finished all their business in the land of the icy noses . . .' Moro was getting bewildered: no one hated him, yet no one wanted him to rule, not even Fatima his faithful and soft-thin wife, whose baby was growing fine under the Mercedes Benz. Moro's government had to go, even though he himself would still be around planting his cola among Pokuaa's politics . . . helping the town, in fact: for after all, if you can't enjoy a width of life and vision when you had immortality, then you were useless. Yet Moro had a stubbornness that even he could not fathom: he still felt that he alone, helped perhaps by Opanin Akorsah, or even Lawyer Tay, could rule or come to an accommodation with Kumasi. He cast his eyes towards Kumasi, even in the sunset, and wondered in his cola language whether that was where his true power here lay . . . There was power in a large cola farm, and he rubbed his elbows together hard. But Donald didn't want to go back to Levensvale. He loved the taste of fresh coconut milk, he felt wonderful with guavas, he played oware, he scattered the ducks that scattered their dung back at him, and he and his Tukwan friend Kofi Boi had almost mastered the intricacies of playing in the maze without getting caught in any dangerous holes. Kofi Boi was one year younger than Donald, depending on which year came first. And Donald had tamed one wild pig with impudent ease. Poor Donald was now hiding among the hihe, refusing to go; and he did his refusal with a coconut and ahe just so fresh. Kofi Boi was of course hiding with him, with his big Boi-bushy hair. They were both eating their favourite kenkey: Osino graphic; and beside them was the stupidity machine enjoying their togetherness. Donald said to Kofi, 'I had a telegram from Sala yesterday on my birthday, saying I should polish my soul here a bit, and eat as many coconuts as possible, and play tumantu too.' Kofi smiled, and said after a pause, 'Let's go and give ourselves up, otherwise your mother will cry when they arrive without you; after all, they will find us anyway.' So they stood on the S machine and were ridden slowly towards the controlled weeds and flowers of the town centre. 'Never miss a coconut,' was what Donald said about nothing in particular. Then they shared a last stretchy mineral between them: what Kofi Boi called: cocacolastic . . . and they gave one lizard and one mosquito to the stupidity machine.

They were putting the usual lavender on the aeroplane. The vulture had left without a word, desperate to land on Kofi Senya's pipe again, and bold enough to fly to Levensvale even though there was autumn there. Several paths around the town and around the lake were changed by Kwaku de Babo. He walked the difference into them: having found spirits quite low in the town, he created different directions for going to the same place for the people; and he raised the hills two more inches with his string of geological love. Everybody was given a small present by Mackie and Babo, from pens to handkerchiefs to Levensvale Rock, hard sugar. 'You have to be toughly Ghanaian,' Kwame Atta was saying to the ever-busy Jock who was trying to use the raw sun to fry his last chips of the visiting season. 'What do you mean you have to be a toffee Ghanaian?' Jock asked absent-mindedly over his unsuccessful fry, 'and if you really are a toffee Ghanaian, then that makes me Scottish sherbet, eh! But leave me alone, my lad, can't you see that I'm trying to utilise the sun freeee?' But Atta had already moved along, among the army of lieutenant-general bustling: they were packing the plane with pineapples, cola, and fish in a military manner; and a few more termites too were included to continue and even increase the nibbling of the European continent by the travelling Tukwan, not forgetting of course Donald's coconuts, see this head-knocking.

Dadoona Tay was there with her intelligent fat, upbraiding Dogo for some extreme bugabuga English. She loved the absence of her husband, but would have been glad to see him back. She was a law unto her house, and she wondered what cheek her son Sala was showing now. When he wrote to her that he hated law, and now wanted science, she loved him more: tweak the father a bit, silly law. 'Dadoona, why don't you fill in the law a bit for your husband while he's not here? Do you think that the church door should be widened again? Or would it be better to go and steal the door of the mosque, so that your increased bulk, alleluya, can pass through to God . . .' said Atta with an impudent hand on his thin hip. Dadoona just ignored him, broadening the snarl on her face, and continuing to check Dogo's language. Atta persisted foolishly: 'Ah, and you my big Doona-day, I understand you have a letter-writing relationship with the great Pokuaa . . . and what exactly is great about Pokuaa? She retains her blandness when she's with the extremely tough people of this world, how sweet is her toffee. And I can vouch that you feel safe with her, especially when you don't meet and continue to write your risky husband-bashing letters . . . but don't forget that Pokuaa has no husband, not even . . .' And Dadoona saw her chance: 'Yes, not even a stupid alanta-legged chofi-chopping fool like yourself, a man a woman would never accept even if he was the last man available to fertilise her!' Atta took on his favourite pained look, which had significant elements of arrogance in the making. He just ran off the tarmac and booted away with a shout the ball that Boi and Shearer, Kofi and Donald, were playing keepie-up tactics with; and that was the best language he could use to reply to Dadoona, boot the words. She shouted with disdain, 'I'm going to church, and no door can stop me . . .' But she had forgotten that she was a member of the farewell committee, so she had to stay, keeping her scowl for Atta at the everready. The S machine took her vital statistics secretly.

'Is everything ready?' Mackie shouted over the tarmac microphone. 'Look, this man doesn't want me to finish my sugar-cane before my emplanement . . .' complained Jock with his toned-down aggressive fish-and-chip style. 'What illusions of grandeur are you having about your enstoolment . . .' Atta asked Jock with the hole in his sock. Jock had given up frying with the sun, and had sworn instead to try the moon later. 'Everybody on board!' shouted Mackie, with some fear that a day longer here would lead to a deep regret at leaving. Go back to Pokuaa, go back to Pokuaa, was all Mackie said to himself to make it easier for him to leave. It was only now that a little drumming started around the freshly cut sugarcane with its guava environs. There was a full general roar because the army of people were happy: the one hundred and first house had just been completed, showing that Atta's invention rate, though erratic and often silly, was bearing fruit by the orange trees. The prisoners were to be dropped by parachute over Kumasi just after the journey started, with a warning note to the authorities there that banishment would continue to be tolerated, but invasion NO. Zolozolo gave Donkor and Koomson their old sense of time back, with a union of shells, cracked palm-nuts, kosee, libation, and deep and dry ginger. There were so many goodbyes that the lower-lip aeroplane couldn't take all the waving. Donald was crying, in spite of himself. Jock couldn't tell whether his fish and chips had failed or not. The stupidity machine was desperate about changing Moro. The plane rose into the afternoon. 'Don't be long in coming back-ooooooh!' was the last huge amplified cry, as Mackie piloted the aeroplane. 'Young boy,' Atta said one thousand feet up, to Donald, 'don't shoogle the plane with your small crying, I beg.' Three arms shot out to comfort Donald, and no one was surprised when they were hastily withdrawn from the small crab crawling on his shoulder. Back to gari, back to Bataan, for the crabs absorbed Donald's crying.

The silly broad wind from the widest street in Tukwan had followed the plane up and was blowing it about see-saw, puff to the aeroplane. When the plane straightened itself again, it received a message from the stupidity machine that Moro's wife Fatima had decided boldly to sit on the Council with her husband to amplify his wisdom a bit, and she had been strongly supported by the stern Maimuna, and Dogo had agreed with a khebab. The sacred duck had refused to go back with the travellers but had sent ahead a quack, air mail, to call the other one in Levensvale to return . . . and the quack was so quick that the aeroplane, now totally domesticated, met the other duck returning to Tukwan after only one hour in the air. Aeroplane and duck crossed wings in an embrace for the sky. 'There's a fish in the jet engine!' Mackie screamed, throwing away the book on theology that he was reading, and giving Jock a wild look of reproach. 'Well, it's not my fish for sure,' Jock replied moving his guilt up and down his frown. 'But I saw you play draughts with fish and chips with Mr Atta,' Donald said, having banished the tears from his face at last. There was a silence as they listened to the changed sound of the engine. 'You are a complete and fried nut, you Jock the strap you,' Mackie said in disgust, losing his rocket-controlled patience. 'Over, over,' came the sudden message from the S machine, 'reverse the engines and blow the horn for five minutes, and the fish will be expelled.' 'Sometimes you just write your silence,' said the exasperated Babo, with his pen poised over nothing. 'Me I want rice and stew, cassava bread, aboloo, abunabu, expertly-fried forest wood-maggots, pigeon-pea bean leaves, akrantie, the under-thighs of an odum squirrel, waakye and abe-wine, fufu and abenkwan gari foto with tilapia-controlled shitoh, green-green with the freshest plantain, akple, groundnut soup with brown rice, banku and okro soup, nkontommire stew with a koobi interregnum, the red and yellow flare of agushie stew with yam so fresh that it shouldn't be born yet, yoo ke gari, smoked deer joined with akyinkyina kyinkyinga, fresh hawk in guava sauce, woodpigeon so green with maximum pepper, Hausa koko in the morning, kenkey and kyenam with deep-fried shitoh, yam and cassava chips, keta-schoolboys soaked in long pepper and oil with a touch of young shrimp, nkautenkwan with chicken, garden-egg stew with the newest sweet-potato, spinach-bokoboko with okro soup and well-fermented kenkey from Yamoransa, wild duck and kpakpo shitoh, plain-soup with cocoyam fufu . . . aaaaaah, I will die!' enthused Atta with his tongue in a mock hang-out. Jock stared at him with disbelief, and said with force, 'But you didn't mention fish and chips!' Donald, Donald, eat your coconuts with your head out of the plane in the rain, and have a bite of that sugar-bread that, when bitten, reveals the shape of your profile exactly in the bite. The moss and heather seats held the coming sleep, a dead owl rolled off the misty wings.

Kwame Atta was the only one awake, fine man. But the trouble with him, alias Old Science, was that sometimes when he smoked a jot, the smoke never came back out immediately . . . but would five minutes later come out of his excuse me to say tu; and being a rascally man with the pretensions of a gentleman, he often stood with one right leg cocked, with the smoke hissing down out of the trouser of the left leg. He believed in his gradually sobering moments that the best thing for his town was benign brain-washing, brain-spinning, brain-drying, and finally brain-freeing. He had this thought thrice with a coolly ascending akpeteshie, spiritually speaking. Your tu. And the mist landed on the sikadimous chin of the co-piloting Kwame, so that he too fell asleep, completely ignoring the NO SNORING sign, O you sky snooze.

So thus freed from human wakefulness, the termites came out in control; they ate the claws of one crab sleeping, and then eased into the sleeping male brains to interpret them . . . the odum tree had brought goodwill to Mackie by its receding leaves, and had travelled in his head from the forests to the savannas while rain was mixing with tears in his living-room in Levensvale. Mackie was sometimes terrified that when he returned to his own town, he would have changed so much and kept such a passion for Tukwan that he would find everything ridiculous there. He had to reverse part of his soul to avoid this. He would send Shebelda a telefart – the wind was getting serious for the termites – that she should expect a changed man coming . . . no my dearest Margaret I do not mean a change of underwear, pioto in Tukwan I believe . . . This new man would still be quite kind with his jumble of sympathy in the ready pocket – cheaper to have sympathy in the pocket than money, sika ye na – but ready to broaden out in all sorts of ways from food to rhythm. And the termites revealed that Mackie was determined to protect the gains of Tukwan and Levensvale to the death, even though he was a thick-set bushy child of immortality: somebody respected by establishments beyond the borders of Levensvale, but keeping a soul absolutely open, so that no one could accuse him anywhere of loving the Tukwan people either from a position of weakness, no status or as a compensatory factor. Christ! When did a human being, in all his potential glory, have to start explaining his quite neutral fascination for a different way of living! Ewurade of the Akwapim ridge save us . . . And one termite was singing: perhaps after all Mackie was a little deeper than his business pleni-potentiary.

Bbbbut Jock was simpler, literally but not metaphorically fishy, with a physical chip on his shoulder. He came from generations of fish and chip sellers originally from Italy, and he never bothered much about the ludicrous immortalities they spoke of: why be immortal when you can fry fish! Jock had never married because basically he didn't want anything to get between him and deep fat; and the once that he fell in love, with

Jennifer, she had so much sole in her face that he ran into a potato field terrified . . . tottering among the tatties, he later said with his thin knees knocking in percussion. Philosophy was a fry, and so was death. And he sold almost all his fish and chips in Tukwan, but they were bought by only three people: Mr K the magistrate who wanted to retire from beans a bit, Dadoona Tay who wanted different types of fat, fat in grades, and then Dogo himself who bought as much as possible so that fewer people would have the taste for it, and thus his kyinkyinga sales would not be affected at all. Babo had matured with a little withdrawnness, had deepened his pen and chalk with a sad and quiet glare over every available horizon with his very round face; and his strong shoulders touched life at six feet in his chalewate, taller and stronger than his brother except for the latter's superchin. And he was more aggressive about fate than he showed. DonaldonaldonaldonaldOnaldoNaldonAldonaLdonalD just loved coconuts, earthworms, crabs, beetles, ducks, vultures, and now termites, especially those that had just left his brain intact. 'Never fart in the east,' Atta said without thinking, and glaring at the wee Jock, 'and I'm saying this because I've worked it out that your body nearly always keeps the same angle to mine if you take the point in space directly horizontal to you. Fart west, go west kwee, because then it will never blow towards me. How on earth, contrey, do you retain this precision in the angle? You are a fish and chip witch, I swear! And don't forget the geography of the wind, OK?' Jock Small just grunted and fell asleep again.

Nana Bontox the bombole was stuck to the ceiling of the Plantain Hotel living-room, legs dangling. Autumn had become too much and he had jumped to escape the cold, not knowing jack frost would follow and stick him to the ceiling. And there was only one way they could get him down: smoke jots and pipes under his feet until he melted a bit and slid down slowly, back into his royal sandals, saaaa. Kofi Senya had taken to making a new pipe to augment the old, from some deep cuttings of his chalewate, so that when he smoked there was a terrible smell of rubber, too mech. He had to smoke his wooden pipe more often again. Senya couldn't help Bontox at first – no ceiling sympathy – because of this flip-flop chalewate technology of the pipe, but Nana thought his wives . . . 'could be misbehaving because it's so long since they mustbehaving me.' When that kind bird flew away again the pin-pine hedge collapsed, prick. Autumn was in paint, and the pigeons sang woodwind there. 'It's time to go back!' Nana shouted as Pokuaa curtsied her disagreement: 'We are waiting for our travellers to return, and then after the conference, we will go back to the land of the warm breeze.' She was too definite for Nana to raise any serious objection against her. Nana's headgear was in second, he rose to his tea, not thinking it odd that these days he almost always wore his full regalia . . . or rather all of how much of it he brought here, including a golden ring that he claimed belonged to Okomfo Anokye. Nana Kasa the Okyeame supported this claim, and in addition was quite confident that Ananse the mythical spider of absolute reality could easily invent steps that continually veered off their landings, and could fashion a man that walked four steps forward, four steps back but felt that he was making great progress for his town. Nana Kasa had some ideas different from his creation of the long uncut cloth that the elders wore at the meeting on the neon-cross hill at Tukwan: autumn nipped him into letting Aba write this for him: Tukwan was deliquescent and Levensvale was efflorescent, and there was a squirrel with nuts that always tried to pull the two words together.

Babo's chalk written with a pen and held by Amoa in his absence was capable of teaching every town that was not double how to cry, every town that was not double like Levensvale and Tukwan: the more contortions you saw in history the greater your mortality became. But these twists and turns had ceased to come through genetic transformations any more; genetics was finished at Levensvale in the autumn. Change was being created by little actions and little dramas that seemed to be turning time slowly away from its abnormal breaking point now in existence, and towards the sludge of the normal. Jack MacTaggart's sad smile in the bulldozer ceased to go together with its machine, and instead formed one image with a ripple on Loch Divina. Time was speeding up into small spaces and pulling things together from farther and farther away, things that may not have been clearly related in the past at all. Even Pokuaa's duku had fallen down to her neck, and was being periodically unfastened and flown away then returned by seagulls with their great noise. The secret was this: once a town had created the new, it had to allow the new to create value and principle by enforcing its own orthodoxy. And this new orthodoxy became only a framework over which all the ordinary everyday living passed. Kofi Senya would often literally run away from such truths, hoping that moving to a new land would somehow stop the inexorable drift towards mortality, and . . . Ewurade! . . . freedom *within* time. His pipe was choked with remorse: both towns would break the immortal through a process they couldn't stop, simply because they thought that was the only alternative available. Only the mad would find a way to march back into time, as if there was not enough energy to do anything else . . . But never mind Murray sitting behind Nana Bontox: he had grown into a punctuation: his life had become the biggest full-stop in the world, unable to find even a small comma past the whisky that blocked it. There was greater grammar in the bottle. He had been dreaming about the Bishop of Brechin who stood before his congregation with two loaded pistols against the Covenant; for Murray thought it should have been two bottles of gin at least, or some seventeenth-century methylated spirits. Pokuaa had chased away the brazen seagulls around her neck yet again.

There was nothing Kofi Senya could do about these dramas, for they were a transitional phase; and he was trying to prepare himself in advance to get tired of eternity. Amoa was getting rather tired too with the weight of Babo's pen-through-chalk. 'What is the use of Babo now having two pens of chalk? If he had only one, then I wouldn't have the kayakaya job of holding one in his absence koraa!' he said, adding 'And besides I would like to continue with lessons from Appa on driving the aeroplane. I too want to exercise some aerial trotro . . . especially Appa's new trick of dropping passengers by parachute if he was in a hurry to move onto the next destination . . .' Pokuaa smiled at Amoa through the interval of wings, cries and dukus, and said, 'Young Agya Amoa, you are lucky that you don't have to bury people from a height by dropping coffins from an aeroplane into graves already dug. You are too young, but this ritual may come when we reach Tukwan again, and time changes . . .' Kofi Senya looked at Pokuaa with surprise, then looked away again, wondering where she got some of her understanding from; but Amoa didn't understand her, he just groaned under the weight of the pen, and wished that it was real chalk that he could at least nibble at to make it lighter.

Sala was getting more and more scientific: he was trying to design a trap for his father to fall into when he was in the middle of a lecture to him on law. And he was dying to see Donald back to see whether he had changed or not. He had become tired of the famous corset. His current drama was thus: rushing around playing ludo with twelve people on four different boards, and then stopping in the middle of each game – he could always tell the end – and then demanding to know the African nature of the game; and after asking this of the ten children and two grandmothers, he would produce an oware board and play it at the same time as the ludo. 'Let's rush off my dear husband before things get out of hand in this kind town,' Akyaa cried one morning when she felt the intimations of her drama coming: an obsession with supervising the workers of the factories so efficiently that much money had been made already. Azziz was flabbergasted at her success, for he certainly didn't know her for her brains. 'My dear wife, David Mackie will be proud of your work when he returns, I swear. You have made thousands of pounds just by standing beside the workers with your chatter-chatter and your great skin . . . and I didn't know that you had made Aba and Angus your secretaries!' Aba hadn't fallen in love yet with poor Angus, who had decided that in the crisis of her temporal unavailability, she should become an ethereal presence. There was some little angelising going on. Opanin Akorsah's ritual now was his determination to be a rhubarb farmer, for the simple reason that he was missing his cassava farming, and he was outraged by the preparations starting for the Conference: instead of practising rhubarb, he was made to be checking the chairs for the conference. Appa had made £70,000 from the trotro, and was getting sick of the kindness of gentle but sarcastic old ladies in the sky, hopping from cloud to cloud to buy their gooseberries. Kofi Senya had sent the termites to England to devour the highest official there if possible, for there were rumours that an invasion force would soon be sent against Levensvale, after the complaints filed by the Immigratis Officers. But they didn't know that Mackie had the support of fifteen canons, who didn't really know how subversive things were in Levensvale, but who loved it for its irreverence.

But the other canons had not of course yet met Pastor Korner Mensah who had turned out, by the authority of his pioto-risky automatic cassock, to be the most sensational import to Levensvale: he had converted no less than two hundred people to his necklace-hill rock-cross religion; and he had created the pastime of walking hills only in circles. And Korner and his new flock worshipped flat on their stomachs. The pastor was surprising himself because he was more radical here than back home. There was a fervour which captivated and evangelised hard-headed and even dour people. Sometimes the most difficult thing to do was to select the right pitch for a clap, to begin the prostrate worshipping. And Korner was glad because the valleys responded by increasing the level of echo decibel; the echoes doubled the commitment, and an accommodation was made with the old churches by squaring the fervour, halving it, doubling it, and then taking away the number of foundation members from the answer . . . after this what fervour was left was translated into the Presbyterian church without tongues: which meant a fine minimum of ten new members for each established church, awam. The stolen tower too was famous, but was causing concern by growing two inches everyday . . . and in addition its steeple would sometimes crow when the town was asleep. The real cocks would then point to the metal cock on the steeple as the guilty beak that sang at the wrong time, and its feathered equivalents would accuse it of insisting that the dawn be brought to its beak to crow into, lazy iron akoko. Revenge: the steeple speared a cock when it was strutting past with a very high crow . . . after which Korner Mensah cut its metal. Women with early fur coats clapped out of rhythm, but this didn't make any difference to the quality of commitment. There were hundreds of flowers on the necklace hill, and there were only three of the Tukwan people who constantly avoided it: Kofi Senya who never went to any church, Babo and Atta. Church was twice a week, but only the most faithful went the second time. Manu the carpenter had announced that the only way to attract more members was to use his new invention: wooden string, which would pull more members in if required. Wooden string? 'Well, it never breaks,' shouted Manu defiantly, 'and you can move it around with some koko manoeuvrability . . . you can even use it to tie laces in shoes.' And once supposed you could make a cross with it, for the brown Jesus would have enjoyed such string . . . would have loved to see Korner among the brambles, elderberries, chrysanthemums, blueasters and pinkasters, delphiniums, gaillardia, and edelweiss, all artificially planted and nurtured by the side of the hill, and at the same points as the pastor's ears were to his head . . . selected bouts of flower power in the bracken.

Angus and Aba were walking hand in hand through the neat streets. The hand of Angus was warmer than the hand of Aba, and so was his heart; for if you had a heart that was stout – guinness – then you could put up with the inspired indifference of Aba. The streets were so clean, and had so many fine and cleverly planted, cleverly watched weeds that it was being considered that one street-taster should be appointed to lick the streets both in Levensvale and in Tukwan. Angus held a half-finished Guinness bottle to his heart, with a slow burp that went on for a minute. Hear his wind. Down by Hornchurch road a barrow boy was taking pomegranates to the doctor who hadn't yet recovered from his Adowa dancing, and had sworn that next time he would keep to the more vigorous Highland fling. The wooden electric poles had heaped between them mounds of unprocessed salt and gravel in early preparation for the winter; bird dung augmented the heaps, but there was a wonderful absence of the usual dog-drops that fouled the streets in the other counties. A selfish bramble was creeping over itself by a wooden fence, and Great Towers avenue had two tiny escalators that actually moved wild roses full of rose-hips in and out of the closes; one or two tenements were bent in the middle in a deliberate bow to the sky which held only nostalgic woodsmoke. 'I'm sure we already have computers to read the taste of salt,' Angus said inconsequentially. His forefinger nail was far smaller than Aba's, but that didn't stop him from making a small dig with it on her wrist. She withdrew her hand but not her smile. 'And an eyelash-lengthening service too exists. Is it not our link with you that will stop this sort of nonsense . . .' 'Angus my old croo, but we have the stupidity machine . . .' ventured Aba. 'Yes but it eats lizards and mosquitoes!' exclaimed Angus, 'which means you have kept your link with the earth around you; and look at your moss and heather seats and all . . .' Footpath number 70 reluctantly crossed footpath number 69. Aba and Angus saw the termites come back from England, carrying a hat, which meant they were successful in their mission of devouring the top official with no extenuating hiccups. The nettles looked extremely flat under the horse's belly.

The success of the factories had already created one new business: a Pubic Hair Stylist, who insisted on his right to be outrageous, and that his business was done in the private anyway. Mortality was coming indeed . . . Sheer Murdoch! was the name of the new entrepreneur. His former business had been arranging meat and creating myths out of mussels from Loch Divina . . . where at this very moment there was a solar display group of senior citizens sunning themselves, for there was nothing wrong with tanning your arthritis in autumn. And there was Murdoch's house with its tartan windows and pebble dashing. Angus usually wondered whether his heart was a rush-hour among the peace around it. And you could see Ma Hol's roses as big as your head, nodding at the sheepskin leather sale that would start at the weekend. Mrs Darling L's tarts were getting quite popular because she would put some soul in them free. Smell the very middle of the scone. 'But Angus, what is that kitikiti dot on the horizon?' asked Aba straining her eyes beyond the hills. Angus made an appropriate squint too. 'O, it's the plane, it's the plane!' shouted Angus. 'And O my god, I'm sure they don't know that Ed Gilmour has moved the tarmac to another place, and planted raspberries there instead . . . we must flash them a message!' Angus and Aba rushed through the town shouting, 'The plane, the plane, have they finished the new tarmac . . .' And Pokuaa ordered the wildest rush to complete the new tarmac – constructed against her wish, but supported by the Levensvale people themselves, for they were dying for raspberries just on that very spot. Ed Gilmour was sweating, full of remorse: what would Mackie say about the tarmac-turning raspberries? And would Jack MacTaggart finish the new tarmac in time . . . or perhaps if the worst came to the worst, the plane could land on top of fresh young raspberries . . . Mackie had already realised what was happening, and was circling angrily over the uncompleted tarmac; and then he burst out laughing to Atta: 'We seem to spend our time landing on new and hastily constructed tarmacs!' Atta raised his eyes to the clouds. 'There, I can see Sala already!' shouted Donald. 'And who the hell has opened the door of my shop?' Jock asked in great agitation, 'I was rejoicing at seeing the heather again, and then somebody gets my dander up by daring to open the door to my sole.' There were spaniels and terriers dashing among the crowd below. MacTaggart almost broke his wife's memory, so fragile, to complete the tarmac. Everybody was waving! – even Akorsah, for he wanted to hop right back on the plane to return to his cocoa wife. Appa came with his nods, shivering his plane with them, and then on a wild impulse, landed right on top of Mackie's circling plane. There was a great roar. 'Land in the conference, it's just starting! Land in the conference!' shouted Amoa with his smile bigger than Babo's chalk.

CLASS ELEVEN

So it was to the two-storey Conference of the humanity, the head and the heart that the lower-lip jet was late; the ground floor was physical, and the other two floors were spiritual, created as wind by Kofi Senya. The aeroplane landed in the opening prayer, preceded by preparations for libation. But it had to free itself first as a mere dot in the perceptions of Aba and Angus, when their eyes were up at the horizon. It thus burst into being over the Plantain Hotel. Pokuaa was under the smoky brown and golden leafed Levensvale sky, and she was agitated: it was painful to start the conference without the travellers, but she just could not wait for the jet: some guests were already in from ordinary time. With the arrival of Babo and co, libation had to be poured. And the gin took the frost quite well. When they were all trying to hug each other, the plane got in the way, so some had to hug a wing, a nose, a bot, or the fuselage instead . . . some unplanned metal embracing. There were so many fine fresh bananas brought by the travellers from Tukwan to increase the chew in the soul that many had a short problem: they could only conceive each other, greet each other, laugh together through the perspective of bananas. There were so many extra skins as the conference slid into gear. There were delegates from Accra, Glasgow, and Kumasi, much to everyone's surprise; but Mackie had been bold, with the help of Pokuaa and Senya: new passports had to be issued, and they had to be ferried across the murky waters of mortality, bang into the living scales of Levensvale and Tukwan. 'I hope it's not going to be just a booklong chatta show,' complained Akyaa, who was often being looked at when she was walking her shoogly walk. Big conference, amaala agbo kpendwe. Accra was foko, nae tother aball, and could have pepper put in its bot easily if it misbehaved; Kumasi was nothing, twiaaa. RUN, Run to the conference! Take tiger-nuts there! The conference was maternal: everything was being looked after, including the flowers: there were, according to Angus, chrysanthemummies and jasmamas. Run, run, run! For goats were running, local governments were running, Fords and liberation theologies were running, squirrels and factories. Run! Do as the Amoas do, run! Do as the Daimlers do, run! Do as Opanin Akorsah does . . . crawls to the conference reluctantly, for he had reached his optimum of angry homesickness. Run with the hidden ancestors past Akorsah . . . and right into Timmy Tale the fair, brown anthropologist born of a Brong father and a Renfrew mother, Tale so excitable that he would fit into a champagne bottle and burst out early. He was at present holding his own waist in exasperation because someone or other had wished him good morning with a nod instead of a smile. Everything was cool against his fire . . . the coolest being Canon Burns who alternated between a deep gravity, and an uncontrollable desire for tea, some doctrinal tea-mania; being sometimes so grave that his nod was a funeral at your feet. Tale was temporarily in Accra, Burns was in Glasgow, and the third person from outside was Kofi Fofie, an ex-aplankey from Kumasi, a young man who had reached but refused to touch twenty years, feeling he deserved to be older. He ended up at the conference by mistake: being an ex-ancestral wizard, he was flying across continents to seek the comfort of a new grave, when the crow he was transporting himself on died over Levensvale, and he in turn fell irrevocably down. He was ex-everything, and had been advised by Kofi Senya to represent Kumasi with his jaw at the conference, so that he would be an ex-delegate too.

'You can't bath in the conference,' Akyaa was telling the newly-arrived Kwame Atta, who was insisting that he had to bath there and then, so he didn't miss anybody's mouth. 'If you want to bath here, then you can have the words for your water,' Akyaa continued, 'and besides all the other travellers have gone to bath their memories of the journey; and you alone want to reveal everything raw-raw to us. Grow up Kwame Atta!' Atta swaggered towards her, and then crept boldly backwards out of the hall, out of her cooling logic and into the bathroom of the Mackies, where he almost saw Shebelda's breasts by accident, but didn't. Meanwhile the Lord Provost couldn't speak for the enormous banana in his mouth, but having been assured that his mouth was capable of devouring it, swallowed the banana under a general motion: 'We move that the Lord Provost may swallow the culprit fruit immediately.' His opening remarks would have the flavour of bananas, undoubtedly, thought Gilmour. And LT had taken it upon himself to interview Kofi Fofie for any credentials that he may or may not find. 'Do you have any idea about the general trend of eternity at this moment, and did you manage to enter through the barrier of immortality here by wizardry or by divine intervention, or you just gave some schnapps to an inquisitive ancestor and he fixed you up sharp?' Kofi Fofie just answered, 'Yes sah boss.' LT went on full steam behind: 'Do you have the intellectual equipment to destroy the primitive purveyors of racism, or do you just live your disagreement with them?' Kofi Fofie just answered, 'Yes sah boss.' Lawyer Tay glared at him with a puzzled squint, and then decided to change his tactics by imitating Fofie: 'Yes sah boss,' said LT. And Kofi Fofie saw his chance: 'Chief, me I think your questions they come from the book of abe, they make proper palm-nut matter. Me I'm not booklong koraa. I dream wizardryyyy, paa. But I hear them say in Kumasi that the world ibi come to an end for a town called Tukwan, ship-sharp! But me I came here to look-aaaa for pure water from Scotland. I fall off my dead crow too mech. And if you want me to take some message back to everybody at Kumasi then tell me quick. I go fly soon midnight, Yes sah boss.' LT adjusted his kente gown, and then declared, 'The interview, I close now now now.' 'YES SAH BOSS!' someone else shouted over the microphone. LT jumped over his Law in disgust, and sat down prominently in a corner. 'But have you finished holding your round-round waist, sir,' the comnipresent Akyaa asked Timmy Tale. He looked at her for a long time, and snarled, 'Young woman, if you are not careful, I may be forced to define you!'

The entering Atta jumped onto Tale's agitation: 'Contrey, I can see your mouth is a book, but let us calm down small with a brotherly smoke. I am very free with your brother the magistrate from Tukwan. I understand you have different fathers . . . very Ghanaian. Put that in your anthropology . . .' Timmy Tale leapt at the throat of Atta inexplicably. There was an uproar as the two men rolled on the floor, with the jot burning a hole in Atta's trousers and a hole in Tale's shirt. After they were separated – with Atta roaring with laughter, especially through the jot hole of his trousers – Tale rushed into some semi-tatale treatise about the need to abolish sociology altogether and substituting anthropology, and not vice versa. 'There is something like roots!' he would shout, in his yellow jacket, with a cream shirt, cream trousers and cream shoes, all dirtied in the scuffle. 'I will never put decorum above energy,' was another of Timmy's sayings. Kwame took to Timmy straight away but was disappointed to find out that Tale did not drink, Koraa. The two of them nevertheless shared a bond of utter scorn, alleviated somewhat by furtive looks of mutual admiration. 'There goes mr yellow jacket coat with his head in Glasgow, Legon, and Oxford,' Atta would shout sarcastically. Tale would snort back, 'Ah the scientist with a chin so strong that the legs can't support them, but the drink can. Wake up!' 'You hold your waist too much, that's your trouble!' would come Atta's reply. Eventually Akyaa assigned the two of them different seats so the canon was finding his way to Pastor Mensah. They both stared at each other's cassocks, Korner Mensah's decorated with bells and beads and still automatic; by the time Mensah had uttered two sentences, it had changed its length four times. They embraced through the nod of Burns and the smile of Korner, but the theology remained stuck to their cassocks: 'I understand the bells on your cassock have established a doctrinal relationship between God in history and God in eternity, through a concept of music and Art in general as intrinsic doctrine,' Canon Burns said rather slowly and drily, trying hard to retain the morgue in his mouth. Pastor Korner stared through the memory of his theological schools, and wondered exactly what experience this tall dour man standing before him had behind his words, then replied, 'The atentenben and the odrogya speak to God directly, through that old African belief that worship is joy . . . please excuse me while I attend to my last sip of Guinness. I swear one day I'll theatricalise God in a bottle before I realise that it's the wrong ablutions I'm doing . . . have you ever danced before the dead?' 'Gentlemen of the cloth, gentlemen! Surely you are wasting your words . . . keep them for the real talking that is following through the microphone,' Pokuaa said with a laugh, coming between Mensah and Burns. Burns turned to his Earl Grey tea, and brushed his hair down with a grave nod. Mensah bowed to Pokuaa ostentatiously, then resumed his smiling. A smell of tobacco and aftershave seemed to emphasise the Canon's chin. Burns gave the impression that he was born to be a bishop, and he always loved the experience, the speed of bypassing Presbyterianism, and ending up panting in the ritual inn of the Episcopacy. Anglicanism added some panache to his kommm tempera- ment, and his bright small wife added even more. He was therefore surrounded by a style and ritual that he had very little of himself. Nevertheless he rejoiced in his own way in his acres of apples and hothouse tomatoes at the rectory. Gladly he was here to represent the other nine canons, for he was especially fond of the adventurous Mackie, Mackie the friend of priests who found him worldly, discerning, and with the right touch of the unconventional. They always thought his life moved faster than he revealed, correct. Korner Mensah was addressing a group of his Levensvale flock, while Burns stared on, intrigued by the fact that a complete stranger had come to this land and increased church membership, even with his bells. And imagine Burns dancing before the dead, I ask you . . . he would rather slip quietly into the box with them.

Jock had been annoyed with Angus because the latter had bumped into him when he was trying to bring his fresh fishery chippings to the conference early. It was all because Angus was concentrating on trying to surreptitiously kiss Aba's elbow, while his lips had cobwebs on them: he had brushed these lips against a spidery wall while conceiving his lips-to-elbow plan; and when the deed was in the midst of being done, Jock spoilt it with his bumping entry of fish and chips. Each blamed the other. But this didn't stop Aba from dragging the head of poor Angus to the mirror in the conference toilet, and triumphantly pointing out the cobwebs more copious on the upper lip than on the lower lip. 'And don't let your words be spiders again after this!' she stormed at him. Angus, in the full view of the conference, suddenly stood on his hands in defiance, and shouted to Aba, 'But how much love do you want to see, lassie, before you just think about returning the weeest bit!' At first there was dead silence, for this scene was an interruption of Tommy Rae the Lord Provost's opening remarks. Then followed the laughter and the roaring, against which Aba stood stiff and indifferent, fingering a small crab. And beside her and the remorseful Angus stood a statue with no eyes, without any lookability at all, for when you see eternity too much, your eyes get finished. Outside, Mackie had a little crisis: the apple trees were demanding the aeroplanes to take them further south as agreed, before the onset of the frost. 'Everything waits for the conference,' insisted Mackie, laying a piece of friendly tweed on each tree to calm it. And the breeze spoke for the trees: package some sunshine-bi and everyone and everything will stay, even beyond the conference. The breeze ducked under a hedge and vanished with a moan. The morning became exceedingly grey, just what Babo loved to think in.

Pamela the Daughter-Lord-Provost was standing with a bouquet of flowers, waiting to give it to Pokuaa at the right time, that is when she gave her kindest most mellow smile. Pamela and Pokuaa were tight friends of course, confreres at the conference, sharing an openness to life that Pokuaa hoped her little friend would keep. With all this going on, Kofi Senya had been amazing twice: he was perched on the eaves, and then he was perched on his own pipe with his vulture, while he was still smoking it. Timmy Tale was refusing to believe what he saw, trying to angle his long brown legs across the roars of joy to stop them. 'Don't dare tell us to believe what we have just seen, ladies and gentlemen!' he shouted, 'Are we here to perceive tricks or to deal with time within a different clock? Do the two towns have any protocol for unity? I deplore the fact that we had to get new passports to come here. And extended family or no extended family, I don't believe that working with antecedents means the same as having decent uncles . . .' 'My dear lad,' interrupted the Lord Provost irritably, 'if you must talk nonsense try and make it an orderly nonsense that we can all under-stand . . .' Tale glared at Chairman Provost the Lord, but the latter's pipe puffed back at him with an easy equanimity. And again Angus was in trouble with Aba: she was sleeping against him, without any such realisation whatsoever, and Angus was finding this unbearable; beside him sat Canon Burns looking stiffly into the afternoon sky overcast with all the actors of the conference; and this was Angus's trouble: being so excited at Aba's closeness, he eyed a rare glass of cider beside the canon on a low table, and he could do nothing as his popylonkwe rose to the left erect and knocked over the glass. The canon, who had seen all that had happened, said not a word, and thanked God instead for sending him little incidents to heighten his ability to hold his nose up in the air at life. Angus Mackie immediately tamed his popylonkwe with a slap, hoping that no one saw him . . . but his eyes just met the glare of Aba looking at him with one eye open. Having looked at Canon Burns carefully to see whether he saw anything or not, Aba too arranged her nose in the air at exactly the same angle. Angus excused himself to stamp angrily among the pines. Jock the zero had nothing now, for he had sold all his fish and chips, and his trousers rustled with pound notes. Canon Burns moved to another seat, right between Azziz and Korner Mensah. He lowered his nose.

The afternoon progressed with a chilly rain. Babo's chalk was wet and shivering in his hand, for he had gone out to assess the grey of the sky to see whether it fitted his mood even better outside than inside; and in his old briefcase brought from Tukwan were souls, reincarnated ancestors, a daytime moon, the history of Tukwan, and very hot yam and chofi. There was a pause inside, and Lawyer Tay slipped his bulk into it: 'Can we discuss God's power in a quadratic equation? for my son wants to carry his science and maths further. What do we mean by quadrupled happiness when the scientist is trying to define the sorrows of the universe? I don't want any bogus inventor like Kwame Atta to attempt to answer the unanswerable . . . besides you either have to mathematicalise the theologians or theologise the mathematicians. I couldn't care less either way. I just want the question answered now.' 'Stick to your law,' Atta growled, sauntering off with a wink at the Canon, whose eyes stared very straight still, for he had never winked before, at least not since he was eight years old. The Lord Provost had now finished his opening remarks, and was having his sweat wiped off his brow by his daughter. He had not tripped publicly for some time, which was fitting for a man with much natural dignity. But he was being bothered by something else: whenever he raised his finger in authority during his last two meetings in the Council gardens, there was either a tiny beetle or a midgie on it. So he wouldn't dare raise his fist for some bigger creature to land on. He therefore winked as the new fashion of authority; for, after all, the success of the factories had made the gift of an African cooler even cooler beside him on the table, he knew Mackie's controlled madness to be useful.

Then the chairs scraped, bumped each other, and halved the conference: those who believed – by the windows with the holly staring in – that they had some sort of head remained UP; and those who felt their hearts were enough went DOWN. 'I insist that I'm head-head enough to be up pronto,' shouted Amoa with his scunner showing. 'Besides, anyone who can learn how to fly an aeroplane in one hour is a bookbook man true!' 'All right all right, take care, take care young Amoa,' said Atta with a pat on Amoa's head. 'If you can answer this coming question, then you can join the booklong people: what is the best way to stop this land here from over-inventing? Is it better to fill the void with an ascending world of spirits, ancestors, gods, sunsum, and owls, that is worlds that make it more difficult to touch the outer and dissect it? Or do you pretend that the spiritual is dead and then walk the wastes of the universe, spreading gadgets with some courage but leaving receding bits of yourself so that in the end there's nothing left of you, but you leave a vast empire as a monument to nothing? C'mon, sharp-sharp, me-you-you, you-me-me.' 'Yes sah boss,' came in

Kofi Fofie who had a passion for interviews that he hated. While he was interrupting Amoa slipped UP the conference and sat imperiously by Korner Mensah, the founder of the double theological school in Accra, with a shrine as an annexe. Fofie continued, 'Chief, I'm looking for a new crow ntemtem, I want to go back to eating fufuo with bigibigi beef. They are telling me to go to the lower end of this bambala room. Me, I will commot my Bible and read you wizard sense one time, no play. Me I answer your lingo kasa to Amoa: break up all the land here and break up all the land there, join them tam! and then leave all the crows to me, I swear.' Kofi Fofie was carried forcibly to the lower half of the hall by the chairs themselves. Could he get a lift to Kumasi from a jackdaw please, after he had eaten haggis and chips?

'You people have shattered me!' began Timmy Tale, 'I have not seen my magistrate brother for years not since he left the big towns in disgust, shouting that he was going to the end of the world. And I had not been to Ghana for at least ten years before now. But how have you managed to build up such fantastic lives here almost secretly in Scotland, and then secretly in Tukwan too? How have you been hiding from the governments? Does your reincarnation create magic? How? Is this what happens when you squeeze up time and soul? How did you manage to tame technology and make it so human? WHO ARE YOU ALL, for God's sake!' There was silence. Tale was shaking alone in the middle of the upper conference 'Dance, dance,' shouted Atta with glee, 'dance the mystery away, and you'll feel better! After all, what do you want to solve?' Tale walked slowly over to Kofi Senya, high up in the caves, looked up to him, and said, 'I congratulate you for being their soul, but can you give me any secrets for my next book? I rejoice to agree with you that their so-called world religions are a matter of culture and not necessarily truth. Just because you have millions worshipping in one way, doesn't mean that one hundred people worshipping another way have less truth. No!' There was another silence, banana.

Canon Burns rose cane-straight sugar, and said sadly, but with a strange mutely agitated strength in his voice, 'I don't believe you have to destroy established religions to prosper . . . there is a promising affinity between the concept of eschatology, and the doctrine of ancestorisation, each being a point in time within different sectors of human history. The more you appreciate other ways, the bigger and better your own becomes . . .' He gave one heavy nod, but Korner Mensah took up the second nod immediately: 'Yes, canon, yes, but help us with the established churches: tell us how much blood they have on their hands, how many betrayals they have caused; please take some statistics of the number of priests that have been racists over the centuries; let us know how often the churches have turned their backs on their true duties. I had a brother once living in the land of London, and he went faithfully to a church for three months; and for these three months, the priest never said a word to him, and once this priest even moved off ostentatiously when it reached my brother's turn to shake his hand. Ewurade Nyankopon! And such a creature has a naming called priest! And even under the beauty of this same sunset that serves all human beings, there was a bishop of the Anglican church somewhere in this Britain that allegedly had sympathy for the ku klux klan. If God had a handkerchief he would cry into it. For Him to see the calibre of most of the men that are running His churches – His? who said? – would make even one hundred handkerchiefs not enough for the crying! And who said the churches had to make compromises with racism and nazism in the so-called real world? Now, my dear canon, what I hate most is this: some churchmen think that the toughest thing to do is to come to compromise with the evil ways of the world, in order to survive. How evil can a church get! You send charity to African children, and then invest millions in a racist system that destroys human beings. You think you are the leader of a very big church, so all you do is some vast public relations with the terror of the oppressed, and about once every few years you come out with some cheap condemnation of some racism somewhere, and you think it's enough. Buei!

'And of course you have your cultivated men and priests who think there's a fine style to intimations of racial superiority. And these intimations come out in extraordinarily messy knots: from the same man or woman you can get the sadism and the brutality, then you get the desire to patronise, then you get the feeling of being charitable to so-called inferior beings, then there's the desire to enter a relationship not deep and on your own terms entirely, and then you have the belief that there's not the subtlety to understand your culture fully, and then there's the physical avoidance, and then you have the feeling that they dare not interfere in your lives, after which you wonder why God created them in the first place, and then when you can't get a biological reason for the so-called backwardness then you look for cultural reasons . . . of course economic ones can't possibly exist, and then you think of the pure English, yes even Scottish, way of life and wonder how many hordes were polluting it . . . My God of great and fiery justice, judge them all! Now my dear Canon Burns, where do you fit into all this? Forgive my passion, but if this is a conference, then it has to have the truth told in conference style. Are you with humanity, or are you not? Are you with the sly and clubby murderers or are you not? Every age should choose the horrors it can deal with, and the most primitive horror now is the racist. Your racism is easy killing: you kill a man for his skin, you disgrace him for his skin, you kill him for no motive at all. And then to top it all in great gari style, you hate the victim even more for making you feel guilty about all this! Yieeee! God help us with history, God better join and judge us in history, for he will have no time to judge us out of it! And our two towns must give each other the greatest thanks for having none of this terrible nonsense with us, none of this horror, none of this assault on the colour of the soul, none of this sly tearing of the spirit!'

Korner Mensah suddenly lay prostrate, licking the reflection of his own tongue in the polished floor and saying prayers in the fashion of his new Necklace Church. Standing above him with a profound stillness was Canon Burns, neglecting the questions he was asked, but holding his hands in prayer also, his spectacles reflecting in his fragrant tea. He was deeply shaken, not because he felt he was guilty of fitting the pastor's speech, but because he wanted to cry at two things: at Korner's tears on the floor, and then at the terrible inaction that he felt his church was caught in. When he felt considerably moved, he always had an urgent desire to have simpler experiences running through his vulnerable inner. The outer could always be tea, a sale of work, a synod, early services, Sunday lunch at a parishioner's house, youth work, ecumenical communion, an appearance or two on television, a visit to Iona every quarter, a single jump to America that hadn't been repeated, and a recital or two for some faithful friends. Now he stood there, the calm fury of his hands not at all reflecting in his cooling tea; and for some reason he had been given two saucers, perhaps one for the turmoil in himself, and the other for the tea of life, for the support of a suddenly overflowing cup. 'But pastor,' said an incongruously beaming Atta, 'surely you have thrown too much at our lugubriously happy priest of stylish dog-collars! He does not look as if the funeral on his chin would allow any sins of the skin koraa. It's now that he is beginning to control his shuddering. You are forcing him to take on the sins of a double-full load of notorious and evil characters who need help: anyone who dismisses or kills a man or feels that the man deserves the way he's being treated, needs not only justice and counter-attack but pity too . . . but surely we are not here for race. Besides the bananas and whisky are getting depleted, O you dear diplos!' When Atta turned round to give the canon a pat he found him absent.

Canon Burns had moved to the centre of the upper conference, still staring at the horizontal form of Korner Mensah. He said in his slow deep voice, 'I have a very old ear for pulpits, I hear what the flock feels as I deliver the words down with that dark manner of mine. I try to make my heart simple many times over so that I can bear the load it carries. But that load is nothing before the shocking crucifixion of the skin that my brother down there was talking about. The Lord gave the different skins!' '. . . and let him protect them then!' shouted Amoa with the confidence of a man of recently double reincarnation. Canon Burns said nothing any more. He just stood there, and he gave way to the sudden impulse to wave to the whole conference, and the whole conference waved back. 'All they are interested in is making goodness glam glamo glamoro glamorous,' said Opanin Akorsah as he avoided a collision with his arch enemy Lawyer Tay. The two of them would never be collinear in life, Akorsah thought, adjusting his Adinkra cloth over his shoulder, cloth in the frost, and he could give anybody the cold shoulder. Pastor Korner Mensah rose from his prostrate berth, his hand above his prostate gland, his tears all finished, and his pioto-short cassock glowing.

'Lunch will be served including brussels sprouts, yam chips, and keta-schoolboys in shitoh,' announced Jock, graduating with a skip beyond fish and chips, and surprising everybody with the store of keta-schoolboys that he brought from Tukwan dried. Timmy Tale had trapped a corner and was talking into it: 'Life itself is one big translation, so I don't really mind whether I speak Engkish or Twi, any lingua franca can do, but the worry starts when all the moral lingo is fracas, when our basis for talking of the good is all gone, when the choice is ultimately between saving a child somewhere or saving an extra pint of beer here for the belly; and of course such a choice exists within a poor society too. Is your Tukwan a poor society? You want to talk generally about life, and I want to talk quite specifically about the two towns. Ampa. I have retained elements of the language. In what year do you exist? How do you achieve your reincarnation? Is your reincarnation related to the morality of the life lived? Has one human being seen another being reincarnated? Do you have a limited number of coffins for the type of lives you lead? How did the link come to be established between Tukwan and Levensvale? How did you manage to be so ordinary in such extraordinary circumstances? At what precise point did you break through time, become immortal, or kill racism? Who are the guiding geniuses of the two towns? When did you . . .' Babo quickly called to Dr Timmy Tale to stop his questions since they were actually making him dizzy: Babo's chalky pen usually wrote the events, wrote the answers, but not the questions. 'And besides, you can address yourself to three people: Kofi Senya, Pokuaa and Mackie.' But Tale was not even listening . . . sometimes he can get so angry at the world that he holds his own collar in fury, in a self-induced makola suspension. He had his own answers very often to his own questions. Even though he was an anthropologist, he believed that ultimate solutions were usually modern. He felt justified in this because of his obsessive fear that any subject of the anthropologist was in great danger of extinction . . . as if anthropology was ultimately archaeology. And then Oxford and Glasgow had some ludicrous views about him: some of them thought that his irascible energy was self-protective and just a matter of having a chip on his shoulder; it was as if you had to show extraordinarily expressive confidence before your gifts were accepted as a human being's gifts, nonsense! They looked at him at random, whether with a plus on Tuesdays or with a minus on Wednesdays. And to survive, he often had to chase them out of the mathematics. Tale's next question: 'What sort of a conference is this with such loose themes?' Atta looked at his friend and replied, 'your fly is just as loose, sir!'

'I must count myself astonished at these proceedings,' the Lord Provost said to the lower conference, 'even though those of us in eternity do not experience surprise very often. I can't understand how the chairs managed to divide the conference thus . . . Pamela my dear, wipe my brow again . . . and of course we must recognise that the upper and lower are merely geographical terms!' Tommy Rae the civic boss then made his way fast to attend to matters of state; but not without David Mackie exchanging a felicitous wink with him, at their mutual success. Hurray to the different cultures! but the wink was dangerous: Mackie found himself with Rae's eye, and Rae found himself with Mackie's eye. They both looked squint for a few seconds; but then the winks closed properly again. The lower conference had been discussing the beauty of each Brussels sprout, wondering whether it was possible to use them as golf balls. Jock was so sorry that his soul would be in sauce for a few minutes when he died; he had even decided to fry his will instead of writing it. Now there he was sitting near Azziz who was sullenly wondering whether his pretty wife was becoming too successful in this cold place. 'Can't we talk about God just as they are doing UP there?' asked Shebelda possibly to make the conversation flow. 'OK, OK, God on the menu!' shouted Appa still smelling of aeroplanes, 'God in the chop-bar! How can we talk about God when mr Jock prefers to give a very brik disquisition on the genetic properties of the onion . . .' 'Leave me out of the onions of God,' wee Jock growled. 'Besides, it's Brussels sprouts that the divine prefer these days, in the absence of ball-rolled bokoboko.' 'Please get your last pronunciation correct mr Jock,' continued Appa regardless and relentless. 'Now who on earth is talking about the Annunciation in the lower and jazzy conference where matters that are obviously syncopatory and pentatonic are in the fashion . . .' said Mackie sweeping the sudden pause at his arrival out of his mouth. Shebelda wanted to bring him an umbrella for his words. 'It is highly dangerous for businessmen to wax lexical,' said the portly LT strolling his mouth around. 'Please gentlemen, do not mix the conference! The chairs are getting restless, and will soon be moving buttocks about by force again,' complained Akyaa. Pokuaa was sitting in the middle of the conference, listening to the long and secret fears of Timmy Tale: he was outraged to discover that his popylonkwe was the same size as his tongue, and he thought his genes should be sued in a court of rational genetics, African if possible. He says your tu. 'Now isn't my wife very very sweet in this good Scotland here?' Azziz asked no one in particular, but was hoping that someone would disagree so that Akyaa could end back up in his syncronous orbit again, merely by having her success unrecognised. Sala and Donald and the other boys and grandmothers moved in and out of the conference with worms, chestnuts, and crabs that Aba caught for them, discarded corsets of historical importance, and sarcastic remarks that the microphone refused to amplify. The three grandmothers added age to everything . . . especially since they knew that very soon they would be reincarnated into beautiful young ladies with cymballaceous hips, clash. 'Ladies and gentlemen, may I have your attention please. I have the pleasure to announce something important,' droned Ed Gilmour into the microphone, 'I wish to announce that profits from our joint businesses so far amount to more than one million pounds each town, not including the aerial transport service . . .' There was a huge roar, and Mackie wanted to look up thankfully at the sky, but when he did, he couldn't: the ceiling got in the way. 'Ah, I will be able to afford different grades of momoni back home,' beamed Atta, widening his big eyes, and substantiating the size of his face with another small smile.

Amoa the temporary renter of the coffin went up to the microphone and shouted, 'We of the lower conference . . .' 'But what is this boy doing? He ran to the upper conference, and now he's identifying himself with . . .' Opanin Akorsah whined. 'Ah, forgive me,' continued Amoa, 'forgive me, I didn't know there was such upper rubbish, so now I am in with the akpeteshie of the lower orders . . . We of the lower conference announce that we recognise that God the Nyankopon is an Appeals Court, and that He is usually Supreme even before the appeal has been heard; and because of this I move . . .' '. . . my bowels!' interjected Appa the Glee. '. . . I move that we come out with separate recommendations to the sky. I also insist that Appa should never ask me to get out of an aeroplane in mid-air again to push . . . have you ever heard of such a something? Pushing a plane in the sky to start it! My first resolution is that we should go back to 99 houses at Tukwan, and retain our immortality . . .' 'Hold it young Amoa, hold it! You are going too fast. We have some distinguished delegates in both the lower and the upper conference. You can't speak for them just like that, Alleluya,' said Pastor Mensah suddenly rushing off into a corner to increase his aggregate of prayers for the two towns. Canon Burns went up to him, waited until he had finished his prayers, and then held his arm and whispered low, 'Can we build a church together on the hill, and utilise the tower there?' 'What a wise and open man you are!' Korner said to Burns, almost lifting the latter off his feet, 'I agree, I agree double. And then we must build one in Tukwan too!' There was an ominous pause, after which the canon added, 'But I want them to be Episcopal churches. Anglican.' There was a much longer pause, as Pastor Mensah's face changed to one of bewilderment. 'Impossible,' was what the pastor said. The two men faced each other with the longest look. 'You know I represent the canons . . .' Burns said. 'Yes,' replied Mensah, his cassock colours dimming with sadness, 'Yes, I know. But I want the freest church possible.' 'Then I must go,' Canon Burns declared, taking off his glasses, but leaving the sorrow in his eyes, 'the canons will communicate with you.' Burns went to look for

David Mackie, who when told, screamed at the canon that surely the buildings should go up and that what was wrong if they were not Anglican. But Burns insisted, and left eternity with his special passport. He was going back to his bright wife to glean some reasonableness from her for his view on the churches; but he was worried about Korner's sorrow and Mackie's anger. Mackie had influence.

The old spaniel of the Gilmours was moving round the conference, barking every time there was a blatant contradiction anywhere. The taped cries of the wild pigs and other animals of Tukwan had not yet been played by Babo, since the travails of the travellers, on their way to Tukwan. The logic-sensitive spaniel barked most when Pastor Mensah made some sudden sortie into a fervour about the need to 'change our minds a little while we are here' by trying to mathematicalise God sharp. He went on: 'Be patient my country people and my cousins of these cold lands. You see, if a woman has no turning point on a curve, if she doesn't coordinate her love for a geometric God, then of course she will end up with negative values. We can express it like this . . . no, no, be patient, I said like this:

$$\frac{dy}{dx} = \frac{1}{x^2 \ln x} + \left(\frac{1}{x}\right) = 0 = \text{God is any number}$$
$$\downarrow$$

BARK!　　　　　　Rain-wet dove here.
$$\downarrow$$
$$= 0$$

Perch on your religion
for there are innumerable pigs
on the way to salvation　　$=$

$$= \frac{d2}{d\,x\,2} = \frac{2}{x\,3}$$

BARK!　　$\left(1 - \ln x + \frac{1}{x\,2}\left(-\frac{1}{x}\right)0,\right.$

when x = e,
and e is eternity
Your jollyjolly is the sum of all pineapples,
Your Jesus is emo tuo on cold Sundays.
$$\downarrow$$

$\frac{1}{x\,2}\left(1 - \ln x = 0\right)$ with x = 1, x = e !!
$$\downarrow$$

God is an African with a tama and a tammy in his hands.
BARK BARK ! = 0

After this you may relegate me back to the pines of my tower and necklace hill, prompt. But it's all love I speak from. I am disappointed in the inability of Canon Burns to move outside his own church.'

And there was Atta outside the conference window, making an experiment: he had half a Vauxhall moving on half an engine, and two side wheels. Termites had choked the carburettor, but a third chamber had been created with a frog's skin. A goat supported the other half of the semi-Vauxhall, cleanly. Scones were passed round, up the conference, down the conference. They were all looking at Atta then at Korner Mensah. What on earth were these two bringing the towns after all? 'I vote that we stop all the experiments since we have some money now, we should *live* on the ideas we have now,' said Manu the carpenter, abolishing his wooden string in a sudden decision. 'Nonsense boogie!' shouted Amoa. 'Double nonsense boogie!' reshouted Appa. 'I agree with the young men,' Kofi Senya said in one of his rare interruptions, 'the big advantage we have – and we have arranged this advantage with this town too, with Mackie's help – is that we have turned our time into cycles: if you go too slow, one cycle will catch up with you; if you go too fast you will bump into another cycle that is not ready for you. But we have yet to solve the biggest trouble: as soon as you enjoy the success of these cycles, then you are in danger of losing your immortality. So the old problem that the gods tested us with has not been solved merely because we have solved another one! And I would like to go back to the shrine at Tukwan. It looks as if any other problem that arises here must be solved from Tukwan . . .' 'But how can you go without us,' said Pokuaa hastily. Her brow looked more worried than her mouth. 'But I would still like to go back to the shrine!' Senya repeated, showing an agitation that was not customary, 'I feel something in my bones.' There were shared silences, the deepest one coming from Pokuaa. 'But the stupidity machine is there shaping things,' Atta said with some pride in his invention. 'Some of the soul I've given it, has to be renewed,' Kofi Senya declared flatly. 'Now what is Papa Senya saying? Is he saying that anything I invent, he must give some soul to? Now why should he do this without telling me? Is he telling me that there is a dimension to my science that I do not know? So the soul is getting finished in the stupidity machine indeed! I would like to see the mechanics and the electronics finishing too! Memmaaaaeeeii! they now want to pollute my science!'

'Calm down Kwame Atta, calm down. I am not reducing your science, I am augmenting it, I am making it longer and stronger in time,' Kofi Senya stated with an authority that was definite and final. Senya was extremely strong under his delicate frame, his soul was electronically wiry, his muscles were as hard as dompe. Siabots would be his sabla, because he was almost more patient than eternity itself. There goes the younger brother of eternity. A man who loved to say: any eternity achieved through science was a bogus and awam eternity! And that any invention had to have parts that were highly perishable, so that the renewal of these parts led to the addition of some soul, some vulnerability before the intimidating neutrality of your own invention. It was so elementary! How could you be intimidated by your own inventions? It was not an intelligent position to be in at all, my brother! Intricate thinking about processes, and a vast and mindless energy were certainly not intelligence! It was in articulating these truths that Senya became passionate and authoritative, his wiry frame looking like hundreds of thousands of restrained diamonds. Mackie had finally given up trying to understand Kofi Senya: he just accepted his uncanny spirituality, and then played the rest by ear, by some inspired Mackie intuition: if the man Kofi Senya said that cycles of time would be the best way of reducing the problems of time, and that adopting these cycles would give direction to an inventive upsurge, while going half-way towards wrestling with the problem of the impending mortality, then he Mackie would certainly go along with that because: one, no one else had any ready answers; and two, when you stretched the everyday step-by-step logic in relation to business and tea-party theology, into long-long millenium-by-millenium moves, then you gave way to the player that could manipulate such a game, even if he had a vulture on his pipe. Ah, there was the honourable Pastor Mensah amening in the distance, polishing his neon buttons, with a belief in the modernity of the cool aluminium Cross of the reincarnated Jesus Christ, whose name was only symbolic for other sons of God, ampa . . . Kofi was a son of God, so was Kobina, and Kwodwo, and Mr X&Y. Sala jumped before God quick to show he was a son too.

Bark, bark! sniffed the spaniel round the conference. It was even sniffing at paradoxes now. Timmy Tale toiled around the dog's tail, to see what the secret of its complexity of truth was. Eventually everyone rowed to bed with a banana, on a sea of tea, sleeping over the trimmed pines, dreaming hard. Very early, there was LT adding himself to the dawn by rising before it; and waiting like a station for the afternoon that seemed so slow in coming. He was worried by the fact that the mortality was not yet solved. He wanted his power in the dynasty of the immortal, even if this meant death and then reincarnation, the present system. No one minded being an ally of death if he or she could rise again and eat abolo noisily if desired. The only thing that kept Lawyer Tay from going too close to Moro in Tukwan was that Opanin Akorsah was also close to Moro. Otherwise he and Moro would have planned something long ago against Pokuaa; and another big reason for his restraint: fear and respect for Kofi Senya, who, LT felt, could see through them all. And the afternoon didn't come before the conference restarted.

There was a reason: the selfish termites had delayed it with their voracious biting, for at that moment there was neither wood nor anything else for them to bite. LT finally fell asleep with little effort, dying to issue a habeus corpus against the body of his own hopes, and snoring too. Yes, Amoa insisted: what exactly had been achieved at the conference, apart from the perpetual astonishment of Dr Timmy Tale, who was deeply proud of being both black and white, but who was also prepared to be ironic about it . . . though he found that with the type of world he had met here, and heard of in Tukwan irony was something that was not deep at all. There were occasions when astonishment was deeper than irony koraa. Babo was asked to examine his chalk to see what the conference had offered to all. He was just about to speak when Timmy Tale interrupted with that quick temper of his: 'Surely as one of only three strangers to witness this ambling conference, I must be given the privilege to say what I have seen. First of all I'm afraid that when they really get to know what you are doing in your towns, they will want to destroy you. But rest assured that I am not going to say anything, even though I would like to broadcast the magnificent openness that I have seen and experienced here. I even had the freedom to attack your eminent but tricky and drunken scientist, my good friend Atta! I am overwhelmed with the absence of guilt, except in the undertones of the desire for power that I thought I saw in one or two of the Tukwan people here . . .' LT raised his eyebrows in utter disdain, and Akorsah gave a snort, perhaps all the way to the ears of Moro, even a Moro reduced by the stupidity machine. Tale continued, 'Now, don't you think that it's time for you to share your penetrations of time with enlightened people outside your two societies? Ahhh, I must be stupid: I've just said that they would attack you for it! So what do you do with your knowledge? . . .' 'Live it,' Babo said simply.

As the conference limped along, waiting for the Lord Provost to come and close it, they all began some body mathematics: Azziz added Manu's shadow to his back: they crossed under the six-o'clock light; Akyaa added her hips to Jock's wee dreams of body and . . . fish, for he had never married, minus Jennifer, and he found her, and Pokuaa, irresistible; Mackie subtracted his glee from the boredom of Akorsah, so that he could enjoy more of it later with Shebelda the Margaret; Kofi Senya was multiplying his reasons for leaving early with his vulture for Tukwan; Babo had divided his chalk into two for any lesser writing needed; and Atta had taken the square root of his inventive capacity, and then lost some hope at the smallness of the number of inventions; Pokuaa had added everyone to her heart, but had given hers to no one, saaaa. And the Lord Provost came and closed the conference; Timmy Tale went swearing to return; and Kofi Fofie left on his new crow.

— 153 —

CLASS TWELVE

Mackie had learnt to grow fine plantain bigger than apem by far, in the new greenhouses of the Plantain Hotel. But this didn't stop the short industry of tears growing in individually designated wet areas of the Levensvale faces. Never being much of a culture for free crying, many hearts were yet stretched to unbearable limits, just because the Tukwan visitors were getting ready to go. It was as if identities, so different, had become one, and thus the parting meant something being wrenched. 'It is the dignity of the parting we're after,' announced Tommy Rae the Lord Provost, who had arranged with his daughter Pamela to do all his crying for him, so that his red eyes would not be seen in politics, no public handkerchiefs. Pamela brought her cheek up to Pokuaa's cheek, and then wet it with a five-minute cry, with Pokuaa holding her like a baby. Donald, much to his own disgust, had dropped an early tear ahead of the dawn, and Sala had sent one back with a sarcastic remark: 'Big scientific boys like us don't have to add to the dew koraa, the world is wet enough.' The energetic groundmothers loved to comfort anyone crying, for that was part of their function. David Mackie stood there tough above the crying: he had initiated this link of the towns with Pokuaa, this link which had stretched above and below time; and thus he certainly was not going to give way to some wild and communal crying. Besides, his worldly eyebrows, the bush of the hour, wouldn't allow it. Shebelda had quite graciously agreed to cry for him if necessary. But it was Alec Murray the ex-bogey that could not be stopped: he diluted his whisky with tears, and followed Pokuaa around whenever he had the chance, bemoaning his missed opportunities, and demanding to be taken back to Tukwan, even if only to sweep the streets. Anything to be near Pokuaa. 'When you people go, they will destroy me with ridicule. I had opened my devastated heart out all these months, but when you go, the closing of it again will surely kill me . . .' Alec the Murray said. Kofi Senya was continuing to be agitated, and he had even driven the vulture off his pipe, while he stood in deep thought . . . with the great bird landing gently and unconcerned on his shoulder instead. Kofi Senya's small thin frame was vulture-proof, and the new hurry in his life had tightened his skin further. Mackie would stare at him and then shake his head.

But it was the happiness, indeed gaiety, of Aba and Angus that surprised everybody. Aba was happy that she was returning to Tukwan, while Angus was happy because she had promised to write what was inside her heart to him, good or bad, when she returned. And Angus was secretly planning to go to Tukwan later by any means possible, local ducks included, if the power of shrines could be put into one. Aba had finally appreciated the devotion of Angus, but didn't know, and hadn't decided, what to do with it. They were becoming so close that she would sometimes wait for him outside the toilet, at his insistence. Then he would regret it: in order that she wouldn't hear any cargo drop in the bowl, he would catch his own droppings one by one in a gloved hand, and then put them much more quietly into the bowl. He was satisfied with the devoted nature of this important interception of the glove between dung and bowl. 'You use the toilet too-too quietly,' was what Aba had said quite innocently. While Appa was bathing the aeroplanes, and getting ready to put copious lavender on them, Aba and Angus were racing crabs in the heather. 'Mine is far faster than yours!' Aba shouted in triumph, dangling her tied crab wisely . . . but not wisely enough, for the small white crab fell down her cleavage, and Angus, to her horror, had his hand down her breasts trying to take out the crab. She pushed him away roughly, and he fell by the bracken, holding the crab. He put his head in his hands, shattered, but not daring to apologise in case he cried. Aba looked at him long and with pity rather than anger. She said, 'I will never allow you to sweet me naked, but I think my tooshies are nicer than Sister Pokuaa's, even though hers are beautiful, heavy and well-shaped. A real African bot!' Angus looked up hopefully as she stood up. She took his hands as he shook in disbelief, placing them first on her breasts, and then down onto her hips. She held his beard hard with a laugh. 'What sort of body is this, what sort of body is this!' Angus cried, not believing the ampleness of her back. They rolled on wild rabbit dung dry, and he gave each breast one hundred caresses, his hands in a joyful and relentless fondling of her hips . . . over but not under her slacks, under but not over her jersey. 'You can't go any further with me,' Aba declared, 'my generosity here now has surprised me enough.' Angus stared, trying to spread his daze equally between his eyes. But they heard a big and sudden roar, and when they looked round and up in consternation, there was Appa laughing in the upper-lip aeroplane, and swooping back up just before the hat of Angus was knocked off by the wing. Appa waved down, down, down, as Aba and Angus strolled off, Aba laughing yet angry at Appa; and Angus acquiring a bold new walk that he hoped would one day lie on Aba perfectly rhythmically still, and in perfect love.

'We are leaving a second stupidity machine here to protect you and your computers,' Atta was saying to Mackie. But Mackie was looking at Pokuaa as if he would never see her again. He said, with a forceful gaze at Atta, 'Thank you, Great Inventor, but I wish you could invent something to open this woman's heart to either of us standing here . . .' Atta looked with great surprise at Mackie, and then roared with laughter when he saw that Mackie was looking perfectly serious. 'So there is a burning heart under these tweeds!' Atta said, laughing so much that Mackie too had to laugh. 'I have always been pottering about this lady's heart, but I knew I would never get it, not even when we were making such a good deal. And if Margaret were to know this, her laughter would be bigger than yours! She would think I was really fancying my chances . . .' Pokuaa took hold of both their arms, and said with a wink, 'Let's go and inspect my aeroplanes, my heart might show under the wings!' 'I told you months back that she was soft!' Atta said to Mackie with triumph, '. . . but I didn't know that you wanted a stake in that softness at all, at all . . .' 'I wish Kwaku Babo were here to write our walk,' said Pokuaa, absent-mindedly quickening her step, and looking down to Mackie, then looking up to Atta.

On the tarmac the durbar was more than ready. Nana Bontox had brought out his fontomfrom drums. Jock was going around offering his last plates of fish and chips, with or without Brussels sprouts. Dogo's export kyinkyinga was all sold. Sala stood stiff beside Donald and Ann and Dizzy and Alex. The grandmothers danced their own way, as did the doctor. Ed Gilmour was seeing to arrangements. There was a telegram of farewell from the canons, including Canon Burns, with a promise to meet later. Azziz was busy dancing with Akyaa in the aeroplane. Nana Bontox was saying, 'I didn't even taste one white woman.' The drums were under the expert hands of Amoa and Manu the carpenter, the drums were giving out messages of farewell, calling on the gods and the ancestors to guard Levensvale and let it prosper. Angus and Aba were an island of happiness, still for different reasons. Different worlds had come together, and there was no need to cry. Shebelda was being wonderfully gracious. She even told David to look how beautiful Pokuaa was looking. Alec the old bogey had slipped his Murray into a glass of whisky, and was sleeping hard. Jack MacTaggart was insisting that he would die next week and join his wife. The Tukwan travellers were on the plane. The Levensvale people waved and waved goodbye with the moist handkerchiefs. And when would they all meet again? And all the waving seemed to give the aeroplane greater height, as if the hands held the fuselage so easily in the palm. The jet emission was full of love spreading down to the good-bye heads below. Kofi Senya was puffing his pipe faster, and he would tell no one what was quickening his soul or his pipe, not even Pokuaa yet, Pokuaa who looked at him silently. The two trailers would pull the planes back if they were going too fast; and two state umbrellas were hooked onto these trailers, partly to protect the things therein, and partly to challenge with their colours any rainbow that would dare to appear in this humble sky. Everybody was quiet in the aeroplanes because the heart had to cool down after rising in the temperature of friendship and love in the cold bracken; and Aba was helping the cooling: by singing religious songs that she grew up with. She was remembering during a particularly contrite piece the erect nature of Angus's popylonkwe which she would not touch; the rising of the erectile memory was equal to the rising of the devotional songs into the state umbrellas. Sala was a credit to sarcasm, for he just used it to fight the feeling of wanting to cry for the memory still hot of his friends, especially Donald. There was Azziz getting Akyaa to count and recount his profits from the pineapples. 'You see woman, my plans are good!' he said. And when you spoke, every sound was to settle in an eventual silence. Only Pokuaa knew in the sky that the grandmothers would lead the repainting of the entire Levensvale in memory of the friendship, and that there would be a properly silly sculpture of the corset. And Pastor Mensah's converts would sing, sing.

The huge door of the sky closed with the advent of this darkness; never mind the stars working as windows, for they opened out and shone into nothing that Kofi Senya's wisdom of the puff could not conceive, pipe down. Dark grey clouds which could convey any memory from any century, surrounded the planes, much like leaves surrounded their kenkey. The single sacred duck that had returned to its twin in Tukwan, had left part of its spirit on the other wing to soothe the vulture if necessary. The termites had vast amounts of digested Europe in their bellies, and Babo was dying to know how their excretions would be felt in Tukwan. Babo too had a long look at Senya, noticing a slight swelling of his cheeks, it could be smoke; and when he asked Papa Kofi what was wrong, he was just given a long painful smile. The vulture had entered the plane again and was holding its master's pipe in its beak; if it was not grapes, then it was pipes. Babo would never forget the day he saw Kofi Senya in the valleys at Levensvale: Senya had accosted a Highland cow, had arrested its tail by holding it hard in spite of the wild kicking, and then moved the tail round in circular motions that stirred time on. A few seconds after this, the dawn arrived one hour earlier, this making it possible for little Pamela Rae to hop along to comfort Pokuaa in the hills, before the latter's consciousness disappeared altogether in a cosmic grief. A little booo can save a heart from dying. And what was Pokuaa saying about aerial burials back in Tukwan? There was something in the air, and Babo felt he had to consider transforming his chalk into a heavier weapon. The night was working hard in its moondial, trying to gather a different time in the sky; the hands of the watches on the travellers that had them, moved very fast, especially on those that were sleeping. Babo peered out of the window, and he had to blink and look again: coming up by the side of the aeroplanes was a sacred duck with a small lit bulb tied to its neck, and holding a large telegram, ten square metres, in its beak. The paper flapped as the wings flapped. It was a message from Fatima, Moro's wife, the new member of the Tukwan Council of Elders. It read in the rather dull light: 'There are some strange movements beyond the maze and the town walls. The magistrate is dead and cannot be reincarnated. Are you not coming yet? Come!' Babo held the duck for Kofi Senya and Pokuaa to read its message; but as he tried to bring it in for a rest, it fluttered off, racing past the planes with two loud cries.

Atta and Appa obliviously piloted the planes, aided by New Pilot Amoa, who jumped from plane to plane, depending on where he was needed most. Babo had barely settled the frown on his face, when an old wise crow from Levensvale flapped with tremendous strength up to the side of the planes, carrying a telegram of similar size to the one just received from Tukwan. It dropped its big paper onto the wing, and raced off without a single cry. The message read: 'Tax men, troops, and Immigrationing officials have gathered at the ramparts of the town. They are preparing to storm us. We will fight.' Babo rose in sweat, pulling the message into the plane for Senya and Pokuaa to see. Pokuaa snapped her fingers, and put her hands at the back of her head in a slow shuffle of pain. 'They will use the stupidity machine to fight, and if we survive, they will survive,' Kofi Senya said flatly. 'If we survive what?' asked Atta, storming up from the cockpit. 'What is going on? And what is this big piece of paper on the moss seat?' Atta read the message. 'At once, we must turn round, and go and help them!' The rest of the travellers woke up. There was chattering and there was the widening of eyes. 'It is our duty to go back!' agreed Manu. 'I told Angus that one day he will meet something more serious than me. Now he has to show whether he has a heart to fight as well as to love,' Aba said, trying to hide a sudden sadness that dropped on her eyelids. The different views, shouted or whispered, moved up and down the aeroplanes. Eventually, Kofi Senya said, 'You cannot know whether we have our own fight on our hands or not. Do you think Mackie will want us to turn back when we are nearer Tukwan than Levensvale? And I've told you that if we survive here, they will also survive there. We have been told by the message of the duck that the magistrate is dead, and that there is something happening beyond our walls. Do you not remember the warning we received from the Kumasi people? We are going to go back to Tukwan to fight the fight that will be the same as the fight of the Levensvale people!' Kofi Senya's small voice stopped, his cheeks had swelled up more.

'Fly faster Appa!' Atta radioed to the upper-lip plane below him. 'All right! I know the magistrate is dead!' came the heated reply. Sala looked at his shirt torn by the toilet door of the plane. He was reluctant to be the air steward, simply because he had been watching carefully how the planes were flown, and he was quite confident that he could fly one now. Lawyer Tay was the only one that continued to sleep through the commotion; and Sala coughed loudly when he caught Opanin Akorsah staring in an evil manner at his sleeping father. 'There's everything to be calm and thoughtful about, my contrymen, be calm,' Kofi Senya said, pressing his cheeks down, and taking his pipe back from the patient vulture. 'You have just dropped some guavas and gooseberries on my plane! What is happening up there?' Appa shouted up to Atta. The bag of frozen fruit had burst, and was dropping its fruit down through the communicating hole in the lower-lip fuselage. Sala saw to the haemorrhaging fruit. 'Let's hope we don't reach Tukwan and find all our precious lives dropped into nothing!' shouted Babo, chewing his chalk, and taking on the residue of Senya's agitation. LT woke up at last, adjusting his eyes to the light, and wondering why there was a new atmosphere in the plane. When he was told, he insisted that the planes turn round, and go to Levensvale. But Kofi Senya looked at him with distressing doubt, knowing that Lawyer Tay may have one reason for insisting that they should go back to the frosty lands; and those of the same view may have other more innocent reasons than his. The lawyer huffed and puffed, but the planes continued to go homewards.

Homewards, homewards was a grab at the sky by the coconut tree, or the royal palm, was the sweep of the higher air by the odum, the baobab tree, or the long thick thorn. The flowers of joy of the Flamboyant were muted without its leaves; and from the lowering height of the aeroplanes, you would think that the hills had collapsed. Babo stared down in disbelief: there was a huge hole in one part of the forest; and at another part, it seemed you could hear a dirge of elephants, and yet at another part the wild pigs continued the cries of other animals. There was a stampede of animal against bush, bush against animal. The rough sly touch of the bush-rat was finished, torn by the lunge of the wild cat. The lowering planes were syncronising their landing. There was a hush in the air, and there was another hush behind that too. Babo ate bread with WHY written into the baking, Jock's work tiiik. The tarmac this time had no fruit on it, only potholes, ash and plantain and cocoyam skins. 'O my God the Ewurade!' screamed Appa. 'My trailer has fallen off, it's going to smash to pieces! Just think of all the presents and breakable things . . .' There was a huge crash, a terrible impact as the trailer broke up, breaking up in turn its own cargo. Babo wondered looking back, as his plane taxied, which animal the bright blood scattered by the wreckage came from. He stared hard again, and when the plane stopped, he rushed back to see, pursued by Atta with a curious expression. The twins stopped abruptly when they reached the spot. They held each other's wrists defensively as they stared, incredulous, at the body before them: there were the disintegrated bones and torn flesh of Alec Murray. Dead, if it was necessary for anyone to ask. Atta held his own head with a wail, shouting, 'But when did this mad whisky man go to hide in the trailer? He said he wanted to come, didn't he, Kwaku, didn't he! If only we had really known, we would have taken him free . . .' Atta ran off still shouting, leaving Babo to look. The smashed mouth had bits of broken glass in it, a tot to the last. Babo's chalk fell in the blood, he would write red until that particular piece finished. The rest of the travellers came with their commotion. Babo moved away with a quietness that came from parched lips. Not a single person had come to meet them, which was very strange. Kofi Senya carefully wrapped up poor Alec Murray's body, while Atta took the broken glass out of his mouth, and marvelled at the tiny stream of whisky coming out of the belly of the body, bogey no more. They took him down the valley in the other trailer.

There was a loud and sudden 'alleluya' that came from beyond the maze; and it was as if the voice, so much like the masculine voice of Maimuna, had been passed through the stupidity machine. There was a crackle to it that spoke of cunning and despair. The weeds, expertly mixed with the tamed flowers, had now overgrown their borders, there was no order to their roots in the avenues. The animals had all rushed to Pokuaa's house, and seemed to be using the same jaw for the different screams and cries. Kofi Senya ordered that all their skins should touch at once; this should be done with meat and leaves put in one place only. When this was done each animal had its jaw back, and the sounds thinned into whimpering, and soft growls, disturbed cheeps for the birds. Pokuaa herself stood guard over the animals. There was an absence of panic among the returned travellers; they simply expected an answer to the strangeness and the silence. The vulture, in a touch of safe but grim irony, was left guard over Murray's body, which had large plantain leaves covering it in the trailer. The sad bogey would not be carrion, not even with the noise of the flies. They all separated to see whether each could trace what was going on in the town. The coconuts were still, had pushed their magic back into their milk, no following Babo. Babo went to the lake and saw just enough water to fill a small pond. The ducks were very high up in the sky, and would sometimes fly down in decreasing circles for a touch of water, and then return to the sky without any welcoming perch on Babo's shoulder. Only the two birds that travelled came down for a few minutes, rubbing their beaks against his legs. The goat was helping Babo to pull the string to raise the hills again, but the string was broken in the middle of the rock, and just led to man and goat falling backwards fast in a useless pull. Maimuna's voice had come again, this time mixed with Fatima's. It was as if they were in the middle of the rocks, some post-travel geological voices. That one fish left in the lake was exhausted with avoiding the beaks of the ducks. One grey elephant and one blue one cried down from Pokuaa's house, so that the thin, brown reeds rustled in their bending. A huge Ghana flag on a huge pole had risen from the maze, with one word written on it: TIME. 'Who raised this flag here?' Atta bellowed, to no one's answer.

LT was in the forest, looking for Moro hard. He trundled his belly among the leaves of law; and he was quite unaware of the intermittent rushes of Kofi Senya into the forest, to watch him. LT had seen that it was the traxcavator that had made the huge hole in the forest; but Kaki was nowhere near it. From another hole near the big one rose Moro with a look of grim determination on his face. Lawyer Tay jumped with surprise. Moro put his finger on his lips to signify silence. 'Akwaaba,' he said to the lawyer. 'Yeewura. What has happened here that we can't see any of you?' The two of them went deeper into the forest to talk. 'I'm ashamed,' said Moro quite suddenly. There was a bewildered pause, into which a dusk mosquito flew to be swatted by LT. 'I know you are with me against the power of Pokuaa and Kofi Senya, but someone has spoiled my plan koraa, my plan to contact Kumasi so that we too we enjoy some of this power . . .' LT stared at him with scorn, saying, 'First when you were given power in our absence, you didn't want it; you wanted a stupidity machine instead. Now too that you may have got another chance, you say someone has spoiled your plans. What two-pesewa plans were these? . . .' 'It was my wife that made up a plan with Maimuna and that mad machine, as soon as she saw groups of Kumasi people beyond the walls. Fatima has her own mind, but she usually gives me love and support. It was that proud man-hating Maimuna plus the machine that pushed her on to plan, even after I had told her that I would take charge of everything.' There was another pause in the deepening forest. 'You see I had tricked Kaki into sending a plan of the maze to Kumasi, but when the invading force arrived, the stupidity machine had already changed the maze at Fatima's insistence. I had arranged for a very big Ghana flag to fly over Tukwan for the first time, but this has just gone up, and at the wrong time on top too. So, my brother, instead of the Kumasi people entering here in triumph to rush under the flag, the same flag served as a warning against a move to invade. Besides, Kaki had betrayed me by crawling in through the barrier of time to reveal some of the fighting secrets of Kumasi . . .'

'So what are you going to do now? Why didn't you wait for me?' Lawyer Tay asked with impatience. 'Me I can't do anything anymore. I will lose my wife . . . I denied I sent Kaki, and she, she believed me as she fed her baby under the Benz,' Moro answered firmly. LT looked at him for a long time, and then said, 'Things are changing. It looks as if mortal time is returning again. Mr K is dead and they can't reincarnate him. The drunken Murray from Levensvale is also dead. No resurrection. So instead of letting you mess things up, we shall wait for our chance. Things are changing!' The two men stared in consternation through the dark as Kofi Senya passed them slowly with a nod and a smile, followed by the longest yawn ever seen in the

forest. 'Kofi Senya!' shouted Moro in desperation, 'I will not betray . . .'
But Senya had vanished, his smile illuminated behind him like the biggest
firefly. Moro stood there at a bad angle to foolishness in the forest, his
woodskin frame touched with the permanence of cola, and his mouth small
with worry. For a man of such firm and stocky build, with a temperament as
solid as the earth he farmed, as solid as his Benz, he found it unbearable that
Fatima would see him as a schemer against the very town that he helped
build with his cola. Fatima suddenly had something which he Moro had
physically but not spiritually: authority. It was the years of subtly bending
to his rolling will that made her so supple; so that when she had to jump into
the Elders' Council primarily to help her husband, she later found it proper
to help him, even against his own inclination. Now stood Moro in the dark
forest, uncomfortable with the ambitious LT before him, and smoking his
pipe at twice the speed. The cinders of the pipe looked like a third,
grotesque slipping eye. He started to walk away from Lawyer Tay. 'I warn
you, Moro, if you reveal my intentions, I will destroy your house and slash
the underwear of your Mercedes Benz. This is between you and me, even
though I know you will want to plan with that hopeless brainless Opanin
Akorsah. He has his angry energy, but like you, he can't plan very well.
He's far worse than you in fact . . . I would tell you to leave him out until we
see the real signs of change that will be to our advantage . . .' Moro the
strong grabbed LT's arm hard in a threatening hold, while LT himself
prepared his massive legal neck for battle . . . though careful to keep his
protruding belly at a safe angle from Moro's hoe-hard hands. There was the
sharp sound of a bell in the forest, followed by the drumming of the
fontomfrom. The two men vanished in different directions. Moro felt fairly
clean under the circumstances, clean like footmarks leaving the front ash of
a baker's mud oven. When Moro heard a loud scream from behind him, he
knew that Lawyer Tay had fallen into the huge hole dug to bury the dead in
the invasion. 'Let him climb out himself!' Moro said to himself, and went
on cursing through his pipe; a newly sad and worried man who had the will
for power but not the temperament. LT crawled out in great mud.

It was when Maimuna and Fatima burst out of the maze, with Dogo the
Khebab following, that the drums began to beat. Pokuaa had left her house
to the animals and to Nana Bontox, and was now down at the maze hugging
the two women. 'Sisters, what was going on? Why the hiding and the
silence? And although we have two deaths on our hands, although we have
some shrow to rub on the dead, I feel that your sudden jump out of the maze
is a triumph for Tukwan!' 'Sister Pokuaa-oooo, Sister Pokuaa! We have
outwitted these Kumasi people! We changed our maze, we fed our stupidity
machine with more and more lizards and mosquitoes, and at last it helped us
to raise the flag of defiance! Once the flag was raised, and the maze was
redesigned by the same machine of love, we could sit and watch half of the

thousand invaders run and scream wounded from our strong and tricky mazes!' rejoiced Fatima, holding Maimuna's hand hard. 'But I haven't seen my Moro for some time. Perhaps he was watching other entrances . . .' Maimuna looked away with a scorn that was intuitive: if Moro was not seen then he was bound to be up to something strange, something this same Fatima wouldn't like. And as they talked, Tukwan now was spilling its people out from the maze; and then its children, animals, and birds from Pokuaa's house. After a ritual libation was poured by Alec Murray's body, it was sent to lie beside Mr K the magistrate's, in Pastor Korner Mensah's narrow-doored church, which already had a huge pine-cone necklace round its beautifully and simply rounded arches. All round it, the sheep and goats cried minus the ducks.

Babo was back round the geology, trying to raise the hills again with a new piece of string; and he was being helped once again with this jutjob by the moral goat with the sideways leaps. And Dovi, exhausted with the ordeal of waiting against the Kumasi people while the stupidity machine, Fatima, and Maimuna did all the planning, had now risen into the hills to help too. He leapt goatwise. 'Pull the string!' came the cry. Some rushed to Babo, others rushed to the lake, many gazed over the maze, and yet others ran to the forest. Kofi Senya sat with stooped shoulders in the middle of the town. He had been talking to Zolozolo, who had fed the stupidity machine faithfully, for he considered it a child of the shrine: Atta took his spirit of invention from the invention room, which was right in a corner of the shrine. But Senya had been agitated on the aeroplane because he knew that Zolozolo had not yet been trained enough to turn the shrine gods to war; he could get them to protect, but not to attack . . . Babo, only your string-O! Pull, pull! The hills rose in grand splendour, with the termites forming a sudden cross at the top; the old neon crosses needed repair, the sacred hill needed joy to regreen its grass. Kwame Atta sat on a horse and a blue elephant at the same time. He only saw the wisdom of the elephants when he saw them amble to the lake, to perform a task: they had swallowed part of the water of the lake in the anger of war, and were now releasing this water in long spouts through their trunks. The gladdened lake multiplied, and its one fish had more space to hide in; the fluorescent eye of the lamppost opened again, in the late afternoon of the next day. There had begun a relentless mortality: when the flies died, they didn't rise again; you could no longer get one time on the left side of the street, and another time on the right side.

There were now one hundred and twenty houses, and there were many millions of cedis and pounds in the banks here and in Levensvale. When Kofi Senya lit his pipe again, this came out with the smoke: the orthodoxy of the new, the little space- and time-breaking dramas of Levensvale were here; and so was a creeping mortality: it would touch some and leave some still immortal . . . some little privilege of the transition of the skin. Senya called Babo from the hills to bring his chalk and write what was both a tragedy and a triumph: change, change that should be living the new way with the old spirit. Senya sat there musing, watching Babo write with his chalk still red from Murray's blood. The town was being tidied up again, and yet he felt that the real war with the Kumasi people, and perhaps even with Accra had not yet started. Thinking in generations for Senya was easier than thinking day to day. It was a wonder to see this small tight frame position itself for a new time. Atta stormed into their silence, shouting, 'Ah, we have two funerals to enjoy! I see Papa Senya that your cheeks are no longer swollen, but what's that strange look on your face? Are you not enjoying the whiff of mortality that we are sharing with Levensvale? Buei! Don't you know that there is greater gin after death? I am dying to reveal the rest of the country! You wait! Here I am holding a telegram from Levensvale, from the great and bushy-eyed Mackie, saying they have repulsed the attack with the help of their stupidity machine and the mad destination – no tram! The Lord be praised if he enjoys the company of a goat by a shrine! Are Mr K and Alec Murray not lucky to be among the first to enjoy this new mortality! Bring on the drums, the houses are growing! Even if we were new before, we are newer now! C'mon my brother and my great uncle, SMILE!' And he rode off on his elephant and his horse, with the dust of a doubtful joy rising after him. He was kicking eternity backwards. Kofi Senya rose, he was going to powder his vulture. Babo discarded his red chalk for something newer. The coconuts knocked against each other wisely. Magic was becoming small steps in rational processes, wrote Babo, and then he fell asleep.

CLASS THIRTEEN

A little bit of perplexity in the gari, for you had to ask what exactly were the gods and the ancestors doing: what was the essence of giving cruel images for the transitional phase between the immortal and the mortal? Cruel: for a whole morning, any man who wanted to shave had to move his jaws up and down against a stationary blade; and women who were bathing had to rub themselves against soap on the bath floor. And try as they could people could not use their hands to eat; they had to put their mouths to the food direct, and this was for a whole day. Dogo too was caught in that mortal mood which joined the disparate more outrageously: he joined religion and goat meat together by making a huge kyinkyinga cross and putting it on one of the hills newly raised by Kwaku Babo. It was to be eaten by especially devout people who were prepared to pay him a small commission afterwards . . . which meant they were to recognise the factor of money in the factor of the holy. The more this sort of thing went on, the more content Lawyer Tay became: he thought that the best way to break the old order, was to encourage these little cycles, these little dramas. Pokuaa and Kofi Senya would have to take an emphatic jump into the present tracks to retain their authority, as LT saw it. Kofi Senya had taken to giving Tay long lugubrious looks, and then bursting into laughter through his pipe, with the vulture almost falling off its perch on the pipe with the force of this laughter. Amoa was in high spirits as usual, especially after learning to fly. But one night he overdid it: he managed to sneak one hundred towels out of one hundred houses, sewed them together, and then hung the lot in one long stretch over the tallest trees in the avenues. But Pokuaa had already jumped playfully onto the new track: when Amoa had been freely abused and had returned home, he was met with a surprise: there was his towel sewed to his shirt sewed to his pioto sewed to his handkerchiefs, and left to hang in a fast blow on the nearest mature abe. Amoa had the capacity to laugh into his pioto by speeding up his innumerable grins.

But now the risks of life were higher, now that death was a permanent possibility; and you couldn't rule out the paradox: the more mortality there was, the greater were the risks taken. Pokuaa had gone straight to the point of having her grave dug and cemented, ready to receive what was now the last mystery, even if she had to wait until she was an abrewa, tooo goood. But LT still lived under three burdens: the great love that Pokuaa still enjoyed from everyone, just because she gave that love straight from her heart too; the scorn of his wife Dadoona Tay, Dadoona who had started suspecting her husband of planning an open rebellion, simply because he still had that revealing habit of talking and answering questions asked by her in his sleep; his fear that Opanin Akorsah would remain immortal while he LT joined the mortal ranks first; and then lastly, the continued ironic gaze of Kofi Senya, whose pipe was more and more becoming a weapon of mockery. 'So did you make the trunk call to Nana Bodo at Fante Newtown in Kumasi, about giving more information on Tukwan?' Dadoona the devout – she was among the first to eat some of Dogo's khebab that crisscrossed the horizon – would ask her sleeping husband, on a lead that he had already provided in his sleep. The sleeping lawyer would answer, 'How could I make a trunk call when the elephants were asleep . . . but that useless Mfantse koyoo Nana Bodo wants money from me before he leads me to higher authority . . .' 'What do you want with the Kumasi people?' Dadoona would continue. 'Power, power, for I see nothing wrong with overthrowing even the most perfect ruling Council!' The outraged Dadoona would answer, 'You, the only power you will ever enjoy is the power of your snoring!' At which point LT would wake up and seriously assess the power of the snores thus defined, without knowing why, because he was now awake. She would give him a doubtful breakfast, and then rush to Pastor Mensah's new all purpose church to pour her heart out to God only, not even to the ancestors. Sala approved of his mother's scorn against his pompous father, growing more and more away from him, with his small anti-law scientific inventions that included an elementary wooden calculator, and an elbow-polishing luxurious machine acting on the funny bone, in a humerus manner. And the harmattan was in, its glut of dust all over the inventions.

Everyday time was serious trouble for Kofi Senya, for his new mockery was a rejection of the desperation he felt at the way the gods were testing him: a simple chew would sometimes have to be taken from eternity, and then translated into the time of seconds, before the poor jaws could even move. He laughed at Pokuaa preparing her grave, for he knew she was still immortal, and could thus eat in peace with her jaw over the centuries. To be in the vanguard of the spirit, as he was, meant that he was the culmination of the transient, with the eternity of truth in one eye, and the lie of mortality in the other eye . . . you Senya with the sparkling eyes with the vulture reflected in them, you Senya with the huge frown that made waves on the constant tides of skin on the forehead. He laughed with that touch of impishness that he kept in his old joromi, a laugh that followed a serious question: was Zolozolo capable of taking over from him if one part of him were to die, and the other half were to stay alive merely to witness this death? Zolozolo had a little money now, and this had the effect of throwing aside his begging and some of his foolishness; and he had been so sobered by the stupidity machine's powers that he truly started to work hard under Kofi Senya the shrinemaster. He would be truer to his bosum. Everyone woke up to a surprise from Zolozolo one morning: he had made terrazzo on the shrine floor, and had transferred the invention room to a fine hut at the back, in which would live the stupidity machine, if it didn't die first of a famine of lizards and mosquitoes later.

Now Corporal Akoss, Nana's favourite wife whose passion for sleep made her miss the journey to Levensvale, was in a great huff with everybody. She was even cool towards Pokuaa who she said was too good to worry over the little things that kept the little people going; little things like sleeping when an important journey was about to be made, with Nana himself unable to recognise her absence. She insisted that Nana Bontox wanted to go without her, so that he could try his hand at the opposite skins that were begotten by cornflakes, mince and tatties, some rough porridge without sugar, potato scones, ritual haggis, and sliced sausages, ampa. However Nana did send three telegrams that she should join them on the back of a duck, but this Akoss refused to do. Besides she knew that the other wives would laugh at her; but she carried herself with such haughty beauty, such domestic efficiency and fairness, that no one dared laugh to her face. And the other wives in fact wished that she should be disappointed more often, since it seemed to transform her into something more mature. But as soon as Nana arrived, she took to her petulance. She melted a bit when she got her presents, including motorised high-heels that Angus had invented in a burst of desire to get Aba to move faster towards him. Nana himself had rearranged his uxorial pecking order, 'in case we are attacked by Kumasi, and I have no time to leave things to the stronger women.' Corporal of course remained at the top, sweeping every other wife under the mat, except Mansa Blue who had to die tragically young when the new mortality struck. So the whole household was mourning, even though Mansa Blue was considered unfaithful to Nana, with her impossible requests and high desires, due, dammirifa due.

The three funerals were beautifully done, with Nana insisting – and getting his way – that Mansa Blue should use the grave dug by Pokuaa for herself. 'But what if I die tomorrow?' she asked, with her finger on her chin. Alec Murray would have enjoyed the dancing and the ritual smearing, the coins and the cloths and the rings put in the box, that box with a bottle of akpeteshie tied to it as a proper salute and a concession to the spirit of

Murray. Pokuaa gave a sharp ration of tears to the man that adored her, and who would have been a good sculptor if his life had taken the right turn. Mr K had done his series of baptisms well enough in the absence of the travellers; but no one knew, not even his troublesome but faithful maidservant, that he had actually killed himself, because he had premonitions that the mortality that he had run away from in other areas was slowly following him to Tukwan. He killed himself with the luxury of crocodile bile, and had insisted, in a note that no one found suspicious, that he should be buried with his pigeon-pea beans freshly picked.

Obaa Yaa, Opanin Akorsah's wife, continued to test his patience by her ability to concentrate on his money, and by openly looking at other men. 'What is wrong with looking?' she would ask, 'after all I'm only looking to make good comparisons in your favour. You are only fifteen years older than me, so why should I be interested in younger men!' 'Then what about my farms and my money? You are always counting my pods and roots, and wondering how much I have in my bank. Sometimes you are so busy staring at my farm produce that you don't even do a foot of weeding . . .' Akorsah would answer, throwing and rethrowing his cloth over his shoulder, 'And how do you hope to give me a child when you won't let me touch you? Have you let me into your bed over the last twelve months? Ewurade! Only the gods know the patience I have for you, I can't understand it. Me Akorsah paaa, I should be bluffed like that by a woman! No bed, poor food, greed, and abuse, walaii! And don't you dare to try to get me to wear jeans again . . .'

Obaa Yaa had a small sharp-featured face, a tall slimness that she had always used to dominate other people's desire. She would sometimes confess to Maimuna and Akyaa that of course she married him for his money, but that a little love had come in for his slim thighs and heavy ankles, and even for his hard work; but that at other times, especially for the last year, she couldn't bear the sight of him. Maimuna in her usual tart way with men, advised her to continue to find her husband unbearable, so that he would realise more readily the worth of her womanhood. Akyaa would laugh and ask, 'But how are you going to have a child with him if you don't let him touch you? Don't think about having a child with anyone else . . . the disgrace they will put on your head will break it.' This time there was a pause from the triple laughter. Obaa Yaa confessed, 'I made love to the dead magistrate Mr K . . .' The two women stared at her with mouths open. 'What are you saying?' asked Akyaa disbelieving. 'But everybody knows that Mr K was unapproachable, a man full of cats and beans and a very stern heart . . . and how could you get past Ama the maidservant? They all say that Ama was his girlfriend . . .' 'Ama wouldn't touch him!' declared Obaa Yaa, 'and you people don't know that it was Ama that arranged for me to embrace him for money . . .' 'For money!' shouted the shocked Akyaa.

Even Maimuna had to concede to the raising of her own eyebrows. 'Then you can never be my friend again!' declared Akyaa, looking that toughly vulnerable way she looked when she was angry. 'O, Akyaa, don't go, I haven't finished . . . you see it was only an embrace, and I needed a new cloth. Later on I started to like this magistrate a bit, and he helped my brother with a case, so there was nothing I could do but to go to bed with . . .' '. . . with your husband?' asked Akyaa looking back. 'O no!' replied Obaa Yaa merrily. 'Not with Akorsah, he will get his turn soon, when I build up the courage to do it. But now I'm sure that I'm expecting the dead man's child . . .' There was a deeper hush, Akyaa stopped walking on, and turned back, saying, 'Well, then hurry up and become one of the new mortal people. That's the only way to solve your problems, you with the tiny baby magistrate in your belly . . .' Akyaa now walked on with hurrying steps, shouting back to Maimuna, 'Don't give her any bad advice-ooo.' 'Now, who do you really love?' asked Maimuna guardedly, pressing the plaster over a cut given her by a trapped Kumasi man during the invasion. 'As soon as the magistrate died, I loved Akorsah better . . . but I wish he would stop smoking the pipe koraa, and he would have a better chance with me if he wore jeans once or twice, even though he is over fifty years old . . .' 'Your mind is a child's mind,' Maimuna declared in disgust, 'but since your Akorsah loves you so much, the only thing you can do is to give in to him, and then let him father the same child a second time. But if you want to grow up a bit, then tell him everything!' 'O I'm not going to grow up just now yet!' Obaa Yaa said in horror. 'With that temper of his, he'll kill me, even if he still loves me!' 'Well, hurry up and make your decision, but let me tell you one thing: once you've made up your okro mind, don't come and tell either Akyaa or me . . . we don't want to share this knowledge with you.' Obaa Yaa now had her turn of presenting an open mouth to the world. She stood there shattered as Maimuna walked off to attend to the Plantain Hotel. 'As for you, your problem is that you don't like men!' Obaa Yaa shouted at the disappearing Maimuna, out of a sudden revenge she felt necessary, to protect her heart.

And Maimuna had a shock when she went to the large dining room of the hotel: there was Kofi Senya there sitting at the table, about to order fufu and abenkwan. 'Yewura Kofi, you have never been here before, what is wrong that you are here today?' she asked with the surprise still on her face. He looked at her with his sparkling eyes. 'I came to thank you for your courage when we were away, and to tell you something too . . .' Senya's voice trailed off, as he took the vulture outside out of a reluctant deference to any prospective diners, and came back in. His step was sprightly, and his skin was glowing. 'Now, my good woman, let me eat first, and then we will talk!' he laughed, adjusting his khaki shorts with an exaggerated pull. Maimuna went into the kitchen to cut garden-eggs to see whether that would keep her patience too cut until Kofi Senya had finished eating. What exactly was he after? He finished more quickly than she thought, and called her through, the vulture back on his pipe. He continued to call her his good woman: 'My good . . . I'll come straight to the point. I want to confirm to you that Pokuaa *is* my daughter!' Maimuna fell back on the stool she was sitting on. She replied with a shaking voice, 'That is a wonderful piece of God's work, Papa Senya, but why are you telling me of all people?' 'Because of your courage,' he answered retaining the same sparkle in his eyes. 'But,' he went on with a long puff at his pipe, 'but it's a long time since I had another child; and with this mortality, I don't want to leave my back empty. I want you to have my second child, because Pokuaa's mother disappeared in another region long ago . . . she found a secret way to escape from my time!' Senya was laughing. Maimuna looked at him with a terrible surprise bordering on horror. 'But I have sworn never to marry . . .' she began. 'The gods have already broken that vow!' he interrupted, 'and I, yes I, am the one to take you. Believe me!' The vulture flew off for a short distance, carrying a bit of his confidence. 'Give me time,' asked the shattered Maimuna, 'give me time.' Senya looked as if he were about to roar with laughter, but said, 'Have your time. I will wait!' Then he left.

Maimuna closed the hotel for the afternoon, without even informing Pokuaa. For the next two hours, she rolled on the floor, beat every table she sat at with her fists, and bit her lip twice at either side. The cooking, cleaning, and serving workers were worried, for they had never seen Manager Maimuna like this before; but they were still glad of a gratuitous holiday, and pushed the snails and dried meat aside to go and enjoy it. As the dusk came – strange that it came on time regularly these days, and no one enjoyed it earlier than anyone else, thought Maimuna – she decided to rush to the house of Akyaa, for it was impossible to go through the night alone without sharing her new burden. The restrained glow of the new street lights made her walk faster, as if she were about to conspire under the lampposts against her will. Mortality meant more light. Approaching Akyaa's pig and pineapple house was not too easy for Maimuna, since Azziz had taken a dislike to her, accusing her of creating a new arrogance, as he put it, in his wife. This was a charge that Akyaa herself did not understand, since a similar charge of excessive success was put on her by the same Azziz in Levensvale over her role in supervising the factories' work force. So the false and rather insulting question that you could ask from seeing this contradiction of Azziz's was this: where did Akyaa's confidence and self-development come from? . . . as if Akyaa couldn't push on her own soul, couldn't guard her own okra.

The moon was generous with the shadows of pigs and pineapples; and Akyaa had achieved something that never ceased to amaze her husband: she had managed to persuade one of the wild pigs in the forest to come and join the domestic ones on the compound, to help with cross-fertilisation for harder stock, on condition that it was never slaughtered. This pig was the leader of the wild pork chorus that was taped for defence purposes for possible use in Levensvale; and it suffered from sartorial hauteur: it insisted on, and got from Mackie during his visit here, a handwoven tweed bow tie which it wore for hot crossing sessions, and which it would take off with great care before any wild confrontations with the domesticated boars. Maimuna found her hand about to knock the front door, but Azziz opened the door first, and she knocked his nose instead, which started a furious exchange of silence, and a tiny sorry from Maimuna. 'I don't know whether Akyaa can come just now since she's cooking a very hot soup and cannot leave the heat in the middle . . .' huffed Azziz with his broad quick frame. 'You Azziz, master of the house, how many years have you not known me that you can keep me standing at your door without giving me a chair to rest in? And yet you were the same man standing beside me to fight against the Kumasi invaders! Hmmm. Give me way to see my bosom sister in her busy kitchen . . .' And with that, she pushed past him, with his mouth open wide enough to swallow half the moon, and went into the kitchen.

Akyaa looked at her with surprise, and got up from the dull stare of ewurofua, the tilapia, just about to be cut up for a soup that would be rich, whether eaten fresh or three days later. She hugged Maimuna with her tomato hands. 'Now my dear dear sister! It wasn't so long ago since we met with Obaa Yaa. What brings you here? And you are panting! Where have your feet been running?' Maimuna returned the welcome with a greeting which shook at the end. She looked behind her furtively to make sure that Azziz was not there. But there he was standing with his hands on his hips, demanding an explanation for the impudent dig that Maimuna's elbow was alleged to have given his ribs in her storm into the house without authority. 'My dear Azziz, your goatee is looking wonderfully fresh this evening, and through our years of being together, I know that this means you are in a happy mood, and that you will be wanting to recount your money in the bedroom, so that I can finish two things very quickly: my soup, and then my small talk with my sister here. We should thank her bebreee, for she is the heroine with Fatima who saved us with your help and Dogo's of course in our little war.' She ended by placing her chin at a terrific angle to his beard. She was after all his favourite space. He would boast early in the marriage that it was the space she filled that he loved, and that if she continued to fill the same space in that marvellous way, he would continue to love her sweet past three score and ten years, koko dedeeede. Exit Azziz with his young nursery beard, trying hard to control the buck of his anger.

'Akyaa, Kofi Senya paid me a visit this afternoon, soon after we parted . . .' 'Is there anything strange about that . . .' butted in Akyaa, still bewildered at the agitation on her friend's face. 'You Akyaa, you are always the same! When you see a bit of excitement you want to add yours to it! Won't you let my mouth finish so that the poor thing can rest from its worries . . .' Maimuna complained. '. . . worries! How can a tuf-tuf fighter have worries so soon after her victory!' Akyaa was being impossible, driving down the wrong side of Maimuna's mouth. Mouth at the wrong time, mouth Maimuna thought. 'Will you listen or will you not?' asked the exasperated Maimuna, with an uneasy hand at her plaited hair. The moon had come right down to the window as a shining example of a dazzling listener; and neither of them could persuade the window to close its light. 'First of all Kofi Senya tells me that Pokuaa is his daughter . . .' 'May the gods save their surprises for our death!' spluttered Akyaa, so loudly that Azziz rushed in to see what was wrong, hoping that the two women were quarrelling, so that he could take his wife's side with alacrity, and get in some heavy abusing against Maimuna . . . and he rushed straight back out when he noticed the strength of his wife's sweet smile. 'Well, many suspected it, but it's no less strange for being confirmed by the rod itself that fathered her . . .' Akyaa continued. 'But is this what has made you so demented at all?' 'My dear Akyaa, you still have the gift of innocence about you . . . No it's not only that . . .' Maimuna wiped one eye with her oblong handkerchief. Akyaa stared long through her, then a sudden feeling of recognition came over her staring. 'I know I know I know! Kofi Senya wants to marry you! Hey Maimuna, we have to tell the truth under the moon, I know! I have known you long enough to read you booklong. We will have a wedding on our hands, but I don't know whether it's the right hand or the left hand, since you haven't spoken yet! Am I right?' Maimuna felt calm and relieved, immediately, adding in a soft voice quite unlike her, 'It's better I say nothing. You can do all the thinking for me. But isn't he too old for me? He has confused me paaa.' 'Too old for you? Why, Papa Senya is the youngest man in Tukwan! Can't you tell by the sparkle and the play in his eyes! Now don't you see where Pokuaa gets her strong, quiet pride and push from? If a man has half the power of spirit that Kofi Senya has, and he asked me to marry him . . .' Akyaa stopped abruptly, as Azziz poked his head round the corner at the last words, and said, 'Is your visitor trying to get you to marry a different man or what! How can you spend so much time with a woman who likes men so little?' 'Precisely because I'm not a man myself, my dear husband! . . .' 'Yes, yes,' broke in Azziz again, 'but you know that she will never marry, don't you? The day Maimuna marries I will shoot my own excuse-me-to-say tu!' The two women stared at him with some hidden triumph that poor Azziz didn't understand. All Akyaa added to her husband's words were, 'Azziz my dear husband, your bottom body is too-too precious for you to point a gun at, let alone shoot it . . .' And then when they were alone again, she said forcefully, 'Marry Kofi Senya immediately, you hear!'

Maimuna was taken aback by the intensity of Akyaa's views on her problem. The main reason that she was considering the proposal at all was that to have a child with a truly historical man was something to be taken seriously piiii. Go to bed with an authority and enjoy some wise flesh, she laughed to herself as she returned to the hotel under the lights that had thrust the dusk aside, and cornered the darkness in pockets of wide glare . . . the same inner-charged glare of Maimuna's necessarily wide-open eyes. She carried the full-turned lanterns of her eyes home, but left some light at the hotel first. It was when she reached her own verandah that she nearly jumped out of her skin: there was that Kwame Atta rushing out of a corner to wish her the fastest good evening yet recorded by Babo at Tukwan. He was standing with one foot far forward, with a smile that felt that it was certainly produced in the best face possible. 'Papa Kofi has sent me to you. Sorry for that free jump you gave me! But being a scientist I can analyse everything: you gave that jump out of fright, yes, but you also gave it because you wanted your feet to be as high as your heart. Love has altitude, and don't I know it, for whenever I try to love Pokuaa from the height of an aeroplane even, I fail miserably, for she always has her feet planted firmly against the ascent of other people's amatory steps . . . just like you I suppose, at least until recently. Kofi Senya has told me of his intentions towards you – he is being intentious! – for he believes that affairs of the heart, when they are at the talking and deciding stage, should be spread among as many people as possible. This openness can either break the prospective union or strengthen it, eh Maimuna! It's the same with me and Pokuaa, only that my boasting that I love her has neither killed nor weakened anything! She has a very good quality in love: neutrality! And let's hope she retains that neutrality, for it wouldn't do if she gave her heart to someone else and not me! But let's get down to business: Papa Senya says that he will be here in a few days to have your answer. Think well, good Maimuna, forget your stern past with men, for the courage of the two of you will be together an advantage to the town. Things are settling! for whoever thought that Papa Senya would want to leave a first child in this universe . . .' 'A second child . . .' Maimuna interrupted before she could stop herself. 'Ah, so you know too, eh! My wife-never-to-be is the daughter of the great man, just as I sometimes suspected in my darkest moods and dreams. This should make it easier for me, but the old man has refused to say a word in my favour to his daughter. They are too close for that, too independent.'

And with that Atta jumped over the verandah dwarf-wall, wishing that he had Alec Murray around to drink with; and that Kofi Fofie could suddenly appear and shout his mad password, 'Yes sah Boss!' And he could just picture Angus dying for a kiss cubed and many fuck factors . . . Atta made his way straight to Pokuaa's house, where he found that her eyes were glowing just like her father's. All she said to begin with was this, 'I am so happy that everyone now knows who my father is! Isn't he great!' Atta looked at her through his jot smoke, wistfully. 'How can you manage to be so innocent, and yet so tough? You are the woman I want, can't you adjust your heart towards my direction or something! That is if you have any haha . . . O and the general mortality has made you even more beautiful, I lie?' Mr Kwame Regret Atta stood there with the smell of elephants and horses on him; his super chin lay quite ordinary in his small hands, his hopes useless in the empty traxcavator with its Kaki asleep beside it, yiw. If his chin remained in his hands any longer, then Pokuaa would start suspecting him of trying to be introspective . . . besides, which market would Atta go and buy his rare bouts of the inner from . . . 'I am getting a bit worried about Kwaku Babo . . .' began Pokuaa, sending her sparkle inwards. 'Worried about that deep man with his constant chalk? . . . He needs nobody, and winds up his heart only once a year for either you or his mother to listen to the faint ticks of, no tocks even . . .' Atta ventured in interruption. Pokuaa held up her hands in exasperation, and continued, 'I'm getting worried because yesterday I saw him with a hundred grains of sand by the one-eyed lake, when I went to see whether I could catch some fish on my own, and I caught only one so I had to put it back, poor fish. It reminded me of Jock . . . He was busy, Babo, writing down different descriptions of each grain of sand. And he told me that when he finished, he would paint each one a minimum of three colours each. What type of soul is he growing? O I know he has been wonderful with the ducks and with the hills, raising them above and below our history, I know all that. But to start painting grains of sand, to start writing minute descriptions of them alone by the afternoon lake . . . I'm sure it made the very twilight worried!' 'Ah Pokuaa the moral and eternal pet! Don't you know that the new mortality is changing everybody! I have now started discovering pure ideas, and I want to leave the inventions to Appa, Amoa and Sala. I have done the same with love: I love you purely now, instead of practically. Believe it or not, I am getting spiritual . . . no no no, I'm not talking about spirit in bottles! Besides I believe, I believe I have fulfilled my invention contract to the town, and I am far too dignified to show the foolishness of my love to you openly like that. I am the scientific hero of Asante! I believe in marrying the soft touch of a dead frog with the special alloys needed for manufacturing aeroplanes. I could be the frog to your aeroplane! Now, listen, my beauty-beauty Pokuaa, let me ask you one question now now now: I have done distinguished work for my hometown; so what is it that really stops you from loving me? I'm not trying to force your hand . . . it is just a pure idea that I would like to understand. Tell me as simply as possible: Why Do You Not Love me? I am tall, semi-handsome, clever, kind, energetic and about to be rich, for some of the patents I left in Levensvale. What exactly haven't I got that you would like? Tell me without shame, without remorse, and without pity, woman!' Kwame Atta stared at Pokuaa in disbelief: there she was before him . . . fast asleep, lips open.

Into the house of pepper plants, arches, and love-grass strode the tall stern and magically straight Maimuna. Atta had fled in disarray from Pokuaa's sleep, but she was now awake. 'Sister Maimuna, come, come and let me embrace you for the way you have been running my hotel. I love your efficiency! How can I thank you enough? Now, are you coming for some money for the usual store of food, or what?' 'Let me sit down my dear Pokuaa, with your freshest palm-wine, never mind the ice-water!' Maimuna was laughing and laughing. Then she said, with a delicate drink of the calabash, 'O, so you have glass calabashes now!' She continued to look gay, saying slowly, 'Pokuaa, your father has proposed to me, but I want you to help me to get rid of the vulture from his pipe first, before I can tell him my mind!' Pokuaa stared stupified as Maimuna generated more laughter, for although others had heard the news, they were all leaving Maimuna to break it. 'And I also want to make one condition: If I'm to marry your father, and I would truly love to!, then you must promise to have one child yourself within one year.' Pokuaa gave one long disturbed yawn, and was about to give another one when she postponed it. 'The ancestors be praised! If my father has chosen you, then I love you both for your courage! I will be a real sister to you. We shall own the hotel together! But as for my having a pikin now, I will tell you a secret: I am already two months pregnant! But I will not tell you who with just yet . . .' Maimuna gave a little scream of joy and surprise, saying, 'What a wonderful way for us to become mortal!'

CLASS FOURTEEN

At the moment Babo's law of life was in his fingernails, for he kept staring at them for the answers to the strong agitation that the receding cycles of immortality created in him. Even Kofi Senya had lost that restlessness before the divine, for his obsession now was to maintain the going pattern, the orthodoxy of the new; and this pattern included his marriage to Maimuna. The quiet traditional wedding was held in the family houses, was held on top of sunflowers, was spread among the frangipani, was danced on the knocking coconuts, was arranged on the ripening bananas, and finally had to burst out of the coins of Pastor Mensah's church; but Senya had not lost all of his stubbornness: he had refused to enter the church and stood at the door until the entire ceremony was completed and brought back out to him still ritually hot; and secondly, instead of parting with his vulture altogether he had merely relegated it to the new golden amulet on his ankle, and he had agreed not to eat with it too often while Maimuna was there in the same room. And at the ceremonies, Kwame Atta kept nudging Pokuaa and whispering to her, 'You see that you have allowed your father to get married before you, wouldn't you like to go through these simple ceremonies with a man like me, instead of sleeping when I'm talking to you. You would think you were pregnant already, the way you catch time and sleep with it!' Pokuaa had to look away quickly with a sudden interest in Maimuna's brilliantly simple cloth.

True, mortality was toffee. It was a dance of glee at the edge of the highest neon-cross hill, for the knowledge of the drop, the death, seemed to add sweetness to the movement of the dance. Babo was terrified that someone was going to reveal some atrocious new information about him that perhaps he himself was not aware of; and his second more serious worry was this: his Minutes Book, his constant secretaryship of the universe had become so heavy that it needed the help of both Amoa and Appah to lift it. And yet this was the time that the two young men had become entirely obsessed with the new freedom of mortality; apart from changing their lives, with a fine amount of success no doubt, they had taken to constant tricks played on each other: Amoa would sneak into Appah's house, nail his sandals down, and then knock his door vigorously so that he would rise, wear his sandals hurriedly, and then go crashing to the ground when the leather wouldn't move with the feet; and then to extend the knocking game, Appah the A-level would control his fast nods of laughter, go and glue Amoa's door and then knock it equally vigorously, for Amoa to spend the next two hours disengaging his door. Appah had finally set up his metal works at which he manipulated the iron in his life, creating imposing metal pieces that included humped beds that rolled you over to a cooler side when your dreams were hot; and creating, with one or two moulds done jointly with poor Murray in bogey style, exquisite popylonkwe and buttock pieces. Two strangers entered the town mysteriously and bought most of Appah's works from his apprentice when he was out, much to his consternation. But few were unduly worried: after all, with the new times, new people coming from Accra or Kumasi or even further, was nothing to squeeze one's face about. But Babo knew that this was the first revelation of Tukwan to the rest of the country, and that they would come in their hordes from Kumasi and Accra, not for war but for curiosity, for a final attempt to reduce Tukwan to the ordinary in case the true freedom there spread. True freedom? The gods would roar with laughter at that, since all they had done to the poor new mortals of Tukwan and Levensvale was to substitute one freedom for another, hoping that elements of both would prevail; and that the paradox of long time and short time would separate and cease to be so, its exclusive elements now being used so distant from each other. Give the gods an aboloo sharp, thought Babo, for what they started as a cultural experiment had now become an ontological one, freeee! . . . And Amoa persevered: he went and blackened Appah's windows, and the metal man slept for two days non-stop, because he thought the night had been extended by one of the short immortal cycles of trickery remaining. Halt! shouted Babo to his mind, for his chalk too was growing heavier and heavier, it had already surpassed the size of Zolozolo's popylonkwe. What a quick life!

As almost everybody lapsed into a narrowing consciousness – with immortality being slowly forgotten, journeys too, and even magic and sacred ducks, but especially the stupidity machine which had tragically become a trick-laden video screen – Babo was left holding the subtleties, the events, the broken heart of his twin when he did discover that Pokuaa was pregnant, and then the telegrams from Levensvale. Poor Mackie the rich mortal was now the Lord Provost, for Tommy Rae's ambition had now led him into the tunnel of time and mortality, and out of Levensvale into the bigger counties for a bigger ambition. There existed this tunnel, the last creation of the Levensvale stupidity machine, which allowed natives out, and allowed strangers in, if both swore to be faithful to the open values of the town whether within it or without it. And the first thing the two strangers from Glasgow said when they entered was, 'How can you keep up with the computers when there is such conscience here, such a balance between the old and the new, such a whimsical reverence for a vital Necklace religion and a culture so wide that almost anything can fit into it?' Mackie now had eyebrows that were so massive that they almost hid his distinguished forehead, and strangers often asked whether the brows were a continuation of his hairstyle. His telegram to Tukwan was this: 'The new mortality is getting out of hand, because people feel freer with it; they think freedom is change, and change is freedom. With the level of wealth and gadgetry, this view is nonsense! We are all well and part of the mad changing of the outer without the inner, but Angus has disappeared without passing through the tunnel of time. Poor Jack MacTaggart is now dead, joined his wife at last, for the poor woman was the first to die without resurrection. They must be driving the bulldozer in the heavenly regions, for Jack insisted that this machine too should be put in a coffin and buried with him, even though it was not his; and you can imagine: the biggest coffin in the world and smelling of oil and fumes too, beside Jack's already prepared simple one. Write soon.' The wind came and blew the telegram into the market.

As more strangers came, the more noise Lawyer Tay made. He had appointed himself as the narrator of Tukwan's history, which in his hands had become a curiosity rather than something vital and organic. In a desperation for allies at this crucial moment when he thought his real chance had come, LT started to exchange notes with Opanin Akorsah about working together, especially when Pokuaa was pregnant and Kofi Senya was busy fathering. Akorsah had his notes translated and written by a nephew and the two conspirators never felt at ease working together, especially when Moro had deserted them under the influence of Fatima, and was exporting his cola direct to Levensvale. Pokuaa just laughed when she realised all this scheming, saying, 'I will bear my child into my authority.' The strangers increased local trade tremendously, but you could see revenge under the trade. And they asked such questions: 'Is it a pregnant woman who has authority in this town? What makes her legitimate?' Babo had refused to write down the new mortality. His book was closed, except for the history, if only that too would survive. He took to counting his grains of sand more and more, trying to grow a passion for optimism.

But one envoy from the authorities in Kumasi had already come to declare openly that a formal invasion was not necessary, and that the so-called strangers coming in would soon swamp Tukwan and destroy its many elements of subversion; and the envoy had eaten at Lawyer Tay's house, from where the outraged Dadoona moved to an empty room in Pokuaa's house, leaving the conspiratorial air of her husband's house . . . and closely followed by Sala who, in spite of his science, had grown a new respect for his mother. LT had rushed to Kumasi in anger, shouting as he went, right outside Pokuaa's window, 'Am I breaking the law by receiving someone from Kumasi? After all, didn't we use to be under them? If I want to speak to someone living in the same region as I am, a Ghanaian after all, can I not! If you my wife, if you think you can desert me because you want to live in the past, you'll regret it! When I have my power and my recognition, you and Sala will come running back to me!' He stormed off with his new bigger belly, its big hump making a fine confidence for what he thought was the future, for was it not one of his laws that the future was a configuration of his belly . . . minus Akorsah's which was even flatter than usual, for he had learnt of his wife Obaa Yaa's pregnancy by the dead Mr K. This news had been broken to him in a half-hidden malicious manner by LT who had overheard Obaa Yaa herself boasting to someone else about it. Akorsah would never forgive LT for venturing this information, for it made him reckless, empty, and a whiny heap of clashing complaints. He thus became completely unsuitable for conspiracy, and acquired a passion for heading unripe cocoa pods off his trees, or at the very worst of times, weeding tiny patches of his land with his teeth. After this, his haughty nephew – the translator of his unfriendly friendship with LT – had stormed to his house and informed him that he was putting the name of the family into disrepute, and that Obaa Yaa was prepared to pacify him if only he could kindly give her half his biggest cocoa farm, and if he could also forget that she was pregnant. Opanin Akorsah thought very hard for two reasons: to regain his sanity, even at the expense of his self-respect, and to enjoy the upmanship of having a wife stay with him, while LT did not. He would consider Obaa Yaa's request, he told his nephew. The sun lay on his farms.

Meanwhile David Mackie had sent across to Tukwan a fine sky of descending sherbet, from a new and useless machine that some naturalised stranger had invented in the thoroughly modern way to titillate bodies that were already more than half shell-so-limited. The ascending sherbet was meant to gorge children, in the company of fruit gums, Caramac, Bounty bars, dairy milk, Mars bars, perspicacious peppermint which could see through everything, and Smarties which knew everything. It was invented as the by-product of a new heart machine, and was thus morally justifiable. Mackie, according to his own testimony, had started to snort at the canons of the many counties for he felt that they should have given more serious thought to the new church in Levensvale, the church left by Pastor Mensah which had rushed some people at great speed back to an organic ritual. Now, Babo was thinking, what was the relationship between this ritual and the current problems that the two towns were facing? During the transitional period when the transition was weighted more to the immortal, then Pastor Mensah's churches there and here had a great evangelising presence. Now, however, the transition favoured the rather obscene swagger of the newer times, Babo complained to himself. Then there were the paradoxes that made poor Babo desperate: what gave the new swagger such power that to merely criticise its thinness meant that one was a serious candidate for reaction? Was it proper to condemn the gods for allowing a mood for mortality to become a new era? Was it simplistic to judge one past time, one epoch, as infinitely better than another? Babo prayed for the speedy advent of the mango season so that the crisis would taste better . . . and something whizzed past him as he sat by the weeds contemplating a coconut: it was Zolozolo passing on a new motor-bike with 'have your spirit now' written on it. Zolozolo motorised, mon hwe.

When Kwaku de Babo went to the house of Kofi Senya with a heavy heart, he saw Senya in a desperate act of self-negation: he was carrying naked around the house, to the tears of Maimuna, a sack of dried cassava in atonement for his failure to attack the newer time and the newer ways and the most impertinent strangers, with greater zeal. Now that Maimuna was pregnant, his fathering was free. She had rushed to put a cloth round his loins when she saw Babo coming. Babo rushed and wiped Maimuna's tears and then hugged the exhausted Senya with joy. 'Papa Senya! So the old spirit is still there! I am so glad that we are not losing the battle by default! Now, the problem is this: we have been very bold, very adventurous; we have travelled to survive, and to broaden our lives and our wealth; we already had a base of originality before we embarked on the journey thank god: But now that we are in a position to create a broad, new, and lasting life, even under the weight of mortality, we are losing our world to something narrow, shallow, boastful and wasteful. And never forget that this is a second-degree invasion: the first invasion was physical and it failed; this second one, as we have been openly warned, is more subtle . . . subtle for the reason that you may feel you are wrong if you fight against it. It is a phantom: ignore it and you look a fool, fight it and you look outdated! Kofi Senya, you can see that I have never spoken so many words at once before, I usually write my mind. But now I have even thrown my heavy book in a forgotten corner, and my chalk is far too heavy to hold alone. Kofi Senya we must come to our senses, and work out a proper compromise with what is happening! Give me a pesewa to talk with! I will not agree with you that this is the period of the orthodoxy of the new . . . it is merely the period when we are losing the great initiative we had! Let's wake up! Are we to allow the bravery of Maimuna and Fatima and Dogo to go free and betrayed? . . .' Babo was in a copious sweat, his large quiet eyes bright with new movement. Kofi Senya put his cassava load down, sat on his stool, and said slowly, 'My dear Kwaku Babo you have spoken my heart for me. You are so right that we are not just trying to go back to an old time, so right. We are trying not to return to the heart of the old ancestors only and the old spirits, but to the new joy that we created less than one handful of years ago. What is the use of creating the new when it doesn't even last one generation? . . . The first thing we must do is to make Pokuaa the formal leader of this town, even in her pregnancy, for she has done so much, and I am certainly not suitable to lead from the front. I will continue to be in the background behind the pregnant president. The next thing is to make Kwame Atta our ambassador to the cities and countries outside us: all the strangers go to him, even though Lawyer Tay tries hard to win them over to himself. The next solution is to create a new maze by spreading the truth of your book, which is a fitting chronicle of all that we have been trying to do, and whose spirit would be behind the most tortuous maze ever created. Then after that we must have an election to choose what to do, where to go with our spirit and morals and inventions, and to decide finally what we can tolerate and what we cannot!' The two men were standing staring at each other. And then Babo asked Senya, without dropping his eyes, 'Where will we get all the power needed to do this that we ought to do? Our power is already disappearing, some cedi note in the water!' 'Is our power disappearing from ourselves? What battles haven't we fought! A residue of immortality is enough! Now, bring me my adoka to drink small!' Babo went away wondering whether Kofi Senya had anything up his sleeve at all, away with his retinue of doubt.

Babo was standing engrossed in smelling guava leaves by a morning-coated avenue when Obaa Yaa went up to him and tapped him on the shoulder. He looked round at her with surprise and distaste, for he had always known that she was one of the biskitisers of life, made everything crumbs and then later complained about the mess; besides she had never spoken to him before. 'You are wondering why me Obaa Yaa, why I want to talk to you. You young men are getting prouder and prouder. You want to know why before I've even said what! I am surprised that you are not married yet. Why didn't you tell me before so that we could get closa, closa!' Babo remained silent after replying to the greeting in falsetto, for no particular reason. 'Only your voice! Kwaku Babo, you duckmaster and book-book secretary, are you trying to charm me with that flying voice or what! I know that your twin brother is troublesome paaa, but you I don't see you do any rufff at all . . . but now you want to start?' Then without warning she burst out crying, explaining her plight between big-big sobs to Babo, and then carefully shining her cheek with her tears. 'They say I look better crying, even my mother used to say that complete . . . but I want you to help me papaapa . . .' Bra Kwaku looked at her suspiciously, knowing that she could very much charm a snake. 'Obaa Yaa what do you want me to do for you that your husband cannot do?' Babo asked sarcastically, and then immediately reduced the sarcasm, chiding himself for letting his mood and his distaste speak for him. 'My husband wants to leave me, even though I'm pregnant, have you ever heard of such a thing . . .' 'What help do you want Obaa Yaa? I know already that your belly-big belongs to someone else, and not to your husband . . .' 'O I know you know, but do you still think that it's right for a pregnant woman to be thrown out of the windows of a marriage? Please help me, because I know my husband still loves me, even though he won't give me half his cocoa farms. All he wants to hear to forgive me is two things: that the baby in my belly doesn't belong to that dead magistrate that lost some cases for him, and that I will announce in public that I love him very much, and that I have always loved him very much, even before I knew him . . . so all I want you to do is to go to him and confide in him that it was you who made me pregnant . . . so that after I give birth I will show my thanks to you by sleeping with . . .' De Babo had stood there open-mouthed while this outburst was in progress. He mumbled a few excuses, and then walked off without any ceremony, adding as an afterthought: 'My brother is very accommodating, provided you get him before he's given some big post . . .' Obaa Yaa called and called and called after him . . .

Then shrugged and went straight to Kwame Atta playing draughts outside his mother's verandah. As soon as he saw her he stiffened and shouted at her, 'Hey woman of the wrong husband, don't come to me with any of your tricks. You've got the wrong husband for two good reasons: you married the wrong man to begin with, and then you became pregnant with the wrong man again. I am beginning to think that it's not the men that are wrong, I am beginning to think that it's you the woman! Please, please take your matter go. I don't want that Akorsah to come along to me brandishing his ridiculously thick gun, accusing me of flirting with the likes of a woman like you . . .' Obaa Yaa was not the least disturbed for she decided to take the bull by the horns: she just walked straight to Akorsah, weeding the farm with his upper teeth, and said bluntly to him, 'You Opanin Akorsah my husband, I can't get anybody to claim responsibility for this bellyfulity. I demand that you accept me back for two reasons: I dreamt last time that you were excuse-me-to-say impotent, and then this morning I really met the ghost of Mr K, and he claimed that it was not him that did the fikifiki with me to commot this pikin koraa! So you hear! Take me back, and I will make you feel like a real husband one time . . .' Akorsah took out a knife threateningly this time . . . but next time she came, he accepted her desperately, trying hard to hold her as she moved back with disgust. He even gave her half his biggest farm, ampa, while his nephew waited impatiently for the other half. Thus Akorsah was neutralised as an ally to the porkul ate Lawyer Tay; but Obaa Yaa kept her pride, ready to snarl at anyone that spoke out of turn to her.

Lawyer Tay kept returning to his house, sometimes even at midnight, to see whether he would see Dadoona and Sala . . . perhaps they would come to the house to get something they left. But what was now worrying him even more was the fact that the strangers from Kumasi and Accra, especially Kumasi, were losing interest in him and his schemes. They were finding Kwame Atta funnier and cleverer; they were in awe of Kofi Senya's mysteriousness; and they found Pokuaa's combination of power and charm fascinating, especially to drink Guinness over. Then they got to hear of Babo's book and were demanding it. Babo was outraged since he felt that the very people causing the dislocation of generations had no good motive calling for the chronicle of a different type of people, a people with a transcendent spirit that barged through time. After all, Tukwan was a new subject in the long timetable of the gods. And what did these swaggering alongi vendors of mortality want with a perspective of eternity, ah? But the more time progressed, the more advantage Kofi Senya saw in the open opening of the Minutes Book, in spite of Bra Kwaku's warning that the book wasn't quite what everyone thought it was, koraa . . . He agreed finally to interpret his book in the open, but by the lake rather than the Necklace Hill, his condition being that Kofi Senya would attempt one last spiritual jut of regeneration for Tukwan.

There were hundreds there by the lake, an unusually cool morning with the fussy dawn mean with its dew, and many frogs ready to blot out the rising sun this Thursday with judicious, solar jumps. The microphones were impatient for the voice of Babo, the man who usually wrote but did not talk, dodo; but Kwaku was not minding them: he moved among the still ducks, stroking them in a calm against the murmuring of the crowd, powdering them and brushing them, while the elephants, with the only blue one left, sprayed their water with the triumph of life, of trunk. Babo was flanked by Appa and Amoa who helped to carry the book; and far off by the Quiet Hill, Babo could see the small form of Kofi Senya busy with Kwame Atta, in a desperate attempt to reach eternity for the last time through a balance of leaves, roots, bark, bolts, new metal, and other machines. There was a strange steam from Senya's forehead. Babo eyed the much-carried book the leaves of which the breeze on leash was blowing up gently. Amoa had a ludicrously serious look on his face, and Appa looked splendid with one of his phallic sculptures slung heavily on his back. The fireflies had refused to move, and had doubled their glowing even though daylight had begun to waste it. There was one tear in Babo's eye which he would not release. 'We are here this morning, my elders, leaders, brothers and sisters, we are here as half a town only; our other half is in Levensvale, and they have the same struggle there . . .' Babo began in his deep faltering voice, his large knees prominent above gnarled but delicate feet without sandals. The only reason we are here is that the African magician of time doesn't invent all the time, there is always a counter-power that restricts his magic and makes nothing of immortality. And we know what palaver we speak when we mention immortality . . .' Babo spoke with a duck in his hand, and he had a sudden need for a corner to stamp his bare feet confidently there, to be the pin-point for the breezes from two directions, Mr Cornerstep nostalgic about wind, big-talk Babo with the spiritual moko in his mouth. 'There's always an advantage about riding free on the back of an intelligent person . . . those strangers who want to join us sincerely can climb on Kofi Senya's back, if there's any left by the time we have been overwhelmed with mortality, and this mortality comes from either Accra or Kumasi, or from the sleeping gods that have decided to toss the coin of life and give us whatever turns up. How could they play with hearts like this! We found out here hundreds of years ago that the different generations are always disconnected by a lack of invention, and you must know that this even affects memories, which end up so much the poorer by tacking their boundaries only with politics and the politicians; and our brothers too from Levensvale will brok you by pointing out all the false historics that they have written in your Glasgows and Edinburghs. But we saw a trick of the mind with Accra and Kumasi: if you allow the experience and memory of the ordinary person to disappear before the dead-end of politics or stagnation or both, then you are left with a mind that may retain its anatomical size, but it will be a mind that will either grab at straws of meaning, or create an easy spiritual mush over everything . . . Kumasi is the land of the semi-distilled mush! After such a fine Asante history, go and look at it now, try and fathom out what the people there are doing with their head-head energy now! . . .'

There was some uneasy muttering from the crowd, especially the strangers; they looked curiously at this intense, coughing, sweating young man, and they didn't quite know whether to take him seriously enough to hoot at some of the things he was saying, or to treat the whole show as a picnic, especially the free beer and kyinkyinga promised by Pokuaa the Pregnant President, when she was in a wise mood of sparkling calm, which she had supported with a generous and mellow palm-wine. 'Let the duck have a rest from your supamoto handling!' someone shouted from the crowd. Babo continued, 'And what is so difficult about keeping a society going in sustained discovery and invention? You people standing here in your Afro styles, in your lavender-supporting cloths, don't you know that it requires less and less brain power from fewer and fewer mosquitoes of the human kind to go beyond a certain minimum of inventive and self-sustaining power? After the initial leap, you can afford to have smaller legs! Wake up out of this tricky cocoon of the sun! Would you find it easy to agree with what David Mackie agreed with in the bracken environs: that the invention of a mud and wood machine for creating instruments is the cerebral bookbook equivalent of the invention of a new process for part of a rocket booster? You don't leave the mind fallow, for if you do, it will leave you fallow too! Obviously what you are all waiting for is for someone to create a ritual and a rhythm to the intellect so that your Accra-KumasiKumasiAccra man or woman can exercise his fundamental gift for giving an organic mould and pattern to everything, especially to the so-called pure and abstract ideas! Don't we want an *additional* dimension to the abstract that will not reduce its quality? Don't you dare, even when working on ideas to develop aeroplanes, to deal only in the "purity" of the idea, you must have some other equally subtle but non-utilitarian being beside the idea, so that when you finish with your invention, it has that inseparable dimension of being in it! We don't want your thin icicles of "modern" invention, icicles in a hot desert that may save diminished bodies, but may ultimately create souls massively dead! . . . Will Dogo please bring me the khebab of an intelligent goat . . .'

The muttering grew, as Dogo brought thirty wheelbarrows of kyink-yinga. 'We all want this marvellous meat of mean men brought in wheelbarrows that look so clean that all the flies have run away to Asafo market! I want that particular khebab with the goat's lips expertly stuck on it. Human lip chews roast goat lip! I am caught in mutton. I can see this as some commot headline in the graveyard of the chip-chop press we have here! My name is Kwasi Poh, I explode every day at the University of Science and Technology, Kumasi. I am paid to teach there, but I want to tell this young man here that as soon as they start paying me better, I'll start inventing what I teach too!' A loud voice shouted from the crowd. Another followed it, 'All of you here take what this young mosquito says seriously especially after you've had a feast with your dictionaries, and swallowed half the talk-talk palaver there. I vote that we have some fufu and dictionary soup at once!' 'Me I don't agree, koraa,' another voice followed, a voice so high that everyone laughed and knew that the truth it wanted to speak was a falsetto truth: 'I feel that this young man here and this whole town want to fool us small. How can he speak of the great Asante as spiritually and intellectually dead? Does he know how many ideas are wasting in the archives? Archives in this country are very useful: immediately someone gets a new idea, it is sent straight to its death in the archives before it's even properly born! So I think this man is talking subversion . . .' 'Shut up with your subversion!' someone else shouted with great heat, 'everything is subversion in Accra or Kumasi! Abenkwan is subversion, kpekple is subversion, sweetapple is subversion so is a harmless man's mouth when it speaks out, so are yoyi, atua and alasa; very soon oware will become so, closely followed by chalewate, piotos; sub-editors will be subversion, and so will subchiefs and submarines! I tire proper, me I am fundamentally fery fed up! Let us join these plop-style people with their new way of life. Can't you see that they have become rich through their thinking and doing? . . .'

LT went up to the platform, and stood beside Babo, looking at the latter with scorn, and saying, 'You have all here seen how this man standing beside me here can insult the generations and feel that he can get away free! His twin brother has even talked my son out of doing Law, how wicked! Instead of keeping the traditions unbroken and the ancestors happy, they want to break and rejoin everything. They are trying to deceive you by saying they are immortal! Who is immortal on this earth? Not even in the cold lands are they immortal. And another thing they have done is to take my wife and child away from me by force . . .'

This was too much for Dadoona Tay. She rushed up to within inches of her husband's belly, pointed to it ostentatiously, and shouted, 'That is where all the lies are! All he wants is power to chop sika, the courtroom is not big enough, he wants the whole world!' There was a surge of laughter which increased to a crescendo when LT imperially raised his hand to speak. 'Let the first speaker finish, let the young man complete his own mouth!' someone shouted. Kwaku Babo looked over at the Quiet Horizon, and saw that Senya and Atta had disappeared, but a dull glow remained there. Babo slowly left the platform to a roar, as Pastor Mensah rushed up, his up-down automatic cassock causing yet another sensation. 'Look at the man of God with his cassock of fantasticalities! But we will have to resew his torn, pale-blue pioto!' a voice rose and fell. 'Where is the beer to intellectually supplement the kyinkyinga?' another voice asked. Uncharacteristically, Pastor Mensah didn't say a word. He stood there with his hands raised as his cassock went on display, going up and down, left and right, semi-sideways and near-laterally, acute- and right-angled. 'God is an omnipresent cassock!' he finally shouted to the sound of huge roars, roars that drove LT out of town, roars that made the cassock syncopated in movement.

There was Aba standing behind the roaring with her Yaa reading a letter from Angus dated two hundred years ago. Aba was overwhelmed with the time-scale, for since she was now mortal, she didn't think Angus's half-wanted touch was so old. Babo had a revelation when he heard of the letter: if Angus and others still had their elements of eternity, why not make use of a large aggregate of time to defeat the Ghana cities? But where did Angus write from? Was he now back at Levensvale? What did the postmark say? It just said: Timeless and Lost. Babo couldn't see Kofi Senya to tell him about the letter. Aba was dressed in bread, selling a slice here, and a slice there, with raw crabs in between as the newest delicacy. She had been helping Maimuna with the hotel cuisine since her return from the stowaway, and the secondhand-removed romance with Angus. Aba's bread was very fresh and very brown; when sliced the bread was the colour of her eyes, and then whole, it was the colour of her skin, which was a deeper brown when guided away from any nearest light, as she herself would say. Most of the crowd had sworn to return to learn more about the new life but Bra Kwaku de Babo knew that this was not a victory: it would be a long curiosity under a short concentration, for wasn't talking more beautiful than doing . . . but they would come back, even in their shallowness, they would prevail over the superficial! Babo was walking slowly home with his unfinished interpretation, bitterly disappointed that Kofi Senya hadn't made an appearance to move the crowd forever away. He hadn't been at his mother's house ten minutes when Kofi Senya rushed in with Kwame Atta, one was breathless for the other. Atta was about to speak, but Senya stretched his mouth first. 'The Quiet Horizon hill gave us enough eternity to keep the local tourists of time away from us, but we were left with the task of gathering some eternity ourselves. I have gathered enough but there's one unit of immortality to get, and . . .' '. . . and we can get it from Angus because he has written to Aba Yaa a letter dated two centuries ago. He has hoarded his immortality, that cunning young man; but how do we trace him at all?' interrupted Babo.

Atta was impatient. He said, 'We will have them running soon, in as peaceful a way as they have threatened to destroy our soul! I believe I have a very good chance of being made a horse- and elephant-riding ambassador plenipotentiary! When and where would I exercise my hot-hot ambassadorship? On the lake with the ducks? Inside Pokuaa's bedroom? Pokuaa breaks my heart twenty times a day! And all I get in return is the gift of someone else's pregnancy with her . . .' 'If Aba Yaa would agree to be used as a travelling bait in the skies for three months, we will trace Angus and try and extract that last element of copious time for our survival,' said Kofi Senya. Sister Mansah came in and looked doubtful: 'This town has really tested my sons! Which one of them is going to persuade Aba to agree to something higher than makola suspension . . .' Papa Ntow came in sleepily, and said, 'The way to greatness is the path of tragedy! My sons have a dimension to life that I never had, let them grow like I never did, and I say this even for the troublesome engineer, that Kwame Atta that's so much like me. And I know that very soon, I will die, happy and honourable in my sons!' Sister Mansah looked at him with moderate contempt, and said, 'The only thing you'll die of is laziness, and that will be long after I'm gone! Stop seeking your daily ration of sympathy from me!'

Aba Yaa finally agreed to haunt the skies in the upper-lip jet with Appa and Sala as pilots, so that she may get Angus to be of use other than love use. They searched and searched the book of clouds where turbulence turns the pages, but found no Angus immediately below any. She had a wonderful time selling bread in the sky, for other pilots bought it, pilots both familiar and strange; Amoa and Dogo now had their own planes on hire purchase, from prototypes made by Atta and Appa, Appa who had already expanded into Nigeria with a fleet of two jointly owned with Atta. Tukwan was expanding so fast that a few miles of it had become close enough to other places to be recorded on the maps, some truncated cartography, sharp. Land moving out, people interfering in . . . how on earth was a town of this nature to survive such extrusions and intrusions? And the odum lived its own history tall.

Some of the old travellers were sitting round a small fire, sparkle crackle crackle sparkle, on a very cool harmattan evening, in Pokuaa's large compound, beyond the pines and the prides of Barbados. Babo was going round the fire, AD 11; but at first he wanted to use a bicycle, for the simple reason that he was agitated: he had caught Pokuaa's eye several times, and she seemed to be looking at him in a new way; obviously, new belly new eyes, true. She should make eyes at the father of her pregnancy, Babo thought to himself. After these quiet years of trying to take her out of his head, she had paid the last respects to his buried love by producing, by some mad magic, a child-to-be before his very heart. So he had to sublimate his suffering by studying the broken heart of his twin brother, broken from the same tragic source, O you Pokuaa the Pregnant President. But what was she planning now with these deep and furtive looks? Was she planning to divorce the baby's father even before it was born? Some odd bon- and bad-fire digamy, I swear. And it wasn't the only digging Pokuaa was doing: she had made a nervous little hole, so uncharacteristic, in the ground, before rising and announcing that she had something to say. Senya was there, Korner Mensah was there, Dogo was there meat and mild, Akyaa, and Nana Bontox too, not forgetting two elephants, several ducks, the vulture, and then Aba and her crabs; and the sound of crickets attacked the fire and was joined inextricably with the flames. 'Say your heart, woman!' Kwame Atta exclaimed, his throat crowded with akpeteshie, and with his new ambassadorial status. Even his nose was different: it had one extra drop of lavender on it, for diplomatic reasons.

'I have a confession to make,' Pokuaa began slowly, having taken on that extra maternal beauty that some women heavy with child took on. There was a peculiar hush, but Kofi Senya was smiling in that utterly calm way of his. Babo rested his AD11 fast. Kwame Atta puffed at his imported Woodbine, three left. Nana exclaimed, 'Can't you people stop the palm trees brushing my head at all, I implore, hey.' Pokuaa's voice took on an incredible gentleness as she continued, 'I had to change the scale of time twice, in what I thought was my own interest, and everybody's interest too, in a way . . . I arranged, by a sharp cut through the calender, for Angus from Levensvale to appear now, yes now, because in a dream, I knew we would need him; besides, he deserved better treatment for his devotion to Aba Yaa, better treatment than losing her . . . so you wouldn't believe it, but Angus is here now in the next room . . .' There was a great roar from different people for different reasons: Senya and Atta and Babo wanted to rush through for the last unit of eternity from the pale eyes of the inventive

Angus. Others just roared out of surprise. But strangely enough, Aba remained sitting, quite calm, looking almost indifferent. She became the focus of stares which she rebuffed with impudence. Pokuaa continued after restraining everyone but her father from going through to Angus: 'I cut the same calendar for Kwaku Babo . . .' Atta stared at his brother with a distant look of recognition. Pokuaa herself was looking at the same Babo, with an intense tenderness. She went on, 'The only way I could stop myself from being pulled towards Kwame Atta, yes I had to stop myself falling in love with his mad ways, the only way was to make poor Kwaku, the one I wanted to love all along, to make poor Kwaku free enough of time to lie down almost helpless with me to father my child. Kwaku Babo is the father of my belly, I swear!' There was a second uproar, this time a deeper one. Then Kwame Atta screamed, 'I will not stand by idle and let my twin brother be loved without authority! I refuse to believe that you can make invisible fornication, sebi, out of a time that you had just cut with scissors. I am outraged koraa . . .' Atta was hastily shouted down, and there was only one way to keep him mute: he smoked two jots and drank one glass of akpeteshie at the same time, to calm his nerves. It was only now that Aba Yaa got up ostentatiously, and shouted, 'I am going to that Angus now. After all if they are all having babies, whether with invisible popylonkwes or what, I will also have one. Angus, prepare your trousers now now now!' Kwaku de Babo stood there speechless, his ducks flapping around him in protective sympathy. Somebody was playing the atentenben in the distance, in a strange rhythm to the fire; there was a confusion of sounds and light, and the harmattan carried its cool dust blatantly into the houses, where any truth available was covered and uncovered. Babo's book seemed to have become considerably lighter, its flapping was a timeless percussion, it caught the silence and then released it in bits. He was caught between jubilation and indignation: did you thank a woman for making the culmination of your love possible, or did you chide her for taking a fundamental decision without you? Kwame Atta, even in his drunken stupor, saw Babo's problem, and so tripped across to the waiting Pokuaa and whispered impossibly loudly, 'My good woman whose heart I almost got, all that you have to do is to go and apologise to Kwaku, even in your elevated position, to go and apologise to him for making him happy! GO AND APOLOGISE TO HIM FOR MAKING HIM HAPPY . . .' Those available were looking at de Babo with a mixture of wonder, pain, and joy. Kwaku de Babo wanted his head under a hat immediately: he considered the back of his head to be extremely vulnerable to fate; fate was a blade that could leave him sakola any minute. He took the hat of his staggering twin brother, went over to Pokuaa, and put his head to the back of her neck. He did not move his head all evening, not even when the two of them sat down. The ducks lay around their feet with all their flapping gone, gone. Nana ordered drums and schnapps.

Angus Mackie came out at last in the company of Kofi Senya and Aba. Each held a shoulder of his. Angus was quite at home, resplendent in his kente joromi, and with a new wise look gained from months of contemplation about his fate with Aba, and from some gratuitous travelling that came from the calendar being cut: he had travelled the same route as his father had done with the Tukwan group, and had found that the desert had changed places with the forest, and that the old mercenaries were all doubly dead, and yet were refusing to rot. When he reached the land of the Football King and the golden-eyed grasscutter, he saw that it was now the grasscutter that was ruling in a true burrowing akrantie fashion with a degree of wisdom that fitted nicely into its silver eye; the awam football matches had ceased, and cassava and even yam had multiplied to such an extent that they threatened the sky with their leaves. And the King was dead: slaughtered on his own slaughter; and the gorge of goats was free! He Angus was here now, rapturous at winning Aba's love, wondering what it would really be like shoogling her wonderful doona with love . . . And he had given his immortality freely, for he wasn't even aware that he still had it. After all, the ancestors had decreed in their diminishing power that any residue immortality ought to be given in transfer not to another human being, but to an idea: the idea that Tukwan should exist at least for the next fifty years with the power to regulate its own rate of change, and its own way of change. Levensvale would plug itself into the same time-scale, enough time to develop new and relatively immortal stupidity machines that would continue to give a tolerable taste to the streets and to the future. Angus had decided immediately to send his parents over by video for his impending coconut-dominated wedding: everything done under the coconut trees, and the fruit of the same trees eaten.

The lake grew wonderfully, a few restrained visitors came and went away enriched, or even stayed. The old free system had come. Akyaa had continued to grow in intelligence past Azziz who had to release his wise pig at last, since it almost took over ownership of the entire sty stylishly. Kwame Atta, having survived the grief of losing Pokuaa to his brother, had made a forcefully ambitious journey to Levensvale in a one-craft, one-time machine that almost didn't survive; but he got there and immediately charmed Donald Shearer's elder sister Joan, and brought her back dangerously to marry her. Appa and Amoa prospered in metal, and began to sell their pranks conditionally with this metal. Dogo had become a meat tycoon across the west coast, and was thinking of turning his chin into kyinkyinga. Lawyer Tay was now domiciled in Kumasi, with little influence, and usually only perked up when Dadoona and Sala the scientist visited him once a month, on a special time-wise crow machine. He was waiting to be thrown into his grave by the kind aeroplanes. Moro had completely forgotten his pointless rebellion. Pastor Mensah had literally made an underground church: he was lowering the necklace, and digging for God at the same time; but he had not yet finished his book on the theology of okros, machines and the African soul. The elephants took the forest from the wild pigs and dominated it. Aba had taken on the baton of pregnancy, but had declared that sex was ridiculous even if you loved the man. Akorsah and Obaa Yaa co-existed; and Zolozolo had acquired a second spiritual motorbike for reaching the ancestors faster. Nana Bontox continued to make his stupidity an art, and had become so close to Corporal that two of his other wives had left. The authority of the termites grew bit by bite. Kaki had become a builder of roads that he immediately dug up and rebuilt. Kofi Senya was obsessed with the sunset, watching it snap over the horizon everyday, and thanking Maimuna for his wonderful new daughter. The vulture ruled the skies, including the aeroplanes. Mackie and Shebelda were overjoyed to find their son Angus alive and newly married. His eyebrows still towered over Levensvale. Pamela was now the new doctor of the town, and Canon Burns was dead.

Dead or alive, an amazing joy held most of them together in the two towns, as did the art of the golden Asante lips. Babo and Pokuaa moved up and down each other's smiles several times in a day. He was busy with work on his new intellectual moulds for Tukwan thought. His Minutes Book was full, and carefully stored by the new vulture egg now hatched beautifully. Pokuaa ruled only when necessary, for joy, even in death, was self-sustaining. She the President gave birth to a boy that looked like Babo. At least they had another fifty years in which to be fine and original, in which to watch the joy of forests and the joy of machines; and this watching was not to be done as mere spectating: it was and was to be a joy of multi-centred dimension, a joy that did not necessarily take knowledge far beyond the knower. 'But the fifty years is a threat,' lamented Pokuaa. 'Lament and groundnuts,' Babo smiled, eating nut by nut. They watched their baby sleep. The sun had slipped into an envelope beyond the paper-shaped clouds. Babo now had a horse on which he sat and did much of his thinking, cantering into the centuries. What a bowlful of abenkwan to enjoy! The quiet man loved his tremendous freedom, even though fate was always a pesewa about to be tossed. The ducks guarded the house, raising their wings to shelter Babo's head. Mr Cornerstep: it was only the universe that was round the corner, a corner very free in creating the breeze for a thousand crows, as Pokuaa slept by the lippy aeroplanes.

GLOSSARY OF GHANAIAN WORDS
AND AUTHOR'S NEOLOGISMS

abe	palm-nut tree
abenkwan	palm-nut soup
aboloo	corn tart
abongo	troubleshooter
abrewa	old woman
abunabu	a soup
adowa	a dance
agushie	a legume for making stew
akoma	heart, patience
akpeteshie	locally distilled gin
akple	corn and cassava staple
alpokplonto	tortoise
akrantie	bush animal used for meat
alagmai	crabs
alanta	knock-kneed
alasa	bitter-sweet fruit
alombo	lover
alongi	longish
ampa	true
ampesi	a staple and stew
anokwere	true
apem	small plantain
asem	matter
asomdwe	peace
atapkame	made of mud
atentenben	traditional bamboo flute
atua	fruit
awam	false, fixed
baako baako	one by one

bambala	large
banku	staple corn food
batakari	smock
bigibigi	big
bigitive	big, pretentious
bio	again
bodamfo	mad
bofrots	doughnuts
bokoboko	spinach
bola	rubbish heap
bosum	a god
bozi	fibroids
brik	clever
bugabuga	broken, illiterate
cedi	Ghana currency
chalewate	slippers
cola	seeds of the cola tree – usually chewed
comadi	*a general doing word*
commot	*a general doing word*
cytoOlogy (from cyto)	study of government schools
dawadawa	large tree
deebi	no
dompe	bone
doona	buttocks
ekusie	bush animal used for meat
enuanono	that's all
Ewurade!	good God!
ewurofua	a type of fish
fokofoko	*expletive*
fontomfrom	talking drum
fufu/fufuo	food made from pounded staples
gari foto	a food
hasmal go-go do (we go do)	*a roar of support/defiance*
hihe	thorn bushes
hu	wonderful
jecko	night lizard

jimi	stupid
jimisokakraba	pee a little (name of a village)
joromi	brightly coloured smock
jot	cigarette
kabasort	part of a woman's cloth outfit
kak	*general doing word*
kakra	a little
kalabule	sharp practices
kapere/kapereba	penny, nothing
kayakaya	porter
kelewele	ripe plantain chopped small and fried
kenkey	staple corn food
kente	colourful traditional cloth
kete	a dance
kitikiti	small, little
koko	porridge, easy
komm	quiet
koobi	dried fish
kooko	illness
koraa	at all
kosee	bean tart
kotiboto	uncircumcised
kpakpo shitoh	round pepper
kpekple	festival corn food
krada	the day on which the soul was born
krontihene	sub-chief
kube	coconut
kwashiorkor	undernourished illness
kwasia	fool, foolish
kwee	let wind escape
kyenam	fried fish
kyere	*an exclamation-cum-expletive*
kyinkyinga	khebab
libilibi	litigious
lingo kasa	talking
logologo	genital (*coined by author*)
Makola suspension	tackle by holding lapel/collar
mogantic	huge
momoni	aromatic fish
mon hive	look!

mon nanti yie	safe journey
motoway	receding forehead
nkantenkwan	groundnut soup
nkonkonte	cassava dough
nkontommire	a stew
nkwasiasem	nonsense
nnipa	people
ntam kese	great oath
ntemtem	quickly
ntromo	sweet potato
nyamanyama	foolish, rubbish
obaa	woman
odoyewu	eternal love
odrogya	bamboo flute
okro	vegetable
okyeamehene	chief linguist
omanhene	paramount chief
oware	a game
oxter	armpit (*Scottish word*)
paa, papaapa	a lot
palava	argument, quarrel
patapaa	quárrelsome
pesewa	Ghana coin, equivalent to penny
pioto	pants
popylonkwe	male organ
rabdopilist	one who gathers walking-sticks
rabjibeeb	second rate
sabe	know
sabla	sobriquet
sakola	bald
salaka	offering or sacrifice
sankofa	a symbol of how the present makes use of both past and future
sapo	sponge
sasabro	rheumatism
scunnered	loathed
sebi	*word with a general euphemistic function*
sheabutter	moisturising cream

shitoh	fried, ground pepper
shoogle	shake
shua	testicles
siabots	be patient
sunsum	soul
tama	waist beads
tatale	mashed fried plantain with ginger
tilapia	fish
tinlegge	thin
titrew	especially
tooshie	buttock
tototicular	sexy
trotro	private van/lorry transport
tu	buttocks
tumantu	hopscotch
undertobolo	small
waakye	rice and beans
wansana pobee	bluebottle (fly)
wo be wi	they will be forced to eat
yoyi	fruit